The Shifting Tide

Anne Perry

First published in Great Britain in 2004
by HEADLINE BOOK PUBLISHING

First published in paperback in Great Britain in 2004
by HEADLINE BOOK PUBLISHING

A HEADLINE paperback

10 9 8 7 6 5 4 3 2 1

ISBN 0 7472 6899 1

Typeset in Times New Roman by
Letterpart Limited, Reigate, Surrey

Printed and bound in Great Britain by
Mackays of Chatham plc, Chatham, Kent

Headline's policy is to use papers that are natural, renewable and
recyclable products and made from wood grown in sustainable forests.
The logging and manufacturing processes are expected to conform
to the environmental regulations of the country of origin.

HEADLINE BOOK PUBLISHING
A division of Hodder Headline
338 Euston Road
LONDON NW1 3BH

www.headline.co.uk
www.hodderheadline.com

F121,741
€ 11·00

To Joe Blades, in appreciation of his help and friendship

Chapter One

❧

'The murder doesn't matter,' Louvain said abruptly, leaning a little over his desk towards Monk. They were both
standing in the big office whose windows faced the Pool
of London, with its forest of masts swaying on the tide
against the ragged autumn sky. There were clippers and
schooners from every seafaring nation on earth, barges
from up and down the river, a local pleasure boat passing,
tugs, ferries and tenders at work. 'I have to have the
ivory!' Louvain gritted the words between his teeth. 'I've
no time to wait for the police.'

Monk stared at him, trying to frame an answer. He
needed this job, or he would not have come down to the
Louvain Shipping Company offices prepared to undertake a task so far outside his usual area of skill. He was a
brilliant detective in the city; he had proved it time and
time again, both in the police force, and later as a private
agent of enquiry. He knew the mansions of the wealthy
and the back streets of the poor. He knew the petty
thieves and informers, the dealers in stolen goods, the
brothel-keepers, the forgers, and many of the general
ruffians for hire. But the river, 'the longest street in
London', with its shifting tides, its constant movement of
ships, and men who spoke scores of different languages,

was strange territory to him. The question beat in his mind, insistent as a pulse: why had Clement Louvain sent for him rather than someone familiar with the docks and the water? The River Police themselves were older than Peel's city police; in fact they had existed since 1798, nearly three-quarters of a century ago. It was just believable that they were too busy to give Louvain's ivory the attention he wanted, but was that really his reason for calling in Monk?

Louvain was standing on the other side of the big, polished mahogany desk, waiting, judging.

'The murder is part of the theft,' Monk replied. 'If we knew who killed Hodge, we'd know who took the ivory, and if we knew when, we might be a lot closer to finding it.'

Louvain's face tightened. He was a wind-burned, slender-hipped man in his early forties, but hard-muscled, like the sailors he hired to work his ships to the East African coast and back, with ivory, timber, spices and skins. His light brown hair was thick and sprang up from his forehead. His features were broad and blunt.

'On the river at night, time makes no difference,' he said curtly. 'There are light horsemen, heavy horsemen, night plunderers up and down all the time. Nobody's going to inform on anyone else, least of all to the River Police. That's why I need my own man, one with the skills I'm told you have.' His eyes swept over Monk, seeing a man reputed to have the same ruthlessness as himself, an inch or two taller, darker, with high cheekbones and a lean, powerful face. 'I need that ivory back,' Louvain repeated. 'It's due for delivery, and the money is owed. Don't look for the murderer to find the thief. That might work on shore. On the river you find the thief, and that will lead you to the murderer.'

Monk would dearly like to have declined the case. It would have been easy enough; his lack of knowledge alone would have provided grounds for it. But many men did know the river and the docks, and there was always someone who would undertake a private commission, for a fee.

But Monk could not afford to point that out. He faced the bitter fact that he must make himself obliging to Louvain, and convince him, against the truth, that it was well within his power to find the ivory and return it to him in less time, and with greater discretion, than the River Police could or would do.

Necessity drove him, the recent spate of trivial cases that paid too little. He dared not go into debt, and since Hester had given her time to the clinic in Portpool Lane, which was wholly charitable, she added nothing to their finances. But a man should not expect his wife to keep herself. She asked little enough – no luxury, no vanity, only to be able to do the work she loved. Monk would have served any man to give her that. He resented Louvain because he had the power to cause him acute discomfort, but, far more than that, he was troubled that Louvain showed more concern to catch a thief who had robbed him of goods than a murderer who had taken Hodge's life.

'And if we do catch him,' he said, 'and Hodge is buried, what evidence do we have? We will have concealed his crime for him.'

Louvain pursed his lips. 'I can't afford to have the theft known. It would ruin me. Would it serve if I swear a testimony as to exactly where I found the body, how and when, and that he was murdered by the thief, and the morgue attendant can swear to his injuries, and you yourself can look too? I'll put it in writing and sign it, and you can have the papers.'

'How will you explain concealing it to the police?' Monk asked.

'I'll hand them the murderer, with proof. What more

3

would they want?' Louvain answered.

'And if I don't catch him?'

Louvain looked at him with a wry, delicately twisted smile. 'You will,' he said simply.

Monk could not afford to argue. Morally it set ill with him, but in practical terms Louvain was right. He must succeed; but if he did not, then, with the possible loss of clues as time passed, the River Police's chances were even less.

'Tell me as much as you know,' he asked.

Louvain sat down at last, easing himself into the padded round-backed chair, and indicating that Monk should sit also. He fixed his gaze on Monk's face.

'The *Maude Idris* put out from Zanzibar fully loaded with ebony, spices and fourteen first-grade tusks of ivory, bound round the Cape of Good Hope and home. She's a four-masted vessel, with a nine-man crew: captain, mate, bosun, cook, cabin boy and four able seamen, one per mast. That's standard for her tonnage.' He was still watching Monk's face. 'She made fair weather most of the way, calling in for supplies and fresh water up the west coast of Africa. She reached Biscay five days ago, Spithead the day before yesterday, and tacked the last few miles upriver with the wind in front of her. Dropped anchor just east of the Pool yesterday, the twentieth of October.'

Monk was listening, and he would remember it, but it meant nothing useful to him. He was certain Louvain knew that; nevertheless they both continued to play out the charade.

'Crew was paid off,' Louvain went on, 'as is usual. Been away a long time, close to half a year, one way and another. I left the bosun and three able seamen on board to keep things safe. One of them was the dead man, Hodge.' A flicker passed across his face. It could have been any emotion at all: anger, sorrow, even guilt.

'Four out of the nine stayed?' Monk confirmed it.

As if reading his thoughts, Louvain pursed his lips. 'I know the river's dangerous, especially for a ship newly come in. All the watermen will know the cargo's still on her. Not much on the river is secret for long, but any fool could work that out. You don't come up this far if you're empty. You're loading or unloading. I thought four men, armed, would be enough. I was wrong.' His face was filled with emotion, but it was unreadable.

'How were they armed?' Monk asked.

'Pistols and cutlasses,' Louvain replied.

Monk frowned. 'Those are close-quarter weapons. Is that all you carry?'

Louvain's eyes widened almost imperceptibly. 'There are four cannons on deck,' he replied guardedly. 'But that's in case of piracy at sea. You can't fire that sort of thing on the river!' A slight flare of amusement crossed his face and vanished. 'They only wanted the ivory, not the whole damn ship!'

'Was anyone else injured apart from Hodge?' Monk concealed his annoyance with an effort. It was not Louvain's fault that he was obliged to work out of his depth.

'No,' Louvain said. 'River thieves know how to come alongside and board in silence. Hodge was the only one they encountered, and they killed him without arousing anyone else.'

Monk tried to imagine the scene: the cramped spaces in the bowels of the ship, the floor shifting and tilting with the tide, the creaking of the ship's timbers. And then would come the sudden knowledge that there were footsteps, then the terror, the violence, and finally crippling pain as they struck.

'Who found him?' he said quietly. 'And when?'

Louvain's face was heavy, his mouth drawn tight. 'The man who came to relieve him at eight o'clock – Newbolt, the bosun. He sent a message to me.'

'Before or after he saw the ivory was missing?'

Louvain hesitated only a second. It was barely discernible and Monk wondered if he had imagined it. 'After.'

If he had said 'before', Monk would not have believed him. In self-preservation the man would have wanted to know what he was dealing with before he had told Louvain anything. And unless he were a complete fool, he would have thought first to make sure the killer was not still on board. If he could have said he had captured him, and kept the ivory, he would have had a very different story to tell. Unless, of course, he already knew all about the theft, and was party to it?

'Where were you when you got the message?'

Louvain looked at him stonily. 'Here. It was nearly half-past eight by then.'

'How long had you been here?'

'Since seven.'

'Would the bosun know that?' He watched Louvain's face closely. One of the ways he could judge the men left on the ship was by Louvain's trust in them. A man in his position could not afford to forgive even error, let alone any kind of disloyalty.

'Yes,' Louvain replied, a flicker of amusement in his eyes. 'Any seaman would expect it. That doesn't tell you what you think it does.'

Monk felt the heat burn up inside him. He was clawing after answers, not grasping as he usually did. This was not the right pace at which to play games of wits with Louvain. He must be either blunter or a great deal more subtle.

'All shipowners are in their offices at that hour?' he concluded.

Louvain relaxed a little. 'Yes. He came here and told me Hodge had been killed and the ivory stolen. I went with him immediately—' He stopped as Monk stood up.

'Can you retrace your steps, and I'll come with you?' Monk requested.

Louvain rose smoothly. 'Of course.' He said nothing else as he led Monk across the rather worn carpet to the heavy door, opened it and then locked it behind them, putting the key in the inside pocket of his waistcoat. He took a heavier jacket from a coat stand, glanced at Monk's attire as if to consider its adequacy, and decided it would suffice.

Monk was proud of his clothes. Even in his most financially restricted times during the past he had dressed well. He had a natural elegance, and pride dictated that the tailor's bill had come before the butcher's. But that had been when he was single. Now he might have to reverse that order, and it already weighed heavily with him. It was a kind of defeat. However, he had realised that a man involved in shipping, as Louvain was, might well have business that required them both to go on to the water, so he had come with that in mind. His boots were heavy and well-soled; his overcoat was easy to move in and would cut the wind.

He followed Louvain down the stairs, and across the outer office where clerks were bent over ledgers or sitting on high stools with quills in hand. The odours of ink and dust were in the air and there was an acrid sting of smoke as he passed the iron heating stove just as someone opened it to put more coke in the top.

Outside in the roadway towards the dock the wind struck them immediately, raw-edged off the river, making the skin smart, whipping the hair back, catching in the throat with the taste of salt on the incoming tide. It was heavy with smells of fish, tar and the sour, overbearing effluent of mud and sewage from above the waterline beyond the wharfs.

The water slurped against the pier stakes in endless movement, the rhythm broken now and then by the wash

7

of barges laden so they sat deep. They moved slowly upriver towards London Bridge. The mewing of gulls was shrill, yet it was a sound that brought back echoes of meaning for Monk, flashes of his life in Northumberland as a boy. A carriage accident seven years ago, in 1856, had robbed him of most of those many-coloured fragments that build the past and form the pictures of who we are. By deduction he had pieced much of it together, and now and again windows opened suddenly and showed him whole landscapes for a moment. The cry of gulls was one of those.

Louvain was crossing the cobbles down to the wharf and striding along it without looking to right or left. The docks, with their vast warehouses, the cranes and derricks, were all familiar to him. He was used to seeing the labourers and watermen and the small craft coming and going.

Monk followed him as far as the end of the wharf where the dark water swirled and slapped under the shadows, its surface spotted with scum and drifting refuse. On the far bank there was a stretch of mud below the tide-line and three children were wading in it, sunk halfway up to their knees, bent over searching with busy, skilled hands for whatever they could find. A snatch of memory told Monk it was almost certainly for coal off the barges, fallen by chance, or deliberately pushed a piece at a time, in order to be picked up by the mudlarks.

Louvain waved his arm and shouted across the water. Within moments a light boat, twelve or fourteen feet long, drew up to the steps with a single man aboard at the oars. His face was weather-beaten to the colour of old wood, his grey beard little more than bristle, and his hat, jammed down over his ears, hid whatever hair he might have had. He gave a brief half-salute of recognition, and waited for Louvain's orders.

'Take us out to the *Maude Idris*,' Louvain told him,

stepping easily down into the boat, adjusting his weight to keep his balance as it tipped and jiggled. He offered no assistance to Monk behind him, either assuming he was accustomed to boats, or uninterested in whether he made a fool of himself or not.

A moment of fear rose in Monk, and embarrassment in case he did it clumsily. He stiffened, and then physical instinct told him that was wrong, and he dropped down loosely, bending his knees, and adjusting with a grace that surprised both of them.

The waterman wove between the barges with practised skill, skirting around a three-masted schooner, her canvas lashed, timbers stained and peeling from long days of tropical sun and salt wind. Monk glanced down and saw the crusting of barnacles below the waterline. The river was too murky for him to see more than a foot or so below the surface.

He looked up quickly as they passed under the shadow of a much larger ship and caught his breath with a sudden thrill as the sheer beauty of her gripped him. She towered into the air, three tremendous masts with yards eighty or ninety feet wide and dark against the grey clouds, sails furled, rigging in fine lines like an etching on the sky. She was one of the great clippers that sailed around the world, probably racing from China to London with tea, silk, spices of the Far East. First one to unload won the stupendous prices, second got only what was left. His imagination teemed with visions of roaring winds and seas, worlds of sky, billowing canvas, spars thrashing in a wild dance of the elements. And there would be calmer seas, flaming sunsets, clear water like glass teeming with creatures of a myriad shapes, and windless days when time and space stretched into eternity.

He jerked himself back to the present and the loud, busy river, the cold spray off the water whipping his face. Ahead of them was a four-masted schooner lying at anchor, rolling very slightly on the wake from a string of barges. She was wide-beamed and quite deep of draught, an ocean-going carrier of heavy cargo, swift under full sail, easy to manoeuvre, and, this close, the gun ports on the foredeck were plain to see. She would be neither caught nor captured easily.

Yet here in her home port she was a sitting target for two or three men creeping up over the black water by night, scaling her sides to the deck and taking an inattentive guard by surprise.

They were almost alongside, and Louvain rose to his feet, balancing with a very slight swaying of his body to the motion of the river.

'Ahoy! *Maude Idris!* Louvain coming aboard!'

A man appeared at the rail, looking down at them. He was broad-shouldered, short-legged, powerful. 'Right, sir, Mr Louvain!' he shouted back, and a moment later a rope ladder hurtled over from the deck and uncoiled down the side. The waterman manoeuvred the boat underneath it and Louvain caught the bottom rung in his hand. He hesitated an instant, as if to question whether Monk was capable of climbing up after him. Then he changed his mind and went without turning round, hand over hand with obvious practice, reaching the top to swing over the rail and stand up on the deck, waiting for Monk to follow.

Monk steadied himself, grasped the rope ladder to hold it firm, then raised his foot as Louvain had done, put his hand out to grip the third rung, and hoisted himself up. He hung suspended for a perilous instant, neither balanced on the boat nor on the ladder. The water churned beneath him. The schooner rolled, swinging him wide, then banging him back against the hull, bruising his knuckles. He threw his weight upwards and took the next rung, and the next, until he too went over the rail and stood up beside Louvain. They had neither of them made any sound.

Monk controlled the breath rasping in his lungs with an effort. 'And how would they do that if no one let down the ladder for them?' he asked.

'The thieves?' Louvain said. 'It must have been more than one, with an accomplice to stay in the boat, possibly hired for the job.' He glanced towards the rail again, and the water beyond. The sun was lowering already and the shadows long, though in the grey light it was not easy to tell. 'They'd climb up ropes,' he answered Monk's question. 'Throw them up from below, grapple the rail. Simple enough.' A brief, hard smile curved his mouth for a moment. 'Ladders are for landsmen.'

Monk looked at Louvain's tight-muscled shoulders and effortless balance, and was quite certain that the lack of a ladder would not have stopped him, had he been intent on boarding. 'Would the grapple leave any marks on the wood?' he said.

Louvain drew in his breath sharply, then let it out again as understanding came to him. 'You think the crew were in on it?'

'Were they?' Monk asked. 'Do you know each one well enough to be certain?'

Louvain thought before he answered. He was weighing some judgement in his mind; his eyes reflected it, and the moment of decision. 'Yes,' he said finally. He did not qualify it or add any assurances. He was not used to explaining himself; his word sufficed.

Monk looked around the deck. It was broad and open, scrubbed clean, but still it was a small space to imagine in the vastness of the ocean. The hatches were closed but not battened down. The wood was strong and in good repair, but the marks of use were clear. This was a working ship; even at a glance one could see the ingrained stains of hands on the surrounds of hatches, of feet on the tracks to and from the way down. Nothing was new, except one piece of shroud going up the foremast high

11

into the rigging to be lost in the web above. Its pale colour marked it plainly.

From the aft hatch, which was standing open, a hand appeared and then a huge body, climbing through and up. He stood well over six feet, his round head was covered in a bristle of brownish-grey hair, his chin similarly. It was a coarse face, but intelligent, and it was apparent he made no move without thought. Now he walked slowly over to Louvain and stopped a little distance short of him, waiting for his orders.

'This is the ship's bosun, Newbolt,' Louvain said. 'He can tell you all he knows of the theft.'

Monk relaxed a little, deliberately. He regarded Newbolt with care: the man's immense physical power; his callused hands; the weathered clothes; dark blue trousers worn and shapeless, but strong enough to protect him against cold or a loose rope lashing. His jacket was thick, and the front of a rough woollen sweater in fancy stitches was visible at the neck. Monk remembered it was an old seafaring habit to wear such garments, the different stitches identifying a man by family and clan, even if his dead body had been in the sea for days, or weeks.

'Three of you here, and the dead man?' Monk asked him.

'Yeah.' Newbolt did not move at all, not even to nod his head. His eyes were fixed on Monk, steady, clever, unreflecting.

'And it was you who found the murdered man?'

'Yeah,' Newbolt said again.

'And where was it you found Hodge's body?' Monk asked.

Newbolt's head moved fractionally to one side, a minute acknowledgement. 'Bottom o' the steps from the aft 'atchway down to the 'old.'

'What do you suppose he was doing there?' Monk asked.

12

'I dunno. Mebbe 'e 'eard summink,' Newbolt answered with ill-concealed insolence.

'Then why didn't he raise the alarm?' Monk enquired. 'How would he do that?'

Newbolt opened his mouth and took a deep breath, his huge chest swelling. Something in his face changed. Suddenly he was watching Monk quite differently, and with far more care. 'Shout,' he answered. 'Can't fire a gun around 'ere. Might 'it someone else.'

'You could fire it in the air,' Monk suggested.

'Well, if 'e did, no one 'eard it,' Newbolt replied. 'I'd guess as they crept up on 'im. Mebbe one of 'em made a noise, like, and when 'e turned ter look, another one whacked 'im over the 'ead. As ter 'is bein' found at the bottom o' the 'atchway steps, that'd be where they threw 'im. If they'd a' left 'im lyin' on deck someone else could've seen 'im, an' know'd there were summink wrong. Thieves ain't fools. Least not all of 'em.'

It made excellent sense. It was what Monk himself would have done, and how he would have answered such an enquiry. 'Thank you.' He turned to Louvain. 'May I see where he was found?'

Louvain took a lantern from Newbolt and moved towards the aft hatch, leaving Newbolt where he was. Monk followed him.

Louvain climbed over on to the steps, twisting his body in a single movement. He went downwards, disappearing into the dense shadows of the interior, only the space around him illuminated by the flame.

Monk followed, with less grace, feeling his way rung by rung. Ahead of him floorboards and bulkheads were visible, and beyond the dark, open maw of the hold, denser outlines of the cargo emerging as his eyes became used to the gloom. He could just make out stacks of timber lashed tight. He could imagine the destruction if it broke loose in heavy seas. In weather wild enough it could pierce the hull and the ship would sink in minutes. Even through the wrappings of oilcloth and canvas, he could smell the strange odours of spices, but they were not strong enough to mask the mustiness of closed air and the sourness of the bilges below. Memory brought back nothing like it. His boating had been above deck, open to the wind and the seas. He had known the coast, not the ocean – and certainly not Africa, where this cargo had begun.

'There.' Louvain lowered the lantern until the light shone on the ledge nearer the steps down on to the floor of the hold. It was clear enough to see the marks of blood.

Monk took the lantern from Louvain and bent to look at them more closely. They were smears, not the still-damp pools he would have expected if a man dead of a lethal head wound had either been killed here, or placed here within moments of being struck.

He looked up. 'What was he wearing on his head?' he asked.

Louvain's face was upward lit, giving it an eerie, mask-like quality that accentuated his surprise at the question. 'A . . . a hat, I think,' he answered.

'What kind?'

'Why? What has that to do with who killed him, or where my ivory is?' There was tension in his voice, but no anger as yet.

'If a man is hit over the head hard enough to kill him, there's usually a lot of blood,' Monk replied, standing up to face Louvain levelly. 'Even when you nick your skin shaving, the head bleeds.'

Comprehension flared in Louvain's eyes. 'A woollen hat,' he answered. 'It gets very cold on deck at night. Air off the river eats into your bones.' He drew in his breath. 'But I think you're right, he was probably killed up there.' He lifted his shoulder slightly and glanced upwards

14

towards the ladder and the darkening square of sky through the hatchway. 'As Newbolt said, they'd have thrown him down here to stop the chance of his being seen by a passing boat, and the alarm raised.' He nodded slightly; it was a single movement, but it was approval.

Monk turned back towards the hold, lifting the lantern higher to see it more clearly. 'How do you unload the timber?' he asked. 'Is there a main hatch which comes off?'

'Yes, but it had nothing to do with this. It's locked fast,' Louvain replied.

'Could that be why they took the ivory? Because it could be carried up the steps and out of this hatchway?'

'Possibly. But so could the spices.'

'What does a tusk weigh?'

'Depends – eighty or ninety pounds. A man could carry them, one at a time. You're thinking a chance thief?'

'Opportunist,' Monk replied. 'Why? What did you think?'

Louvain weighed his answer carefully. 'There's a lot of theft on the river, everything from piracy to the mudlarks, and people know when a ship comes in and has to be at anchor before she can find a wharf to unload. It can be weeks, if you're unlucky – or don't know the right people.'

Monk was surprised. 'Weeks? Wouldn't some cargoes rot?'

Louvain's face was sardonic. 'Of course. Shipping is not an easy business, Mr Monk. The stakes are high; you can win a fortune, or lose one. No errors are forgiven, and no mercy is asked or expected. It's like the sea. Only a fool fights with it. You learn its rules and if you want to survive, you keep them.'

Monk believed him. He needed to know more about crime on the river, but he could not afford to expose his ignorance in front of Louvain. He loathed being obliged to court a job and equivocate about his own abilities in order to do it.

'Could anyone assume you would be anchored here for several days before being able to unload?' he asked.

'Yes. That's the only reason I can put off my buyers,' Louvain answered. 'You've got no more than ten days at the outside to find my ivory and get it back, whether you get the thief or not. We can prove his guilt later.'

Monk raised his eyebrows. 'Of murder? Wasn't Hodge your man?'

Louvain's face hardened, his eyes cold and hollow as a winter sky. 'How I deal with my men is not your concern, Monk, and you'd be advised to remember it. I'll pay you fairly, or better, and I expect the job done my way. If you catch the man who murdered Hodge, so much the better, but I'm concerned with feeding the living, not avenging the dead. You can take your evidence to the River Police. They'll hang whoever's responsible. I assume that is what you want?'

A sharp retort rose to Monk's tongue, but he bit it back, and merely agreed. 'Where is Hodge's body now?' he asked instead.

'At the morgue,' Louvain answered. 'I have made arrangements for his burial. He died in my service.' His mouth formed a thin line, as if the knowledge caused him pain, but there was a hard thread of anger as well.

Monk found it the first comforting thing he had seen in Louvain. He no longer feared that Hodge's killer would escape any kind of accounting. It might be river justice, so the burden upon Monk to make sure he had the right man was even greater, but perhaps he should have expected that. He was dealing with men of the sea, where judgements had to be right the first time because there was no mercy, and no appeal.

'I need to see him,' Monk said. He made it an order rather than a suggestion. Louvain would have no respect for a man he could dominate, and Monk could neither afford his contempt nor stomach it.

Wordlessly Louvain took the lantern from him and turned to begin the climb up the ladder again through the hatch and out on to the deck. Monk followed after him. Up on deck the wind was harder, like a whetted knife edge as the tide came in. The heavy grey skies made it close to darkness already, and there was a smell of rain in the air. The wash from a string of barges made the ship strain a little at the anchor and set the boat rocking where it was waiting for them, the waterman steadying it with his oars.

Newbolt was still on deck, his arms folded over his barrel chest, swaying to keep his balance.

'Thank you,' Monk said to Louvain. He looked at Newbolt. 'Was there a change of watch during the night?' he asked.

'Yes. I did eight till midnight. Atkinson was on midnight to four, Hodge from four till eight,' Newbolt replied. 'Then me again.'

'And no one came on deck before eight in the morning when you found Hodge?' Monk let his surprise show, and a degree of contempt, as if he considered Newbolt incompetent.

'Course they were on deck!' Newbolt growled. 'Nobody went down the 'old, so they didn't find 'Odge's body.' His eyes were level and grey, the way a man's eyes are if he has been unjustly accused – or is lying.

Monk smiled, showing his teeth a little. 'What time?'

'Just arter six,' Newbolt replied, but his face betrayed his understanding. 'Yeah . . . the thieves came arter four an' afore six, an' that's cuttin' it fine.'

'Why wouldn't they come between midnight and four?' Monk asked him, temporarily ignoring Louvain. 'Wouldn't you . . . if you were a thief?'

Newbolt stiffened, his big body motionless. 'What are you sayin', mister? Exact!'

17

Monk did not flinch or move his eyes even a fraction. 'That either we have the facts wrong, or we have a most unusual thief who either chooses, or is obliged, to carry out his robberies on the river in the last couple of hours before dawn, rather than the middle of the night watch. Do you disagree with that?'

'No . . .' Newbolt admitted reluctantly. 'Mebbe 'e'd tried other ships an' either the watch were too spry, or they din't 'ave nothing as he wanted or could move easy. We was 'is last chance for the night.'

'Perhaps,' Monk agreed. 'Or could he have picked Hodge's watch for some reason?'

Newbolt understood immediately. 'Yer sayin' as 'Odge were in on it? Yer wrong, mister. 'Odge were a good man. I know'd 'im fer years. An' if 'e were in on it, 'ow come the poor sod got 'is 'ead bashed? Don't sound ter me like a bargain even a fool'd make!' He sneered at Monk, showing strong, yellowish-white teeth.

'No, it wouldn't be Hodge's arrangement,' Monk agreed.

The dull colour rose up Newbolt's face. 'Well, it bloody in't mine, yer son of a bitch! 'Odge is family ter me! I know'd 'im twenty years, an' 'e's married ter me sister!'

Monk felt a stab of regret. He had not even thought of personal loss until this moment. 'I'm sorry,' he said quickly.

Newbolt nodded.

Monk considered the information. It was possible all of it was true, some of it, or very little. Atkinson might have been in collusion with the thieves, and been caught by Hodge at any time from midnight until four, or possibly even later.

Monk turned to Louvain. 'Get me Atkinson,' he requested.

Atkinson was a tall, lean man. The scar that ran from his brow across his cheek to his chin now showed livid

18

through the stubble of his beard. He moved easily with a feline sort of grace and he regarded Monk with faint suspicion. He looked to Louvain for orders.

Louvain nodded to him.

'What time did Hodge come to relieve you from watch?' Monk asked, although he knew the answer was of little use because he would have no idea if it was the truth or not.

''Bout 'alf-past three,' Atkinson replied. ''E couldn't sleep, an' I were 'appy enough ter let him do my last 'alf-hour. I went away ter me bed.'

'Describe the scene you left,' Monk requested.

Atkinson was surprised. 'Nothin' ter tell. All quiet. Weren't nobody on deck but me an' 'Odge. Nobody near on the water neither – least, not that I could see. Course, anyone could be there wi'out ridin' lights, if they was daft enough.'

'Did Hodge say anything to you? How did he look, sound?'

Newbolt was watching him, his eyes angry.

'Same as any time,' Atkinson answered. 'Much as you'd be if yer'd come out o' yer bed at 'alf-past three in the mornin' ter stand on a freezin' deck an' watch the tide rise and fall.'

'Sleepy? Angry? Bored?' Monk pressed.

''E weren't angry, but yeah, 'e looked rough, poor sod.'

'Thank you.' Monk turned to Louvain. 'May I see Hodge's body now, please?'

'Of course, if you think there's any point,' Louvain said with frayed patience. He walked over to the rail and shouted for the lighter to come back, and waited while it did so. He swung over the rail, grasped the ropes of the ladder, nodded at Newbolt, then disappeared down.

Monk went after him, a great deal more carefully, scraping his knuckles on the way, and bruising his fingers as he was bumped against the ship's hull by the movement of the water.

Once down into the boat he sat, and he and Louvain were rowed wordlessly back to the wharf.

At the top of the steps up, a shorter distance with the turned tide racing in, the wind was keener and edged with rain turning to sleet.

Louvain put up his collar and hunched his shoulders. 'I'll pay you a pound a day, plus any reasonable expenses,' he stated. 'You have ten days to find my ivory. I'll give you twenty pound extra if you do.' His tone made it plain he would not accept negotiation. But then a police constable started on just under a pound a week. He was offering seven times as much, plus a reward at the end if Monk were successful. It was a lot of money, far too much to refuse. Even if he failed, the rate was better than for most jobs, although the penalty afterwards to his reputation might be dear. But he also could not afford to think of the future if there were no present.

He nodded. 'I'll report to you when I have progress, or need more information.'

'You'll report to me in two days regardless,' Louvain replied. 'Now come to see Hodge.' He swivelled on his foot and marched along the wharf all the way to the street without looking back. As Monk caught up with him they crossed together, picking their way between the rumbling wagons. It was almost dark, and streetlamps made ragged islands as the mist blew in and the cobbles glistened underfoot.

Monk was glad to be inside again, even though it was the morgue, with its smell of carbolic and death. The attendant was still there; perhaps this close to the river there was always someone present. He was an elderly man with a scrubbed, pink face and a cheerful expression. He recognised Louvain immediately.

'Evenin', sir. You'll be after Mr 'Odge. 'Is widder's 'ere,

poor soul. In't no use in yer waitin'. She could be 'ere some time. I reckon as she's makin' 'er peace, like.'

'Thank you,' Louvain acknowledged. 'Mr Monk is with me.' And without waiting for the attendant to show him, he led the way to a room where a large, raw-boned woman with grey hair and a fine, pale skin was standing silently, her hands folded in front of her, staring at the body of a man lying on a bench. He was covered up to the neck with a sheet, which was stained and a little thin at the edges. His face had the lividity of death, and the strangely shrunken absent look of the shell no longer inhabited by the spirit. He must have been large in life – the frame was there, the bones – but he seemed small now. It took a force of imagination to think of him as having been able to move and speak, to have will, even passion.

The woman looked briefly at Louvain, then at Monk.

Monk spoke to her first. 'I am sorry for your grief, Mrs Hodge. My name is William Monk. Mr Louvain has hired me to find out who killed your husband, and to see that he answers for it.'

She looked at him with leaden eyes. 'Mebbe,' she answered. 'Don't make much difference ter me, nor me kids. Don't pay the rent nor put food in our mouths. Still, I s'pose 'e should swing.' She turned back to the motion-less form on the table. 'Stupid sod!' she said with sudden fury. 'But 'e weren't all bad. Brought me a piece a wood back from Africa last time, all carved like an animal. Pretty. I never 'ocked it afore. S'pose I'll 'ave ter now.' She glanced at the corpse. 'Yer stupid sod!' she repeated helplessly.

Monk's anger at the thief stopped being a matter of law, and became suddenly hate, and deeply personal. Hodge was past injury, but this woman was not, nor her children. But there was nothing useful for him to say, nothing that would help now, and he could give her no assistance in her poverty.

F121,741

He looked instead at the dead man. He had thick hair and the back of his head rested on the table. Monk reached across and lifted the head very slightly, feeling underneath for the extent of the injury. He had seen no blood on the top of the steps to the hold, and none on the deck. Scalp wounds bled.

His fingers found the soft, broken skull under the hair. It had been an extremely hard blow. Something heavy and wide had been used, and by a person either of a good height, or else standing slightly above. He looked at the attendant. 'You cleaned him up, washed away the blood?'

'A bit,' the attendant answered from the doorway. 'There wasn't much. Just made 'im presentable, like.' There was nothing in his face to indicate whether he knew the man was a victim of murder or accident. There were probably many of the latter on ships, and especially on the docks, where heavy loads were moved, and sometimes came loose.

'Not much blood?' Monk questioned.

'He had a woollen hat on,' Louvain explained. 'I'm afraid it must have been lost when we were carrying him here. I can describe it for you, if you think it matters.'

'There was no blood on deck,' Monk pointed out. 'And very little where he was found. It might have been helpful, but it's probably not important. I've seen all I need to.'

He thanked Mrs Hodge again, then went out ahead of Louvain, back to the outside room.

'I want the attendant's testimony in writing, and yours.'

A brief smile flickered across Louvain's face, some oblique, inner humour he would not share. 'I've not forgotten. You'll get your pieces of paper. Dawson!' he called the attendant. 'Mr Monk would like our testaments of Hodge's death on paper to help him in his work. Would you be good enough, please?'

Dawson looked slightly taken aback, but he produced paper, pen and ink. He and Louvain both wrote their statements, signed, and witnessed by each other, and Monk put them in his pocket.

'Did it tell you anything?' Louvain asked when they were on the pavement. The rain had now eased off and the wind slackened, allowing the mist to drift up off the water, wreathing the lamps and obscuring the roofs of some of the buildings nearby.

It had told Monk that someone was lying. Hodge had not been struck on deck and then carried below by a single thief. There was no blood on deck, no trail across the boards. Either Hodge had not died there, or there were more than two thieves, one from the boat and two on deck, or at least one of the crew had been involved. He decided not to say that much to Louvain.

'Possibilities,' he answered. 'I'll start again in the morning.'

'Report to me in two days, regardless of what you have,' Louvain reminded him. 'Before, if you have the ivory, of course. I'll pay you five pounds extra for every day short of ten that you recover it.'

'Good,' Monk said levelly, but he felt the money slip out of his grasp as he walked forward in the darkness and wondered how far he would have to go to find an omnibus back towards his home. He should not spend money on hansoms any more.

It was nearly seven o'clock by the time he alighted from the final leg of his journey, with the two pounds that Louvain had given him still unbroken. He was in Tottenham Court Road with only a hundred yards or so to walk. The mist had settled, obscuring the distances. It smelled of soot from the chimneys and the horse manure of the day, which had not yet been cleared, but he knew the way almost to the step. It would be warm once he was inside.

There would be food prepared, if Hester were in. He tried not to hope too fiercely that she was. Her work at

23

the clinic was of intense importance to her. Before they had met seven years ago she had nursed in the Crimea with Florence Nightingale. On her return to England she had worked occasionally in hospitals, but her independence on the battlefield had made her intolerant of being reduced to cleaning, stoking fires and rolling bandages. Her temper had cost her more than one position.

As a private nurse caring for individual cases she had been far more successful. But now, married to Monk, it was no longer acceptable to either of them that she reside in the home of the invalid, as was necessary. She had turned her attention instead to helping prostitutes who were injured in the course of their trade, and had nowhere to turn. Hester had first set up the clinic almost in the shadow of the Coldbath Prison, then – in a stroke of brilliant opportunism – moved it to a large house nearby in Portpool Lane. Monk's only objection was that the very urgency of the need for such a place meant that Hester spent more hours there than Monk really liked. Indeed, when there was a serious case, she was there even longer.

He reached the front door and slipped his key into the lock. Inside the lights were on, only dimly, but it must mean she was at home. She would never have left them to burn otherwise.

He walked through quickly, a surge of pleasure welling up inside him. It was far more than simply the warmth of being protected from the wind and enclosed by his own home, or even knowing that a long, comfortable night lay ahead of him.

She was in the sitting room, which was always tidy, always heated because it was the room in which he saw clients. It was Hester, years before they were married, who had insisted it to be so. It was she who had placed the chairs either side of the fireplace and put the bowl with flowers on the table.

Now she dropped her book and stood up, her face full of pleasure. She came straight to him, expecting him to put his arms around her and to kiss her. The sheer certainty of it was almost as sweet to him as the act itself. He held her closely, kissing her mouth, her cheek, her closed eyes. Her hair was untidy. She never cared about it much. She smelled faintly of carbolic from the clinic. No matter how much she scrubbed, it never entirely went. She was a little too thin to be womanly. He had always thought it was something he did not like, and yet he would not have changed her gangling grace or her fierce, tender emotion for the most beautiful woman he had ever seen or dreamed of. The reality was always better, sharper, more surprising. In loving her, he had discovered a fire and delicacy within himself he had not known existed. She infuriated him at times, exasperated him, excited him, but never, ever bored him. Above all – more precious than anything else – in her presence he could not be lonely.

'The shipowner gave me the job,' he told her, still with his arms around her. 'His name is Louvain. He's lost a cargo of ivory, and the thieves murdered the night watchman to get it.'

She pulled back to look at his face. 'So why doesn't he call in the River Police? Is it even legal not to?'

He saw the anxiety in her eyes. He understood it uncomfortably well.

'He needs the ivory back more quickly than they'll be able to get it,' he explained. 'There are thefts up and down the river all the time.'

'And murders?' she asked. There was no criticism in her, but there was fear. Did she know how narrow their finances were now? The bills were paid for this week, but what about next week, and the one after?

She loved the clinic. It would be a defeat of all they had tried to do if she had to give it up in order to earn money as a paid nurse again. It would not survive without her. She was not only the one reliable person there with any medical experience, hers was the will and the courage behind the whole venture.

They had managed through the harder, earlier times with the financial help of Lady Callandra Daviot, who had been a friend to Hester for years, and to both of them since long before their marriage. But it was a step Monk was very loath to take, to have to go back to her now – when she was no longer actively involved in their cases, and certainly could not help in this one – simply to ask her for money he knew perfectly well he would not be able to repay. And could Hester ever accept that, either?

He touched his fingers gently to her hair. 'Yes, of course murders,' he answered. 'And accidental deaths, which is what the authorities seem to be assuming this one is so far; Louvain has not told them otherwise. When I catch the thief and can prove his guilt, then I can prove the murder as well. I have Louvain and the morgue attendant's statements on paper.'

He hated the thought of working secretly from the River Police. He was not a lover of authority, nor did he take orders with ease, or grace, but he was a policeman by training, and even if he despised some of them for lack of imagination or intelligence, he still respected the concept of an organised force, both to prevent and to detect crime. Deceiving them, even obliquely or by omission, disturbed him.

Hester did not argue. That in itself betrayed her understanding of their financial need. He wished she had not known. He was afraid she would give up the clinic, but he did not know what to say that would not drag the issue out into the open. He did not want to be in a position where he had either to lie, or to tell her other truths he would rather conceal unless they became

26

unavoidable – things about the river and his own ignorance of it, and the fear inside him that he might never find the ivory.

'I'm hungry,' he said with a smile. 'What is there to eat?'

Chapter Two

In the morning the mist had blown away. Monk left the house by seven to begin his investigation, and his learning of the river and its customs. Hester slept a little later, but by eight she too was on her way to the house in Portpool Lane, almost under the shadow of Reid's Brewery. The journey was over three miles, and necessitated the use of two omnibuses, and then a walk, but she was too aware of the expense to waste money on a hansom, except in the middle of the night.

She arrived just before nine to find Margaret already there, having made a note of the night's work, and busy considering what might best be done for the day. She was a slender woman in her late twenties. She had the confidence that goes with a degree of money and education, and the vulnerability of a woman who was not yet married, and had therefore failed to fulfil her mother's ambition for her – and indeed her own for her social and financial survival.

She was dressed in a plain wool skirt and jacket, and had a pencil and piece of paper in her hand. Her face lit when she saw Hester.

'Only one admission during the night,' she said. 'A woman with a serious stomach ache. I think it's largely hunger. We gave her porridge and a bed, and she looks better already.' There was a shadow in her face, in spite of the harmlessness of the news.

Since the move from Coldbath Square there was no need for rent to be paid, so Hester knew it was not that which caused Margaret's concern. This building was theirs – or, more accurately, it belonged to Squeaky Robinson, who remained out of prison and with a roof over his head strictly on condition that they had the sole use of it for as long as they should wish. It had allowed them to expand their work, and now a greater part of London was aware that here prostitutes who were injured or ill could find help, without religious conditions attached, or any questions from police.

The building was a warren of rooms and corridors. Originally it had been two large houses with appropriate doors or walls knocked down to turn it into one, and it possessed an adequate kitchen and excellent laundry. Its use in Squeaky Robinson's time had been as a brothel; the laundry in particular was an inheritance from that time. Ideally, if more walls were removed they could turn rooms into wards, which would make it far simpler to care for patients, but that would cost money they did not have.

As it was, it was getting more difficult to afford the necessities: coal, the raw materials for laundering, cleaning and lighting and food. Too little money seemed to be available for medicine.

'Where did you put her?' Hester asked.

'Room three,' Margaret answered. 'I looked in on her half an hour ago, and she was asleep.'

Hester went to see anyway. She opened the door softly, turning the handle with no noise, and stepped inside. The place was still well furnished from its original use, which had been only a matter of months ago. There was quite a good rug, albeit made of bright rags, but it kept the warmth, and there was old paper on the walls, which was better than bare plaster. Now the bed was made up with sheets and blankets, and a young woman lay sound asleep, curled up sideways, her hair knotted loosely at the back of her neck, her thin shoulders easily discernible through the cotton nightgown. It was one belonging to the clinic. She had probably come in wearing her own gaudy street dress, which would be showing too much flesh, and giving no protection from the cold.

Hester touched the thin neck with the back of her fingers. The girl did not stir. She looked about eighteen, but more likely was far less. Her collarbone protruded and her skin was very white, but her pulse was steady enough. Margaret was probably right, and it was no more than chronic hunger and exhaustion. When she woke up they would give her more to eat, but after that she would probably have to go. They could not afford to feed her regularly.

Hester wondered who she was: a prostitute without the skill or the prettiness to make enough to live on; a servant thrown out because she had lost her character, either willingly or unwillingly involved with one of the men in the house; a girl who had had a baby, and perhaps lost it; an abandoned wife, a petty thief – the possibilities were legion.

Hester went back out and closed the door. She returned to the main room, which had been created with rather simplistic carpentry from two smaller rooms a few months ago. Margaret was sitting at the table and Bessie carrying a tray from the kitchen with a teapot and two cups. Bessie was a big woman with a fierce countenance and hair that she screwed back off her brow and twisted into a tight knot on the back of her head. She would never have said so – it would have been a sign of unforgivable sentimentality – but she was devoted to Hester, and even Margaret was earning considerable favour in her eyes.

'Tea,' she said unnecessarily, putting the tray down in the middle of the table. 'And toast,' she added, indicating the rack with five pieces propped up to remain crisp. 'We in't got much jam left, and I dunno where we're gonna get any more, less we get it given us! An' 'oo's gonna give jam ter the likes of us? Beggin' yer pardon, Mrs Monk!' And without waiting for an answer she swept out.

'Are we really out of jam?' Hester said unhappily. 'And so low we can't afford any more?' She would like to have brought some from home, but she was far more aware of the need for economy there than she had allowed Monk to know. She had already bought less meat, and cheaper cuts; and herrings more often than cod or haddock. She had told the woman who came in to do the heavy cleaning that she was no longer needed, and when she had time she meant to do it herself.

Before Margaret could answer there was a sharp bang on the door and a moment later, without waiting for an answer, Squeaky Robinson came in. He was a thin man, dried up and bent over. He was dressed in a very old velvet jacket that had lost whatever its original colour had been. His trousers were thick and grey and he wore slippers on his feet. He carried a leather-bound ledger in his arms. He put it on the table, eyeing the tea and toast, and sat down in the third chair opposite Hester.

'We cut it down,' he said with satisfaction, 'but you'll have to do better.' He had the air of a schoolmaster with a promising student who had unaccountably fallen short of expectation. 'You can't put out more'n you get in.'

Hester looked at him patiently, but it required a certain effort. 'You've balanced the books, Squeaky. What do we have left?'

'Of course I've balanced the books!' he said with satisfaction, even if he was making it by a pretence of being offended. 'That's what I'm here for!' He was here under constant protest, because at first he had had nowhere else to go when Hester and Margaret had very neatly tricked him out of his appalling brothel business, and at a stroke gained the building for use as the clinic. But as he had busied himself with small jobs here, he had gained a certain pleasure from it, even if he would sooner have given blood than admitted it.

'So how much have we left?' she repeated.

He looked at her lugubriously. 'Not enough, Mrs Monk, not enough. We'll manage food for another five or six days, if you're careful. No jam!' He pulled his lips down at the corners. ''Cepting for yourself, p'r'aps, and Miss Ballinger. No jam for these women! And careful with the soap and vinegar and the like.' He took a breath. 'And don't tell me you got to scrub! I know that; just scrub careful. And boil them bandages up and use 'em again,' he added unnecessarily. He nodded, pleased with himself.

He was becoming more and more proprietorial each time they discussed the subject. The patients here were the same women whom less than a year ago he had blackmailed into prostitution against their will. Now he gained a secret pleasure – and it was secret – in scrimping halfpennies to feed them and heal their injuries. He still spoke of them as if they were both useless and contemptible, but Hester had more than once caught him boxing the ears of a delivery boy daring to do the same. He had defended himself, saying the boy had been insolent to him, but Hester had heard the truth.

'Carbolic?' she asked.

'Oh – some,' he conceded. 'But we need more money, and I dunno where you're going to get it, 'less you let me follow a few ideas of my own?'

Margaret raised her cup to conceal a smile.

Hester could make an educated guess as to what Squeaky's ideas might be. 'Not yet,' she said firmly. 'And we don't need to attract any attention that we could avoid. Give Bessie what she'll need for food, but be sure to keep back at least two pounds. Tell me when we get that low.'

'I can tell you now,' Squeaky said, shaking his head. 'It'll be the day after tomorrow.' He sniffed. 'Sometimes I think you live in a dream. You need me to wake you up, an' that's a fact.' He rose to his feet slowly, clutching the book. There was an air of profound satisfaction in him, the ease of his body, the smug line of his lips, the way his hands folded over the ledger.

Remembering his previous occupation, and his outrage at being tricked into yielding the house and all its furniture, which was his entire livelihood, Hester smiled back at him. 'Of course I do,' she agreed. 'That's why I kept you.'

His satisfaction vanished. He swallowed hard. 'I know that!'

'I'm glad you do it so diligently,' she added.

Mollified, he turned and went out, closing the door with a snick behind him.

Margaret put down her cup and her face was grave. 'We do need to get more money,' she agreed. 'I've tried the usual sources, but it's getting more difficult.' She looked rueful. 'They're all generous enough when they think it's for missionary work in Africa or somewhere like that. Speak about lepers and they're only too willing. I began two evenings ago at a soirée. I was with . . .' she coloured very slightly '. . . Sir Oliver, and the opportunity presented itself to approach the subject of charitable gifts without the least awkwardness.'

Hester bit her lip to disguise her smile. Oliver Rathbone was one of the most brilliant – and successful – barristers in London. He had not long ago been in love with Hester, but an uncertainty about a step as irrevocable as marriage, and to someone as unsuitable in her outspokenness as Hester, had made him hesitate to ask her. Not that she would have accepted him. She could never have loved anyone else as she did Monk, in spite of their continual quarrels, the erratic nature of his income and his future, let alone the dark shadow of amnesia across his past. To marry him was a risk; to marry anyone else would have been to accept safety and deny the fullness of life, the heights and the depths of emotion, and the happiness that went with them.

Now she believed that Rathbone could find that same joy with Margaret. And deep as her friendship with him still was, being a woman, she felt most sensitively for Margaret, and read her with an ease she would never have betrayed.

'But the moment they knew that it was for a clinic for street women here,' Margaret went on, 'they balked at it.' She bit her lip. 'They make me so angry! I stand there feeling like a fool because I'm full of hope that this time they'll give something. I know it shows in my face, and I can't help it. I'm trying to be polite, and inside I am veering wildly between pleading with them, thanking them overmuch as if I were a beggar and the money were for me, and fury if they refuse me.'

She did not add that she had been acutely conscious of Rathbone beside her, and what he would think of her manners, her decorum, her suitability to be his wife. But on the other hand, would he lose all respect for her, and she for herself, were she to do less than her best for a cause she believed in so passionately?

'And they say "no"?' Hester said gently, although something of her own anger crept into her tone. Cowardice and hypocrisy were the two vices she hated the most, perhaps because they seemed to give rise to so many others, especially cruelty. They were woven into each other. She had learned how many men used the street women, and she refrained from judgement on that. She also knew that quite often their wives were perfectly

34

aware of it, even if only by deduction. What she hated was the hypocrisy of then turning and condemning those same women. Perhaps the interdependence was what frightened them, or even the knowledge that what separated them was often an accident of circumstance rather than any moral superiority.

Where there really was a moral honour, a cleanness of spirit, she had found there was also most often a compassion as well. Margaret was an example of exactly such singleness of intent.

'And then I feel so ridiculously disappointed,' Margaret answered, looking across at Hester and smiling ruefully at herself. 'And I'm disgusted to be so vulnerable.' She did not mention Rathbone's name, but Hester knew what she was thinking. Margaret caught her eye and blushed. 'Am I so obvious?' she said softly.

'Only to me,' Hester answered. 'Because I've felt just the same.' She finished the last of her tea. 'But we do need more money, so please don't stop trying. You know me well enough to imagine what a disaster I would be in your place!'

Margaret laughed in spite of herself. Seeing her amusement it flashed across Hester's mind to wonder if Rathbone had ever told her of some of the social catastrophes Hester had precipitated in her single days when she had been newly home from the Crimean battlefields and, still full of indignation at incompetence, she had burned with belief in her power to move people to change, to reform. She had wanted to sweep away vested interest and follow discovery and truth. She had spared no one with her tongue, and achieved very few of her dreams.

'I suppose so,' Margaret conceded. 'I hold my tongue far more than you do. I don't think I like that in myself. I'm thinking just the same as you are, I'm just too used to not saying it.'

'It doesn't achieve anything,' Hester admitted. 'In the end it is self-indulgent. You feel wonderful for a few minutes, then you realise what you've lost.'

Margaret rubbed her hand over her brow. 'I hate having to swallow my beliefs, and be civil to people because I need their money!'

'The women need their money,' Hester corrected her. She leaned forward impulsively and put her hand on Margaret's. 'Don't be as frank as I was – it horrified Oliver. The fact that most of what I said was true made it worse, not better. Give him time to come to it himself. Believe me, he is a lot more liberal than he used to be.' Memory lit sharply in her mind, and she found herself almost laughing. 'A year ago he would have been paralysed with horror at the idea of what we did to Squeaky to get this place – but I think honestly he rather enjoyed it!'

A smile lit Margaret's face, making her eyes dance. 'He did – didn't he?' she remembered.

Bessie came in, as usual without knocking, to say that there was a young woman looking for help. 'Like an 'a'penny rabbit, she is,' she said wearily. 'All skin an' bone. Never make a livin' like that! In't 'ad a square meal in weeks, shouldn't wonder. White as a fish's belly an' wheezin' like a train.'

Hester stood up. 'I'll come,' she said simply. She glanced back once at Margaret, and saw her go to the medicine cupboard and unlock it to check what they had, and what they might afford to buy.

She followed Bessie, and found the girl standing in the waiting room shivering, but too wretched to be frightened any more. She looked much as Bessie had described. Hester estimated her to be about sixteen.

Hester asked her the usual questions and studied her as she answered. She was slightly feverish and had heavy congestion in her lungs, but her principal problems were exhaustion and hunger, and now also cold. Her thin dress and jacket were useless against the late October rain, not to mention the freezing fog, which would come up from the river most nights. If only they had money to give her a hot bath, and decent clothes! But the source of what little there was was already in jeopardy.

Hester dearly wanted Margaret to marry Rathbone, but if she did then she might well no longer be able to work here. At best her time would be restricted. As Lady Rathbone she could hardly spend as many hours here as she did now. She would have social obligations, and of course pleasures she had certainly earned. Rathbone had more than sufficient financial means to give her all she could wish of position and comfort – not like Monk, who understood both hardship and work only too intimately.

And then why should she not have children? That would end her connection with the clinic altogether.

But it could not be fought against, nor would Hester have wanted to, even were it possible.

She told Bessie to put the kettle on again and use the warming pans to heat a bed for the girl. She could at least stay here and sleep until the bed was needed for a more serious case. A little hot water and honey would ease her chest, and a couple of slices of bread her hunger. It is hard to sleep well on an empty stomach.

'We in't got much 'oney left,' Bessie said warningly, but she was already on her way to the kitchen. This was one she could help.

By the time Hester left in the late afternoon to go home, the regular costermonger, Toddy, had called by to give her the bruised apples he could not sell, and the heavier vegetables it was not worth his while to take all the way back home again. He had consulted her about his cough, his bunions and the blister on his hand. She had looked at them all and assured him they were not serious. She recommended honey for his throat, and he went away happy.

Effie, as the new girl was named, was still sound asleep, but her breathing was less noisy and there was a look of deep peace in her white face. The other patients were well enough, and Margaret was renewed in her determination to hold her tongue at social events, no matter what it cost her temper or her indignation. Squeaky was still grumbling about the responsibility of balancing the books, but if there were a man in London who could do it, it was he.

Hester was pleased to arrive home, even though she was aware that Monk would probably not be there. At least he had a case to work on, rather than looking for business, hoping and failing. Although as she cleared out the grate and lit a low fire, being careful from habit to use no more coal than necessary, in spite of their suddenly improved circumstances, she could not help her thoughts turning to the problems he would face in an area so unfamiliar to him.

She lit the fire and watched the slow flame seeking the wood sticks, then the smaller pieces of coal. The danger was that he would fail. His ignorance of the nature of crime peculiar to the river might mean there were things he did not see, or saw but did not understand. A greater danger was the risk of violence, and the fact that he was even more alone than in the city. From the little he had told her, he was working not exactly against the River Police, but at least without their knowledge, and on a case that was rightly theirs. Was it disloyal to be afraid for him? Was she doubting his ability?

The fire was not catching. The flame had sunk to a smoulder. Hester bent on her hands and knees and kneeled forward to blow gently at the small part that was still alive. She knew the trick of placing an open newspaper over the whole front of the fireplace, to make the chimney draw, but she had no newspaper. It was an extra expense unnecessary at the moment. Anyway, she was too busy to take much interest in the world and its troubles. There was no time to read such things.

The flames licked up again.

When Monk came in she must not let him see that she was concerned. The last thing he needed was his faith in himself undermined. She must behave as if she believed in him, without stating it. She would face disaster only if it came.

This was the season of year when stew was a very welcome meal, and if the big pan were left on the back of the stove, she could add vegetables to it every day, and it kept perfectly. It also meant that whatever time Monk came home, it was hot and waiting. This time she felt free to add a nice amount of fresh meat, and when she heard his key in the lock shortly after seven, it was cooked.

'Well?' she asked when they were seated at the table and the bowls were steaming in front of them.

He thought before he replied, watching her reaction. 'I've never been so cold in my life!' he answered, then smiled widely. 'At least not that I can remember . . .' Since recovering so much of his past in the recent railway case, the fact of his amnesia no longer haunted him as it had done from the time of the coach crash that had caused it a month or two before they had first met, now nearly seven years ago. It was as if the ghosts were laid, the worst known and faced, and it had been not giants but ordinary weaknesses after all, frailties that could be understood, pitied and healed. The horror had shrunk to human proportions, into tragedy rather than wickedness. Now he could joke about it.

She smiled back. A long-borne weight was gone. 'Is the river very different from the streets?' she asked.

'It feels different,' he replied, taking another mouthful of stew and savouring the richness of it compared with their recent frugality. 'Everything's governed by the tides;

all of life seems to revolve around them. Ships go upstream and downstream with the ebb and flow. Get caught at low water and you run aground, but try to pass under the bridges at high water and you break your masts. The rivermen know it to the foot.' He thought for a moment. 'But the water has a beauty the streets don't. There's a feeling of width; the light and shadow are always changing.'

She looked at his face and saw the awe of it in him. There was something in the elements of the river that had captured him already. Again the fear touched her that he was out of his depth. Might he be too occupied in seeing what was physical to be aware of the differences in the minds of thieves and receivers, the subtleties of deceit and violence whose warnings he might not recognise because they were unfamiliar?

'You aren't listening,' he accused her.

'I'm trying to picture it,' she said quickly, meeting his eyes again. 'It doesn't sound like the city at all. Where do you start to look for the ivory? Can you trace where people have passed when there are no tracks, no footprints?' Then she wished she had not asked, because how could he know? It was too soon.

He looked rueful. 'I learned that today. I spent most of the time just walking around the docks. I've lived in London for at least fifteen years, but I had no idea how separate a world the docks are. Thousands of tons of cargo go through them every week, from every part of the world. It's amazing there isn't more lost.' He leaned a little forward over the table towards her, his food temporarily forgotten, his voice rising in urgency. 'It's the gateway to the world, in and out. Ships have to wait to unload until they can find space at one of the wharfs. Sometimes it's days, sometimes weeks after they drop anchor. There are people on the water all the time – little boats, ferries, tugs, quite apart from the barges—'

'How are you going to find out who took the ivory?' she interrupted.

He took another mouthful of stew. 'I'm not sure that I can begin there,' he replied. 'I think I'll have to come at it the other way, find out where it went, and trace back from there to who took it. I need the thief because he killed Hodge, otherwise I wouldn't care about him. But he sold the ivory to someone, or he will do. Everything that's stolen gets sold sooner or later, unless you can eat it, burn it or wear it.'

'Burn it?' she said in surprise.

'Coal,' he explained with a sudden smile. 'Most of the mudlarks on the banks are after coal. Some are looking for nails, of course, or anything else you can use.'

'Oh . . . yes.' She should have thought of that. She tried to imagine wading up to your knees in the winter river, bending to search for bits someone would buy. But perhaps it was no worse than walking the alleys at night in the rain, hoping to sell the use of your body for half an hour. Poverty, and the need to survive, could change your view of a lot of things. Thank heaven that if Monk did not find the ivory, at least they could turn to Callandra Daviot to help them, temporarily. That is, if Monk could bear to ask her.

Perhaps Hester should go to her and ask for something for the clinic? Callandra, of all people, would understand. She had worked ceaselessly for the good of the hospital, and never shrank from asking anyone for money, time, or anything else she needed. She had shamed many a society matron into a larger gift than the woman had ever intended.

Hester stood up and cleared away the plates. She had a hot bread and butter pudding in the oven, and she brought it through and served it with considerable pride. Making it so well was a very recent achievement. She watched Monk eat it with pleasure, noting the amusement

41

he strove to hide, not with great success. She caught his smile, and shrugged a little ruefully.

They were still at the table when there was a firm rap on the front door.

Monk stood up immediately, but there was surprise in his face. It was too late for anyone to call socially, and he expected no information on his case for Louvain yet. Either the caller was for Hester, to do with some emergency at Portpool Lane, or a new case for him.

Hester picked up the dirty dishes and carried them out to the kitchen. When she returned, Callandra Daviot was standing in the sitting room. Her hat was askew and her hair was as wildly untidy as usual, curling in the damp and falling out of its pins, none of which mattered in the slightest. Her eyes were bright and her cheeks flushed. She had one glove in her hand and the other one was nowhere to be seen. She was glowing with happiness.

Hester was delighted to see her. She went forward and put her arms around her, feeling Callandra's quick response.

'How are you, my dear?' Callandra said warmly.

'Very happy to see you,' Hester replied, letting her go and standing back. 'Would you like a cup of tea?'

Callandra looked startled. 'Oh! No, thank you, my dear.' She stood still in the middle of the floor as if unable to make herself sit down, the smile still wide on her face. 'How are you both?'

Hester thought of lying politely, but she and Callandra had known each other too long and too well for such a thing. The generation between them had not affected their friendship in the slightest. It had been Hester, rather than anyone Callandra's own age or social class, who had watched her heart-breaking love for Kristian Beck, and understood it. It had been Hester and Monk to whom she had turned when Kristian had been accused of murder, and not only because of Monk's skill, but because they were friends who would not mock her loyalty, or intrude upon her grief.

Hester could not deceive her. 'We are struggling to make ends meet in the clinic,' she answered. 'Victims of our success, I suppose.' However deep their friendship, she would not tell her that for Monk work had been poor of late. He could do so if he wished; for her to do it would be a betrayal.

Callandra immediately turned her concentration to the subject.

'Raising funds is always difficult,' she agreed. 'Particularly when it is not a charity they feel comfortable boasting about. It's one thing to tell everyone at the dinner table that you have just given to doctors or missionaries scattered across the Empire. It can stop conversation utterly to say you are trying to save the local prostitutes.'

Hester could not help laughing, and even Monk smiled.

'Do you still have that excellent Margaret Ballinger with you?' Callandra asked hopefully.

'Oh yes,' Hester said with enthusiasm.

'Good.' Callandra lifted her hand as if she should have had an umbrella in it, then remembered that she had left it somewhere. 'I can give her some reliable names for raising contributions. You had better not be the one to ask.' A smile of profound affection softened her face. 'I know you too well to delude myself you would be tactful. One refusal, and you would render such an opinion of them as to make all future approaches impossible.'

'Thank you,' Hester said with mock decorum, but there was something in Callandra's words that disturbed her. Why did Callandra not offer to ask them herself? In the past she had not been hesitant, and she could surely see in Hester's face that she was already busier than she could manage with comfort.

Callandra was still standing in the middle of the room

as though too excited to sit. Now she was searching in her reticule for something, but since it was more voluminous than most, and obviously overfull and in no sort of order at all, she was having difficulty. She gave up. 'Have you a piece of paper, William? Perhaps you could write them down for me?'

'Of course,' he agreed, but he glanced at Hester rapidly and away again before he moved to obey.

Hester was on the edge of asking what it was that had brought Callandra, unannounced, and was so clearly momentous to her so that all her usual care was scattered to oblivion. But to do so might be intrusive. She was a dear friend, but that did not destroy her right to privacy.

Monk brought the pen and paper, and an inkwell, and set them on the table for Callandra. She sat down at last and wrote the names and addresses herself, and then after a moment's thought, with a flourish added what sums she thought they could comfortably contribute. She held it up in the air and waved it for the ink to dry, since Monk had brought no blotting paper, then she handed it to Hester. 'Don't lose it,' she commanded. 'I may not be able to replace it for you.'

Monk stiffened.

Hester looked up at him slowly, hardly breathing.

Callandra's eyes were bright. It was with happiness and tears, as if she were on the edge of some tremendous step and she was clinging to the last moments of the familiar, because it too was dear to her and she could not let go without pain.

'I am going to Vienna,' she said with only the slightest tremor in her voice. 'To live there.'

'Vienna!' Hester repeated the word as if it were close to incomprehensible, and yet it made the most devastating sense. Vienna was the original home of Kristian Beck, before he had left with his wife to come to London. Then he had met Callandra, his wife had been murdered, and

44

grief and the shattering revelations had followed. Perhaps as difficult as those of his dead wife's character had been the discovery of Kristian's own origins, turning upside down everything he had previously believed. But was Callandra going to Vienna because Kristian had decided to return? What was his part in her decision? Hester was already dry-mouthed with fear that Callandra would be hurt yet again, and she had borne so much already.

But Callandra's eyes were shining, not, it seemed, with a wild hope, but rather with a steady understanding. 'Kristian and I are going to be married,' she said softly, her voice tender, and absolutely sure. 'He has decided that he needs to face the past, look at it honestly and discover the answers, whatever they are.'

She turned from Hester to Monk. 'I'm sorry, William. Sharing cases with you gave me interest and purpose during many years when I would have had neither without you. Your friendship has meant even more to me – as much, in its own way, as Hester's. But Kristian will be my husband.' She coloured very slightly. Her eyes flickered down, and then up again. 'I wish to be with him, and if leaving my home and my dearest friends here is the price, then I will pay it willingly. I thank you with all my heart for the love you have given me in the past, and for your skill and loyalty in defending Kristian . . . and me. I know what we would have suffered without you.'

Hester went forward and put her arms around Callandra, holding her tightly, and feeling Callandra's eager response. 'I couldn't be more delighted for you,' she said honestly. 'Go to Vienna, and be happy. And whatever Kristian finds there, help him to remember that he is not responsible for the sins or the ignorance of his fathers. None of us is. We cannot ever undo our own pasts, let alone anyone else's. But we have the future, and I am so glad yours is with Kristian. That couldn't be better.' She kissed Callandra on the cheek, hugged her hard for a moment longer, and then stepped back.

Callandra turned to Monk, her face still touched with uncertainty.

He did exactly as Hester had done. 'Go and be happy,' he said sincerely. 'I can't think of anyone who deserves it more than both of you. And when you've solved the problems of the past, there'll be other good causes to fight for. If there's anyone who knows that, I do.'

Callandra sniffed hard, gulped, and gave up the battle. She let the tears flow, standing quite still, her face smiling in spite of them. Then as Monk pulled out a handkerchief, she accepted it and blew her nose.

'Thank you,' she said, handing it back to Hester. 'I apologise. But I cannot add stealing your clothes to my general desertion. My carriage is waiting. Will you allow me to retreat with what dignity I have left?'

'Of course,' Hester said, her own voice thick with emotion. 'Goodbyes are ridiculous. One is quite sufficient.'

'I'm most grateful,' Callandra said, and with her eyes brimming again.

She dug in her reticule and this time quite easily found what she was looking for. She brought out two small packages, handsomely wrapped and tied up in ribbon. She glanced at them, then handed one to Hester and the other to Monk. From the expectancy in her face she was obviously waiting for them to open the gifts now.

Hester started with hers, undoing the ribbon and paper carefully. Inside was a box, and within it the most exquisitely carved cameo, not of the usual head of a woman, but of a man with an elaborate helmet and flowing hair. It was mounted in rich filigree of both yellow and rose gold.

Hester gasped with delight, then looked up at Callandra, and saw the answering pleasure in her eyes.

Monk unwrapped his more impatiently, tearing the paper. His was a gold watch, a perfect piece of both art and workmanship. His appreciation was abundantly clear in his face even before he spoke to thank her.

'So you will remember not only me, but how much I care for you both,' she said a little huskily. 'Now I must go. This has already continued too long. I hate people who say goodbye and then seem incapable of actually leaving.' She smiled once more and then swept out of the door as Monk held it open for her. Her skirts were crooked, her jacket not quite matching, and her hat had slipped to one side, but her head was high. She did not look behind her, even once.

Monk closed the door and returned to the fire, the watch still in his hand. Hester was still clasping the cameo. She was thrilled for Callandra. Her friend had loved Kristian profoundly and hopelessly for so long that to have wished her anything but success would be unthinkable. But she was aware, with the cold from the open door still sharp in the air, just how alone it left them. She was not sure what to say. The awareness of the difference it would make, especially now, was like a third presence in the room between them.

'It had to happen,' she said, lifting her gaze slowly to meet his. 'We couldn't have wished it differently. If the position were the other way around, and it were you and I in their place, and they in ours, I should go to Vienna, or anywhere else, if you needed me – or wanted me with you.'

He smiled slowly. 'Would you?'

She knew he was joking, fighting the fear so she could not see it. She pretended she had not. 'I'd like tea,' she remarked. 'Shall I fetch some?'

By ten the following day when Monk was back at the dockside, Hester was going through the cabinets in the main room at Portpool Lane. There was conspicuously less of almost everything than there had been the day before. No later than tomorrow they would have to buy more disinfectant at least, carbolic, lye, vinegar and candles. It would be nice to have brandy as well, and fortified wine to add to beef tea – she could list another dozen helpful things.

The girl who had come in the day before was still deeply asleep, but her breathing was easier and there was already a little colour in her skin. If they could have afforded to feed her for a week or two, she would probably have recovered completely.

Hester had turned away from the cupboard and was going to the drawer of the desk when Bessie came in. She had her sleeves rolled up and an apron tied around her waist. There was an old smear of blood across the centre of it.

'We got another of 'em as can 'ardly breathe,' she said wearily, her face puckered in anger because the problem was too big. She had spent as long as she could remember trying to cope with it, and as fast as she cured one, another turned up, if not two. 'Why couldn't the Good Lord 'a' designed us better?' she added tartly. 'Or else done away wi' winter. 'E can't 'a' not see'd this comin'! It 'appens every year!'

Hester did not bother with an answer – not that she had one anyway. The question was rhetorical. She turned from what she had been going to do and followed Bessie to the entrance room, where a middle-aged woman in brown was sitting hunched up on the old couch, her arms folded protectively across her chest. She breathed slowly and with obvious difficulty. In the candlelight her face was colourless; her fair hair, liberally streaked with grey, was piled on her head like so much old straw.

Hester looked more carefully at her pinched face and saw the whiteness about her lips and around her eyes, and the slight flush in her cheeks. Her problem was probably bronchitis, which could turn to pneumonia.

'What's your name?' she asked.

'Molly Struther,' the woman answered without looking up.

'How do you feel, exactly?'

'Tired enough ter die,' the woman replied. 'Dunno why I bothered ter come 'ere, 'cept Flo tol' me ter. Said as yer'd 'elp. Daft, I call it. Wot can yer do? Gonna change the world, are yer?' There was no mockery in her voice; she had not the energy for it.

'Find you a warm, dry bed – undisturbed for the most part – and some food,' Hester replied. 'Plenty of hot tea, with maybe a nip of brandy in it, at least until the brandy runs out.'

Molly drew in a deep breath of amazement, and broke into a fit of coughing until she all but gagged. Hester fetched her some hot water from the kettle, with a spoonful of honey in it, and held it out for her. Molly sipped it gratefully, but it was several minutes before she tried to speak again.

'Thanks,' she said finally.

Hester helped her to one of the rooms with two beds, while Bessie went off to heat a warming pan. Half an hour later Molly was lying on her back, blankets up to her chin, eyes still wide with surprise and the sheer unfamiliarity of it.

'We gotter get more money!' Bessie said to Hester when they were back in the kitchen. She poked tentatively at the stove, wondering how long it would burn without adding more coke to it. It was a fine balance between the minimum it would take to keep burning, and so little it actually went out.

'I know,' Hester admitted. 'Margaret's trying, and I've got a list of names to go on with, but people are uncomfortable about giving because of the women's occupation. They feel better about sending their offerings to Africa, or somewhere like that.'

49

Bessie made a snarl in her throat that was eloquent of contempt. 'So they think them Africans is better than we are?' she demanded. 'Or they're colder, or 'ungrier, or sicker mebbe?'

'I don't think it's got anything to do with that,' Hester replied, warming her hands above the cast-iron surface of the stove.

'O' course it ain't!' Bessie snapped, filling the kettle up again from the ewer of water in the far corner near the stone sink, and putting it back on the hob. 'It's ter do wi' conscience, that's wot it's ter do wi'! It in't our fault if Africans starve or die, it's too far away for us ter feel bad about it. But if our own is freezin' an' starvin', then that's summink ter feel bad abaht, aw right. 'Cos mebbe we should 'a' see'd they wasn't like that in the first place.'

Hester did not answer.

'Or mebbe it's 'cos they in't no better than they should be,' Bessie went on, drying her hands on her apron. 'They sell their selves on the street, which is sin, in't it? An' we might get our skirts dirty if we 'ave anythin' ter do wi' the likes o' them! Never mind our 'usbands go ter them poor sods fer a bit o' wotever we don't wanter do – 'cos we got an 'eadache, or it in't decent, or we don't want no more kids!' She slammed the grate door shut on the stove. 'It in't nice ter know about things like that, so we pretend as we don't! So o' course we don't want 'em fed or nursed; we'd rather play at it as they in't real. Gawd 'elp us, it in't our daughter, or sister, or even our man!'

'That's probably more like it,' Hester agreed, hoping the kettle would boil soon. A hot cup of tea would warm her through before she went round collecting the linen to wash, and turned her thoughts to what they could fall back on if Margaret failed. She didn't want an idle mind, or it would be too quickly filled with thoughts of how Monk was progressing on the docks in the blustering rain, searching for evidence he might not even recognise if it were there in his hands.

''Course it is,' Bessie retorted. 'Stick yer 'ead in the coal cellar, and then tell the world there in't nobody there, 'cos you can't see a bleedin' thing! Gor, I dunno! Are they stupid, or just frit out o' their brains?'

Hester did not reply, and she was upstairs changing beds ready to wash the linen when Bessie came tramping up again about two hours later.

'I'm here!' Hester replied, coming to the door.

'Got another sick one, poor cow,' Bessie said cheerfully. 'Looks like death on a bad day, she do. Shoot 'er'd be the kindest thing.' She caught a stray length of hair and tucked it behind her ear. 'Mind, I've felt like that at times. It don't last for ever, jus' seems like it. But she got a feller with 'er wot's askin' real nice, all proper dressed an' all. An' 'e says 'e'll pay us wot it costs ter look arter 'er, an' more besides.' She waited expectedly for Hester's approval.

Hester felt a stab of pity for the woman, but she could not help the flood of relief that washed over her that someone was here this minute with money – not the promise but the actuality.

'Good!' she said enthusiastically. 'Let's go and see him. Whoever he is, he's come to the right place!' And she followed on Bessie's heels as they went downstairs and back to the front room.

The man was standing looking towards them. He was a good height, not unusually broad, but strong and supple. His light brown hair was thick with a slight wave to it, but cut shorter than most, and sprang up from his brow. His skin was weather-burned, his eyes blue and narrowed, as if against light that was harsh.

'Mrs Monk?' He stepped forward. 'My name is Clement Louvain. I've heard that you do a great work here for women of the streets taken ill. Am I told rightly?'

51

Louvain! She was uncertain whether to show that she knew his name or not. 'You are told rightly,' she replied, intensely curious to know why he was here with a woman who was obviously extremely ill. Even at the slightest glance that Hester had been able to afford her, she looked fearful. She was all but fainting where she sat on the couch and she had not even raised her head to look at either Hester or Bessie. 'We help all those we can, particularly if they have not the money to pay a doctor,' she told Louvain.

'Money is not the problem,' he countered. 'I shall be happy to pay whatever charges you consider reasonable, as I told your woman. Plus a contribution so you can care for others. I imagine such a thing would be welcome? Folks can be hard to persuade when they can excuse themselves by a nice moral judgement.' There was a bitter humour in his eyes, and he knew Hester understood his meaning precisely. He was speaking to her as an equal, at least on the subject of irony.

'It would be welcome,' she agreed, warming to the intelligence in him, and the dry wit. 'Without money we can help no one.'

He nodded. 'What would be fair?'

She thought rapidly. She must not pitch it too high or he would be angry and refuse to pay, but she wanted as much as possible; at least sufficient to look after the woman well, feed her, give her clean linen and such medicines as would ease her distress. 'Two shillings a day,' she replied.

He seemed pleased. 'Good. I will give you fourteen shillings, and come back again in a week, although I imagine it will be unnecessary. She has family who will come for her before then. It is simply a matter of caring for her in the meantime. And I shall donate five pounds to your charity, so you can care for others as well.'

It was an enormous sum. Suspicions flickered in Hester's mind as to why he would give so much, and who the woman really was. But the money would keep them open for another two weeks at least, and she could not afford to refuse it. After that surely Margaret would have succeeded in persuading at least one benefactor from Callandra's list who would give something.

'Thank you,' she accepted. Equivocation or a refusal for the sake of courtesy would be absurd. 'What can you tell me about her so that we can do the best for her we are able?'

'Her name is Ruth Clark,' he replied. 'She is . . . was . . . the mistress of a colleague of mine. She has become ill, and he is no longer interested in her.' His voice carried emotion, but no anger that she could see. There was an intense pity in him, just for a moment; then he realised she was watching him, and he controlled it until it was hardly discernible. He was not a man who wished to have any softness seen in him, even here. 'He put her out,' he added. 'I have sent letters to her family, but it may be a few days before anyone can send for her. They live in the north. And at present she is too ill to travel.'

Hester looked at the woman again. Her face was flushed deep red and she seemed to be so consumed by her suffering that she was almost oblivious of her surroundings.

'Can you tell me any history of her illness?' Hester asked quietly. Even though she thought the woman was not listening to her, she still disliked speaking of someone as if they were not present. 'Anything you can tell me may help.'

'I don't know when it began,' he replied, 'or if it was slow or sudden. She seems to be feverish, barely able to stand, and since last night when I took her from his keeping, she has had no desire to eat.'

'Is she sick, vomiting?' she asked.

He looked at her quite steadily. 'No. It seems to be a matter of fever and dizziness, and difficulty in breathing.

I dare say it is pneumonia, or something of the sort.' He hesitated. 'I don't wish her in a hospital with their rigid moral rules. They would despise her for her circumstances, and rob her of any privacy.'

Hester understood. She had worked in hospital wards and knew the pages of directions, the things patients must do, and could not do without removal of privileges, freedoms. Many of them were to do with morality, in someone's strict opinion.

'We'll do everything for her that we can,' she promised. 'Rest and warmth, with help and as many hot drinks as we can persuade her to take, will help. But if it is pneumonia, it will have to run its course, until the fever breaks. No one can tell whether that will be good or ill, but we will do all that can be done. And I can promise you that at least she will be eased in her distress.'

'Thank you,' he said quietly and with a suddenly intense feeling. 'You are a good woman.' He put his hand into the pocket inside his jacket and pulled out a handful of money. He placed five gold sovereigns on the back of the couch, and then counted out four half-crowns and four separate shillings. 'Our agreement,' he said. 'I shall return in a week. Thank you, Mrs Monk. Good day to you.'

'Good day, Mr Louvain,' she replied, but already her attention was on the sick woman. She picked up the money and put it in the pocket of her dress, then rearranged her apron over it. 'Bessie, you'd best help me get Miss Clark along to a room and into bed. The poor soul looks fit to pass out.'

And indeed Ruth Clark seemed so deep in her distress as to be beyond helping herself. When Hester bent to half lift her on one side, with Bessie on the other, it was all they could do to get her as far as the first bedroom. Bessie propped her up, sagging against the door frame, while Hester freed one hand to open the door, and then together they half lifted, half dragged her across to the bed. She fell on it heavily. Her eyes were still open, but she did not seem to see anything, nor did she speak.

She was a dead weight, and with considerable difficulty, in spite of much practice, Hester took her outer clothes off while Bessie went to get half a cup of hot tea with a drop of brandy in it.

When she had removed all but Ruth's undergarments, and eased her into the bed, and put the covers over her, she took the pins out of her hair so she would be more comfortable. She touched her forehead. It was very hot, her skin dry. She studied her face for a little while, trying to assess what sort of woman she was, and how long she had been ill.

The pneumonia must have come on very rapidly. Had it been slow – a sore throat, then a tight chest, then fever – surely Louvain would have brought her sooner. She did not look to be a woman of delicate constitution, or prone to infection. The skin of her arms and body was firm and her neck and shoulders had a good texture, not the loose, thin, slightly bluish look of someone frequently ill. Her hair was thick; indeed, it was very handsome, dark brown with a heavy wave, and when she was well it would probably have a gloss to it. Her features were regular and pleasing. What kind of a man would have cast her off like this, simply because she was ill? It was certainly not chronic. If she recovered she would again be a healthy, vital woman, and she was not beyond her mid-thirties.

Was she some shipowner's mistress whose circumstances made it impossible for him to give her the care she needed? Was he afraid she was going to die, and he would be unable to explain the presence of her body in his house?

Or was she Louvain's own mistress, and for some reason he was unwilling to admit that?

Had the reputation of the clinic spread so far that even

55

on the dockside Louvain had heard of it? Or had Monk mentioned something of it when accepting his new job?

Perhaps none of that mattered now. Hester did not ask questions of the other women who came. Their recovery was all that concerned her; why should this woman be different?

Bessie came with the tea, and between them they propped Ruth up and – a teaspoonful at a time – managed to persuade her to take it. Finally they eased her down again, put the covers right up to her chin, and left her to sink into a sleep so profound she seemed close to unconsciousness.

Outside the room Hester fished in her pocket and took out the money. She gave one of the sovereigns and the fourteen shillings to Bessie. 'Go and get food, coal, carbolic, vinegar, brandy and quinine,' she ordered. She added another sovereign. 'Enough for the rest of the week. Thank God there isn't rent to pay! I'll give this to Squeaky. That should make him smile!' And with a lift of hope she followed down the corridor after Bessie.

Chapter Three

Monk left the house before daylight on his second day on the Louvain case, so he was on the wharfside by sunrise just before eight o'clock. It was a bright, sharp day with a blustery wind from the fast-flowing tide, and the light glittered in jagged patterns on the waves. The barges going slowly upstream were dark; the broadening dawn had not yet lent anything colour. Greys, silvers and looming shadows were cut by the dense blackness of masts sweeping the sky lazily, barely in motion, yardarms lumpy with sails lashed to them. The hulls of the ships were indistinguishable except for size, no features clear, just a shape: no gun ports, no figureheads, no timbers.

He had learned a little yesterday, but most of it only emphasised how different the river was from the city, and that he was a stranger with no old debts or favours to call in.

People stole things for many reasons: because they wanted them for themselves; because they could sell them to others; to deprive the owner of them; perhaps destroy them if they were dangerous, such as letters or markers of debt; or simply out of hate, to punish someone. Only two of those he considered likely where Louvain's ivory was concerned. The thief could sell it for profit, or he had some personal quarrel with Louvain and had taken it merely to make him suffer, possibly knowing that he had already committed it to a particular buyer.

Monk needed to know more about the receiving of stolen goods on the river and, even more than that, about Louvain himself, his friends, his enemies, his debtors and creditors, his rivals.

Yesterday Monk had realised that he could not spend time around the dockside without a reason that would occasion no comment, so he had come dressed as if he were a gentleman fallen on times hard enough to drive him to seek work. He had noticed several such men the day before, and studied their manner and speech well enough to imitate them. He had good boots to keep his feet dry, old trousers and a heavy jacket against the wind. He had bought a second-hand cap, both to protect his head and to disguise his appearance, and a woollen muffler and the kind of mittens that allowed a working man to use his fingers.

He found a cart selling hot tea and bought a mugful. He contrived to fall into conversation with a couple of other men who appeared to be hoping for a day's work when unloading began shortly. He was careful not to let them think he had any plans to jump his place in their queue.

'What's the cargo today?' he asked, sipping the hot tea and feeling it slide down his throat and warm him inside.

The larger of the two men pointed. 'The *Cardiff Bay* down there,' he replied, indicating a five-masted vessel fifty yards away. 'Come in from the China Seas. I dunno wot they got, but they'll likely be keen ter get it orff.'

The other man shrugged. 'Could be teak from Burma,' he said unhappily. 'Damn 'eavy stuff that is, an' all. Or rubber, or spices, or mebbe silk.'

Monk looked further out where another vessel was riding at anchor, this one with six masts.

'The *Liza Jones*?' The first man raised his eyebrows. 'South America – I 'eard Brazil. Dunno if that's right. Could be a load of 'ogwash. Wot der they bring in from Brazil, Bob?'

'I dunno,' Bob answered. 'Wood, coffee? Chocolate, mebbe? Don't make no difference ter us. It'll be all 'eavy an' awkward. Every day I say I'll never carry that bleedin' stuff again, an' then every night I get so cold I'd carry the devil piggyback just fer a fire an' a roof over me 'ead.'

'Yeah . . . an' all,' his friend agreed. He gave a warning glance at Monk. 'First come first served, eh? Remember that, an' yer won't come ter no 'arm. 'Less yer fall in the water, like, or some bastard drops a load on yer foot.' The implied warning was as clear as the hard light on the water.

Actually, Monk had no desire whatever to work at the backbreaking job of unloading, but he must not appear unworthy, or he would awaken suspicion. 'That would be very foolish,' he observed.

They went on talking desultorily, speaking of cargoes from all around the world: India, Australia, Argentina, the wild coasts of Canada where they said tides rose and fell forty feet in a matter of hours.

'Ever bin ter sea?' Bob asked curiously.

'No,' Monk replied.

'Thought not.' There was a benign contempt in his face. 'I 'ave. Seen the fever jungles o' Central America, an' I in't never goin' there again. Frighten the bleedin' life out o' yer. Sooner see the midnight sun up Norway an' the Arctic, like. Freezin' ter death'd be quick. Saw a feller go overboard up there once. Got 'im out, but 'e were dead. The cold does it. Quicker than the fever, an' cleaner. If I got the yellow fever I'd cut me own throat sooner'n wait ter die of it.'

'Me an' all,' his friend agreed.

They spoke a little longer. Monk wanted to ask about

cargoes being stolen, and where they would be sold, but he could not afford to arouse suspicion. They were all facing the water when a barge went by, and they could not help seeing the 'lumpers' knock a few pieces of coal off into the shallow water where at the next ebb it would be low enough for the mudlarks to find it and pick it up. No one made any remark. It was an accepted part of life. But it stirred a thought in Monk's mind. Could the ivory have been moved like that, dropped off the *Maude Idris* in the dark on to barges on their way up or downstream? It would take only moments to move canvas to conceal it. He must find which lightermen were out that night and follow it up.

The foreman came from one of the loading gangs, looking for two men. Monk was intensely relieved he did not want three, but he affected disappointment – although not deep enough for the men to start thinking of another ship which might want him.

He did not manage to avoid a small errand, for which he was paid sixpence. He spent the next two hours asking about which barges moved at night, and learned that it was very few indeed, and only with the tide, which at the time of Hodge's death would have been upstream, towards the morning high water. Painstakingly he accounted for all of them.

He bought a hot pie and a piece of cake for lunch, with another cup of tea. It was late, after one o'clock, and he had never felt colder in his life. No alley in the city, however icebound, wind-funnelled, could match the cutting edge of the wind off the water and the sting of the salt. His recent cases of petty theft, when he had spent his time in offices and the servants' quarters of other people's houses, had made him soft. He realised it now with acute discomfort.

He sat down on a pile of timber and old ropes that was sheltered from the wind, and began to eat.

He was halfway through the pie, relishing the hot meat, when he realised that the shadow next to the pile of boxes to his left was actually a small boy with a ragged coat and a cloth cap pulled over his ears. His feet were bare, streaked with dirt and blue with cold. He should share his cake with the child, who could not be more than nine or ten. After all, Monk would eat when he went home. He would have a warm bed.

'Do you want some pie?' he said aloud. 'Half?'

The child looked at him suspiciously. 'Wha' for?'

'Well, if I were you I'd eat it!' Monk snapped. 'Or shall I give it to the gulls?'

'Yer don' wan' it, I'll take it,' the child replied quickly, stretching out his hand, then pulling it back again, as if the thought were too good to believe.

Monk took a last bite from the pie and handed it over. He drank the rest of the tea before his better nature lost him that as well.

The child sat down beside him on a stump of wood and ate all the pie solemnly and with concentration, then he spoke. 'Yer lookin' fer work?' he said, watching Monk's face. 'Or yer a thief?' There was no malice or contempt in his voice, simply enquiry as one stranger might make of another, by way of introduction.

'I'm looking for work,' Monk replied. Then added quickly, 'Not that I'm sure I want to find any.'

'If yer don't work, an' yer in't a thief, where'd yer get the pie?' the child said reasonably. 'An' the cake?' he added.

'Do you want half?' Monk asked. 'When I say I don't want work, I mean I don't want to load or unload cargo,' he amended. 'I don't mind the odd message now and then.'

'Oh.' The child thought. 'Reckon as I might 'elp yer wi' that, now and then, like,' he said generously. 'Yeah, I'll 'ave a piece o' yer cake. I don' mind if I do.' He held out his hand, palm upward.

Monk carefully divided the cake and gave him half. 'What's your name?' he enquired.

'Scuff,' the boy replied. 'Wot's yours?'

'Monk.'

'Pleased ter meet yer,' Scuff said gravely. He looked at Monk, frowning a little. 'Yer new 'ere, in't yer?'

Monk decided to tell the truth. 'Yes. How did you know?'

Scuff rolled his eyes, but a certain courtesy prevented him from replying. 'Yer wanna be careful,' he said, pursing his lips. 'I'll learn yer a few things, or yer'll end up in the water. Ter begin wiv, yer needs to know 'oo ter speak ter, an' 'oo ter stay clear of.'

Monk listened attentively. At the moment all information was a gift, but more than that, he did not want to be discourteous to this child.

Scuff held up a dirty hand less than half the size of Monk's. 'Yer don' wanna know the bad ones – more'n that, yer don' want them ter know you. That's the night plund'rers.'

'What?'

'Night plund'rers,' Scuff repeated. 'Don't you 'ear too good? Yer better watch it! Yer gotta keep yer wits, or yer'll end up in the water, like I said. Night plund'rers is them wot works the river at night.' There was an expression of infinite patience on his face, as if Monk were a very small child in need of constant watching. 'They'd kill yer for sixpence if yer got in their way. Like the river pirates used ter be, afore there was ever River P'lice special, like.'

Another string of coal barges passed, sending their wash slapping against the steps.

'I see,' Monk replied, his interest engaged.

Scuff shook his head, swallowing the last of the cake. 'No, yer don't. Yer don't see nuffing yet. But if yer live long enough mebbe yer will.'

'Are there a lot of night plunderers?' Monk asked. 'Do

they work for themselves or for others? What kinds of things do they steal and what do they do with them?'

Scuff's eyes opened wide. 'What der you care? Yer in't never goin' ter even see none of 'em, if yer've any sense. Don' yer go lookin' into fings like that. Yer in't got the wits fer it, nor the stomach neither! Yer stick ter wot yer can do – wotever that is!' He looked distinctly dubious that that was anything at all.

Monk bit back the reply that rose to his lips. It irritated him surprisingly deeply that this child's opinion of him was so low. It was an effort not to justify himself. But he did need this information. The theft from the *Maude Idris* looked like exactly the sort of thing such men would do.

'I'm just curious,' he replied. 'And yes, I mean to avoid them.'

'Then keep yer eyes shut – an' yer mouf – all night,' Scuff retorted. 'Come ter that, yer'd better keep yer mouf shut most o' the day, an' all.'

'So what do they take?' Monk persisted.

'Anyfing wot they can, o' course,' Scuff snapped. 'Why wouldn't they? Take yer 'ole bleedin' ship, if yer sloppy enough ter let 'em.'

'And what do they do with what they take?' Monk refused to be deterred. This was no time for delicate feelings.

'Sell it, o' course.' Scuff looked at him narrowly to see if he could really be as stupid as he appeared.

'To whom?' Monk asked, keeping his temper with difficulty. 'Here on the river, or into the city? Or to another ship?'

Scuff rolled his eyes. 'Ter receivers,' he replied, 'depending on wot it is. If it's good stuff, ter the op'lent geezers, if it's poor, ter the cov'tous. They pick up the other bits. Or the rev'nue men, o' course. But they more often take just a cut. In't easy ter sell stuff, 'less yer got the know-'ow, or the connections.' He shook his head. 'Yer in't never gonna last 'ere, mister. Leavin' yer 'ere is like puttin' a babe out by 'isself.'

'I've done all right so far!' Monk defended himself.

'Yeah?' Scuff said with heavy disbelief. 'An' 'ow long is that, then? I know everyone around 'ere, an' I in't never seen yer afore. Where yer gonna sleep, eh? Yer thought o' that, then? If it rains, an' then freezes, which it will sooner or later, them as in't inside somewhere is gonna wake up dead!'

'I've got a few contacts,' Monk invented rashly. 'Maybe I'll go into receiving. I know good stuff from bad – spice, ivory, silk and so on.'

Now Scuff was really alarmed. 'Don' be so bleedin' daft!' His voice went up into a squeak. 'D'yer think it's a free-for-all, or summink? Yer go inter the cov'tous stuff an' the Fat Man'll 'ave yer feet fer doorstoppers. An' if yer try the op'lent stuff Mr Weskit'll fix yer fer the rest o' yer life. Yer'll wake up wi' a splittin' 'ead in the 'old o' some ship bound for the fever jungles o' Panama, or some place, an' nobody'll never see yer again! Yer wanna go back ter thievin' wi' bits o' paper, or wotever it is yer done afore. You in't safe 'ere!'

'I have seen something of life!' Monk retaliated at last. He had had enough of being considered a fool. 'Meet me here tomorrow. I'll bring you a damned good lunch!' It was a challenge. 'A whole hot pie for yourself, tea and cake with fruit in it.'

Scruff shook his head disbelievingly. 'Yer daft,' he said with regret. 'Don' yer go an' get caught. It in't no better in gaol than it is 'ere, rainin' or not.'

'How do you know?' Monk challenged.

''Cos I keep me ears open an' me mouf shut,' Scuff retorted. 'Now I got work ter do, if you ain't. Those lumpers put coal out. It in't gonna sit there all bleedin' day. I gotter go fish it up.' And he rose to his feet swiftly, looked once more at Monk and shook his head, then disappeared so rapidly Monk was not sure which way he went. But he determined to keep his word, however inconvenient, and be there the following day with exactly what he had said he would have.

Monk spent the afternoon further along the docks to the north side of Louvain's offices where barges might have put in on the morning high tide. He tried to blend in with the other labourers, idlers, thieves and beggars who populated the area. He took Scuff's warning very seriously.

He stood half sheltered behind a bale of wool ready for loading; it served the double purpose of concealing his outline and protecting him from the worst of the wind. He watched the men with backs bent under the weight of coal sacks, and hoped profoundly he would not have to resort to such a task to preserve his anonymity. He saw the intricate outlines of winches and derricks bearing heavier loads out of ships' holds alongside the wharfs. Everywhere were the sounds of shouting, the cry of gulls and the slap of water. Barges moved in long strings, piled high with coal or timber. A three-masted schooner was tacking up towards the bridge. Ferries were weaving in and out like beetles, oars shining as they rose and dipped.

He watched the River Police patrolling so close to the shore that he saw their faces as one turned to another with a joke, and they both laughed. A third made some remark and they shouted back at him, the waves drowning their words, but the good nature of it was obvious.

Monk felt suddenly isolated on the dockside, as if the warmth and the meaning of life were out there on the water, in comradeship and a shared purpose. There had been much about working in the police that had infuriated him, as well as the restrictions, the answerability to men of limited vision and unlimited vanity, sometimes the monotony of it. But the very boundaries were also a shape and a discipline. The same man whose weakness curtailed his freedom also supported him when he was vulnerable, and sometimes covered his failures. He had been intolerant then. He was paying some of the price for that now as he stood alone on the dockside, having to learn everything for himself in a new, alien and bitterly cold world where few of the familiar rules applied.

About mid-afternoon, when his legs seemed frozen immobile and he realised he was shivering and all his muscles were locked, he saw a man walk up to another and accost him in an obvious bad temper. The second man answered him fiercely. Within moments they were shouting. Two or three bystanders joined in, taking one side or the other. The quarrel swayed backwards and forwards and looked like developing into an ugly incident. More than half a dozen men became involved and the crowd swirled around a group of labourers unloading brassware.

Monk moved forward, mostly to stretch his limbs and try to get the feeling back in his feet. No one noticed him; they were all watching the quarrel. One of the men took a wild swing at another and connected with his jaw, sending him staggering backwards to knock over a third man. A fourth let fly his own punch, and then it was a mêlée. It was by chance that Monk saw two men detach themselves and with remarkable speed and skill pick up four of the brass ornaments and slip them sideways to a youth and an old woman among the bystanders, who promptly turned and walked away.

Monk left as well, before the police could come to part the combatants and restore peace. He could not afford to be caught on the outskirts of the crowd. 'Scuffle-hunting' was a trade he had seen a hundred times before, and the brass would never be found. But as he walked back along the quayside towards Louvain's offices, he resented the fact that he was in effect running away from the band of men he used to be one of; indeed, to command. It was a bitter taste to swallow.

He was acutely mindful of the fact that he had to report to Louvain today, and he had nothing remotely useful to tell him. The search for evidence of barges unloading surreptitiously had been fruitless. He had no facts at all, and not a great deal of deduction. He walked slowly as he thought about it, the sounds of the riverside all about him, the clang of metal, creak of wood, hiss and slurp of water. The tide was turning, sweeping in again upriver, driving the mudlarks up the shore and lifting the ships higher at anchor. The dusk seemed later this afternoon because the sky was streaked with clear, pale strips to the west, and the water was all greys and silvers, dotted by riding lights burning yellow.

What had he deduced? That the ivory could have been taken by any of the thieves on the river, and almost certainly ended up with one of the 'opulent receivers', who would sell it on to . . . whom? Who would buy ivory? A dealer, to pass it on to jewellers, carvers of ornaments or chess pieces, makers of piano keys, any of a dozen artists or artisans.

That led him to the crux of the question: was it a theft of opportunity, or a planned crime with a particular receiver in mind? The hour it must have happened, according to Hodge's death, indicated the former. If it were the latter, then Monk had very little chance of recovering it because it was almost certainly well beyond the river by now.

He crossed the street and walked along the narrow footpath as a cart rattled over the cobbles. The lamp-lighter was busy, tipping his long pole to touch the wicks and bring the gift of sudden vision and the illusion of warmth. There was no mist off the water, just the clean, driving wind and the faint haze of smoke that there always was. To the east, where it was darkest and the river wound beyond Greenwich and the estuary to the sea, a few stars glittered sharp and brittle.

Monk turned the corner into the wind again, pulled his coat collar higher and tighter around his neck, and quickened his pace to Louvain's offices. He was obliged to wait in the foyer for a quarter of an hour, pacing back and forth on the bare floor, before Louvain sent for him. But he would know there was no news yet. Had there been, Monk would have come earlier.

The office was warm, but Monk could not relax. The force of Louvain's personality dominated the room, even though he looked tired. The lines on his face were deeper than before, and his eyes were pink-rimmed.

'What have you got to tell me?' he asked.

'I'm here because I said I would be,' Monk replied. 'I need to cultivate informants—'

'Is that an oblique way of saying you want more money?' Louvain looked at him with undisguised contempt.

'Not more than I have,' Monk replied coldly. 'If I do, then I'll tell you in a manner you won't mistake.' He looked at Louvain more closely. He would be a fool to miss such an opportunity to observe him. The theft might have been by chance, but it was equally likely to have been deliberate. He could not afford any kind of ignorance.

Louvain stood in front of his desk now, with his back to the gaslamp on the wall. It was an easy and perfectly natural position, but it also concealed his expression, giving his features an unnatural and sombre look.

'And how long does this process take?' he asked. There was an edge to his voice, anxiety and perhaps tiredness making it rough. He worked long hours. It was possible more of his fortune rested on recovering the ivory than he had told Monk.

'I should reap some benefits tomorrow,' Monk replied rashly.

'Do you have a plan?' Louvain enquired. Now his face

was softer, something like a lift of hope in it. Perhaps his contempt was to conceal the fact that he was dependent upon Monk. He employed him, and could pay him or not, but he would not find his ivory without help, and they both knew that.

Monk weighed his answer carefully. The tension in the room prickled as each watched the other, weighing, judging. Who had the strength of will to bend the other? Who could harness his vulnerability and disguise it as a weapon?

'I need to narrow down the kind of receiver who could handle a load like that,' Monk said levelly. 'A man with the connections to sell it on.'

'Or a woman,' Louvain amended. 'Some of the brothel-keepers are receivers as well. But be careful; just because they're women doesn't mean they wouldn't slit your throat if you got in their way.' The vaguest smile crossed his face and then vanished. 'You're no use to me dead.'

If it happened it would anger him, but it would not lie on his conscience. There was a certain respect in him now, a levelness in the gaze, a candour he would not have used to a lesser man, although one could not call it warmth.

Monk refused to be ruffled. He glanced around the office at the pictures on the walls. They were not of ships, as he might have expected, but wild landscapes of fierce and alien beauty, stark mountains towering above churning water, or barren as the volcanoes of the moon.

'Cape Horn,' Louvain said, following his look. 'And Patagonia. I keep them to remind me who I am. Every man should see such places at least once, feel the violence and the enormity of them, hear the noise of wind and water that never stops, and stand on a plain like that, where the silence is never broken. It gives you a sense of proportion.' He hunched his shoulders and pushed his hands into his pockets, still staring, not at Monk, but at the pictures. 'It measures you against circumstances so you know what you have to do – and what it will mean to fail.'

Monk wondered for an instant if it was a warning, but when he looked at the intense concentration in Louvain's face, he knew he was speaking to himself.

'It's a cruel beauty,' Louvain went on, his voice touched with awe. 'There's no mercy in it, but it's also freedom, because it's honest.' Then, as if suddenly remembering that Monk was a hired hand, not an equal or a friend, he stiffened and the emotion fled from his face. 'Get my ivory back,' he ordered. 'Time's short. Don't waste it coming here to tell me you've got nothing.'

Monk swallowed the retort that came to his lips. 'Good night,' he answered, and before Louvain responded he turned and went out.

He hesitated in the street. It was bitterly cold; the wind was knife-edged, and a sickle moon was rising across the water. Ice rimed over the cobbles, making them slippery, and his breath was a plume of vapour in the air. The thought of going home was sweet, like a burst of warmth inside him, but it was too soon to give up on the day. It was only a little after six, and he could put in at least another two or three hours. The thieves would already have got rid of the ivory by now, and the receiver would be looking to place it. He needed to find it before then.

He walked back along the street towards the public house on the corner, pushed the door open and went in. It was warm and noisy, full of shouts, laughter, and the clink of glasses. The floor was covered with dirty straw. People jolted each other to move closer to the bar, and in the lantern's yellow light the barman's face gleamed with sweat above the tankards topped with foam. It all smelled of ale, the steam from hot, weary bodies, wet clothes, mud and horse manure on boots.

Monk waited his turn, moving slowly closer to the

70

front of the queue, all the time listening and watching. There were street women among the men, garish in red and pink dresses, low on the shoulder, faces painted with false gaiety. Their voices forced the laughter, and their eyes were tired.

He listened to snatches of conversation, straining to link them together and make sense of them. He had worked many years in the city; he knew receivers of stolen goods by instinct. It was not in their appearance so much as in their manner. Some were hearty, some furtive, some talked a great deal, others were terse. Some offered magnificent prices and sang praise of their own generosity, and how it would ruin them; others haggled over every halfpenny. But they all had a watchfulness about them; they did not miss a word or a gesture from anyone, and they could assess the monetary worth of anything in seconds.

The receivers were apparent also in the defiance, the cautious caginess with which other people approached them, not as friends but always with a mind to business.

Monk saw several transactions, some with a discreet hand in and out of the pocket, a piece of jewellery shown, or a trinket of some other sort; some were merely words. If one of them had concerned Louvain's ivory he would not have known, but only a fool buys something he has not seen, and fools do not survive long in such a trade.

He reached the front of the queue and bought his ale. Then he found a place to sit and drink it, next to a man with a scar down his cheek and an empty left sleeve of his jacket.

Monk took the opportunity to strike up conversation. Within half an hour he had refilled his own glass and the man's, getting them both a pork pie at the same time. It was an expense that could go on Louvain's bill.

''Course we still get some like it,' the sailor said, taking up his tale where he had left it when Monk stood up. 'But

71

not like the old days. Real pirates, they were.' His watery eyes were bright with memory. 'Me granpa were one o' the first in the River P'lice; 1798 that were. In them days there was crime on the river you wouldn't believe!' He nodded. 'Not now, seein' as 'ow it's all tame an' respectable, like. Near 'alf the men in the docks was thievin' back then.' He held up his fingers. 'Two men, they were – 'Arriott an' Colquhoun – set up the p'lice. Got rid of ninety-eight out of every 'undred o' thieves, they did, in jus' one year!' He stared at Monk challengingly. 'Think on it. Don' it eat yer 'eart out, eh? They was real men.' He said it with a fierce, happy sense of pride.

'Were you in the River Police?' Monk enquired with interest.

The man laughed so hard he all but spilled his ale. 'No! No, I in't an oggler, bless yer. I bin ter sea most o' me life, till I lorst me arm. But that were river pirates, an' all. Comin' back from the Indies, we were.' He leaned forward confidentially, his voice quieter and more urgent as memory flooded back. 'Java way. Them China Seas is summink 'orrible in bad weather, an' swarmin' wiv pirates.' He took a long swig of his ale and wiped the back of his hand across his mouth. 'Don' trust nobody. Keep a watch on deck all hours, an' keep yer gun loaded an' yer powder dry. But we made it all the way 'ome, down the Indian Ocean.' He made a circular movement with his finger. 'Round the Cape o' Good 'Ope, and up the Atlantic past the Skeleton Coast o' Africa, across Biscay . . . are yer followin' me, like?'

'Yes, of course.'

'An' 'ome ter Spit'ead,' he said triumphantly. 'Five-masted schooner, we was, wiv a good set o' guns fore an' aft. We passed Gravesend, tacked up Fiddler's Reach, past the marshes on either side of us, safe as 'ouses. Gallions Reach right up ter Woolwich.' He sniffed lugubriously. 'Could smell 'ome, it was that close.

''Eave to for the night off Bugsby's Marsh ter make the Isle o' Dogs an' the Pool the next day. Damn it if we weren't boarded in the middle watch by 'alf a dozen river pirates, an' cut loose.' He banged his fist on the table. 'Tide took us onter the mud banks an' by dawn there weren't a bleedin' thing left o' the cargo they could shift, the sons o' bitches. The man on the watch raised the alarm, poor sod! Cost 'im 'is life. An' we all come up on deck wiv pistols and cutlasses, an' it were a right battle. But yer can't fight them bastards an' the wind an' the tide at once.'

Monk imagined it, the ship drifting, picking up speed with the current, the men fighting desperately on deck, trying to swing swords in the narrow spaces, seeking to shoot at moving, uncertain targets in the swaying lantern light, the violence, the fear, the pain.

'What happened?' He had no need to pretend interest.

'We killed three of 'em,' the man replied with satisfaction, licking his lips after the last mouthful of the pork pie. 'Lost two o' us, though. Wounded two more o' them pretty bad, an' put 'em over the side. They drowned.'

'Then what?'

''Alf a dozen more of 'em, weren't there,' he said bitterly. 'I 'ad me arm gashed so bad I bled like a stuck pig. Got it all stitched up like, but went wi' the gangrene. Took it off, they did. 'Ad ter, ter save me bleedin' life.' He said it wryly, as if it were a long time ago and hardly mattered any more, but Monk saw the pain in his eyes, and the memory of what he had been.

Monk did not know how to respond. Should he acknowledge the pain he had seen, or was it better to behave as if he had not noticed?

'Are there still pirates on the river, even today?' he asked. It was an evasion, but it was the best he could do.

'Some,' the man answered, the brilliance of hurt fading

from his eyes. 'The ogglers is pretty good, but even they can't do it all.'

'Are there pirates this far up the river?'

'Prob'ly not. Up to Lime'ouse and that way it's opium eaters an' them kinds o' things. But yer never know. There's other folks as 'as 'ad a few run-ins wiv 'em, 'part from me.'

'Louvain?' The moment Monk had said it, he wondered if it were wise.

The man's face lit up with pleasure. 'Clem Louvain? Yer damn' right! 'E cut them up summink beautiful, 'e did. Yer never seen a better man wiv a cutlass than Clem. They rued the day they messed wiv 'im.' He sniffed cheerfully. 'Mind, that's a few year ago now, but it don't make no diff'rence. Summink like that yer don' forget. They don' mess wiv 'im still, an' all.'

Monk measured his words carefully. 'I'm surprised they don't want revenge,' he said with a deliberate lift of curiosity.

The man grinned, showing gapped teeth. 'Come up from 'ell ter ask for it, yer reckon?'

'Dead?' Monk was surprised.

''Course dead!' the man said contemptuously. 'Two killed right there on the deck o' the *Mary Walsh*, and two 'anged up Execution Dock. I see'd it meself. Went ter watch, I did. Rare sight, that.'

'No one left to . . . want payment for it?' Monk pressed.

'Not for that bleedin' lot o' sods.' The man upended his glass to drain the last of his beer. 'Reckon as Mr Louvain's 'ealth were drunk right well in a few 'ouses up an' down the river that night.' He took his mug and pushed it an inch closer to Monk without looking at him. 'River's full o' tales,' he added.

Monk took the hint and fetched them both another pint, although he had no capacity or wish to drink any more himself. But he was prepared to listen for another hour at least.

His companion settled down to picking from his memory tales of violence, humour and vast wealth, failed robberies and successful ones, and eccentric characters in the last fifty years along the river.

'Most o' them back then,' he said gleefully. He wiped the back of his hand across his mouth. Monk had bought him a second pie. The colour with which he painted the river life contained many warnings that might prove useful, and it gave Monk a far better understanding of the intricacies of illicit trade, of light horsemen, heavy horsemen, lumpers, plunderers and crooked revenue men. Monk heard stories, some about the legendary receivers, including the present-day Fat Man, the most famous opulent receiver along this stretch of the water.

Monk did not arrive home until after nine o'clock, by which time Hester was concerned. The dinner she had made was far past its best and barely still edible.

'I'm all right,' he assured her, holding her as closely as he could until she pushed him away to search his face. 'Really,' he repeated. 'I was in a public house down by the docks, listening to an old sailor telling me tales.'

Her face was very serious. 'Mr Louvain came to the clinic today.'

'What?' He was incredulous. 'Clement Louvain? Are you sure? What for?' It disquieted him, although he did not know why. He did not want Louvain anywhere near Hester. And even as the thought was in his mind he knew it was absurd. Hester dealt with the ugliest and most tragic elements of life every day. 'What did he want?' he demanded, taking his coat off and hanging it up.

She was frowning. 'He brought in a woman who was sick.' She said it as if it were simple, and quite obvious. 'He said she was the mistress of a friend, who's cast her off, but her family will come for her in a few days. He paid for her, and made a very generous donation as well.' She bit her lip. 'We're finding it hard to get people to give.'

He heard the anger in her voice and he understood it. 'Why didn't he take her to a hospital?'

'He would have to register her there, and tell them his own name. Anyway, he might be known. He's an important man. They would ask who she was, and they might not believe he brought her for someone else.'

He smiled, touching her cheek gently. 'Did you?'

She shrugged. 'I don't care. And I won't repeat it to anyone except you. Did you learn anything more about the ivory?'

'Not specifically, but I gained an informant.'

'Good. You're cold. Are you hungry?'

'Not very, but I'd like some tea.'

He followed her through into the kitchen, telling her about Scuff as she filled the kettle and put it on the stove, fetched milk from the pantry and set out the teapot and cups on a tray. He told her many of the things he had seen and heard, but not about Louvain and the river pirates. There was no need to waken fears in her that she could do nothing about.

She laughed at some of the descriptions: the eccentricity, the imagination and the will to survive. They went to bed, tired from the work of the day, and happy to be close not only in mind but in the warmth of touch.

In the morning he woke before she did. He slipped out of bed, and washed and dressed without disturbing her, not shaving in order to keep his image for the dockside. Downstairs he riddled the stove and carried out the ashes. It was not a job he was accustomed to doing, but it was heavy, and he knew she had dismissed the woman who came to help. Louvain's payment was generous, but it must be made to last as long as possible. He had no idea where the next reasonably sized sum was coming from. The rewards for the solving of domestic issues and small robberies could be counted in shillings rather than pounds, and some of them were paid only if he was successful. Failure gave him nothing. For that matter, the major payment from Louvain would come only if he found the ivory. Perhaps any future jobs on the river were dependent on that as well.

He filled the kettle and set it on the hob, then went back upstairs to waken Hester and say goodbye to her. He had given a great deal of thought to how next to proceed, and only one answer pushed itself to the forefront of his mind. He needed to find the receiver. Reluctantly he went to the drawer of his dresser, took out the gold watch Callandra had given him, and slipped it into the top pocket inside his jacket.

Ten minutes later he was out in the grey light of the October street, and half an hour after that he was back on the dockside again. The air was still, almost windless, but the damp penetrated the flesh till it felt as if it reached the bone. He huddled into his coat, turning up the collar and shivering. He pushed his hands deep into his pockets and stepped over the puddles from the night's rain. It was a while since he had had a new pair of boots, and it might be even longer before he did again. He needed to take care of these ones.

The more he considered the ivory, the more he believed the thieves would have taken it to a specific 'opulent receiver', capable of selling it on to the highly specialised markets that could use it. There were a limited number of such people along the river. It was not finding them that was the major issue, but proving that they still knew where the ivory was, and with each day passing his chances of success were reduced.

He started at one of the better pawn shops, took out the gold watch and asked what they would give him for it.

'Five guineas,' was the answer.

'And if I have more?' he asked.

The pawnbroker's eyes widened. 'More like that?'

'Of course.'

'Where'd you get more like that?' Disbelief was heavy in his face.

Monk looked at him with contempt. 'What do you care? Can you deal with them or not?'

'No! No, I in't in that business. You take 'em somewhere else,' the pawnbroker said vigorously.

Monk put the watch back into his pocket and went out into the street again, walking quickly, avoiding the close walls and skirting wide around the entrances of alleyways. He thought of word spreading and his being robbed, or even killed, and it sent colder knots clenching in his stomach than even the raw air could produce. But he knew of no other way to draw the attention of a receiver. He could not afford the time to play a slow, careful game, and he had no police knowledge or help to guide him. Far from going to them, as would have been his instinct, he was obliged to avoid them, to watch for them and take another path, as if he were a thief himself. Once again he cursed Louvain for not being able to use the regular, lawful means.

He kept his promise to Scuff, and was at the same time and place on the dockside with hot pies, tea and fruitcake. He was absurdly disappointed to see no one there waiting for him. He stood in the grey, colour-bleached clearing amid the old boxes. He could hear nothing but the lost cry of gulls above and the wail of foghorns as mist rose from the water, choking the light and muffling sound. The rising tide slapped against the pier stakes, and in the distance men shouted at each other, some of them in languages he did not understand.

A string of barges made a wash that hit the shore sharply, and then died away again, swallowed in the fog.

'Scuff!' he called.

There was no answer, no movement except a rat

scuttling into a pile of refuse twenty yards off.

If Scuff did not come soon, the pies would not be warm any more. But then the boy would have no way of telling the time – even if he could. It was stupid to have expected him to be here. He was an urchin just like any of the petty thieves who roamed the alleys of the city, picking pockets or running errands for forgers, card-sharps and brothel-keepers.

Monk sat down unhappily and began to eat his own pie. There was no point in allowing that to get cold, too.

He was halfway through it when he was aware of a shadow across his feet.

'You eaten my pie?' a voice said disgustedly.

He looked up. Scuff was standing in front of him, his face filthy, his expression full of reproach. 'You didn't oughta do that,' he accused.

'If you want yours cold, that's up to you,' Monk said, overwhelmed with a relief it would be absurd to show. He held out the other pie. It was twice the size of yesterday's.

Scuff took it solemnly and sat down cross-legged, holding the pie with both hands as he ate it. He said nothing until the last mouthful was gone, then he reached out and took the tea and cake. When that was finished he spoke.

'That was good,' he said with satisfaction, wiping the back of his hand across his mouth.

'You were late,' Monk remarked. 'How do you know the time, anyway?'

'Tide, o' course,' Scuff replied with exaggerated patience for Monk's stupidity. 'I come at the same 'eight o' the water.'

Monk said nothing. He should have thought of that. If there was anything a mudlark would know, it was the rise and fall of the water.

Scuff nodded. 'Yer bin runnin' more errands?' he asked, glancing at the cups that had held the tea.

'Not today. I'm looking for a receiver who'll deal in good stuff, maybe gold or ivory.'

'Lots o' gold,' Scuff said thoughtfully. 'Dunno nob'dy wot 'as ivory. Worth a lot, is it?'

'Yes.'

'The Fat Man. 'E knows most things wot goes on. But yer'd best stay clear of 'im. 'E's a right bad bastard, an' yer in't no match for 'im.' There was a gentle pity in his voice, and Monk was almost sure it was concern in his eyes.

'I need to find some ivory,' Monk confided. He knew he was being rash telling this young mudlark information he could not afford to have spread everywhere, but the desperation was mounting inside him. His efforts of the morning had not so far led him to a single receiver. 'Who'd sell it?'

'Yer mean cheap?'

'Of course I mean cheap,' Monk agreed witheringly. 'If I don't go to the Fat Man, who else?'

Scuff considered for a few moments. 'I could take yer ter Little Lil. She knows most o' wot's fer sale. But I can't jus' do it, like. I gotta make arrangements.'

'How much?'

Scuff was offended. 'That in't nice. I trust yer like a friend, an' yer go an' insult me.'

'I'm sorry,' Monk apologised with genuine contrition. 'I thought it might cost you something.'

'I'll 'ave another pie – termorrer, like. I can do a pie fer me lunch real nice. Come back 'ere at 'igh tide.'

'Thank you. I shall be here.'

Scuff nodded his satisfaction, and a moment later was gone.

Monk returned to his round of pawn shops, and saw at least three he was certain were receivers of one sort or another, but only of petty goods. He was followed for almost a mile by two youths he believed would have robbed him if they could have caught him alone in one of the narrow alleys, but he took care to see that they did not. He in turn took care to keep well away from the occasional police patrol that he saw. It riled him to do it, but he had no choice.

By four o'clock he was back on the dockside again and found Scuff waiting for him. Wordlessly the boy led the way along the wide street parallel with the river, up a flight of stone steps, and along an alley so tight that instinctively Monk tucked his elbows in. The smells of old cooking, effluent and soot almost choked him. They were twenty yards in from the river, and yet the damp seemed to be absorbed into the stones and breathed out again in a fog as the dust settled and the few streetlamps made yellow islands in the gloom. There was no sound but a steady dripping from the eaves.

Finally they came to a doorway with a painted sign above it, and Scuff knocked. Monk noticed that his dirty, clenched fist was shaking, and realised with a stab of amazement that Scuff was afraid. Of what? Was he betraying Monk to be robbed? The thought of losing Callandra's watch made him so angry he would have lashed out at anyone who attempted such a thing. The gift was immeasurably precious, the token of a friend-ship that mattered more than any other, except Hester's. It was also an emblem of success, elegance, the kind of man he wanted to be, and who could face Oliver Rathbone as something like an equal. He stood stiffly, ready to fight.

Or was Scuff afraid for himself? Was he doing some-thing dangerous in order to cement his new friendship? Or perhaps as a matter of some obscure kind of honour to repay the man who had given him hot pies? Or even simply to keep his word?

The door opened and a large woman stood just inside, her hands on her hips. Her red dress was brilliant in the light of the streetlamp, and there was red paint on her mouth and cheeks.

'I'nt yer a bit young fer this?' she said, eyeing Scuff wearily. 'An' if yer lookin' ter sell yer sister, bring 'er an' I'll take a gander, but I in't promisin' nothing.'

'I in't got no sister,' Scuff said immediately, but his voice rose into a squeak, and his face pinched with anger at himself. 'An' if I did 'ave,' he added, 'it'd be Miss Lil 'erself as I'd wanna see. I got a gennelman as is lookin' ter buy summink else.' He gestured to Monk, half obscured in the shadows behind him.

The huge woman stared, screwing up her face in concentration.

Monk stepped forward. He considered smiling at her, and decided against it.

'I'm looking for certain merchandise,' he said in a low, level voice, overly polite. He allowed an element of threat to show in his unblinking stare.

She stood still. She was about to speak, then said nothing, waiting for him.

Scuff looked very white, but he did not interrupt.

Monk said nothing more.

'Come in,' the woman said at last.

Without any idea of where he was going, Monk accepted, leaving Scuff in the street behind him. He went through the doorway into a narrow passage and then up a creaking flight of stairs, across a landing hung with pictures, and into a room red-carpeted and with papered walls and a good fire burning in the grate. In one of the soft, red armchairs a tiny woman sat with a piece of richly detailed embroidery spread across her lap, as if she had been stitching it. It was more than three-quarters completed, and the needle threaded with yellow silk was stuck into it. She had a thimble on one finger, and the scissors lay beside her on top of a basket of skills.

'Miss Lil,' the huge woman said softly, 'this one's fer

you.' She stood back to allow her employer to see Monk and make her own decision.

Little Lil was in her forties at least, and she had once been very pretty. Her features were still neat and regular. She had large eyes of an indeterminate hazel colour, but her jawline was blurred now, and the skin on her neck had gone loose, hanging from the shrunken flesh underneath. Her little hands were clawlike with their long fingernails. She regarded Monk with careful interest.

'Come in,' she ordered him. 'Tell me what yer got as I might like.'

'Gold watches,' Monk replied, obeying because he had left himself no choice.

She held out her hand, palm upward in a clutching gesture.

He hesitated. Had it been any gold watch it would still have caused him concern, but Callandra's was precious in a different and irreplaceable way. He took it out of his pocket slowly and held it up, just beyond the grasp of her hand.

Her big eyes fixed on him. 'Don't trust me, then?' she said with a smile showing sharp, unexpectedly white teeth.

'Don't trust anyone,' he replied, smiling back at her.

Something in her changed; perhaps it was a flash of appreciation. 'Sit down,' she invited.

Feeling uncomfortable, he did as he was told.

She looked at the watch again. 'Open it,' she ordered.

He did so, turning it carefully for her to inspect, but keeping a firm hold on it.

'Nice,' she said. ''Ow many?'

'Dozen, or thereabouts,' he answered.

'Thereabouts?' she questioned. 'Can't yer count, then?'

'Depends on your offer,' he prevaricated.

She chortled with laughter, which was high-pitched like a little girl's.

'Do you want them?' he asked.

'I like you,' she said frankly. 'We can do business.'

'How much?'

She thought about it for several seconds, watching his face, although it seemed she was doing it now for the pleasure it gave her more than any need for time to think.

Monk wanted to come to the point and then leave. 'I have a client looking for ivory,' he said a bit abruptly. 'You wouldn't have any advice on that, would you?'

'I'll ask fer yer,' she said in a whisper, unexpectedly gentle. 'Come back 'ere in three days. An' bring me some o' them watches an' I'll pay yer nicely.'

'How much?' he asked. She would expect him to haggle, and Callandra's watch must have cost at least thirty pounds.

'Like that? Twelve pound ten,' she replied.

'Twelve pound ten!' he said in horror. 'It's worth more than twice that. Twenty, at the very least.'

She thought for a moment, looking at him through her eyelashes. 'Fifteen,' she offered.

'Twenty?' He could not afford to lose her, or to appear to give in too easily.

This time she considered for longer.

Monk felt sweat break out on his body in the warm room. He had made a mistake. He had let his desperation push him into going too far. Now he had no retreat.

'Seventeen,' she said at last.

'Right,' he agreed, his mouth dry. He wanted to escape this stifling house and be outside alone in the street to think of a way to extricate himself, and still be able to hear any information Little Lil might give him. 'Thank you.' He inclined his head slightly, and saw her acknowledge it with a gleam of satisfaction. She liked him. He despised himself for playing on it, at the same time as he knew he had to.

In the street he was barely beyond the ring of the

lamplight when Scuff materialised from the darkness.

'Yer got anyfink?' he asked eagerly.

Monk swore under his breath.

Scuff giggled with satisfaction. 'She like yer, does she?' he said.

Monk realised Scuff had expected it, and he reached out to clip him over the ear for the acute embarrassment he had suffered, but Scuff ducked sideways and Monk's hand missed him. Not that it would have hurt more than a slight sting. He was still laughing.

They reached the main street running parallel with the docks and crossed into the better light. Monk turned to Scuff again, and realised he was not there. He saw a shadow in front of him, a row of buttons gleaming on a dark jacket, a solidity, a confidence to him.

'Has his wits about him more'n you have, Mr Monk,' the man observed.

Monk froze. The man was River Police, he knew it with certainty; more than the uniform it was the quiet authority in him, the sense of pride in his calling. He did not need to threaten, not even to raise his voice. He was the law and he understood its worth. If only Monk had that same dignity, the fellowship of all the other quiet men who kept order on the river and its immediate shore. Suddenly the reality of his aloneness was almost beyond bearing.

'You have the advantage of me, sir,' he said stiffly, with more than necessary politeness.

'Durban,' the man replied. 'Inspector Durban, of the River Police. I haven't seen you here before a couple of days ago. You say you're looking for work, but it doesn't seem to me like you want it. Why would that be, Mr Monk?'

Monk ached to tell him the truth, but he dared not. He was committed to Clement Louvain, and to his own need.

'I'd rather work with my brain than bending my back,'

he replied, putting an edge of truculence in his voice that he did not feel.

'There's not much call for brain work down on the docks,' Durban pointed out. 'Least, not that's legal. There's a lot that's not, as I'm sure you know. But I wonder if you really know how dangerous that is? You wouldn't believe the number of dead bodies we pick up out of the water, an' there's no one to say how they got in there. I wouldn't like yours to be one of 'em, Mr Monk. Just be a little bit careful, eh? Don't go messing with the likes of Little Lil Fosdyke, or the Fat Man, or Mr Weskit. There's no room for more opulent receivers than we've already got. Do you take my meaning?'

'I'm sure there isn't,' Monk agreed, hating the lies. 'My interest is in running errands, and being of service to people who can't do all their own jobs. I don't buy or sell goods.'

'Really . . .' Durban said with disbelief. His face in the near darkness was almost unreadable, but his voice was sad, as if he had expected better – fewer lies, at least.

Monk remembered with a jarring urgency being in exactly the same position, seeing a man well-dressed, well-spoken, hoping he was in the run-down alley only by chance, and realising within minutes that he was a thief. He remembered his disappointment. He drew in his breath to explain himself to Durban, and then let it out again in a sigh. Not until after he had earned Louvain's money.

'Yes, really,' he said tartly. 'Good night, Officer.' And he walked away down the street towards the lighted thoroughfare to catch an omnibus, and then another, home.

Chapter Four

❧

Oliver Rathbone sat in the hansom as it moved with relative ease through the London traffic from his own home towards that of Margaret Ballinger. He was going to take her as his guest to an evening concert given by a very fine violinist at the home of Lady Craven. The concert was in aid of a worthy charity, and many people of social importance would attend. Rathbone was dressed in the height of elegance, fashionable enough to occasion admiration, and yet not so much so as to look as if he cared. A real gentleman did not need to make an effort to please, it was a gift with which he was born.

And yet Rathbone was not at ease. He sat upright rather than relaxed into the padding of the seat. He had plenty of time, but he could not help looking out of the windows to see where he was, watching the yellow glitter of the streetlamps reflected on the wet surfaces of the road through the drifts of rain, and noting the familiar landmarks.

It had been a hurried invitation, offered to her yesterday somewhat impulsively. He could not remember exactly what the conversation had been, but certainly something to do with the clinic in Portpool Lane, as their conversation so often was. Were anyone else so single-minded it would almost certainly have been tedious, but he still found pleasure in seeing the animation in her face when she spoke of the work there. He even found himself involved with the welfare of certain of the patients she described, anxious for their recovery, upset at the injustices, happy for any success. Such a thing had never happened to him before. He governed his professional life with strict emotional discipline. He engaged his extraordinary skill in the service of those who needed it, by its nature those accused of some crime, but he kept his personal feelings well apart.

But then had anyone a few months ago outlined to him the plan by which Hester and her colleagues obtained the use of Squeaky Robinson's establishment for the clinic he would have been horrified. So far from joining in, or in any way whatever assisting them, he would have struggled with his conscience as to whether he should actually report them to the police.

He blushed even now, sitting here alone in the dark, islanded from the noise and bustle of anonymous traffic outside. He felt the heat well up in his face, and no one but Hester, Margaret and Squeaky Robinson, and possibly Monk, knew what had taken place. But there had been a sublime kind of justice in it. He did not realise that he was smiling as he recalled Squeaky's face, his horror at being so brilliantly and completely outmanoeuvred. And it was Rathbone, not Hester, who had delivered the ultimatum to him, and cornered him so he could not escape. It was exquisitely satisfying. He was profoundly embarrassed for allowing himself to be involved in such dealings. He would be mortified if any of his professional colleagues were to know. Yet he was also obscurely proud of it. That was the most remarkable thing, the incomprehensible thing. How he had changed! One would not have recognised him from the man he had been even a few months ago.

He was at the Ballinger house already and the hansom was drawing up. He did not feel completely prepared for the visit. He had no conversation on his tongue for Mrs Ballinger. She was a type of woman he had encountered numerous times before. After all, he was an exquisitely eligible bachelor, and she had an unmarried daughter. Her ambition was so naked as to be beyond embarrassment. Not that there was any society matron in London whose ambition was any different, so attempting to conceal it or place it behind a mask of decency was really irrelevant. It would simply have spared Margaret.

As he stepped out of the carriage on to the glistening footpath and felt the cold air on his face, Rathbone remembered the anger he had felt on Margaret's behalf the very first time they had met. It had been at a society ball, and Mrs Ballinger had been praising Margaret's virtues to a degree that mortified her so deeply that she had been on the point of refusing to dance with Rathbone when he asked her. He remembered even now the stark honesty of their conversation as they had swirled around the floor, heads high, feet in perfect rhythm, words anything but the trite courtesies other dancers were murmuring to each other. He did not know what he had said, but in his mind he could still see her eyes, dark grey-blue and so very level and angry, full of hurt at being paraded like some piece of merchandise, overpraised in order to be sold quickly. He had burned with resentment for her.

He went up the steps and pulled the doorbell. A moment later the footman opened it and ushered him in across the hall to the rich, dark withdrawing room where Mrs Ballinger was waiting for him.

'Good evening, Sir Oliver,' she said with more guarded enthusiasm than on their earlier encounters, since he had not yet met her expectations regarding her daughter, and he had had more than adequate opportunity. However, the brightness was still there in her eyes, the single-minded concentration. She was a woman who never forgot her purpose.

'Good evening, Mrs Ballinger,' he replied with a slight smile. 'How are you?'

'I am in excellent health, thank you,' she said. 'I am most fortunate in that respect, and I thank God for it every day. I see friends and acquaintances around me who suffer from this and that.' She raised her eyebrows. 'So wearing, I always think, don't you? Headaches and shortness of breath, exhaustion, or even palpitations. Such a difficulty, don't you find?'

He was about to say that he had never suffered such afflictions, when he realised the double meaning in her words. She was not really referring to herself, or to tediousness for the hundreds of women who were so troubled. She was telling him, in her own way, that Margaret was from good stock, not only healthy by nature, but not brought up to indulge herself in fancies and complaints.

He bit back the reply that came to his tongue. 'Yes,' he agreed. 'One should be most grateful for such excellent health. Unfortunately it is not enjoyed by all. But I am happy for you.'

'How generous you always are,' she said without hesitation. 'I find rudeness so unattractive, don't you? It speaks of a selfishness of nature, I always think. Please sit down, Sir Oliver.' She gestured towards the chair nearest the fire with its embroidered armrests and an antimacassar over the back to protect it from gentlemen's hair oil. 'Margaret will be a few minutes yet. You are delightfully punctual.' She suited her own actions to her words, spreading her wide silk and lace skirts around her.

It would have been impolite for him to decline. He sat opposite her and prepared to indulge in chatter until Margaret should appear. He was very used to guarding himself. He hardly ever spoke without thought. After all, his profession, at which he was one of the most gifted men of his generation, was to plead the cause of those accused of crime and against whom there was sufficient evidence for them to stand trial. No society matron was going to discomfit him, let alone outwit him.

'Margaret tells me it is a most charming event to which you have invited her this evening,' Mrs Ballinger observed. 'Music is so civilised and yet speaks to the romantic in us at the same moment.'

He found himself irritated and defensive already. 'It is a function at which they hope to raise a considerable amount of funds for charitable work,' he replied to her.

She smiled, showing excellent teeth. 'How I admire you giving of your time to such a cause. I know it is one of the qualities Margaret finds most worthy in a man. Many people who are successful in life forget those who are less fortunate. I am so pleased to see that you are not such a one.'

She had placed him in an impossible position. What on earth could he say to that? Any answer would sound ridiculous.

She nodded. 'Margaret has such a noble heart. But I am sure you are already aware of that. Good works have brought you together so many times.' She made it sound as if he had somehow contrived to see Margaret at every opportunity. He had not. Indeed he still saw quite a variety of other ladies, at least two of whom might be considered eligible for marriage, even if they were widows.

He wondered suddenly why he did that. He had no intention whatsoever of marrying either of them. They were agreeable friends, no more. He had known their husbands, or brothers, or they had some cause in common. And, of course, he still saw Hester and Monk now and again. They would always have the friendship born in their battles shared in the pursuit of justice.

Did he spread his attentions in order to retain for

himself some kind of safety from precisely the entrapment Mrs Ballinger was trying to close on him?

She was waiting for him to reply. His silence was beginning to look like disagreement.

'Indeed she has,' he said with more fervour than he had meant to. 'And what is more unusual, she has the courage and the selflessness to pursue it, and create of it deeds that are far-reaching.'

A shadow flashed across Mrs Ballinger's face. 'I am so pleased you mentioned it, Sir Oliver.' She leaned forward towards him. 'Of course I am happy that Margaret devotes her time to worthy causes rather than frittering her hours away with mere entertainment, as so many young women do, but this latest cause of hers does alarm me more than a little. I am sure it is very noble to be concerned for the morally unfortunate, but I think she could place her care to better advantage in something a little more . . . salubrious. Perhaps with your influence you could suggest to her other avenues that you may be aware of? I expect you know many ladies who . . .'

Rathbone found himself suddenly furious. He knew exactly what she was doing. At one stroke she was manipulating him into spending more time with Margaret, not because he wished to but as a moral obligation to her mother, and also reminding him of social pressures and duty in general. It was unbelievably condescending to Margaret. He could feel the blood rising in his face and his body so stiff his hands were locked where they lay on his knees.

'I came to see Margaret because I enjoy her company, Mrs Ballinger,' he said with as much control as he was able to muster. He saw her eyes gleam with satisfaction, and alarm rose up inside him as he realised what he had committed himself to, but he did not know how to stop. 'I would not presume to influence her in her choice of causes. She feels intensely about the clinic, and I believe

she would regard any interference from me as imperti-
nent, and I should lose her friendship.' He did not know if
that were true, but even the possibility struck him with
extreme unpleasantness. It surprised him how very sharp
it was.

'Oh, she would not be so foolish.' Mrs Ballinger
dismissed the idea with a light laugh. 'Her regard for
you is far too deep for her not to listen to you, Sir
Oliver.' Her voice was warm, full of assurance, as if she
too held him as dearly.

He wished that that were true. Or did he? Hester would
have been furious with him if he had tried to dictate
matters of conscience to her. She would not have allowed
even Monk to do that. In fact, he could very clearly
remember a good number of occasions when Monk had
been unwise enough to try!

'I have too much respect for Margaret to attempt to
influence her against her beliefs, Mrs Ballinger,' he
replied, anger on Margaret's behalf making him say
something far beyond the degree to which he had wished
to commit himself. And yet it was true, and it rang in his
ears with a certainty he could not have retracted.

Mrs Ballinger looked both alarmed and excited, as if
she had gone fishing and caught a whale she had no idea
how to land, nor on the other hand to let go. She started
to say something, then changed her mind and sat on the
edge of her seat, her lips a little parted.

'Added to which,' Rathbone went on, unable to endure
the silence, 'her clinic is run by one of my dearest friends,
and I would not dream of attempting to rob her of her
most loyal supporter. It has been the calling of great
women down the centuries to care for those less fortunate,
and to do it with compassion and without judgement. No
doctor demands first whether his patient is worthy of
healing, only whether he needs it. The same is true of
those who nurse.'

'My goodness!' she said in amazement. 'I had no idea you were so deeply involved, Sir Oliver. It must be a far more noble endeavour than I had appreciated. You work very closely with it, then? Margaret did not make me aware of that.' She was quite breathless at the thought.

Rathbone silently swore to himself. Why on earth was he being clumsy? In court he could see a pitfall yards off, and evade with such elegance it exasperated his adversaries. And he had outwitted matchmaking women like Margaret's mother for twenty years or more, admittedly not always with quite such grace, although his skill had increased with time.

'I don't work with it at all,' he denied firmly. 'But I have occasionally been of assistance with advice, because of my long friendship with Mrs Monk.' As soon as the words were out he was ashamed of them. It was cowardly. He had been the prime mover in obtaining the premises for them, even if it was Hester who had put the words into his mouth. And it had been for Margaret's sake that he had abandoned all his life's careful rules to do it. And if he were truly, scrupulously honest, he would also admit that for a few wild moments he had thoroughly enjoyed it. He had often heard it said that a really good barrister must have something of the actor in him. Perhaps that was truer than he had appreciated.

'It is through her that I am aware of the work,' he added defensively. 'And of course Margaret has also told me, from time to time. I have the deepest admiration for them.' That was true, and he met her eyes as he said it. His mind was filled with memories of Hester, not only at the clinic, but in all the other battles they had fought together for all manner of causes. She would risk herself to struggle against injustice with a passion he had seen in no one else. Her courage was supreme; nothing daunted her, although she must have been afraid at times. He had seen her exhausted, discouraged, cold and hungry, and so furious she could hardly speak, but never had he heard self-pity in her voice or seen it in her eyes.

Of course she had made some wild mistakes. He shuddered to think of those he had seen. And she was anything but tactful! He had loved her, and yet hesitated to propose marriage. Could he really face such a wilful companion in his life, a woman with unreasoning, unturnable conviction, such fierce hunger of the soul?

Mrs Ballinger was staring at him, confused by his words, and yet also satisfied. She felt the emotion in him, even if she did not understand it, and she interpreted it as she wished.

There was a slight sound behind him as the door opened and Margaret came in. He rose to his feet and turned to face her. She was dressed in a deep plum pink, a colour in which he had never seen her before. It flattered her wonderfully, giving her skin a glow and making her eyes look bluer. He had never thought of her as lovely until now, but quite suddenly he realised that she was. It gave him extraordinary pleasure to see her. There was a gentleness in her, a dignity in the way she stood waiting for him, confident and yet not eager. She would not allow her mother's ambition either to embarrass him or to move her to defend herself and retreat. There was a pool of calmness inside her that made her nothing like Hester, and it was that serenity that he loved. It was unique to her.

'Good evening, Miss Ballinger,' he said with a smile. 'It would seem redundant to ask if you are well.'

She smiled back at him, her colour heightening so slightly as to be almost imperceptible. 'Good evening, Sir Oliver. Yes, I am indeed well. And ready to face the arbiters of both musical and charitable taste.'

'So am I,' he agreed. He inclined his head to Mrs Ballinger and she rose to escort them out, proprietorially, beaming with an imminent sense of victory.

'I'm sorry,' Margaret murmured as they crossed the hall and the footman assisted her with her cloak, then opened the front door for them.

Rathbone knew precisely what she meant. 'It is merely habit,' he assured her, equally softly. 'I no longer notice.'

She seemed about to respond, perhaps even to say that she knew he was lying to comfort her, but the footman had gone with them to the waiting hansom and was well within hearing.

Once they were seated and moving it seemed ridiculous to pursue what had been only a politeness after all. He was aware of her sitting next to him. She wore very little perfume. He detected only what might have been the faintest breath of roses, or merely the warmth of her skin. It was one of the many things about her that pleased him.

He wanted the enjoyment of conversation. They had little enough time together uninterrupted by the necessities of good manners when they were in company, but he was too aware of Mrs Ballinger's expectations, and his own feelings crowding in upon him. The strength of his emotions disconcerted him. If he spoke candidly he might betray himself, and then find restraint impossible.

'How is Hester?' he enquired.

'Working very hard,' Margaret replied. 'And concerned for the financial management of the clinic. Although we have just admitted a woman who seems to be in a very bad way with what looks like pneumonia, and the man who brought her gave us an extremely generous donation, as well as paying for her keep. That will enable us to continue for a couple of weeks at least.'

Her voice was polite, concerned, and he could not see her face clearly in the flickering light of streetlamps and other carriages as they passed. It was tactless of him to have asked after Hester so quickly, almost as if she were the one in his thoughts, and not Margaret.

'Two weeks?' he said aloud. 'That's not very long.' He

was anxious for her, and he was startled to realise that he was worried for the clinic as well. 'I did not know it was so . . . so narrow a margin.'

'People are more willing to give to other causes,' she explained. 'I have tried most of those I know of, but Hester has a list from Lady Callandra, and we are going to try that.'

'We?' he said quickly. 'It would be far better if it were you alone. Hester is . . .'

'I know.' She smiled with both amusement and affection, which lit her face till the gentleness in her seemed to be something so powerful he could almost have reached out and felt its warmth. 'I was using the plural rather loosely,' she went on. 'She has given me the names, I shall approach them as I have the opportunity.'

'Why does Lady Callandra not do so herself?'

'Oh, you didn't know?' She seemed surprised. 'She is leaving England to live in Vienna. She is to marry Dr Beck. I expect Hester will tell you as soon as she has the chance to. She is delighted for her, of course, but it does mean that we do not have Lady Callandra to turn to any more. She was superb at raising funds. We shall just have to do it ourselves from now on.' She looked away from him, forward and a little sideways as if she had some interest in the passing traffic.

Was she self-conscious because she had spoken of marriage? Had she been thinking of it? Was it really what occupied the minds of all young women? If he asked her to marry him, she would undoubtedly accept. He could not be unaware of her regard for him. And he was supremely eligible. Of course, that did not mean that she loved him, only that time was on her heels and society expected it of her.

He realised with an immense jolt that he did not wish to marry unless he loved as deeply and wholly as it was in his ability. And if that were so, if he was not loved in return with the same fervour, it would be a unique and awful kind of suffering.

Was he really prepared for such a thing? Did he wish to disrupt his very successful and satisfactory life in order to involve himself in such possibilities for pain he could not deal with, pain that would invade every part of his being, and very possibly cripple his ability even to think?

'I am sure you will succeed,' he said rather shiftly. 'I must write immediately and congratulate Callandra. I hope I am not too late. I dare say her household will know where to forward a letter to reach her.'

'I imagine so,' she replied, keeping her face towards the window.

Ten minutes later they alighted and were welcomed to the soirée. The large withdrawing room was already crowded with people: men in the traditional black and white, older women in rich colours like so many autumnal flowers, the younger ones in whites and creams and palest pinks. Jewels glittered in the gleam of chandeliers. Everywhere there was the hum of conversation, the occasional clink of glasses and trill of slightly forced laughter.

Rathbone was aware of Margaret's sudden tension – as if she were about to face some kind of ordeal. He wished he could have made it easier for her. It hurt him that she should have to protect herself from speculation, rather than gain the kind of respect he knew she deserved. She had courage and kindness far deeper than any of the achievements that passed for value here. And yet to say so would have been absurd. It would have been so very obviously a defence where no attack had been made.

Lady Craven came forward to welcome them.

'Delightful to see you, Sir Oliver,' she said charmingly. 'I am so pleased you honoured us with your company. We don't see you nearly often enough. And Miss – Miss Ballinger, isn't it? You are most welcome. I hope you will enjoy the music. Mr Harding is a highly talented violinist.'

'So I have heard,' Rathbone replied. 'I expect the evening to be a complete success. No doubt a great deal of money will be raised for good causes.'

Lady Craven was a little taken aback at his bluntness, but she was equal to any social occasion. 'We hope so. We have been careful in our preparations. Every detail has been attended to with the greatest thought. Charity is surely next to godliness, is it not?'

'I believe it is,' Rathbone agreed warmly. 'And there are a great many sorely in need of your generosity.'

'Oh, I dare say. But it is Africa we have in mind. So noble, don't you think? Brings out the very best in people.' And with that she sailed away, head high, a smile on her lips.

'Africa!' Margaret said between her teeth. 'I wish them well with their hospitals, but they don't have to have everything.'

They took seats in the very front row.

'Are you sure?' Rathbone said, thinking of less obvious seats further back.

'Perfectly,' she replied, sitting down gracefully and with one simple movement rearranging her skirts. 'If I am here right in the middle it will be impossible for me to speak to anyone without being appallingly rude to the artist. I shall have to listen to him with uninterrupted concentration, which is exactly what I should like to do. Even if anyone should speak to me, I shall be completely unable to reply. I shall look embarrassed and regretful, and say nothing at all.'

Perhaps he should have hidden his smile – people were looking at him – but he did not. 'Bravo,' he agreed. 'I shall sit beside you, and promise not to speak.'

It was a promise he was happy to keep because the music was indeed superb. The man was young, wild-haired and generally eccentric in appearance, but he played his instrument as if it were a living part of himself, and held the voice of his dreams.

An hour later, when silence engulfed them the moment before the eruption of applause, Rathbone turned to look at Margaret, and saw tears on her cheek. He lifted his hand to touch hers, then changed his mind. He wanted to keep the moment in memory rather than break it. He would not forget the wonder in her eyes, the amazement, or the emotion she was not ashamed to show. He realised that he had never heard her apologise for honesty, or pretend to be unaffected by pity or anger. She felt no desire to conceal her beliefs or affect to be invulnerable. There was a purity in her that drew him like light in the darkening sky. He would have defended her at any cost, because he would not even have thought of himself, only of preserving what must never be lost.

The applause roared around them, and he joined in. There were murmurs of approval gaining in volume.

The artist bowed, thanked them and withdrew. For him to play was the purpose and the completion. He did not need the praise and he certainly did not wish to become involved in chatter, however well-meaning.

Lady Craven took the artist's place and made her plea for generous donations to the cause of medicine and Christianity in Africa, and in turn was greeted with polite applause.

Rathbone felt Margaret stir beside him, and was sure he knew what she was thinking.

People began to move. Of course, no one would do anything so vulgarly overt as put their hands in their pockets and pull out money, but promises were being made, and bankers would be notified, footmen would be sent on urgent errands tomorrow morning. Money would change hands. Letters of credit would make their way to accounts, in London, or Africa, or both.

Margaret was very quiet. She barely joined in the conversation that continued around them.

100

'Such a worthy cause,' Mrs Thwaite said happily, patting the diamonds around her throat. She was a plump, pretty woman who must have been charming in her youth. 'We are so fortunate, I always think we should give generously, don't you?'

Her husband agreed, although he did not appear to be listening to what she said. He looked so bored his eyes were glazed.

'Quite,' a large lady in green said sententiously. 'It is no more than one's duty.'

'I always feel that in the future our grandchildren will consider our greatest achievement was to bring Christianity and cleanliness to the Dark Continent,' another gentleman said with conviction.

'If we could do that, it would be,' Rathbone agreed. 'As long as we do not do it at the cost of losing it ourselves.' He should have bitten his tongue. It was exactly the sort of thing Hester would have said.

There was a moment's appalled silence.

'I beg your pardon?' The woman in green raised her eyebrows so high her forehead all but disappeared.

'Perhaps you would care for another drink, Mr . . .?' The bored husband suddenly came to life. 'Then again perhaps not,' he added judiciously.

'Rathbone,' Rathbone supplied. 'Sir Oliver. I am delighted to meet you, but I cannot have another drink until I have had a first one. I think champagne would be excellent. And one for Miss Ballinger also, if you would be so kind as to attract the footman's attention. Thank you. I mention losing that sublime charity because we also have a great many good causes at home which need our support. Regrettably, disease is not confined to Africa.'

'Disease?' The bored husband directed the footman to Rathbone, who took a glass of champagne for Margaret, then one for himself. 'What kind of disease?' he pursued.

'Pneumonia,' Margaret supplied, taking the opening Rathbone had given her. 'And of course, tuberculosis, rickets, occasionally cholera or typhoid, and a dreadful amount of bronchitis.'

Rathbone let out his breath. He did not realise he had been holding it in fear she would mention syphilis.

The bored husband looked startled. 'But we have hospitals here, my dear Miss . . .?'

'Ballinger,' Margaret said with a smile Rathbone knew was forced. 'Unfortunately there are not enough of them, and too many of the poor have not the financial means to afford them.'

The pretty wife looked disturbed. 'I thought there were charitable places provided. Is that not so, Walter?'

'Of course it is, my dear. But her tender heart does Miss . . . credit, I'm sure,' Walter said hastily.

Margaret was not going to be silenced. 'Charitable places require charity. I work for a clinic in Portpool Lane, specifically for poor women in the area, and we are continually seeking funds. Even the smallest donation would be sufficient for food, or a little coal. Medicines can cost more, but vinegar and lye are cheaper.'

Walter seized on the one thing he had not understood, and felt he could take issue with. 'Surely vinegar is unnecessary, Miss Ballinger? Can you not feed them simpler food? If they are ill, what of gruel, or something of that nature?'

Rathbone was aware of Margaret's hesitation, and knew it was to control her anger. Hester would have retorted with an answer that stung Walter so sharply he would have remembered it for weeks. Rathbone let out his breath in a sigh of relief for Margaret's smoother temper, and smiled without realising he was doing so.

'We do not eat vinegar,' Margaret replied, forcing herself to speak softly. 'It is to keep things clean. We do use a lot of gruel, and porridge when people are a little stronger, or for those who are injured rather than ill.'

Walter was plainly disconcerted. 'Injured?'

'Yes. Women are quite often involved in accidents, or attacked. We do for them what we can.'

His expression filled with distaste. 'Really? How . . . very unpleasant. I imagine it must be difficult for you. I prefer to make my donations to those who are spreading the light of Christianity to those poor souls who have not already had the opportunity and spurned it. One must not waste precious resources.' He inclined his head as if he were about to leave.

Margaret stiffened.

Rathbone put his hand on her arm, tightening his fingers a little in a warning to her not to respond.

'I know,' she said under her breath. Then, as soon as Walter had retreated to another group where he would not be disturbed by unpleasant thoughts, she added, 'I would love to tell him what I believe, but it would ruin all future chances of help. Don't worry, I shall bite my tongue.' But there was no smile on her face, and she did not turn to look at him.

Her next attempt fared little better. They were engaged in polite but trivial conversation with Mr and Mrs Taverner, Lady Hordern and the Honourable John Wills.

'Such a wonderful man,' Lady Hordern said enthusiastically, referring to one of the doctors in Africa. 'Prepared to give his life to saving people he does not even know, body and soul. Truly Christian.'

'Most doctors save people they do not know,' Rathbone pointed out.

Lady Hordern looked a little bewildered.

'At least they know who they are,' Wills argued. 'And of course they are paid for it.'

'Sometimes,' Rathbone said. 'When it is charity they are not.'

'All that is necessary is to know that they are ill and in trouble,' Margaret said with a smile.

'Quite,' Wills agreed, as if she had made his point for him.

Rathbone hid a smile. 'I think what Miss Ballinger means is that we should also give generously to other causes as well.'

Lady Hordern blinked. 'Whose cause?'

'I was thinking of those who work in such places as the clinic run by my friend Mrs Monk, who treats our own Londoners,' Margaret responded.

'But we have hospitals,' Mr Taverner pointed out. 'And we are Christian already. It is very different, you know.'

Margaret bit her lip. 'There is something of a difference between having heard of Christ, and being a Christian.'

'Yes, I suppose so.' He was patently unconvinced.

She scented an opportunity. 'Surely one soul is as valuable as another. And to save those in our own community will have excellent effects all around us.'

'Save?' his wife asked suspiciously. 'From what, Miss Ballinger?'

Rathbone felt Margaret's arm tense and heard her indrawn breath. Was she going to make a tactical error?

'From behaviour unworthy of a Christian,' Margaret replied sweetly.

Rathbone let out his breath in a sigh of relief.

Lady Hordern's pale eyebrows rose very high. 'Are you referring to that place which caters to women of the street?' she asked incredulously. 'I can hardly imagine that you are asking for money to support . . . prostitutes?'

Mr Taverner turned a dull shade of red, but whether his emotion was fury or embarrassment it was impossible to say.

'I believe that for the most part they support themselves,

Lady Hordern,' Rathbone interposed, hearing Hester's voice in his head exactly as if she had prompted him. 'Which is the heart of the trouble, I imagine. The clinic you are referring to is to help street women who are injured or ill, and therefore cannot obtain their usual employment.'

'Which is devoutly to be wished!' Mrs Taverner snapped.

'Is it?' Rathbone asked innocently. 'I do not admire it as a trade – nor the fact that so many men patronise it, or it could not exist – but neither do I think that attempting to do away with it would be a practical solution. And as long as there are such people, it becomes us to treat their illnesses as effectively as we may.'

'I find your opinions extraordinary, Sir Oliver,' Mrs Taverner responded icily. 'Most particularly that you should choose to express them in front of Miss Ballinger, who, after all, is unmarried, and I assume you regard her as a lady?'

To his amazement Rathbone was not furious, he was suddenly and intensely proud. 'Miss Ballinger works in the clinic,' he said clearly. He wanted to say it again, with more volume in his voice so everyone might hear. 'She is more aware of the nature of these women's lives than any of us. She knows the beatings and stabbings they endure, the privations of insufficient food and poor shelter and exposure to disease.'

Mrs Taverner looked profoundly shocked, and insulted.

'The difference,' Rathbone concluded, startled at the passion in his voice, 'the difference is that she chooses to do something to help, and we have yet to avail ourselves of that opportunity.' He felt Margaret's hand close tightly on his arm and was ridiculously elated.

'I choose to give such gifts as I do to a worthier cause,' Lady Hordern said stiffly.

'Are the Africans worthier?' Rathbone enquired.

'They are more innocent!' she snapped back. 'I presume you would not argue that?'

'Since I am unacquainted with them, I cannot,' he responded.

Wills tore his handkerchief out of his pocket and buried his face in it, his shoulders shaking. He was obviously laughing uncontrollably.

Lady Hordern looked very steadily at Margaret. 'I can only assume, Miss Ballinger, that your poor mother is unaware of your present interests, both personal–' she glanced at Rathbone and back again to Margaret– 'and occupational. I think, in the service of your future, it would be the act of a friend to inform her. I should not like to see you suffer more than is already unavoidable. I shall call upon her tomorrow morning.' And with that she swept off, the stiff taffeta of her skirts rattling.

Mr Taverner was still scarlet in the face. Mrs Taverner wished them good evening and turned away, leaving her husband to follow.

'You are worse than Hester,' Margaret said between her teeth, but now it was not laughter she was stifling, it was fear. If her mother forbade her, it would be very difficult to continue seeing Rathbone, and perhaps impossible to work in the clinic. She had no independent means, not even a home apart from that of her parents.

He looked at her and saw the sudden change in her. 'I'm sorry,' he said gently. 'I have indulged my anger at your expense, and made it impossible for you, haven't I.' It was an acknowledgement of fact, not a question.

'It was impossible before that,' she admitted, refusing even to think of the meaning far deeper than the loss of tonight's contribution. 'I have a strong feeling that Mr Taverner may already make his contribution to their keep and Mrs Taverner is quite aware of it.'

'I dare say it is her acceptance of it that she resents the most,' he agreed. Then he hesitated. 'Margaret, will your mother listen to Lady Hordern and believe her? Do I need to make myself a great deal more respectable in her eyes in order to be permitted to see you again? Should I . . .' he swallowed '. . . apologise?'

'Don't you dare!' She lifted her chin a little higher. 'I shall speak to Mama myself.'

It was exactly the sort of thing Hester would have said: brave, angry, and unwise, but so intensely from the heart. Did Margaret feel that in some way she was standing in for Hester in his regard, that she was here as a substitute and not for herself? It was untrue. He knew it with overwhelming conviction. He loved the courage and the honesty in Margaret that were like Hester's, but there were also other qualities of gentleness and honour, modesty and inner sweetness that were nothing to do with anyone else at all. One did not love people because they reminded one of somebody else.

She turned slowly, her eyes wide, questioning.

'It is what you would say that I care about.'

'Is it?'

'Yes, of course it is.' He was overcome with a tingle of fear at just how far he was committing himself.

She looked away again, smiling, her eyes bright. 'I am afraid we have not been very successful at inspiring donations, have we?'

'I have been a liability so far,' he confessed. 'I shall endeavour to do better.' He offered her his arm and she took it. Together they walked towards a large group of people, ready to try again.

Chapter Five

❧

Hester arrived at Portpool Lane by half-past eight on the third morning after Monk accepted the job for Clement Louvain. The very first thing she did was sit down with Bessie in the kitchen and have a hot cup of tea and a slice of toast while she listened to the report of what had happened during the night.

In its time as a brothel very little cooking had been done here. Most of the prostitutes who inhabited the place had eaten what meals they had somewhere in the street, before their working hours began. There had seldom been more than three or four people to cater for at any one time: just Squeaky Robertson himself, and a few women kept on and off for cleaning and laundry, and a couple of men to deal with any customers who got rough and needed throwing out, or who were a trifle slow in settling their bills. It had never been necessary to enlarge what was essentially a family kitchen. The laundry was another matter; that was enormous, and excellent, with two boiling coppers for the vast numbers of sheets used, and a separate room for drying them.

Bessie looked profoundly tired. Her hair was scraped back so tightly it looked painful, but large strands were looped carelessly as if she had pushed them back in irritation, simply to get them out of her way. Her skin was pale, and every now and then she could not stifle a yawn.

'Been up all night?' Hester said, more as a statement than a question.

Bessie took a third mouthful of her tea with a sigh of satisfaction. 'Them two from a couple o' nights ago are getting better,' she replied. 'One poor little cow only needed a spot o' food, an' a couple o' nights' proper kip. Put 'er out again termorrer. Knife wound's 'ealin' up nice.'

'Good,' Hester nodded. However, she expected the woman Louvain had brought in to be worse – in fact she was afraid she might be one of those they could not help beyond giving her as much comfort as possible in her last hours. At least she would not have to die alone.

'But we got up of a dozen in, an' there's a bleedin' lot o' washin' ter do,' Bessie answered. 'I bin up all night wi' that Clark woman. In't much yer can do fer 'er, 'ceptin' cool towels like yer said, but it seems ter 'elp. She still looks like the undertaker should 'ave 'er, but 'er fever in't so bad, so I s'pose she's on the mend. Temper in 'er, mind! Ruth's too good a name for 'er. I'd a called 'er Mona if it'd bin up ter me.'

Hester smiled. 'I expect she was christened long before she could speak.'

'Pity we can't take 'er back ter then!' Bessie grunted.

'Rechristen her?'

'Nah – just keep 'er mouth shut.'

'Finish your breakfast and get some sleep,' Hester advised. 'I'll do the laundry.'

'Yer can't do that all on yer own.'

'I won't need to. Margaret will be in later. I'll just get it started.'

'Yeah? An' 'oo's gonna fetch the water fer yer?' Bessie asked.

Hester smiled more widely. 'Squeaky. It'll do him good.

A bit of fresh air and exercise.'

Bessie laughed outright. 'Then tell 'im if 'e squawks I'll come an' beat 'im over the 'ead wi' a saucepan!'

When Hester spoke to Squeaky ten minutes later he was horrified.

'Me?' he said incredulously. 'I'm a book-keeper. I don't fetch water!'

'Yes, you do,' she answered, handing him two pails.

'But it'll take ten loads of that to fill the bleedin' copper!' he said furiously.

'At least,' she agreed. 'And another ten for the other one, so you'd better get started. We need them washed today, and dry by tomorrow, or the day after.'

'I'm not a bleedin' water carrier!' He stood rooted to the spot, indignation filling his face.

'Right, then I'll fetch the water,' she said, 'and you change the beds. Remember to pull the bottom sheets straight and tight, and tuck in only the ends of the top ones. You'll have to work around the sick women, but I expect you know how to do that. Then you can mix the lye and potash and—'

'All right,' he said angrily. 'I'll get the water. I'm not dealing with sick women in bed!'

'Bit modest, aren't you, for a brothel-keeper?' she asked mockingly.

He gave her a filthy look, picked up the two pails, and stormed out.

Smiling to herself, Hester went back upstairs with a pile of clean sheets and pillowslips to begin changing the beds. Fevers made people sweat, and it was inevitable that linen soiled quickly.

She began with the girl who had come in exhausted, and who was already so much better she could be sent back out again today or tomorrow.

'I'll 'elp yer,' she offered straight away, rolling over and getting to her feet. She steadied herself with one hand on the bed frame, then wrapped a shawl around her shoulders and prepared to begin.

Hester accepted. All such duties were a great deal easier with two. They changed the linen on that bed, then went to the next room, and the woman with more severe congestion. She was feverish and in considerable discomfort. They took off the damp and crumpled sheets, easing her from one position to another, and replacing the old with new. It was an awkward task, and at the end of it, when the woman sank back, dizzy and gasping for breath, Hester and the girl were also glad of a moment's respite.

Hester helped the sick woman to take a few sips from the beaker of water on the table, which had once been hot and was now tepid. Then they left her and went to the next one, and so on until they were all finished.

'Can I help yer wash 'em?' the girl offered, pointing to the sheets.

Hester looked at her pale face and the slight beading of sweat on her brow. 'No, thank you. Go back to bed for a while. It doesn't take two to do this.'

That was not strictly true – it would have been much easier with someone else to assist her – but she carried the sheets down, stuffed into two pillowslips and put over her shoulder.

Once in the laundry room she checked the coppers, and found the first one more than half full. Squeaky must have been working swiftly, in spite of his complaints. She undid the sheets and put all the linen into the copper, stirring them around with a long wooden dolly until they were thoroughly soaked. She brought another scuttle of coke across and added it to the boiler, then carried the empty scuttle back.

Next she took the last of the soap to add to the water in the copper, and set about one of the jobs she disliked most, the making of more soap. It was not a difficult task so much as a heavy and tedious one. They bought the potash from a dealer a few hundred yards along the street, in Farringdon Road. It was made from burned potato stalks, not necessarily the best, but the cheapest, because they produced a dozen times as much as the same weight of any wood. One pound of caustic potash combined with five pounds of clear grease would make five gallons of soft soap. For the clinic's purpose the smell of it was unimportant, and funds did not run to adding perfume.

While Hester was working Squeaky came in with two more loads of water, scowling so hard she was surprised he could see where he was going. 'I hate that stuff!' he said, wrinkling his nose. 'When we were a proper brothel we bought soap.'

'If you've got money to spare I should be delighted,' she replied.

'Money! Where'd I get money?' he demanded. 'Nobody around here makes bleedin' money. You all just spend it.' And before she could make any reply he tipped the pails of water into the second copper and marched out again.

They admitted two more women in the middle of the day, and in the early afternoon Margaret came in and willingly helped scrub the kitchen floor with hot water and vinegar. Later she took another two pounds and went to pay the coal merchant's bill, and bring back a pound of tea and a jar of honey.

Another woman came in with two broken fingers on her right hand, which took all Hester's skill to set and bind. The woman was exhausted with the pain of her injury, and it was some little time before she was composed enough to leave.

At quarter to six Margaret went home. Hester intended to take a few minutes' sleep herself, see Ruth Clark for the last time today, and then go home, but she woke with a start to find it completely dark outside, and

Bessie standing over her with a candle in one hand, her face creased in concern.

Hester pushed her hair out of her eyes and sat up. 'What is it?' she said anxiously. 'Another admission?'

'No.' Bessie shook her head. 'It's that Clark woman. Wot a miserable piece o' work she is, an' no mistake! But she's real poorly. I think as yer'd better come an' take a look at 'er.'

Wordlessly Hester obeyed. Without bothering to pin up her hair she put her boots back on and followed Bessie to Ruth Clark's room.

The woman lay half on her back, her face flushed, her hair tangled. The sheet was crumpled where her hands had clenched on it. Her eyes were half open but she seemed only barely conscious of there being anyone else in the room.

Hester went over to her and touched her brow. It was burning.

'Ruth?' she said softly.

The woman made no answer except to move her hands fretfully, as if the touch bothered her.

'Get me a fresh bowl of cold water,' Hester directed. The woman's condition was serious. If Hester could not get the fever down at least a degree or two she might well become delirious, and die.

Bessie went immediately, and Hester picked up the candle on the bedside table and looked more closely at Ruth Clark. She was breathing erratically, and her chest seemed to rattle as if it were full of congestion. Pneumonia. The crisis might well come tonight. Hester could not leave to go home. If she did everything she knew, she might save her. She looked a robust woman, definitely someone's mistress rather than one of the women who walked the streets, selling their bodies to anyone with the money to pay. Often the latter spent their nights cold and hungry, and in bad weather with

113

wet feet and possibly wet clothes altogether. Hester put the candle back.

Bessie returned with the water and cloths and set them down on the floor.

Hester thanked her and told her to go and see what she could do for the other patients, then take a chance to sleep herself.

'Not while yer tendin' to 'er all on yer own,' Bessie said indignantly.

'This isn't a job for two,' Hester answered, but smiled at her loyalty. 'If you rest now, you can take a turn in the morning. I'll call you if I need you, I promise.'

Bessie stood her ground. 'I'll never 'ear yer.'

'Take the room opposite, then you will.'

'Yer'll call?' Bessie insisted.

'Yes, I will. Now get out of my way.'

Bessie obeyed, and Hester put the cloth in the cold water, wrung it out and placed it on the sick woman's forehead. At first it seemed to irritate her and she tried to turn away. Hester moved the cloth and very gently put it over her throat. She wrung it out again and tried her forehead a second time.

Ruth groaned and her eyelids flickered.

Again and again Hester dipped the cloth in the water, wrung it out and bathed the woman with it, at first only her face and neck. Then, as that seemed to have little effect, she stripped back the sheet and blankets and laid the cloth over the top of her chest as well.

The time crept by. She looked at her watch and it was ten in the evening.

Then some time around midnight she became aware that Ruth had not moved for a while, perhaps ten or fifteen minutes. Hester leaned forward. She could not see the rise and fall of her breathing. She was far too familiar with death for it to frighten her, but it never left her without sadness. She put out her hand and touched the woman's neck, just to make sure there was no pulse. Ruth's eyes opened.

'What is it?' she whispered crossly. It was the first time Hester had heard her speak and her voice was startling. It was low, soft and pleasing, the voice of a woman of some education and culture. Hester was so startled she flinched backwards.

'I . . . I'm sorry,' she apologised, as if rather than ministering to a sick patient she had crept into someone else's bedroom. 'I wanted to see if you were still feverish. Do you feel better? Would you like something to drink?'

'I feel awful,' Ruth answered, still speaking as if her throat were parched.

'Would you like some water?' Hester repeated the offer. 'I'll help you sit up.'

Ruth frowned at her. 'Who are you?' She looked around the room as much as she could see without moving her head. 'What is this place? It looks like a brothel!'

Hester smiled. 'That's because it is – or was. Now it's a clinic. Don't you remember coming here?'

Ruth closed her eyes. 'If I remembered coming, I wouldn't ask.'

Hester was taken aback. She realised with a shock how used she had become to gratitude from the sick and injured who regularly found shelter here. She had come to take it for granted, and this woman looked at her with no admiration at all, no sense of respect towards a rescuer.

Was that because she was used to being courted by whoever's mistress she had been? Was she usually the one with power in the relationship, and she had possibly even temporarily forgotten, in her fever, that her lover had thrown her out? Or did she recall it very well, and her anger and sense of being rejected made her lash out now at Hester, simply because Hester was here?

'Do you remember Mr Louvain, who brought you here?'

The change in Ruth's face was subtle, so slight it could have been no more than the struggle to focus her mind, or the fear that she was losing control of what was happening to her.

Hester could not help her thoughts racing as to what had brought this woman to becoming a cast-off mistress, rescued by a man she barely knew, and brought, desperately ill, to a charity clinic for women of the street. She had obviously been educated; she was handsome, perhaps more than that when she was well. Had she fallen hopelessly in love with a man she could not marry? Or who would not marry her? Or had she escaped genteel poverty by accepting a life many would regard as sin? How? Accident? Deliberate choice? An adventuress, a victim? Both? Or Louvain's own mistress?

'He brought me here?' Ruth said quietly.

'Yes.' Hester should have asked again if she wanted water, but curiosity stayed her for another moment, waiting.

An odd smile touched Ruth's face, ironic, as if there were a terrible humour to it that even in her state of wretchedness she could still appreciate. 'What did he say?' Her eyes meeting Hester's were hard and angry. She would accept help, but she would not be grateful for it.

'That you were the mistress of a friend of his, who had put you out because you were ill,' Hester replied. The answer was cruel, but surely a woman who had followed such a path, chosen or not, must be used to facing truths.

Ruth closed her eyes as a wave of pain washed over her, but the smile did not fade away entirely.

'Mistress – is that what he said?' she whispered derisively.

'Yes.'

'Did he pay you? Is that why you sit here nursing me?'

116

'He did pay us, yes. Or more accurately he gave me a donation sufficient to cover the cost of caring for you, and for several other women as well. But we would have taken you anyway. We have plenty here who have nothing to give.'

Ruth was silent. She was finding it difficult to breathe again and her face was very flushed. Hester stood up and fetched a half-glass of water from the stand and brought it back. 'You should take this. I'll help you to sit up.'

'Leave me alone,' Ruth said irritably. 'You've been paid to look after me, consider yourself acquitted.'

Hester controlled her tongue. 'You'll feel better if you take some liquid. You have a high fever. You need to drink.'

'A fever! I feel worse than I ever thought a human being could—'

'Then stop being so perverse and let me help you take a little water,' Hester insisted.

'Go . . . go to . . .' Ruth was gasping for breath again and her face was scarlet.

Hester put the cup down, leaned forward and put her arms around Ruth's shoulders, heaving her up and sliding another pillow behind her. With great difficulty she put the cup to her lips. The first mouthful was lost, sliding down her neck on to her chest; of the second she swallowed at least half. After that she yielded and took almost all of the rest, and finally lay back exhausted.

Hester took away the pillow, and helped her lie back, then began again with the cloth and the cool water.

A little after two she left her for a while and went around the other patients, just to make certain that everyone else was as well as was possible. Then she went down to the kitchen and boiled the kettle. She made herself a cup of tea and had drunk most of it when there was a banging at the front door. She roused herself to go and answer.

117

There were two women on the step: Flo, whom Hester had seen many times before; and leaning against her, white-faced and holding her arm in front of her, cradling it with the other, was a younger woman with auburn hair and frightened eyes. The sleeve of her dress was scarlet and blood was dripping on to the step.

'Come in,' Hester said instantly, stepping back to make room for them to pass her. Then she closed the door and bolted it, as she always did after dark. She put her arm around the injured woman and turned to Flo. 'Bessie's asleep in the room to the left at the top of the stairs,' she directed them. 'Please go and waken her and ask her to put more water on to boil, and get out the brandy—'

'She don't need no more brandy,' Flo interrupted her, glancing at the injured woman impatiently.

'It's not to drink,' Hester replied. 'It's to clean the needle if she needs stitching up. Just get Bessie, please.'

Flo shrugged, pursing her lips. She was somewhere in her mid-thirties, dark-haired and with a mass of freckles. She had a long, rather lugubrious face, and no one could have called her pretty. But she was intelligent and had a quick tongue and, when she could be bothered, she had a certain charm. She had sent or brought a number of women here, and once or twice she had even come with money. Hester was grateful to her for that.

'I'll put the water on,' she said gruffly. 'Yer think I don' know where ter find it, or I can't lift a pan?'

Hester thanked her and helped the other woman to sit down in the chair in the main room, still nursing her arm, her face pasty white at the sight of so much of her own blood.

Hester lit more candles and began to work. It took her over an hour to stop the bleeding, clean the wound and stitch it, bandage it and get the woman, whose name was Maisie, into a clean nightgown and to a bed, at least to lie in the relative warmth for a while.

'Yer look 'orrible yerself,' Flo observed when the two of them were alone in the kitchen. 'I'll make yer a cup o' tea. Yer fit ter drop, an' if yer do, 'oo'll look arter the rest of us then, eh?'

Hester was about to refuse, instinctively, then she realised the stupidity of it. She was so tired the room seemed to waver around her, as if she were seeing it through water. She did not want to disturb Bessie, who had more than earned her sleep. 'Thank you,' she accepted.

'Then yer should catch a bit o' kip yerself,' Flo added. 'I'll wake yer if anythin' 'appens.'

'I've got a very ill woman upstairs; I must see how she is. We have to keep the fever down if we can.'

Flo put her hands on her hips. 'An' 'ow yer goin' ter do that, then, eh? Work a bleedin' miracle, will yer?'

'Cold water and cloths,' Hester said wearily. 'I'll look in on her, then maybe I'll take an hour or so. Thank you, Flo.'

But that was not how it transpired. Hester drank her tea, looked in on Ruth Clark and saw her sleeping, then went to a room two doors along and sank gratefully on to the bed. Pulling the blankets over herself, she allowed oblivion to claim her.

She woke reluctantly – she had no idea how much later – to hear women's voices raised in fury. One was louder than the other, and unmistakably Flo's; the other was quieter, deeper, and it was a moment before Hester could place it. Then it came to her with amazement as she sat up. There was no light except the small amount that came from the candle in the passage. The other voice was Ruth Clark's, and the language was equally robust and abusive from both of them. Words like 'whore' and 'cow' were repeated often.

Hester stood up, still dizzy with tiredness, and stumbled towards the passage. She blinked as she reached the brighter lights. The noise was worse. How could Bessie sleep through this?

119

It was coming from Ruth's room – of course it was. She was far too ill to be out of her bed. Hester strode along and pushed the door wide. Helpful or not, she would tear Flo to pieces for this!

The scene that met her eyes was extraordinary. Ruth was propped up on several pillows, an empty cup in her hands. Her hair was wild, her face pale but for the hectic flush in her cheeks, and her expression was one of unmitigated rage.

A few feet away from her Flo stood, her lips drawn back in a snarl. Her hair was half down as if someone had torn at it, and the whole of the front of her dress was soaked in water.

'Stop it!' Hester said in a tone of voice she had heard used in the army during her time on the Crimean battlefields.

Both women stared at her. It was Ruth who drew breath to speak first. 'You're paid to look after me,' she said raspingly. 'Get this whore out of here!'

'Who are you calling an 'ore? Yer nothing but a fancy slut yerself, fer all yer airs!' Flo retorted. 'Think 'cos yer lies wi' sailors that makes yer summink diff'rent? Well, it don't. Yer an 'ore, jus' like the rest o' us. An' keep a civil tongue in yer 'ead an' speak nice ter Mrs Monk, wot's keepin' yer from dyin' in the gutter where yer belong, or I'll fetch a bucket o' slops an' toss it right back at yer, yer manky bitch.'

'I'm sure you have plenty of slops to spare,' Ruth said icily. 'You smell as if you bathe in them.'

'Silence!' Hester raised her voice sharply.

But it was to no effect. Flo lost her temper and hurled herself forward on to the bed, landing on Ruth, then raising her hand to hit her.

Hester grabbed it, catching it almost across her own face, and was dragged forward and off balance, half on to the floor. Both Flo and Ruth were still cursing each other, but Ruth had no strength to lash back physically.

It was at that moment that Bessie burst in, saw the scene and charged across to pick Flo up bodily, swing round with her and drop her on the floor.

'Wot the bleedin' 'ell d'yer think yer doin', yer crazy lard-arse?' she yelled at Flo. Then turning on Ruth she went on, 'An' as fer you, yer spotty slag, you mind yer tongue or I'll put yer out inter the gutter, money or no money. In't surprisin' yer lover threw yer out, yer iggerant mare. Yer got a mouth on yer like a midden. One more order out o' yer, an' I'll throw yer out meself. Just shut yer face, y'ear me?'

There was total silence.

Slowly Hester climbed to her feet. 'Thank you, Bessie,' she said gravely. She stared at the woman in the bed. Ruth was flushed and weak, but her eyes were spitting venom. 'Miss Clark, go back to sleep. Bessie will come to see you in a while. Flo, you come with me.' And seizing her by the arm, she strode out, half dragging her along, down the stairs and into the kitchen before she spoke again.

'Kettle,' she commanded. 'Make some tea.'

'In't surprised 'e threw 'er out, the turd,' Flo retorted, but she did as she was told. 'Din't give yer much of a kip, did she? Ungrateful trollop.' She took the kettle from the stove. 'Thinks 'cos one man keeps 'er, not twenty, that she's suffink special. Talks like she was a lady – she's a common slut, like the rest of us.'

'Probably,' Hester agreed, too tired to care what it was about this time. It was thirty-five minutes since she'd lain down on the bed upstairs. She felt as if she could have slept on the kitchen table – or the floor, for that matter.

'An' yer got rats,' Flo called, pouring water out of the pail into the kettle. 'Yer'll 'ave ter get the rat-catcher in. D'yer know one?'

'Of course I do,' Hester said wearily. 'I'll send a message to Sutton in the morning.'

'I'll take it,' Flo offered. 'Yer don't want no more tea, or yer'll be up an' down all night like a dancer's knees.'

'What "night"?' Hester responded bitterly.

Bessie came into the room, her face scrubbed and ready for business.

'I'll go an' see 'er in a couple of hours,' she announced, looking at Hester. 'Me an' Flo'll take care o' the rest o' the night.' She glared at Flo. 'In't that right?'

'Yeah,' Flo agreed, grinning at Hester and showing several gaps in her teeth. 'I won't kill 'er, honest. Swear on me mother's grave.'

'Yer ma in't dead,' Bessie growled.

Flo shrugged and put the kettle on to the stove, then bent to open the range and poke the coals to make them burn up. 'Yer need more coke,' she said with a sniff. 'S'pose that's why yer 'as ter take that kind o' pig.'

Hester went back upstairs again with profound gratitude, and sank into a dreamless sleep until nearly seven o'clock, when the day's duties began. Mercifully when she looked in on Ruth, she seemed to be quite quietly asleep, hot but not delirious, and breathing fairly well.

Downstairs in the kitchen Bessie was making gruel for those who were well enough to eat, and Flo was asleep in one of the chairs, her head fallen forward on to the table.

When Margaret arrived shortly after ten o'clock, she took one look at Hester's face and then Bessie's. 'What's happened?' she asked, her eyes wide with alarm.

'We need more 'elp,' Bessie replied before Hester could say anything.

'And the rat-catcher,' Hester added. Flo was already fetching more water from the well along the street.

Margaret made a slight flinch of distaste, but she was not surprised. Rats were a condition of life in places like Portpool Lane.

'How's Ruth Clark?' she asked Hester.

'She'll live, more's the pity,' Bessie replied. She jerked her head towards Hester. 'Bin' up most o' the night, wot wi' m'lady Clark, 'er an' the poor bint wot come in wi' a knife cut in 'er arm. Which 'minds me, I in't never took 'er no breakfast yet.' And suiting the deed to the word, she ladled out a dish of gruel and went out of the room with it, leaving Hester and Margaret alone.

'We do need more help,' Hester admitted. 'But we've got no money spare to pay anyone, so it'll have to be voluntary. Heaven knows, it's hard enough to get money. I've no idea how we're going to persuade someone to give up their time to a place like this.' She glanced around the candlelit kitchen with its stone sink, pails of water, and wooden bins of flour and oatmeal. 'Unfortunately heaven's not telling me.'

Margaret made tea for both of them, and toast from one of the loaves of bread she had brought. She even had a jar of marmalade, taken surreptitiously from her mother's kitchen. She had left a note in the larder, in case the cook or one of the other servants got the blame for its disappearance.

'I'm not sure where I'll ask,' she said when they were both sitting down. 'But I have one or two places at least to start. There are women who have no money they can dispose of without their husbands' approval, but they do have time. It is possible to be very comfortably off, and bored silly.'

Hester was in no position to quibble. She would be very grateful for any help at all, and she said so.

It was a hard day. Two more women were admitted with bad bronchitis, and a third with a dislocated shoulder, which took Hester and Bessie considerable difficulty to reduce, and, of course, was extremely painful for the woman. She let out a fearful scream as Hester laid her on the ground, put her foot as gently as she could into the woman's armpit and then pulled steadily on the hand.

Flo came rushing in, demanding to know what had happened, and then was furious to discover it was nothing she could do anything about. The woman, gasping to frame abuse, staggered to her feet, and only then realised that her shoulder was back to normal.

Just before five there was a knock on the back door and Hester opened it to find the costermonger in the yard, his barrow behind him.

'Hello, Toddy, how are you?' she asked with a smile.

'Not bad, missus,' he replied with a lop-sided grin. 'Just got me usual. Yer don't think as it's summink serious, do yer?' A flicker of anxiety showed for a moment in his eyes.

She affected to give his aches their proper consideration. 'I'll get you some elder ointment that you can rub in. Bessie swears by it for her knees.'

'That's right nice o' yer,' he said, obviously comforted. 'I got 'alf a dozen pounds o' apples it in't worth me takin' 'ome. More trouble than it'd be worth. D'yer like 'em 'ere?'

'That would be very nice,' Hester accepted, going back inside to fetch the ointment. She returned and gave it to him in a small jar, and found him standing there with the apples, and a small sack of mixed potatoes, carrots and parsnips.

Margaret left to go home at eight o'clock, and it seemed a long night. Hester, able to snatch no more than an hour or two's sleep, in bits and pieces, catnapped when the chance arose. Flo fetched and carried, but her quarrel with Ruth Clark rumbled on, and by daylight everyone was exhausted. The best that could be said was that none of the patients gave cause for fear that they were close to death.

At half-past ten Margaret arrived, bringing with her two women. They walked into the clinic behind her, then stood in the main room, the first staring quite openly around with a look of disdain. She was a tall, rather thin woman with dark hair, and she was considerably broader at the hip than the shoulder. Her face had been handsome in her youth, but the marks of discontent detracted from it now that she appeared to be in her middle forties. Her clothes were smart and expensive, even though she had clearly selected her oldest skirt and woollen jacket in which to come. Hester knew at a glance that they were well made and of good fabric. Five years ago they had been the height of fashion.

The woman behind her was different in almost every respect. She was at least two inches less in height. Her face was soft featured, but there was great strength in the broad cheekbones and the chin. Her hair was honey-brown and had a heavy natural curl. Her clothes were also of good quality, but less fashionable in cut, and looked to be no earlier than last winter's in style. She seemed to be the more nervous of the two. There was no discontent in her face, but a profound apprehension, as though she feared the place as if there were something in it that was dangerous, even tragic.

'This is Mrs Claudine Burroughs,' Margaret introduced the older woman to Hester. 'She has very generously offered to help us at least two days a week.'

'How do you do, Mrs Burroughs?' Hester responded. 'We are very grateful to you.'

Mrs Burroughs looked at her with growing disapproval. She must have seen the exhaustion in her face, her hair untidily caught up and her hands red from scrubbing the floor and feeding hot, wet sheets through the mangle. There was a tear in the shoulder seam of her blouse from reaching to winch up the airing rack to try to get the bed linen dry before it was needed again.

'It isn't the sort of charity work I usually do,' Mrs Burroughs said coolly.

'You will never do anything which will be more valued,' Hester replied with as much warmth as she could manage. She could not afford to offend her, full of misgivings as she was.

'And this is Miss Mercy Louvain,' Margaret introduced the other, younger woman. 'She has offered to be here as long as we need her. She will even sleep here if it would be helpful.' She smiled, searching Hester's eyes and awaiting her approval.

'Louvain!' Hester was incredulous. Was she related to Clement Louvain? She must be – a much younger sister, almost certainly. They had the same look and it was hardly a common name. Was it possible she knew Ruth Clark? If she did, it might be an embarrassing situation, especially if Ruth were really Louvain's mistress and not that of some fictional friend.

She smiled back, first at Margaret, then at Mercy Louvain. 'Thank you, that is extraordinarily good of you. Night times can be hard. We appreciate it very much indeed.' Not once had Mercy looked around the room as Mrs Burroughs had; it was almost as if she were very little interested.

Hester did not express her gratitude to Margaret in words, in case the depth of her feeling alarmed the two new volunteers, but she allowed it to show in her eyes for a moment when their glances met. Then Hester took the women to show them the house, and introduced them to their first tasks.

'For heaven's sake, don't you have servants here of any sort?' Mrs Burroughs demanded when they were in the laundry. She gazed at the stone floor and the pile of linen on it, awaiting washing, and then at the huge copper with the steam rising from it, her nostrils flaring at the vinegar and caustic in the air. She looked at the mangle between the two deep wooden tubs as if it were some obscene instrument of torture.

'We don't have money for them,' Hester explained. 'We need all we can get for medicine, coal and food. People are very unwilling to give to us because of the nature of our patients.'

Mrs Burroughs snorted, but made no direct reply. Her eyes went further around the room, noting the pails, the sack of potash, the vat of lard and the large glass flagons of vinegar, the scrubbing brushes and the rags for wiping up.

'Where do you get water?' she asked. 'I see no taps.'

'From the well down the street,' Hester replied.

'Good heavens, woman! You want a carthorse to labour here,' Mrs Burroughs exclaimed.

'I want a lot of things,' Hester said ruefully. 'I'll accept what I can get, and be most grateful for it. Bessie usually fetches the water. You don't need to concern yourself with it.'

'Bessie? Is she the big woman I saw on the landing?'

'Yes. She would do most of the laundry usually, but we have a lot of sick and injured here right now, and she has learned a little nursing, so I need her to help with that.'

'Skilled, is it?' Mrs Burroughs asked disbelievingly.

'Yes, some of it is,' Hester replied, again finding it difficult to remain civil. 'Some of it isn't, like cleaning up blood or vomit, emptying slops, that sort of thing.'

Mrs Burroughs jerked up her chin. 'I'll do the laundry,' she stated.

Hester smiled back at her. 'Thank you,' she accepted sweetly.

If Mercy Louvain saw any humour in Mrs Burroughs' reaction there was no reflection of it in her grave face. Hester showed Mrs Burroughs where everything was, and the exact proportions to be mixed, and put into the coppers. She demonstrated how to use the wooden dolly to move the linen, how long to leave it and at what temperature. She would have to return in order to help her move it all to be rinsed and then mangled, folded and the airing rack winched down, the linen put on it, and winched back up again and lashed tight. It was obvious Mrs Burroughs had never so much as washed a handkerchief. She had a great deal to learn, if she were to be of use.

Mercy Louvain was of a totally different character, but it did not take Hester long to see that she also was completely inexperienced in any domestic work. She had seldom visited a kitchen, but when Hester showed her the saucepans, oatmeal, salt, flour, split peas and vegetables, she seemed to grasp the essentials at least willingly, even if she needed to ask a great many questions. Hester finally left to go back upstairs, wondering if it would not be easier to do it all herself than accept such unskilled help.

However, in the middle of the afternoon she was grateful to leave Bessie to teach Mrs Burroughs how to clean up the laundry, and Flo to give Mercy Louvain a lesson in peeling potatoes, and go upstairs to take a couple of hours' rest.

Darkness was coming earlier each evening as autumn moved towards winter, and by six o'clock it was both dark and cold. They bolted the doors at eight, and Hester thought with a shiver of those outside walking the streets, looking and hoping for the trade that kept them alive.

She went upstairs to see how Ruth Clark was.

She had been well enough to take a little very thin broth, and had expressed her disgust with the quality of it. Hester wondered again how much of her temper was really directed at the man who had apparently loved her, or at least desired her, and then when she was ill had put her out on the street to depend upon strangers and the pity of those who wished to do good. Were she in the same position, she might resent it just as deeply, and with as bitter a tongue. Had she loved the man? Or was he no more than a means to live well? If she had cared for him, had even hoped there was something real in it that would last, no wonder she was raw with pain.

Then she heard Flo shrieking again, and she strode upstairs to find her standing over Ruth's bed swearing at her. Ruth had malice bright in her eyes and her fist was clenched on long dark hairs.

Hester lost her own temper. 'Stop it!' she shouted, exhaustion draining her voice until it was sharp and high-pitched. 'Stop it this moment! This is a hospital, not a bawdy house!'

'Of course it's a bawdy house,' Ruth snapped back. 'It's a house full of whores – and thieves!'

'I'm no thief!' Flo said furiously, her body shaking with emotions. 'I never stole nothin' in me life. An' yer in't got no right ter say I did. I in't seen yer bleedin' ring. We took yer in 'cos yer was threw out an' yer should be glad to be 'ere.'

'Instead of where – this cesspit?' Ruth retorted, heaving herself up on the pillows. 'And you are a thief.'

There was a slight noise in the doorway and Hester swivelled round to see Mercy Louvain standing behind her.

'Yer never 'ad a ring, yer lyin' cow!' Flo yelled, her face red. 'Full o' yer airs an' graces – an' yer in't no better'n the rest o' us. For all I care, yer can leave any time yer can stand up an' get out,' she went on viciously. 'Only yer can't, can yer? Yer man tossed yer out, an' yer in't got no place else ter go. We're the last ones as'll 'ave yer, yer scabby mare!'

'And who has ever wanted you, you ignorant, pox-ridden trollop?' Ruth demanded.

Flo started forward to attack, just as Mercy Louvain stepped past Hester to stand between the two women, only it was Ruth she was facing. Flo nearly fell over her, instead veering sideways and bumping into Hester, who gripped her arms.

129

'Hold your tongue,' Mercy said in a hard, quiet voice. 'You're sick and in need. These women have taken you in to look after you. They owe you nothing. They have no need to sit up all night caring for you, and you'd best remember that. You can be put back out into the street to be alone, and there's no reason except kindness why they shouldn't do exactly that. So unless you want to exchange this bed, with someone to care for you and feed you, for the street corner, you'd better mind your tongue.'

Ruth stared at her in disbelief. She could hardly comprehend what had happened.

'Do you hear me?' Mercy said sharply.

'Yes . . . of course I hear you,' Ruth replied. 'I haven't—'

'Good,' Mercy cut her off. 'Then behave as if you do.' She turned away, apparently amazed, and now self-conscious at her own words. She looked at Hester in some embarrassment. 'I'm sorry. Perhaps . . .'

Hester smiled at her. 'Thank you,' she said quietly. 'That was more effective. Flo, you had better go and see the rest of the women, and keep out of here.'

Flo glared at her. She took it as a reproach, a granting of Ruth's wishes. 'I in't no thief,' she said hotly. 'I in't.'

'I know that,' Hester answered her. 'Do you think you would be welcome here if you were?' She could not afford to have Flo walk out.

Somewhat mollified, Flo stared once more at Ruth, then swept out, whisking her skirts behind her. Hester and Mercy set about changing the linen on Ruth's bed and making her as comfortable as possible. She was still an extremely ill woman, and running a high temperature.

Chapter Six

꧁❦꧂

Monk was becoming used to the dampness in the air and the smell of the tide, the movement and the constant sound of water. There was something vaguely comfortable about it, like the beating of a heart. The light was different from that in the streets; it was sharper, cleaner, full of angles and reflections. At dusk and dawn it shone back off the polished surfaces of the water in flashes of pink and primrose. It took far longer to fade than it did over the dense rooftops of the city.

Now he had something urgent to do. He knew enough to realise that seeking the thief directly would be pointless. He must anticipate his movements and be a step before him when he sold the ivory. If it were not already too late.

But failure was not something he could afford to think about; it was crippling, robbing him of the strength even to try. If the ivory had been taken by someone who knew of it and already had a buyer, there had never been any chance of getting it back. On the other hand, if the theft were a crime of opportunity it would be far harder to sell, and it was likely that it had not yet been moved more than to keep it safe.

And tomorrow Little Lil should send for him. What

would she have to say? The thought was not entirely a pleasant one.

The first lift of hope came in the middle of the morning when Monk was sharing a sheltered spot out of the damp wind off the outgoing tide with one of the men he had seen in the scuffle-hunting gang. He had just mentioned Louvain's name.

The man jerked his head round, anger and fear in his face. 'Yer workin' fer 'im?' he snarled.

Monk was uncertain whether to admit or deny it. 'Why?' he asked.

'In't nothin' ter do wiv me,' the man said quickly.

'What isn't?' Monk demanded, moving a step towards him.

'Get off me!' The man lifted his arm as if to shield himself, and took a quick, scrambling step sideways and backwards. 'I dunno nuffink.'

Monk went after him. 'About what?'

'Clem Louvain. I don't touch nuffink ter do wiv 'im. Get off me!'

Monk snatched the man's arm and held it. 'Why not? Why not Louvain?'

The man was frightened. His lips were drawn back from his teeth in a snarl, but his body was trembling. There was hate in his eyes. He glared at Monk for a moment, then his free hand went into his pocket. An instant later Monk felt a stinging pain in his upper arm even before he saw the knife. Partly to defend himself, but at least as much in sheer fury, he lifted his knee and sent the man staggering backwards, clutching himself and squealing, tears running down his face.

Monk looked at his arm. His jacket was sliced open and there was a stain of blood spreading on to his shirt and the fabric of his coat.

'Damn you!' he swore, looking at the man now half crouched over. 'You stupid sod! I only asked you.' He turned and walked away as quickly as he could, aware that he must get his arm seen to before he lost too much blood or it became infected.

He was a hundred yards along the street, and realised he had no specific idea where he was going.

He stopped for a moment. His arm was painful and he was becoming worried in case it hampered his ability to go on as he had intended. One-armed, he was at a disadvantage he could ill afford. Where was there a doctor who could bind up his wound, stitch it if need be?

Would the Portpool Lane clinic have helped him? Or was it open only to women of the street? Pity it was too far away. He had not been aware of doing it, but he was holding his arm and the blood was oozing stickily through his fingers. He must find a doctor.

He turned and walked back to the nearest shop, and went in. It was stacked with ironmongery of every sort: pots, pans, kitchen machines, gardening tools, but mostly ships' chandlery. The air was thick with the smell of hemp rope, tallow, dust and canvas.

A little man with spectacles on his nose looked up from behind a pile of lanterns. 'Oh dear, now, wot's 'appened ter you, then?' he asked, looking at Monk's arm.

'Thief,' Monk replied. 'I shouldn't have struggled with him. He had a knife.'

The man straightened up.'Oh dear. Did 'e get your money?'

'No. I can pay a doctor, if I can find one.'

''Ere, sit down, afore yer fall. Look a bit queasy, you do.' He came out from behind the lanterns and led Monk to a small hard-backed chair. 'Mouthful o' rum wouldn't do yer no 'arm, neither.' He turned round to face the door at the back of the shop. 'Madge! Go an' fetch the crow. Quick on your way. I ain't got no time ter mess abaht!'

There was a call of agreement from somewhere out of sight, and then the patter of feet and a door slamming.

133

Monk was glad to sit down, although he did not feel as bad as the proprietor seemed to think.

'You jus' stay there,' the man told him with concern, then bustled away to sell a coil of rope and two boxes of nails to a thin man in a pea jacket, then a packet of needles for stitching sails, a couple of wooden cleats and a coal scuttle to a sailor with a blond beard.

Monk sat thinking about the response the man on the dockside had made to the mention of Louvain's name. He had been angry, but, more than that, he had been genuinely afraid. Why? Why would a scuffle hunter be afraid of a man of power? Louvain was someone whose influence could help or hurt many he would barely even know. Monk had seen that kind of fear when he had been in the police, in small men without defence who had hated and feared him because he could injure them and he let them know it. He had thought it was the only way to do the job, but the price was high. Was that true of Louvain also, a shadow of the same knowledge and responsibility, and use of power? But the scuffle hunter and a man of Louvain's stature – how would their paths even have crossed?

There were facts about Louvain that Monk did not know – ones that he should learn, both practically and morally. Ignorance was dangerous, and he was floundering in unfamiliar surroundings, among thieves with whom he had no connection and no leverage. In a way it was like the first months after his injury, when everything had been strange. He had not known friend from enemy and he seemed always to be at a disadvantage.

Somehow it was harder trying to do it a second time. His innocence then had been a kind of protection. He felt wearier and more vulnerable now.

The smells of rope, oil and tallow were overpowering. How long had he been here? Had he even the slightest chance of finding Louvain's ivory? For that matter, was there any proof that it actually existed? He had only Louvain's word for it. Perhaps he had put ashore somewhere else and sold it, and was employing Monk as a façade to dupe the London buyer.

''Ere 'e is.' A small, high-pitched voice jerked him out of his thoughts.

Monk looked up to see a child about eight or nine years old, her hair tied up in a piece of string, her face grubby, her skirts down to the top of her boots. But the fact that she had boots was unusual here. She must be Madge.

Behind her was a man of about thirty, with sleek black hair almost to his shoulders, and a wide smile. He looked relentlessly cheerful.

'I'm the crow,' he announced, using the cant word for a doctor – or a thieves' lookout. 'Bin in a fight, 'ave yer? Let's see it then. Can't do nothin' useful through all that cloth.' He regarded Monk's jacket. 'Pity, not a bad bit o' stuff. Still, let's 'ave it off yer.' He reached out to help Monk divest himself of it, taking it from him as Monk winced at moving his injured arm.

Madge turned and ran off, coming back seconds later with a bottle of brandy. She held on to it, cradling it in her arms like a doll, until it should be needed.

The 'crow' worked with some skill, pulling the cloth of the shirt away from the wound and screwing up his face as he peered at it.

Monk tried not to think about what training the man had, if any, or even what his charges might be. Perhaps he would have been wiser to have taken a hansom to Portpool Lane after all, whatever the time or the money concerned. In the end it would have been safer, and maybe cost no more. But it was too late now. The man was already reaching for the brandy and a cloth to clean away the blood.

The raw spirit stung so violently that Monk had to bite

his lip to stop himself from crying out.

'Sorry,' the doctor muttered with a wide smile, as if that would be reassuring. 'Could 'a' bin worse.' He peered closely at the wound, which was still bleeding fairly freely. 'Wot've yer got worth puttin' up that kind o' fight for, eh?' He was making conversation to keep Monk's mind off the pain, and possibly the blood as well.

Monk thought of Callandra's watch, and was glad that he had put it away in the top drawer of the tallboy in the bedroom. He smiled back at the doctor, though it was rather more a baring of teeth than an expression of good humour. 'Nothing,' he replied. 'I made him angry.'

The doctor looked up and met his gaze, curiosity bright in his face. 'Make an 'abit o' that, do yer? I could make me livin' orff you, an' that's a fact. O' course, that's only if you din't go an' die on me. Don' make nobody angry enough ter stick it in yer throat next time.' He was pressing hard to stop the bleeding as he spoke. 'Put yer other 'and on that,' he ordered, directing Monk to a pad of cloth above the wound. ''Old it.' He pulled out of his pocket a fine needle and a length of catgut. He washed them in the brandy, then told Monk to release the pad. Quickly and deftly he stitched first the inside of the wound, then the skin on the outside. He surveyed the result with satisfaction, before winding a bandage around it and tying the ends. 'Yer'll 'ave ter 'ave that changed termorrer, an' every day till it's 'ealed,' he said. 'But it'll do yer.'

'My wife will do it,' Monk replied. He was beginning to feel cold and a little shivery. 'Thank you.'

'She don't come all over faint at the sight o' blood, then?'

'She nursed in the Crimea,' Monk replied with fierce welling up pride. 'She could amputate a leg if she had to.'

'Jeez! Not my bleedin' leg!' the doctor said, but his eyes

were wide with admiration. 'Really? Yer 'avin' me on.'

'No, I'm not. I've seen her do something like it, on the battlefield in the American War.'

The doctor pulled a face. 'Poor sods,' he said simply. ''Oo did yer get across, then? Yer must 'ave done it good ter make 'im do this to yer?'

'I don't know. Some scuffle hunter.'

The doctor squinted at him, studying him with interest. 'Yer in't from round 'ere.' It was a statement. 'Down on yer luck, eh? Yer speak like yer come from up west, wi' a plum in your mouth.' He regarded Monk's shirt, ignoring the torn and bloody sleeve. 'Cardsharp, are yer? Yer in't no receiver; yer in't 'alf fly enough. Daft as a brush ter get sliced like that.'

'No,' Monk said stiffly. The wound was painful now and he was feeling colder with every passing moment. Discretion was gaining him little. 'The man who stabbed me did it because I asked him about Clement Louvain.'

The doctor's eyes opened even wider. 'Did yer?' he said, making a faint whistling sound between his teeth. 'I wouldn't do that if I was you. Mr Louvain in't one ter meddle wi', an' yer won't cross 'im twice, I'd put money on that.'

'But he has friends?'

'Mebbe. Mostly there's them as 'ates 'im, an' them as is frit of 'im, an' them as is both.' He reached for the bottle of brandy and offered it to Monk. 'Don't take more'n a swig or two, or yer'll feel even worse, but that'll get yer on yer way. An' I'll give yer summink else fer nothin': don' meddle wi' Clem Louvain. Anybody crosses 'im up an' 'e's like a pit bull wi' toothache. If yer wanter keep yer other arm, yer'll steer clear of 'im.'

Monk took a swig of the brandy and it hit his stomach like fire.

'So whoever crosses him is either very brave or very stupid?' he asked, watching the doctor's face.

The doctor sat back and made himself comfortable against a pile of rope.

'Did you?' he asked candidly.

'No. It was a thief, and I'm trying to get the stuff back.'

'Fer Louvain?'

'Of course.'

'Off one of his boats? Likely the *Maude Idris*.'

'Yes. Why?'

'What were it?'

'Ivory.'

The doctor made another shrill whistle between his teeth.

Monk wondered if the loss of blood had weakened his wits. He should not have said so much. Desperation was making him careless. 'So either someone is sitting on a pile of ivory wondering how on earth to get rid of it without betraying who they are and bringing down Louvain's vengeance on them,' he said very quietly. 'Or else someone with a great deal of power, enough not to need to be afraid of anything Louvain can do to them, is feeling very pleased with themselves, and perhaps very rich.'

'Or very 'appy ter 'ave scored one off Louvain,' the doctor added.

'Who would that be?'

The doctor grinned. 'Take your pick – Culpepper, Dobbs, Oldham. Any o' them big men along the Pool, or the West India Dock, or even down Lime'ouse way. I'd go back 'ome, if I was you. Yer in't suited fer this. River's no place fer gennelmen. Cut-throats is still two a penny, if yer knows where ter find 'em.'

Monk gritted his teeth as pain from his arm washed over him.

'Let Louvain clean up 'is own mess,' the doctor added.

'How much do I owe you?' Monk asked, rising to his

138

feet slowly and a trifle unsteadily.

'Well, you prob'ly owes 'Erbert 'ere fer 'is brandy, but I don't need nuffink. I reckon yer worth it fer interest, like. Crimea, eh? Honest?'

'Yes.'

'She know Florence Nightingale?'

'Yes.'

'You met 'er?'

'Yes. She has a pretty sharp tongue in her, too.' Monk smiled, and winced at the memory.

The doctor pushed his hands into his pockets, his eyes shining.

Monk thought of telling him about the clinic in Portpool Lane, then changed his mind. It was only pride that made him want to. Better to be discreet, at least for now. 'What's your name?' He would do something later.

'Crow,' the doctor said with a huge smile. 'At least that's what they call me. Suits me profession. Wot's yours?'

Monk smiled back. 'Monk . . .'

Crow roared with laughter, and Monk found himself oddly self-conscious, in fact he felt himself colouring. He turned away and fished in his pocket to pay Mr Herbert for his brandy.

Herbert refused it, and Monk gave Madge sixpence instead, and another sixpence when she brought him water and soap to clean up his jacket before he walked outside. There was a bitter wind coming off the tide, but its chill revived him.

But with a sharper mind and slightly clearer head came the awareness that if he were going to go back to see Little Lil, then he had to have at least two or three gold watches to sell her. Not even to earn Louvain's money was he going to part with Callandra's watch. The only person whose help he could ask for now was Louvain himself. The thought choked in his throat, but there was no alternative. The sooner he did it, the sooner it would be over.

'What?' Louvain said incredulously when Monk told him.

Monk felt his face burn. He was standing in front of Louvain's desk and Louvain was sitting in the large, carved and padded chair behind it. Louvain had already remarked on Monk's torn sleeve, and Monk had dismissed it.

'I need to convince them that I have stolen goods to sell,' Monk repeated, staring back at him unblinkingly. He knew exactly what Louvain was trying to do by his demeanour because he had exercised exactly that kind of domination of will over others when he had been in the police and had the power to back it. He refused to be cowed. 'Talk means nothing,' he answered. 'I have to show them something.'

'And you imagine I'm fool enough to give it to you?' There was a bitter derision in Louvain's voice, and perhaps a disappointment as well. 'I fund four or five gold watches for you, hand them over, and why should I ever see you again, let alone my watches? What kind of an idiot do you take me for?'

'One who does not hire a man to retrieve his stolen goods without first finding out enough about him to know whether he can trust him or not,' Monk replied immediately.

Louvain smiled, showing his teeth. There was a flash of respect in his eyes, but no warmth. 'I know a great deal more about you than you do about me,' he conceded with a touch of arrogance.

Monk smiled back, his look hard, as if he also had secret knowledge that amused him.

Louvain saw something and there was a subtle change in his eyes.

Monk smiled more widely.

Suddenly Louvain was uncertain. 'What do you know about me?' he asked, no timbre or lift in his voice now to indicate whether the answer mattered to him or not.

'I'm not concerned with anything except what has to do with the ivory,' Monk told him. 'I need to know your enemies, rivals, people who owe you, or whom you owe, people who think you have wronged them.'

'And what have you found out?' Louvain's eyebrows rose, interest sharper in him.

Perhaps if Louvain were to succeed in the hard and dangerous trade he had chosen then he needed to appear a man no one would dare cross, but was there a gentle man behind the mask? Was he capable of softer passions as well – of love, vulnerability, dreams? Was the woman he had taken to Portpool Lane the mistress of a friend for whom he would perform such a service? Or was she perhaps his own mistress, and he had had to protect his family, whoever they were – wife, children, parents?

'What have you found?' Louvain repeated.

'Don't you know?' Monk asked aloud.

Louvain nodded very slowly. 'Then if I get the watches for you, you'll know that if you steal them, England won't be big enough for you to hide in, let alone London.'

'I won't steal them because I'm not a thief,' Monk snapped. He was overpoweringly aware of the difference in wealth between them. He lived from week to week, and Louvain would know that, whereas Louvain owned ships, warehouses, a London home with carriages, horses, possibly even a house in the country somewhere. He would have servants, possessions, a future of as much certainty as was possible in life.

Louvain raised his eyebrows, but there was a flicker of humour in his face. 'Perhaps no one else was rash enough to give you gold watches?'

'I have never worked for anyone who lost a shipment of

ivory before,' Monk snapped back. 'I tend to specialise in murders.'

'And minor thefts,' Louvain added cruelly. 'Lately you've retrieved a couple of brooches, a cello, a rare book and three vases. You have failed to retrieve a silver salver, a red lacquer box and a carriage horse.'

Monk's temper seethed. Only knowledge of his own dependency on the payment for this job kept him in the room. 'Which begs the question why you asked me to find your ivory, rather than the River Police, as any other victim of crime would have done!' he said bitterly.

There were many emotions in Louvain's face, violent and conflicting: fury, fear, a moment of respect, and a mounting frustration. He realised Monk was still staring at him and that his eyes read far too much. 'I'll give you forty guineas,' he said abruptly. 'Get what you can. But if you're going to sell them around here, you'd better go the south side of the river to buy them. The pawnbrokers and receivers all know each other's business on this side. Now go and get on with it. Time's short. It's no damned use to me finding out who took my ivory if they've already sold it on!'

He stood up and went to the safe in the far corner, unlocked it with his back to Monk, took out the money and locked it again. He faced Monk and counted out the coins. His eyes were as hard as the winter wind off the Thames, but he did not repeat his warning.

'Thank you,' Monk accepted, turning on his heel and leaving.

Louvain was right that there was no time to lose; also, that he would be far wiser to buy his watches on the south side of the river, perhaps as far down as Deptford, opposite the Isle of Dogs. He walked briskly back along the dockside, guarding his injured arm as well as he could. He should find a tailor to stitch up the gash in his coat, but he had no time to spare now. The cut was surprisingly small for the pain the knife had inflicted on his flesh.

It was growing dusk already, even though it was mid-afternoon. He had missed lunch, so he bought an eel pie from a pedlar on the kerbside. Only when he bit into it did he realise how hungry he was. He stood on the embankment side near the stone steps down to the water, waiting until he saw a ferry that would take him across. It was half-tide and the smell of the mud was sour. It seemed to cling to skin, hair, cloth, and be with him even when he left the river to go home.

The air was damp; the sound of water slapping against the stones was as rhythmic as the blood in a living thing. Faint veils of mist hung over the slick river surface. The wind-ribbed shafts of silver were bright one moment, vanishing the next. Far to the south, along the curve of Limehouse Reach, a foghorn sounded, drifting like a cry of loss.

Monk shivered. As the wind dropped the mist would increase. He had no desire to be caught trying to cross back again if there were a real pea-souper. He must go as quickly as possible. Without reasoning the advantage to it, he walked to the edge of the steps and down the first two or three, parallel to the wall, rail-less, the black water swirling and slopping a dozen feet below him.

There was a boat twenty yards away, a man sitting idly at the oars. Monk cupped his hands around his mouth and called out to him.

The man half turned, saw where Monk was standing, and dug the oars in deep, pulling the boat towards him.

'Wanter cross?' he asked when he was close enough to be heard.

'Yes,' Monk shouted back.

The man drew the boat in and Monk went down the rest of the steps. It was going to be less easy with one stiff arm, but he had to move it in order to keep his balance.

The man watched him with a certain sympathy, but he was obliged to keep both hands on his oars to control the boat.

'Where yer goin'?' he asked when Monk was seated and pulling his coat collar up around his ears.

'Just the other side,' Monk replied.

The man dug his oars into the water again and bent his back. He looked to be about thirty or so, with a bland, agreeable face, skin a little chapped by the weather, fair eyebrows, and a smear of freckles across his cheeks. He handled the boat with skill, as if it were second nature to him.

'Been on the river all your life?' Monk asked. A man like this might have seen something of use to him, as long as his questions were not so obvious as to make his purpose known.

'Most.' The man smiled, showing a broken front tooth. 'But yer new 'ere. Least I never seen yer afore.'

'Not this stretch,' Monk prevaricated. 'What's your name?'

'Gould.'

'How late do you work?'

Gould shrugged. 'Bad night, go 'ome early. Got a good job, stay late. Why? Yer wanter come back across late?'

'I might do. If I'm lucky I ought not to be long.' He must phrase his questions so as not to arouse suspicion. He could not afford word to spread that he was inquisitive. He had already made one enemy in the scuffle hunter, and the last thing he wanted was to be tipped overboard into the icy water. Too many bodies were fished out of the Thames, and only God knew how many more were never found.

'Isn't it dangerous at night?' he asked.

Gould grunted. 'Can be.' He nodded towards a pleasure boat, lights gleaming on the water, the sound of laughter drifting across towards them. 'Not for the likes o' them, but down in the little boats like us, yeah, it can be. Mind yer own business and yer'll be all right.'

Monk heard the warning, but he could not afford to obey it. 'You mean river pirates use little boats?' he asked.

Gould tapped the side of his nose. 'Never 'eard of 'em. In't no pirates on the Thames. Odd thieves an' the like, but they don't kill no one.'

'Sometimes they do,' Monk argued. They were about halfway across and Gould was weaving in and out of the vessels at anchor with considerable skill. The boat moved almost silently, the dip and rise of the oars indistinguishable from the sounds of water all around them. The mist was drifting and most of the light was smothered by a clinging, choking grey mass that caught in the throat. The hulls of the ships loomed up as only a greater density in the murk, one moment clearly seen, the next no more than shadows. Foghorns echoed and re-echoed till it was hard to tell which direction they came from.

What had it been like on the night of the robbery? Had someone cleverly used the weather to their advantage? Or stupidly even chosen the wrong ship?

'Could you find a particular ship in this?' he asked, moving his head to indicate the mist swirling closer around them.

'Course I could,' Gould said cheerfully. 'Know the boats on the river like me own 'and, I do.' He nodded to one side. 'That's the *City o' Leeds* over there – four-master she is, come in from Bombay. *Liverpool Pride* twenty yards beyond 'er. Come from the Cape o' Good 'Ope. Bin stuck 'ere three weeks waitin' for a berth. Other side's the *Sonora*, foreigner from India, or some place. I gotter know 'em ter the yard or so, or I'll be rowin' straight into 'em in this.'

'Yes . . . of course.' Monk's mind was racing, picturing the thieves creeping through the wreaths of vapour, finding the *Maude Idris*, having marked her carefully in

145

daylight. Would it have had to be a bigger boat than this to carry two men, or even three, and the tusks as well? He looked at Gould, his powerful shoulders as he heaved on the oars, his agility as he made a sudden turn, swivelling the blade to change the boat's course. He would have the strength to climb up the side of a ship, and to carry the ivory. He would have the strength to beat a man's head in, as Hodge's had been.

'Where yer wanna go?' Gould asked.

Monk could see little distinguishable in the dark blur of the shoreline. What he needed was a good pawnbroker who asked no questions, and would decline to remember him afterwards, but if he had ever had any knowledge of the south side of the river, he had forgotten it now. He might as well make use of Gould's help.

'Pawnbroker,' he replied. 'One that has some good stuff, but is not too particular.'

Gould chortled with hilarity. 'Will yer want one on the souf side, eh? I could tell yer a few good ones on the norf. In't none better'n Ol' Pa Weston. Give yer a fair price, an' never ask no questions as 'ow yer got it, wotever it is. Tell 'im yer Aunt Annie left it yer, an' 'e'll look at yer as solemn as an owl, an' swear as 'e believes yer.'

Monk made a mental note that Gould had almost certainly tried that a few times himself. Perhaps he was a heavy horseman on the side, with all the specially built pockets in his clothes, or simply a scuffle hunter, like the man who had stabbed him. He was glad he did not have Callandra's watch with him now.

'Rather the south side,' he answered. 'Better for me at the moment.'

'I unnerstand,' Gould assured him. 'In't everything as is easy ter place.' He made a rueful gesture, a kind of shrug, and as he leaned forward a ship's riding lights caught for a moment on his face, and Monk saw his expression of frustration, and a wry, desperate kind of

146

self-mockery. He wondered what trinket Gould was trying to pawn. Presumably the description of it was already known to the police.

They were only a few yards from the shore now, and Monk saw the steep bank rise ahead of them and heard the water slapping on the steps. A moment later they were alongside, and with an expert turn of the oar Gould bumped the boat gently against the stone so Monk could get out.

'Wot yer done ter yer arm, then?' he asked curiously, watching Monk wince as he fished in his pocket for money to pay his fare.

Monk raised his eyes to meet Gould's. 'Knife fight,' he said candidly, then he passed the money over, plus an extra sixpence. 'Same for the way back, if you're here in a couple of hours.'

Gould grinned. 'Don' slit nobody's throat,' he said cheerfully.

Monk stepped out on to the stairs and began to climb upward, keeping his balance on the wet stone with difficulty. Once on the embankment he walked to the nearest streetlamp and looked around. He could not afford the time to explore, he needed to ask, and within a matter of minutes he found someone. Everybody was familiar with the need to pawn things now and then, and an enquiry for a pawnbroker was nothing to raise interest.

He was back at the stairs an hour and three-quarters later, and within ten minutes more he saw Gould's boat emerge from the mist and the now total darkness of the river. He did not realise how relieved he was until he was seated in the boat again, rocking gently with its movement in the water, three gold watches in his pocket.

'Got wot yer wanted then, 'ave yer?' Gould asked him, dipping the oars and sending the boat out into the stream again. The mist closed around them and the shore disappeared. In a matter of moments the rest of the world vanished and there was nothing visible except Gould's face opposite him and the outline of his body against the dark pall of the mist. He could hear the water, and now and again the boom of a foghorn, and smell the salt and mud of the fast-running tide. It was as if he and Gould were the only two men alive. If Gould robbed him and put him over the side, no one would ever know. It would be oblivion in every sense.

'I kept my word to someone,' he replied. He looked directly at Gould, staring at him with the hard, level iciness that had frozen constables, and even sergeants, when he had been in the police. It was the only weapon he had.

Gould might have nodded, but in the dark Monk could barely make out his figure. It was only the regular rhythmic movement of the boat that assured him he was still rowing. For several moments they moved in silence except for the water, and, away, the foghorns.

But Gould knew the river and Monk should not waste the opportunity to learn from him. 'Are there boats on the water all night long, even shortly before dawn?' he asked.

Gould hesitated a moment or two before answering. 'There's always thieves on the lookout for a chance,' he replied. 'But 'less yer know wot yer doin', an' can look arter yerself, better be in yer bed that hour.'

'How do you know that?' Monk said quickly.

Gould chuckled deep in his throat. 'I 'eard,' he answered, but the laughter in his voice made the truth obvious.

'Thieves around? Dangerous ones,' Monk said thoughtfully.

Gould was still amused by Monk's naivety.

'In their own boats, or borrowed?' Monk pursued. 'Or stolen for the night? Anybody ever steal your boat?'

'Nah!' Gould was indignant. It was an insult to his ability and his worthiness to be on the river.

148

'How would you know if somebody'd had your boat, at say . . . three or four o'clock in the morning?' Monk asked dubiously.

'I'd know if somebody'd 'ad me boat any time.' Gould said it with complete confidence. 'I leave 'er tied wi' me own kind o' knot, but at four in the mornin' I'd be in 'er meself.'

'Would you.' It was an acknowledgement more than a question. 'Every morning?'

'Yeah – jus' about. Why? Some mornin' yer got special, like?'

Monk knew he had gone far enough. Gould was probably familiar with many of the river thieves; he might even be one of them, as an accomplice. The question was, did Monk want to risk word of his hunt getting back to whoever had taken the ivory? Except that they almost certainly knew already.

The large bulk of a schooner loomed up ahead of them, almost over them. Gould made a hasty movement with the oars, throwing his weight against them, to turn the boat aside. Monk found himself gripping the sides. He hoped in the darkness that Gould had not seen him. He half expected the shock of cold water on his skin any second.

It was worth the risk – maybe. He could spend weeks here going round and round the subject, and discovering what had happened to the ivory when it was too late. How would he survive anything if his reputation were ruined? He lived on other people's perception of him as a hard man, ruthless, successful, never to be lied to.

'October the twenty-first,' he answered. He wanted to add, 'And look where you're going!' but tact told him not to.

Gould was silent.

Monk strained his eyes ahead, but he could not see the opposite shore yet, although in this murk it could be twenty feet away.

'Dunno,' Gould replied at last. 'I were down Greenwich way around then. Weren't up 'ere. So come ter fink on it, nob'dy could 'a' 'ad me boat. So wotever it was as was done, it weren't done in my boat.' His voice lifted cheerfully. 'Sorry, I can't 'elp yer.' And the next moment the dark wall of the Embankment was above them and the hull of the boat scraped gently against the stones of the step. 'There y'are, mister, safe an' sound.'

Monk thanked him, paid the second half of his fare, and climbed out.

It was another miserable night, because Hester was not home. He knew that the reason would be illness at Portpool Lane, people she could not leave because there was no one else to care for them, but it did not ease his loneliness.

He slept in, largely by accident because his arm kept him awake until long after midnight, and disturbed him after that. He was undecided where to go to have the bandage changed. He kept telling himself to go back and find Crow. He might learn more from him. But even as he did so he was putting on his coat, mitts and muffler and walking towards the omnibus stop in the direction of Portpool Lane.

It was raining steadily, a persistent, soaking rain that found its way into everything, and sent water swirling deep along the gutters. Even so, he strode down the footpath under the shadow of the brewery with a light step, as if he were going home after a long absence.

He entered the clinic and found Bessie in the main room, sweeping the floor. She glanced up and was about to berate him when she realised who he was, and her face broke into a transforming smile.

'I'll get 'er for yer, sir,' she said immediately. 'She'll be that glad ter see yer. Workin' like a navvy, she is.' She shook her head. 'We got more in 'ere sick than yer ever see'd. Time o' year, I reckon. An' you look starvin' cold, an' all. D'yer like an 'ot cup o' tea?'

'Yes, please,' Monk accepted, sitting down as she disappeared out of the door, still carrying the broom as if it were a bayonet.

He had little time to look around him at how it had changed since he had last been here – the addition of a new cupboard, a couple of mats salvaged from somewhere – before Hester came in. Her face filled with pleasure at seeing him, but it did not disguise the tiredness in her. He was alarmed at the pallor of her skin and the very fine lines around her eyes. He felt a lurch of tenderness, realising how much of herself she spent in the care of others.

He stood up to greet her, keeping his injured left arm a little further away, in case she touched the wound.

She noticed it at once. 'What have you done?' she demanded, her voice sharp with anxiety.

'A slight cut,' he replied, and saw her disbelief. 'I had a doctor stitch it up for me, but it needs looking at again. Will you, please?'

'Of course. Take your coat off and sit down.' She took the jacket from him. 'And look at this,' she said crossly. 'It's ruined that sleeve. How am I going to mend that?' Her voice caught and he realised she was close to tears. It had nothing to do with the jacket and everything to do with him, but she would not say so, because she knew he had no choice.

'It'll stitch,' he replied calmly, not referring to the jacket, either, but to his arm.

She took a deep, shivering breath and went to the stove for hot water, keeping her back to him. She picked clean bandages out of the cupboard, and began to work.

It was early afternoon by the time Monk went a second time to Little Lil's establishment, and was admitted. His arm was feeling a great deal easier. The bleeding had stopped and it smarted a bit, and was stiffer than usual, but apart from that it was little handicap. Hester had said the cut was not very deep and in her opinion Crow had made a good job of stitching it up. Above all, it was clean.

Lil was sitting in exactly the same place as before, with the same piece of embroidery in her lap. The fire was burning and the dim, crowded-in room had a reddish glow. She looked like an old, smug little cat, waiting to be served up another portion of cream. Or possibly another canary. Louvain had warned Monk not to underestimate the violence of an opulent receiver, just because she might be a woman.

Lil looked up at him, her large eyes bright with anticipation. She regarded his hair, his face, the way he stood, the fact that he had taken his muffler and mitts off to come into her presence. She liked it. 'Come in,' she ordered him. 'Sit down.' She looked at the chair opposite her, no more than four feet from her own.

He obeyed her, thanking her quietly. She did not turn straight to business, and he felt more than the heat of the fire as he realised what she was doing.

''Eard yer got knifed,' she said, shaking her head. 'Yer wanter look after yerself. A man wi' no arms is a danger to 'isself.'

'It's not deep,' he replied. 'It'll be healed in a few days.'

Her eyes never left his face. 'Mebbe yer shouldn't be workin' by yerself?'

He knew what she was going to say next. Long before the words were framed, it was there in the appetite in her face. But he had invited it and there was no escape now.

'The river's an 'ard place,' she continued. 'Yer should think on workin' wi' someone else. Keep an eye on yer back for yer.'

He had to pretend to consider it. Above all he must

draw some information from her. If she wanted flattery, attention, and heaven knew what else, then that was the price he must pay.

'I know the river's dangerous,' he agreed, as if admitting it reluctantly.

She leaned forward a little.

He was acutely uncomfortable, but he dared not seem to retreat.

'Yer should think abaht it. Choose careful,' she urged.

'Oh yes,' he agreed with more emotion than she would understand. 'There are a lot of people up and down this stretch I wouldn't want to go against.'

She hesitated, weighing her next words. 'Got no stomach fer it, 'ave yer?' she challenged.

He smiled widely, knowing she would like it. He saw the answering gleam in her, and masked a shudder. 'Oh, I like to be well thought of,' he said. 'But I want to live to see it.'

She giggled with pleasure. It was a low noise in her throat like someone with heavy catarrh, but from her eyes it was clear that she was amused.

He spoke again, quickly. 'Who do I keep clear of?'

She named half a dozen in a low, conspiratorial whisper. He had no doubt they were her rivals. It would not do to let her think he believed her unquestioningly. She would have no respect for that. He asked her why, as if he needed proof.

She described them in vicious and picturesque detail. He could not help wondering if the River Police knew anything like as much about them.

'I'm obliged,' he said when he was sure she had finished. 'But there are more than receivers to be careful of. There are one or two shipowners I don't want to cross.'

Her big eyes blinked slowly. 'You frit o' them?' she asked.

'I'd rather swim with the tide than against it,' he said judiciously.

Again she gave her strange, deep-throated giggle. 'Then don' cross Clem Louvain,' she told him. 'Or Bert Culpepper. Least not until yer sees 'oo wins.'

He felt a prickle at the back of his neck. He must not betray his ignorance to her. 'My money's on Louvain,' he said.

She pulled her mouth into a thin line. 'Then yer knows summink as I don't. Like where 'is ivory went ter, mebbe? 'Cos if 'e don't get that back afore Marchment closes in on 'im, 'e won't 'ave the money ter pay 'is debt. 'E'll lose 'is ware'ouse, an' he won't be able ter pay up fer that damn big clipper as is comin' up for sale, when she makes port. An' ol' Bert Culpepper'll get it, sure as God made little fishes. An' then where'll Clem Louvain be, eh? I'll tell yer: a week be'ind, for the rest of 'is days. An' you an' I both know wot good a cargo is a week be'ind! So yer put yer money on Clem Louvain if yer want, but I'm keepin' mine in me pocket till I sees which way the cat jumps.'

Monk smiled at her very slowly. 'Then so will I,' he said softly. It was what he wanted at last.

She was uncertain just how deep his agreement was. She wanted it all, but she knew she had to play it slowly. She had reeled in many fish in her day, and this was a tasty one.

Monk sat back again, still looking at her. 'You said something about watches.'

She moved her fingers gently on the fabric of her embroidery. 'Yer got watches?'

'Three . . . for now.'

She held out her hand.

He gave them to her, one at a time, hoping she would either give them back to him, or pay him something like their worth. If not, the information would be bought at a price he could not afford.

It took him nearly an hour to haggle with her, and she relished every moment of it, as if it were a kind of game between them, as the haggling had been when he'd shown her the watch Callandra gave him. She sent for a bottle of gin and it was brought by a thin man with muscles like cords in his neck, and a knife scar over the crown of his shaven head. He brought it with ill grace, and Lil barely looked at him. She was bored with him, and her appetite was sharp for Monk.

They sat in front of the fire, sipping gin, arguing back and forth. She leaned forward so close to him he could smell the warmth and the staleness of her, but he dared not let her see that. He could feel the sweat trickling down his body and knew it was caused as much by revulsion as by the heat of the room. He had walked into this knowingly, using what he saw in her face, and now he did not know how to get out. He was tempted to settle for less than the watches were worth – anything to escape. But if he did that she would know why and not only despise him for it but be insulted, which would be far more dangerous. Every instinct in him screamed that a woman rebuffed was an enemy no man could afford. Better a man robbed of his goods, or insulted in his honour, better almost anything than that.

The minutes ticked by. She sent for the man with the corded neck again to fetch more coal. Apparently his name was Ollie.

He brought it. She told him to stoke the fire. He did so. She dismissed him.

'Forty pound,' she said as Ollie closed the door behind him. 'That's me last offer.'

Monk pretended to weigh it very carefully. He had asked forty-five, three pounds more than the forty guineas Louvain had given him, expecting to have to come down. This would mean he lost two pounds, but he would not do better. 'Well . . . I suppose there's more to a price than money,' he said at last.

She nodded with satisfaction. 'Gimme.'

He passed over the watches, and she stood up and went to a locked box over in the far corner of the room. She opened it and brought back forty sovereigns, counting them out for him.

He took them and put them in his own inside pockets. He knew better than to leave instantly. It was another five minutes before he rose to his feet, thanked her for her hospitality and said he would be back the next time he had business of a similar nature.

He walked briskly to Louvain's office, tense all the way, thinking he heard footsteps behind him. He could not afford to lose the money. He went in with a sense of relief so overwhelming it was like exhaustion suddenly catching up with him. He asked to see Louvain immediately, and was shown in within ten minutes.

'Well?' Louvain demanded, his face dark with anger and impatience.

Monk realised how glad he was that he had something positive to report, and that the coins were in his pocket. He took them out and put them on the desk. 'Forty pounds,' he said. 'I owe you two. It bought me information that you should have told me in the first place.'

Louvain looked at the coins for a moment, then picked one up, scraped his fingernail across it, then put them in his pocket. 'What information is that?' he said quietly. There was a rough, dangerous edge to his voice and his eyes were cold, but he did not ask for the other two pounds.

'That your warehouse is surety for a loan from Culpepper, and if you don't redeem it you can't put it up for collateral to buy the clipper when she comes up for auction,' Monk told him.

Louvain let out his breath slowly, his jaw clenched so

156

the muscles stood out. 'Who told you that? And what you say had better be the truth.'

'An opulent receiver,' Monk replied. 'If you want to know who else knows, I can't tell you. I didn't learn that.'

'So now they know you're my man.'

'I'm not your man. And no, they don't know.'

'You're my man until I say you aren't.' Louvain leaned forward over his desk, his hands, callused and scarred by ropes, spread wide on the polished wood. 'How does knowing about Culpepper and the clipper get you any further? I told you I needed to deliver the ivory because it was due. I hadn't time to tell you all my enemies along the river. I have crossed every man on it, one time or another. And they've crossed me. It's not a trade for the squeamish.'

'Because if you'd told me about Culpepper I could have started to trace the ivory from the other end,' Monk answered with equal bitterness. 'Following the ivory from the ship I'm always at least two days behind.'

A dull flush spread up Louvain's cheeks. 'Well, go and get on with looking at Culpepper, but for the love of God be careful. You're no use to me at the bottom of the river with your throat cut.'

'Thank you,' Monk said sarcastically, then turned on his heel and went out. He felt safer now he had only a little silver and copper change in his pocket, but he still kept to the middle of the road all the way back to the omnibus stop.

He was standing waiting, hunched against the wind, when another man came up, presumably to wait also. Only when he stood beside him was Monk suddenly aware of a weight pressing into his side. He turned to complain, and saw the hatred in the man's eyes. He had a hat on covering his shaven head, but Monk recognised the strangely muscular neck, his jaw and mouth. It was Ollie, who had waited on him at Little Lil's.

'Yer in't ready ter go 'ome yet, Mr Busybody,' Ollie

hissed softly, as if someone might overhear him. 'Fancy yerself, do yer? Think our Lil'd give yer more'n the time o' day, do yer? Well, yer in't gonner 'ave the chance, see, 'cos yer comin' wi' me fer a little trip down Lime'ouse Way.' He jerked the knife in his hand a little more sharply into Monk's ribs. 'An' there in't nob'dy listenin', so don' bother yellin' out, or thinkin' as mebbe I wouldn't stick yer, 'cos I would.'

Monk did not doubt it. He might get a chance to overpower him later, but certainly not now. And his mind was filled with the memory of the knife in his arm as a scream fills silence. Obediently he turned from the omnibus stop and walked back along the dark, gusty street, the wind in his face, the stones slick under his feet.

They were alone, practically side by side, Ollie close and a little behind, always keeping the knife bumping Monk's back. He must have done such a thing before, because all the way along the road, across the dark inlet to the Shadwell Docks and beyond towards the curve southward of Limehouse Reach, he never let Monk move far enough from him to turn or escape the prodding blade.

Monk saw the cranes and warehouses of the West India Dock ahead. The rain was spitting in the two men's faces and the air was pungent with the smells of fish and tar when Ollie ordered him to stop.

'Yer goin' fer a nice little swim, you are,' he said with malicious delight. 'Mebbe our Lil won't fancy yer so much when they fish yer out.' He laughed, with a sound like a clearing of the throat. 'That's if they do, like. Sometimes bodies get caught up in the piers an' no one ever finds 'em. They stay there for ever.'

'I'll make damn sure you come with me!' Monk retorted. 'Is that what Lil wants?'

'Don't yer talk abaht 'er, yer . . .' Ollie's voice shook with rage.

Monk felt the knife point prick him. He moved towards the broad surface of the wharf where it stretched out ten or twelve yards into the dark water before dropping off abruptly, nothing beyond but the creaking, dripping stumps, poking up like dead men's bones. The smell of woodrot was heavy in his nose. It was dark but for the riding lights of a ship twenty yards away.

'Garn!' Ollie prompted, shoving him forward with the knife blade. He was too close behind for Monk to twist and lunge back at him. He stepped down as he was told, and felt the boards slippery under his feet. The wood was pitted and slimy with age. He could hear the river swirling and sucking round the stakes, only a few feet below him now. Would he have any chance of swimming in that current? Could he catch hold of the next stake as he was carried against it? If it were that easy, why did people drown? Because the tide was fast, and the eddies pulled you away, clothes soaked with water were too heavy to move in, and they pulled you under, no matter what you did.

He had to fight now or not at all. And Ollie knew that, too. He gave another stiff prod and Monk stumbled forward on to his knees and rolled over rapidly, in a single movement, just as Ollie flung himself into the place where he had been, knife blade arcing in the air and stabbing downward.

Monk scrambled to get up as a board cracked under his weight and swung for a moment, then plunged into the water below.

Ollie was on his feet again. He grunted with satisfaction. He knew the pier, where the rotten planks were, and he had the knife. He was between Monk and the way back, but at least there was space between them now and Monk could make out his shape in the darkness. Would that be enough? It was a long time since he had fought for his life – in fact, not since that dreadful night in Mecklenburgh Square before his accident, and he remembered that only in flashes.

Ollie was balancing on the balls of his feet, preparing to lunge.

This was ridiculous. If he were not facing death it would be funny. He was fighting a man he did not know for the favour of a woman he would have paid not to touch! And if he told Ollie that, Ollie would be so insulted for Lil, he would murder Monk in outrage.

Monk gave a bark of laughter at the sheer lunacy of it.

Ollie hesitated. For the first time he was faced with something he did not understand.

Monk moved a step sideways, away from the board he knew was rotted, and closer to the way back.

Ollie froze, looking beyond Monk.

It was then that Monk turned and saw the other figure in the gloom, solid, menacing, huge with the riding lights behind him. Monk broke out in a sweat of panic – then the instant after, when the figure moved, recognised the slightly rolling gait of Durban from the River Police.

'Now then, Ollie,' Durban said firmly. 'You can't take us both, an' you don't want to finish up on the end of a rope. It's a bad way to go.'

Ollie remained motionless, his jaw hanging.

'Put that away an' go on home,' Durban went on, moving a step further towards Monk. His voice held such certainty it was as if there were no question in anyone's mind that Ollie would obey.

Ollie stood still.

Monk waited.

Underneath them the water sucked and belched, swirling around the pier stakes, and somewhere something fell in with a splash and was washed away.

Monk was shuddering with cold, and relief.

Ollie made his decision. He lowered the hand with the knife in it.

'Into the water,' Durban directed.

Ollie squawked with indignation, his voice high and harsh.

'The knife,' Durban said patiently. 'Not you.'

Ollie swore, and tossed the knife. It fell into the water with only the faintest sound.

Monk stifled a laugh that was far too close to hysteria.

Ollie turned and stumbled up towards the street, and the darkness swallowed him up.

Another figure appeared behind Durban, slighter, and moving with an ease that suggested he was also younger.

'You all right, sir?' His voice was concerned, challenging.

'Yes, thank you, Sergeant Orme,' Durban replied. 'Just Ollie Jenkins getting a bit above himself again. Thinks Mr Monk here has designs on Little Lil.' There was humour in his voice but it was soft and oblique.

Sergeant Orme was satisfied. The rigidity in him relaxed, but he did not leave.

'What exactly is it that you're doing here, Mr Monk?' Durban asked. 'What are you looking for?'

'Thank you,' Monk said with profound feeling. It was embarrassing being rescued by the River Police. He was used to being the one who helped, who did the favours and found the solutions. It was made the more so because he respected Durban and loathed not being able to be honest with him. This secrecy was a kind of grubbiness he would have paid a great deal to avoid.

'What are you looking for?' Durban repeated. The water gurgled around the pier, the wash from something passing in the gloom sloshed against the stakes and the wood creaked and sagged sideways. 'I know you're a private agent of enquiry,' Durban said in an expressionless voice. What he thought of such an occupation could only be guessed at. Did he think Monk was a scavenger in other people's misery, or a profiteer from their crimes?

161

'Stolen goods,' Monk answered the question. 'So I can return them to their owner.'

Still Durban did not move. 'What sort of goods?'

'Anything that belongs to one man, and has been taken by another.'

'You're playing with fire, Mr Monk, an' you aren't good enough at it, at least not down here on the river,' Durban told him softly. 'You'll get burned, an' I already have enough murders on my stretch without you. Go back to the city, and do what you know how.'

'I've got to finish this job.'

Durban sighed. 'I suppose you'll do whatever you want; I can't stop you,' he said wearily. 'You'd better come with us back along the river. Can't leave you around here or somebody might attack your other arm.' He turned and led the way out towards the river edge of the wharf to where the police boat was waiting, on the high tide close enough to the banks to jump down into.

Monk followed and Sergeant Orme offered him a hand, so he balanced himself in the dark. He landed moderately well in the boat, at least not falling over any of the oarsmen, or pitching beyond into the water.

He sat quietly and watched as Orme, who was apparently in charge, gave the order and they put out again and turned upriver towards the Pool. They moved swiftly on the still-incoming tide, the men pulling with an easy rhythm, with that special kind of unity that comes with practice and a common purpose.

They manoeuvred with skill, making little of the art and the knowledge required to weave their way between the anchored ships without hitting one of them. Now and then someone made a joke and there was a burst of laughter, a comfortable sound in the wind and the blustery darkness lit only by the glimmer of riding lights.

They called each other by nicknames, which were

often derogatory, but the affection was too plain to need display. The mockery was their way of robbing the fear from the reality of violence and hardship. Monk knew that as he listened to them and remembered all the better parts of his own police days, things he had forgotten until now, and lied to himself that he did not miss.

They put him off at London Bridge and he thanked them, climbing out stiffly, then walked towards the nearest omnibus stop.

He was glad to feel the solid earth under his feet, but his mind was in turmoil, his emotions raw. He hated having appeared such a fool to Durban. Even when the time came that he could tell him the truth, it might not sound a great deal better, even though ideas were at last becoming clearer in his mind. There were threads to follow, something definite to do.

Chapter Seven

Monk returned home for the night, but Hester was not there. The emptiness of the house oppressed him and he found himself anxious for her, thinking how tired she must be. At least she was in no danger, and Margaret Ballinger and Bessie would look after her as much as they could.

In the morning he dressed, choosing another jacket, with no tear, then went downstairs and cooked himself kippers and toast for breakfast. At eight he set out to pursue the ideas he had formed from the knowledge gained the day before. He began by enquiring for the exact location of Culpepper's warehouse, then taking a boat down the river to Deptford Creek, just short of Greenwich.

He went ashore on the south bank and walked slowly along the street past ironmongers', ships' chandlers', sailmakers' and general stores, making a note of the local public house, and then went and stood on the dockside as if waiting for someone. After a little while watching the labourers come and go, he began to appreciate how many men worked for Culpepper in one way or another. He was obviously an ambitious man.

In the public house at lunch time again he listened,

then when he had heard enough, he contrived to fall into conversation with a disgruntled dock labourer who said his name was Duff.

'It's hard,' Monk sympathised with him. 'Good work isn't easy to come by.'

'Good work!' Duff exploded. 'They're a bunch o' cut-throats, the whole poxy lot of 'em.'

'Pity they don't cut each other's throats, and save us all grief,' Monk agreed.

'Could 'appen.' Duff looked suddenly cheerful at the thought. 'Culpepper and Louvain, any road. That'd be a start.'

'That's what I heard,' Monk agreed. He leaned forward confidentially. 'I have interests. I need to be sure I put them in the right place. Can't afford to back a loser.'

Duff's eyes brightened and he sat forward a little. 'Prepared ter pay a little for yer information, are yer?'

'If it's accurate,' Monk answered. He made no threat as to what would happen if it were not, but he looked steadily at Duff's narrow face, and held his gaze. 'And I keep my promises, good and bad.'

Duff swallowed. 'What is it yer need ter know, like?'

'I'll take a little at a time, and test it,' Monk replied. 'If it's true, I'll pay in gold, if it's false, you'll pay in blood. How's that?'

Duff swallowed again. 'I got friends, too. If yer gold in't the real thing, yer'll never dare come back 'ere. River's eaten more'n one gent as thought 'e were an 'ell of a clever sod.'

'I'm sure it has. Let's start with saving me a bit of time. How many properties does Culpepper have, where are they, and what does he have his eye on to buy next?'

'Easy.' Duff listed three wharfs, a couple of warehouses and a lodging house as well as a good-sized dwelling. 'An' 'e wants the clipper, the *Eliza May*, soon as she comes up for sale.' He grinned. 'So does Clem Louvain. We'll see 'oo 'as the money on the day, eh? She's a beauty! Cut their sailing time by a week or more from the Indies. Worth thousands o' pounds, that is, with a good load. First in makes a fortune, second counts fer nothin', a few 'undred.'

Monk knew that already. He needed to learn if Culpepper had either hired the thieves who had taken the ivory, or had bought it from them afterwards, knowing that it would be the beginning of defeat for Louvain.

He stayed questioning Duff for another half-hour, passed him a gold guinea, and sent him to find out more about recent cargoes. A mass of questions that he asked disguised the one that mattered.

He spent the afternoon further down the river, watching, making notes of cargoes, times of comings and goings, and began to amass enough information to tell him how far Culpepper's empire stretched.

The following day he returned with more money to pay Duff. By now he was learning enough of Culpepper's trade to see how important it was to his future profits that he, and not Louvain, purchased the *Eliza May*.

'Course 'e wants 'er,' Duff said bitterly. ''E won't be top dog down 'ere any more, 'less 'e gets 'er. Louvain neither.'

'There'll be other ships, won't there?' Monk asked, leaning on the railing of the pier and watching the dark water churn beneath him. The barges going past, following the tide, were so deep laden that in places the decks were awash.

''Course, but losin' counts,' Duff replied, pulling a clay pipe out of the pocket of his coat, knocking the dottle out, then shredding tobacco with his other hand before stuffing it into the bowl. 'Lose one fight, an' the next time you start out two steps be'ind, like. People don' back yer no more. Folks as used ter be scared o' yer, all of a sudden find out they're more scared o' someone else.' He put the pipe in his mouth and struck a match to light it, inhaling slowly. 'Winnin' an' losin' as their own rules,' he went on. 'The more it goes one way, the more folks foller the tide, like. When it turns, that's it. Yer don' wanna lose, mister. Like rats, they are. The cowards leave yer, the bad ones turns on yer, all teeth an' claws. If yer made enemies, losin' is the beginnin' o' the end. The big bastards can't afford ter lose. The likes o' you an' me, it don't matter; we done it afore, an' we'll be low a while, then we'll come back.'

Monk could see the profound truth of that. No wonder Louvain needed his ivory back. And that explained why there was no word of it anywhere along the river. It had not been sold; it was stored, hidden so the loss of it wrought the more damage to Louvain.

He thanked Duff and left. He needed to know more about Culpepper so he could find out where the ivory was. It would mean endless small questions. He would have to disguise them, or word would creep back to Culpepper. At best he would move the ivory and Monk would have to start all over again. If he were nervous, or angry enough, he might even sink it in the Thames mud, and it would never be found. There was the chance he had done that anyway, but surely he would not willingly destroy a cargo of that much value?

Monk tried several inventive stories, mostly about an heiress who had eloped, in order to question rivermen as to who and what they had seen on the river around Culpepper's wharfs on the morning of 21 October. For the rest of the day he stood in the cold, asking painstaking questions and noting the answers almost illegibly, his hands were so stiff, his body shivering. The steps were slimy with salt and weed, wooden piers creaked and sagged under the weight of years. The wind scythed in off the river, knife-sharp, always the light shifting in blues and greys cut with silver shafts.

Then that evening, 29 October, he sat at home, the

kitchen stove open and stoked high, the kettle steaming, putting together all he knew to make sense of it. He had his feet in a bowl of hot water and a pot of tea on the table, and three slices of toast made, when he saw the one fact that connected everything.

The boatman Gould had told him that he could not have seen anyone rob the *Maude Idris* in the early hours of 21 October. Monk had verified that Gould had indeed been in Greenwich. But only in checking the ferries and lightermen in Greenwich did Monk realise that Gould had taken no fares that day. His boat had been at Greenwich, certainly, but idle! What boatman could afford that, unless he were being paid more than for working?

It had been at Culpepper's wharf early in the day, and then disappeared without passengers. It had been seen as usual up in the Pool of London the day after. It answered every question if his were the boat in which the thieves had crept up to the *Maude Idris*, taken the ivory, and then carried it down to Culpepper at Greenwich. Whether they had done so to order, or simply taken advantage of a supreme opportunity, hardly mattered. If Louvain's cargo had been betrayed to Culpepper by someone in his own company, that was Louvain's problem to discover and to deal with. Once Monk had retrieved the ivory and taken it back, he had discharged his obligation. He anticipated the relief, the sudden weight lifted from him almost as if he were free to breathe again, to stretch his shoulders and stand straight.

He went to bed early, but lay awake staring at the faint light on the ceiling thrown up from the streetlamp a few yards away. He had plenty of blankets on the bed, but without Hester there was a coldness he could not dispel. Before his marriage he had dreaded the loss of privacy, the relentless company of another person preventing him from acting spontaneously, curtailing his freedom. Now loneliness crowded in on him as if he were physically chilled. When he held his breath there was silence in the room, a cessation of life itself.

Perhaps he would not have asked her what his next step should be, possibly not even told her much about the river, to save her worry when she had so many of her own anxieties to deal with. But he resented the fact that he was robbed of the choice.

And it hurt that Gould, whom he had liked, was one of the robbers who had beaten the night watchman to death. The theft of the ivory was a crime in an entirely different way – Louvain could do what he liked about that – but Hodge's murder must be answered for to the law. It was Monk's business to see that it was.

He would have to be careful in capturing Gould. With the rope waiting for him he would fight to the death, having nothing to lose. Monk could not ask Durban for help before he had forced Gould to tell him where the ivory was and got it back to Louvain. After that he must take Gould to the police.

Whose help could he ask? Crow? Scuff? He turned over idea after idea, none of them making complete sense, until he fell asleep. His dreams were crowded with dark water, cramped spaces, shifting light and flashes of a knife blade ending in pain as he turned on his wounded shoulder.

In the morning he was on the dockside at daybreak. The tide was flowing in fast, filling the hollows of the mud, creeping up the stone walls, and drowning the broken stumps on the old pier. The air was bitter. The broadening light had the clarity of ice and the hard, white fingers of dawn found every ripple on the water's face. The spars and rigging of the ships etched complicated, exquisite black lines against the sky, and the wind tasted of salt.

Monk stood alone staring at it as the sun below the

horizon started to burn the first colour into the day. Perhaps by tonight he would have finished all he had to do here. He would be paid, and back to the streets he was used to, where he knew the thieves, the informers, the pawnbrokers and receivers, even the police. He would be able to work openly again, even if most of the cases were small.

He breathed in the icy air, savouring it, watching the light spread across the water. He would miss this. One could never stand alone in a street and see this kind of beauty.

There was life on the river already, more than just the first strings of barges, low in the water, humped with cargo. A loan boatman was busy, oars working rhythmically, rising with the eastward blade dripping diamonds.

As he looked downriver a ship caught his sight. She was just a flash of white at first, but growing as she came closer until he could make out the five tiers of sails on the towering masts: courses, lower topsails, upper topsails, topgallants and royals, billowing to catch the surprise wind. She was a shining thing, a creature of dreams, all power and grace.

He stood spellbound, oblivious of everything else: the rest of the river, other traffic, people, anyone on the dockside near him. Not until the sun was fully risen and pouring light into every corner, showing the shabby and the new, the idle and the labouring, and the clipper was at last at anchor, did he even notice that Scuff was standing next to him, his face transfigured.

'Jeez,' he sighed, his eyes huge. 'She's enough ter make yer b'lieve in angels, in' she?'

'Yes,' Monk replied, for want of anything better to describe her. Then he decided that that was quite good enough. There was something of the divine in anything that was such a perfect blend of power, beauty and purpose. 'Yes, she is,' he said again.

170

Scuff was still rapt in the awe of the moment.

Monk understood why Louvain was obsessed with the passion to own such a ship. It was far more than money or success, it was a kind of enchantment; it captured the glory of a dream. It spoke to a hunger for great space and light, a width of freedom impossible in any other way.

He shook himself from the thought with difficulty. He could not lose himself in it any longer. 'I need to find someone to help me, for nothing,' he said aloud.

'I'll 'elp yer.' Scuff drew his eyes away from the river reluctantly. Reality had governed him too long to allow self-indulgence. 'Wot d'yer want?'

'Unfortunately, I need a grown-up.'

'I can do a lot o' things yer wouldn't believe. An' I'm nearly eleven – I think.'

Monk judged his age was probably closer to nine, but he did not say so. 'I need size as well as brains,' he softened the blow. 'I was thinking a man called Crow might help. Do you know where I could find him – without anyone else knowing?'

'The doc? Yeah, I reckon. Yer won't get 'im in no trouble, will yer?' Scuff asked anxiously. 'I don' think 'e's no fighter.'

'I don't want him to fight, just to offer to buy something.'

'I know where 'e lives.' Scuff appeared to be turning something over in his mind. Loyalties were conflicting with one another, new friends against old, habit against adventure, someone who healed him when he was sick as opposed to someone who shared food with him.

'Tell him I'm here, and I'd like to see him urgently,' Monk requested. 'Then we'll have breakfast before we go. I'll fetch us some ham sandwiches and tea. Be back in an hour. Do you know an hour?'

Scuff gave him a filthy look, then turned and ran off.

Fifty minutes later he was back, and a highly curious

171

Crow with him. He was dressed in a heavy jacket, his black hair hidden by a cap and mitts on his hands. Monk had the sandwiches, but was waiting to buy the tea fresh and hot. He gave Scuff the money and sent him off to fetch it.

Crow looked him up and down with interest, his eyes bright. 'How's the arm?' he asked. 'You never came back to get the bandage changed.'

'I had my wife do it,' Monk replied. 'It's fine, a bit stiff, that's all.'

Crow pursed his lips. In the clear morning light, no softness in its glare, the tiny lines were visible on his skin. He looked closer to forty than the thirty Monk had assumed, but there was still a fire of enthusiasm in his expression that made him uniquely alive. 'So what is it you want me for?' he asked.

Monk had been thinking how to broach the subject, and how much to tell him. He knew nothing about this man; he had made his decision on a mixture of instinct and desperation. Would he take caution as an insult or a sign of intelligence?

'I need someone to make an offer for me,' he replied, watching Crow's expression. 'I can't do it myself, they wouldn't believe me.'

Crow raised an eyebrow. 'Should they?'

'No. What I'm looking for was stolen from a . . . an associate of mine.' He could not bring himself to call Louvain a friend, and he was not yet willing to let Crow know that he was a client. It raised too many other questions.

'Associate,' Crow turned the word over. 'An' yer want to buy it back? Now what kind o' thing would you buy back, if it were yours in the first place? And what kind o' people do you "associate" with who are happy to buy back things that was stolen? An' then why use you – why not do it 'emselves? You don' do it fer nothin', do yer?'

172

Monk grinned. 'No, I don't. And no, I'm not going to buy it back. When I know where he's put it, I'm going to take it, but he's got it well hidden. I need you to make an offer to buy some of it so he'll go there.'

Crow looked dubious. 'Doesn't 'e have a receiver for it 'isself? If you're threatening to cross up one o' the receivers along here you're daft, an' you won't last long.'

'I think it was stolen to deprive the owner of its use, not to sell on,' Monk explained reluctantly. 'I just want you to offer for one tusk.'

Crow's eyes widened. 'Tusk! Ivory?'

'That's right. Will you do it?'

Crow thought for a moment or two. He was still considering it when Scuff returned with the tea, carrying it carefully in three mugs.

Crow took one, warming his hands on it, and blowing at the steam rising from the top. 'Yeah,' he said at last. 'Someone needs to look after you, or we'll be fishin' you outa the water and telling the police who you were.'

'Yeah,' Scuff added with sage concern.

Monk felt both cared for and diminished, but he could not afford the luxury of taking offence. Apart from that, they were right. 'Thank you,' he said a trifle tartly.

'In't nuffin'.' Scuff brushed it aside generously, and took a huge bite of his ham sandwich.

'So who do I 'ave to ask for the tusk?' Crow enquired.

'Gould, the boatman.'

''Oo works from the steps 'ere?' Crow said with surprise. 'Knew 'e was a thief, o' course, but ivory's a bit much for 'im. Yer sure?'

'No, but I think so.'

'Right.' Crow finished his sandwich and his tea and rubbed his hands together to signify he was ready to begin.

Monk looked at Scuff, who was waiting expectantly. 'Will you come with me, and when I'm sure where Gould is leading us, take a message to Mr Louvain and tell him where we are, then go and fetch Inspector Durban of the River Police, so we can arrest Gould and get the ivory back?'

Crow's eyes widened. 'Louvain?' he said with a sharpness to his voice, a sudden wariness as if it changed his perception.

'It's his ivory,' Monk replied. 'I'm going to return it to him. That's what he hired me for.'

Crow whistled through his teeth. 'Did he? You do this kind o' thing often?'

'All the time, just not on the river before.' He tried to judge whether Crow would consider it a compliment or an insult to be offered money. He stroked his face, and had no idea of the answer.

Then Crow grinned hugely, showing magnificent teeth. 'Right.' He rubbed his mittened hands together. 'Let's go and find Mr Gould. I'm ready! By the way, how am I supposed ter know if 'e's got ivory?'

'From an informant who is unusually observant, and whom it would be more than your life's worth to name,' Monk said with an answering smile.

'Yeah. Right.' Crow put his hands in his pockets. 'But if yer comin' after me, I'd be 'appier if you 'ad a boatman I could trust. I'll get Jimmy Corbett. 'E won't let you down.' And without waiting for Monk's agreement he strolled over towards the edge and started to walk along, scanning the water.

Scuff picked up the mugs and returned them, at a run, and he and Monk set off a comfortable distance behind Crow as he went to search for Jimmy Corbett, and then for Gould.

It took them nearly an hour before this was accomplished, and Monk and Scuff saw the lanky figure of Crow finally step down into Gould's boat, pull away just to the east of Wapping New Stairs, and turn back upstream, not down as they expected. They climbed hastily into Jimmy Corbett's waiting boat and pulled away into the traffic on the river, turning west as well. This was going to prove an expensive business.

'I thought you said Greenwich,' Scuff said urgently.

'I did,' Monk admitted, equally surprised.

A pleasure boat passed them, moving swiftly. People were lining the decks, scarves and ribbons fluttering. The sound of music drifted across the water from the band on deck. Some people were waving their hats and shouting.

There were ferries in the water, lighters, all kinds of craft about their business. It was not always easy to keep Gould in sight, although the tall figure of Crow in the stern helped.

Monk and Scuff sat in silence as they wound through the anchored ships, Monk wondering where they could be going. Where was there upstream where Gould would have hidden a boatload of ivory? Why would he not have left it near Culpepper's warehouses, if not actually in one of them?

Jimmy was taking them steadily closer to the middle of the river, and then towards the south bank. They must be almost in line with Bermondsey by now.

'I know where we're goin',' Scuff said suddenly, his face earnest, his voice strained. 'Jacob's Island! It's an awful bad place, mister. I in't never bin there, but I 'eard of it.'

Monk turned to look at him and saw the fear in his face. Ahead of them Gould's boat was swinging round, bow to the shore where rotting buildings leaned out into the water, the tide sucking at their foundations. Their cellars must be flooded, wood dark with the incessant dripping and oozing of decades of creeping damp. Looking at it across the grey water, Monk could imagine the smell of decay, the cold that ate into the bones. Even in the city he had heard its reputation.

He looked again at Scuff's face. 'When the boat drops

me off, go back and tell Mr Louvain to come immediately,' he said. 'Tell him I've got his ivory, and if he doesn't want the police to take it as evidence, to come and collect it before they do. Do you understand?'

''E won't know where,' Scuff protested. 'I gotter foller yer till I sees where yer goin'.' He clenched his jaw tight in frightened refusal.

Monk looked at his stubborn face and the shadows in his eyes. 'Thank you,' he said sincerely.

They were pulling in close to the shore now. Ahead of them Gould was only feet from landing on a low, almost water-logged pier. He reached it and scrambled out, tying his boat to a rotted stake and waiting while Crow climbed out after him. Monk could tell by the way he moved that he was nervous. His legs were awkward, his back stiff as though he half expected to have to defend himself any moment. Was it insane to have come here alone?

Too late to change the plan now. Monk told Jimmy to put him ashore at the next landing steps onward, around the jutting buttress of the warehouse and out of sight of Gould. 'Go and get Louvain,' he hissed at Scuff, who was making ready to follow him. 'Now! Then get Durban!'

Scuff hesitated, glancing at the dark waste of timber ahead, the alleys, sagging windows and doorways, the rubbish and the water seeping everywhere.

Monk refused to follow his eyes, or to let his imagination picture any of it. 'Go!' he ordered Jimmy, and pushed Scuff's thin shoulders until he overbalanced back into the boat and it pulled away.

He turned back to Jacob's Island in time to see Crow follow Gould between two of the buildings and disappear. He hurried after them, trying to move soundlessly over the spongy wood, afraid with every step that it would give way beneath him.

As soon as he was in shadow he stopped again to accustom his eyes to the gloom. He heard movement ahead of him before he saw Crow's back just as he turned another corner and was gone. The smell of rot was heavy in the air, like sickness, and as Monk went under a broken arch into one of the houses, everything around him creaked and dripped. It seemed as if it were alive, beams settling, the scuffle and scratch of clawed feet. He imagined red eyes.

He went after the sounds of footsteps ahead of him, and now and then, as he climbed up or down steps, or went around a corner, he saw Crow's back, or his black head with its long hair under his hat, and knew he had not lost them yet.

Was Crow a fool to trust Monk to rescue him if Gould suspected he was being tricked? Louvain would never find them here. Or was Monk the fool, and had Crow already told Gould exactly what he was really here for? Should he leave now, while he could, and at least get out alive?

Then he would never be able to work on the river again. His name would be a mockery. And if he ran away from this, what would he stand and face in the future? Would he run away next time, too? The thoughts raced in his mind but his legs were still carrying him forward. The light was dim through broken windows and here and there gaping walls. He could barely discern the figures of Gould and Crow going through a door at the end of the passage.

Monk hesitated, sweat running down his back in spite of the clinging chill, then he went after them. He pushed the door open. Ahead was a small room, dim in the grey light from one window. Gould was pulling a sack away from a pile of something that lay on the floor. One long white tusk protruded. The outlines of others beyond were plain enough to see. Monk thought for an instant of the creatures that had been slaughtered and their carcasses robbed, then he remembered his own peril, and stopped abruptly.

But it was too late. Gould had seen his shadow against the door lintel and jerked his head up. His face froze.

Monk walked forward slowly. 'You had better leave,' he told Crow. 'I'll talk with Mr Gould about the ivory and what should happen to it.'

Crow shrugged. His relief was almost palpable, and yet the darkness was still in his eyes. He looked at Monk as if he were trying to convey something he could not say in words. It might be a warning of some sort – but what? That they were watched? That Gould was armed? Time was short – there was no way back. Might there also be no way forward?

Help would come only from the river, when Scuff fetched Louvain.

''Oo are yer?' Gould demanded, glaring at Monk. 'I'll sell yer one tusk each, but if yer think yer gonna rob me, yer stupider than yer got any right ter be an' stay alive.' His eyes flickered from one to the other of them nervously.

'Who am I?' Monk was taking as long as he could. 'I'm someone interested in ivory, especially that shipment from the *Maude Idris*.'

Gould's face showed no added fear, no sudden change at the mention of what he must know was murder. Monk felt a stab of regret that it meant nothing to him. All he thought of was the money. Monk kept his back to the door, straining to hear anything human among the rat feet, the dripping wood and the slow subsidence of the fabric of the building into the mud of Jacob's Island.

''Ow d'yer know it's from the *Maude Idris*?' Gould asked, his face puckered with suspicion.

'Get out!' Monk said again to Crow, hoping that now he would go and bring the nearest police, river or land.

''Oo are yer tellin' ter get out?' Gould said angrily. 'Yer got money ter buy all this then, eh? An' don' think yer can rob me, 'cos yer can't. I in't alone 'ere. I in't that daft!'

'Nor am I,' Monk said with a slight laugh he hoped was believable. 'And I don't want more than one tusk, and only that if the price is right.'

'Oh yeah? An' what price would that be, then?' Gould still had confidence.

'Twenty pounds,' Monk said rashly.

'Fifty!' Gould retorted with undisguised derision.

Monk pushed his hands into his pockets and stared at the pile of tusks thoughtfully, as if considering.

'Forty-five is the lowest I'll go,' Gould offered.

Monk was disgusted, but he dared not show it. He thought of Hodge lying on the step above the hold, his head broken, his brain crushed.

'Twenty-five,' he said.

They argued back and forth, up a pound, down a pound. Monk realised that Crow had gone – please God to fetch help, though he owed Monk nothing, no friendship, no loyalty. But he prayed that Scuff had managed to get Louvain. Durban would not need to be asked more than once.

'It's worth more than that,' Gould said angrily when Monk refused to go any higher, afraid of agreement and the end of the conversation. 'I worked bleedin' 'ard fer it,' Gould went on. 'You any idea 'ow 'eavy them things are?'

'Too heavy for one man,' Monk responded. 'Someone helped you. Where is he? Behind me? Or are you planning to cut him out of the deal?'

There was a faint movement in the passage ten or fifteen feet beyond the doorway. Now he wished Crow had not gone – although there was no guarantee of which side he would have been on. Perhaps, Monk speculated, a thieves' quarrel was his best chance. 'Were you the one who went into the hold of the *Maude Idris*?' he asked, his voice louder than he meant, and unsteady. He wanted to know who had killed Hodge. He would have no guilt in killing him in return if he had to, in order to escape with his own life. Where the hell was Louvain? He had had time to get here by now.

'Why'd you care?' Gould's eyes narrowed.

'Were you?' Monk demanded, taking a step forward.

'Yeah. So wot of it?' Gould challenged.

'Then it was you who murdered Hodge!' Monk accused. 'Perhaps your partner won't be so happy to share the rope that's waiting for you, along with the price of your tusks?'

Gould froze. ''Odge? I never murdered no one! 'Oo's 'Odge?' He sounded honestly confused.

'The night watchman whose head you beat in,' Monk said bitterly. 'Did that slip your mind?'

'Jeez, I din't bash 'is 'ead in!' Gould's voice rose to a screech. 'There weren't nothin' wrong wiv 'is 'ead.' He looked grey-white, even in the gloom, his eyes wide with horror. Had he not seen Hodge's body himself, Monk would have sworn it was genuine.

'Rubbish!' he barked, rage welling up inside him for the lie as much as the violence. It was twisting his own emotions because he wanted to believe the boatman, and it was impossible.

'So 'elp me Gawd, it's the truth!' Gould ignored the ivory and stepped forward towards Monk, but there was no threat in him, it was urgency, even pleading. ''E were lyin' there on the step. I thought 'e were dead drunk till I touched 'im, then I saw 'e were dead for real, but there weren't nothin' wrong wiv 'is 'ead. He must a' fell from the top an' broke 'is neck.'

Monk hesitated. Was it conceivable? Gould looked not only frightened and indignant, but shocked as well. For this moment at least, he seemed truly to have forgotten the ivory. 'Did you look at the back of his head?' he asked.

'There weren't nothin' wrong wiv it,' Gould insisted. ''E might 'a' banged it bad, I dunno, but it weren't bashed so's I could see. 'Ow'd you know, anyway?'

'I'm looking for the ivory because I'm paid to,' Monk said bitterly. 'But I'm looking for whoever killed Hodge because I want him to answer for it.'

'Well, it in't me,' Gould said desperately. ''E were dead when I found 'im, an' I never touched 'im, 'cepting to make sure as 'e weren't gonna wake up an' raise the rest o' the ship an' set 'em onter me.'

Monk stood still, his back to the door jamb. It was bitterly cold in here, so cold his fingers were dead and his feet were growing numb. The damp was everywhere, heavy with the reek of mud and effluent and the sweet stench of rot. Everything was sagging, dripping, full of slight sounds like the soft tread of feet, rat feet, human feet, creaking like the shifting of weight, and always water oozing and trickling, the slow sinking of the land and the rising of the river.

He tried to clear his head. He was beginning to believe Gould, and yet it made no sense. Who would beat in the head of a man already dead?

There was a distinct sound about a dozen yards away, a movement too big to be a rat. Monk swivelled round to look. The shadows changed. Was there someone there, a man coming this way, creeping step by step? The sweat broke out on his skin, and his body was shaking. He backed further into the room, looking at Gould. 'Someone'll hang for it,' he said softly. 'The police are coming, and they'll make sure of that. It'll be prison, then trial, then three weeks' waiting, and one morning they'll take you for the short walk, and the long drop – into eternity, darkness . . .'

'I didn't kill 'im!' Gould's cry was stifled in his throat, as if he could already feel the rope.

At that moment the other man reached the doorway just behind Monk. Monk saw it in Gould's face, and twisted away as the man behind him lunged forward

181

and Monk caught him a glancing blow on the side of the head, bruising his own hand.

Gould stood frozen, indecision wild in his face. Were the police really coming? Crow was gone and he knew where to lead them back.

Monk waited, his heart pounding.

The man started to get up. Gould swung his arm and hit the man hard, sending him backwards, his head thudding against the floor, and he lay still. 'I din't kill nobody!' Gould said again. 'But they'll kill you if yer don't get out of 'ere. C'mon!' He started to move past Monk.

'Wait,' Monk commanded. 'I need one tusk to prove to the police that they were here.' He stepped back and picked up the largest one from the pile. It was startlingly heavy, cold and smooth to the touch. He hoisted it on to his shoulder with difficulty, the effort tearing at his injured arm, then he staggered after Gould, leaving the other man senseless on the floor. They did not go the way they had come in but, awkwardly veering a little from right to left under the burden of the tusk, up a short flight of steps.

At the top Monk leaned against the wall and the rotted panelling gave way behind him. He swung around and let the tusk slip into the cavity, easing the crick out of his shoulder, then turned to see if it was still visible. It wasn't, but he could feel it. He would be able to show Durban where it was.

He hurried after Gould along the corridor. Broken windows let in the grey light. He caught up with him going down another stair with iron rails, then through a door on to an open patch of ground overgrown with weeds just as Louvain and four of his men emerged from the ruins of a warehouse at the other side. They were wind-burned, brawny men dressed in seamen's jackets.

Monk and Gould stopped abruptly, five or six yards from them.

'Well?' Louvain said grimly. 'What have you got? I don't see anything.'

'Thirteen tusks of ivory,' Monk replied. He jerked his hand. 'Back there. You might have to fight for them.'

'Thirteen?' Louvain questioned, his face darkening. 'Do you think you're keeping one for yourself? That wasn't the bargain.'

'One for the police, for evidence,' Monk replied. 'Or would you rather the thieves got away with it?' He let a slight sneer into his voice. 'That's not good for business. You'll get the last one back when the case is over. Keep it for a memento. You've got away cheaply. A damned sight cheaper than Hodge.'

Louvain looked puzzled for an instant, then realisation flooded his face. 'Who's he?' he demanded, indicating Gould with a jerk of his head.

Instinct made Monk lie. 'He's with me. Did you think I'd come here alone?'

Louvain's face relaxed. He did not ask who had killed Hodge, and the omission angered Monk. 'Right. We'll take the ivory. I want to be gone before the police get here. No questions. Come to my office tonight and I'll pay you.' It was curt, dismissive. He strode past Monk and into the shadows of the building, leaving his men to follow.

Durban should be here any time now. Monk glanced at Gould, who was white-faced, shifting from foot to foot.

'Don't think of it,' Monk warned. 'You'd be hunted down like a rat.'

'I didn't kill 'im.' Gould's voice was hoarse with fear and his eyes begged for belief. 'I swear on my life!'

'Very appropriate,' Monk said drily. 'Since it's with your life you'll be paying for it.' But he felt a tug of pity he had not expected. Was it even imaginable that one of

183

the crew had killed Hodge? A quarrel of some sort? Perhaps there had even been a traitor in the crew, and Hodge had seen him, and would have told Louvain, so Hodge had been killed?

There was no point in asking Gould; it would be offering him an obvious avenue of escape, and naturally he would take it. And why should he, Monk, involve himself in looking for the last shreds of truth and untangling them to save a thief?

Because the man might not be a murderer, and no one else would bother to help him.

'Someone beat his head in,' he said aloud. 'If it wasn't you, then it was somebody else on the *Maude Idris.*'

'I dunno!' Gould was desperate. 'Yer can't . . . Oh Jeez!' He said nothing more.

They stood on the damp, sour earth and waited. Neither Louvain nor any of his men passed them. They had found another route to take the ivory, swiftly and unseen from here, no doubt expecting Durban to come from this side.

Five minutes later Monk heard Gould gasp as if he were choking, and his breath caught in a sob. He looked round and saw Durban's distinctive walk as he came out of the shadow of the building ahead, Sergeant Orme and a constable behind him.

'Go with him,' Monk said quietly to Gould. 'I'll do what I can.'

'Good day, Mr Monk,' Durban said curiously, stopping a couple of yards away. 'What are you doing here?'

'Recovering stolen goods,' Monk replied. 'One very handsome ivory tusk. But the point is that the night watchman on the *Maude Idris* was killed in the theft.'

Durban's face was comical with understanding and scepticism. 'That why they took only one tusk, is it?'

Monk knew without question that Durban did not believe it. He knew exactly what Monk had done. 'I imagine so,' Monk said smoothly. 'Maybe there was a bit of double-crossing going on. Gould says he didn't kill Hodge, but somebody did. I'll show you where the tusk is.'

Durban signalled for his man to take Gould, who let out a cry and swivelled to look at Monk, and was jerked sharply to face forward as manacles were put on his wrists.

Monk turned and led Durban back into the far building, going slowly, partly because he was uncertain of the way, but mostly because he wanted to be sure that Louvain had had sufficient time to move all the tusks and leave no trace for Durban to catch him. It also crossed his mind to wonder if, now that he had his ivory back, he would cheat on the payment, but he refused to dwell on that. If Louvain did, then Monk would open up the Hodge murder case in such a way that Durban would plague Louvain until he wished he had not paid Monk to retrieve the ivory in the beginning. But even as he thought that, he knew what a dangerous thing it would be to do. It would be a last resort, only to be adopted in order to save his own reputation; not for the money, but for all future work.

They were inside the long corridor again and the gloom closed in on them. Monk walked slowly, picking his way by touch as well as sight, stepping carefully to avoid the rotted boards, the refuse, and the weeds that had grown up through the floor and died, their stems slimy.

He found the place where he had left the tusk, recognising it by the newly broken wood. He pointed to it, and allowed Durban to dislodge it and pull it out.

'I see,' Durban said expressionlessly. 'So who does it belong to when we've finished with it? I assume he's going to press charges, apart from the murder of the watchman?'

'Clement Louvain,' Monk replied. He wished he could be more open with Durban. Every lie scraped at him like an abrasion to the skin, but he had left himself no room to manoeuvre.

At Durban's instruction Sergeant Orme hoisted the tusk on to his shoulder and Durban turned to walk back again. Monk followed him, wanting to say something, anything to let Durban understand, and knowing he could not.

He found Louvain in his office after dark that evening. The room was warm. A fire was burning briskly in the grate under the ornate mantel, the light of the flames dancing on the polished wood of the desk. Louvain was standing by the window with his back to the sombre view of the river. It was too dark to see anything but the yellow eyes of other windows and the riding lights of ships at anchor.

He was smiling. He had a decanter of brandy on the small table – and two glasses out, polished to burn like crystals in the reflected fire. A small leather purse sat beside them, its soft fabric distorted by the weight of coins inside.

'Sit down,' he invited as soon as Monk had closed the door. 'Have some brandy. You've done well, Monk. I admit I had doubts at times, I thought you weren't up to it. But this is excellent. I have my ivory back, bar one tusk for evidence, and when Gould comes to trial, other thieves will know not to meddle with me again.' He nodded, smiling, and there was no curb or evasion in it. 'You couldn't have done better. If I get another problem I'll send for you. As it is, I'll recommend you to everyone I like.' He smiled, showing his teeth. 'And I'll hope my enemies never find you.' He poured a generous brandy for Monk and passed it to him, then one for himself. He raised the glass. 'To your continued prosperity – and mine.' He drank with relish. 'There's an extra ten guineas in the purse for you. I like you, Monk. You're a man like myself.'

186

It was a generous compliment, and honest.

'Thank you.' Monk picked up the purse and put it in his pocket. Quite apart from the money in it, it was a beautiful piece of leather. It was a generous gesture. He raised his brandy and took a mouthful. It was exquisite, old, mellow and full of warmth.

Chapter Eight

❧

Squeaky Robinson staggered into the kitchen at Portpool Lane and heaved two baskets of shopping on to the table. His fingers were still bent from the weight of them.

'Have you got any idea how heavy that lot is?' he demanded, looking at Hester indignantly.

'Of course I have,' she replied, barely turning from the stove where she was straining beef tea. 'I usually carry it myself. I just haven't had time to go out lately. Unpack it, will you? And put everything away.'

'I dunno where it goes,' he protested.

'Then this is an excellent time to learn,' she told him. 'Unless you'd rather do something else? Like laundry, or scrubbing the floor? Or we could always do with more water. We seem to be using a great deal at the moment.'

'You're a terrible hard woman,' he grumbled, picking the items out of the baskets one by one.

Claudine Burroughs came in from the laundry, her face pinched with distaste at the smell, her sleeves rolled up above the elbows and her hands and lower arms red.

'I have none of that stuff – potash,' she said to Hester. 'I can't work without supplies.'

'I got some,' Squeaky said cheerfully. 'Here.' He pointed to the bag on the floor. 'I'll take it down for you.

We're gonna have to use a little less of all this, least until we get some more money. I dunno where folks' hearts is any more. Hard, they are. Hard like flint. Come on, missus, I'll give you a hand.'

Claudine looked at him in disbelief. She drew in her breath to rebuff him for his familiarity, but he was impervious to it. He picked up the large bag of potash, lifting it with some effort, although he had carried it all the way from the next street with greater ease. Claudine let out her breath again and, with as big an effort as his, she thanked him and followed him to the laundry.

Flo came in, carrying a full scuttle of coal, a grin on her face.

'Learnin' 'er 'ow the other 'alf lives, is she?' she said with relish. 'If ol' Squeaky spoke to 'er in the street she'd 'ave kittens.'

'We need her,' Hester pointed out. 'Thank you for getting the coal in. How much have we left?'

'Need more day arter termorrer,' Flo replied. 'I know where ter get more cheap. Yer want it?'

'No, thank you. I can't afford to have the police here.'

'I said cheap.' Flo was insulted, not on behalf of her honesty but her intelligence. 'I din' say free.'

'Do what you can,' Hester accepted. 'Sorry.'

Flo smiled patiently. 'That's all right. I don' take no offence. Yer can't 'elp it.'

Hester finished the beef tea, put more water in the kettle and replaced it on the stove, then with the tea in a large cup she went up the stairs to see how Ruth Clark was this morning. Bessie had been up with her most of the night, but had reported she now seemed no worse than some of the other women with fever and bronchitis.

'If yer ask me,' Bessie said briskly, ''alf 'er trouble's that 'er lover threw 'er out. Took in someone else with a softer tongue, I dare say, an' 'oo knows wot side 'er bread's buttered on. Now she's got no bread at all,

189

buttered or not, an' she's crosser'n a wet cat. She in't no sicker'n nobody else.'

Hester did not argue; there was no time and no point. At the top of the stairs she met Mercy Louvain with an armful of dirty laundry.

'I've left most of it,' she said with a smile. 'That Agnes is feeling pretty bad, and I changed hers. She's got a very high fever. I don't think the poor creature has had a decent meal in weeks, maybe months. I'll take these to Claudine.' A flash of amusement crossed her face. She said nothing, but Hester knew precisely what was in her mind.

'Perhaps you can give her a little help?' she suggested. 'Especially with the mangle.'

'I'm no better at it,' Mercy confessed. 'I got my apron caught up in it yesterday. Tore the strings off and I had to stitch them back on again. And that's something I'm not very good at, either. I can paint pretty well, but what use is that?'

'Everything that's beautiful is of use,' Hester replied. 'There are times when it is the only thing that helps.'

Mercy smiled. 'But this certainly isn't one of them. I'll take these down and help Claudine mangle the last lot. Between the two of us we'll make a passable job of it. I might even make her laugh, although I doubt it.' She dropped one of the sheets and bent to pick it up again. 'Although if she gets herself caught in the mangle again, it might make me laugh. And if Flo's there, she'll never stop.' She gave a tiny little giggle, then it died as she heard someone along the passage call out and Hester went to her.

Margaret came in just after midday, bringing with her a bag of potatoes, three loaves of bread, two very large mutton bones, and three pounds, six shillings and ninepence in money. She was dressed for work and she looked vigorous and ready to tackle anything, and enormously pleased with herself.

Hester was so relieved she almost laughed just to see her.

'I've got jam,' Margaret said conspiratorially. 'And I bought a couple of slices of cold mutton for your lunch. Eat it quickly, there isn't enough to share. It was all I could take without getting Cook into trouble. I made a sandwich for you.' She unwrapped it as she spoke. 'When did you last go home? Poor William must think you've abandoned him.' She passed the sandwich across. It was sliced a little crookedly, but made with plenty of butter, mint jelly and thick meat. Hester knew Margaret had done it herself.

'Thank you,' she said with profound gratitude, biting into it and feeling the taste fill her.

Margaret made fresh tea and brought it to the table, pouring a cup for each of them. 'How is everyone?' she asked.

'Much the same,' Hester replied with her mouth full. 'Where did you get the money?'

'A friend of Sir Oliver's,' Margaret answered, colouring a little. She looked down at her cup. She was annoyed with herself that her feelings were so clear, and yet she also wanted to share them with Hester. There was a need in her not to be alone in the turmoil, the vulnerability she felt, and the acute anxiety in case Lady Hordern carried out her threat to call on Mrs Ballinger and repeat the conversation at the soirée. She had actually broached the subject herself, in order to forestall disaster, but she was not at all sure that she had succeeded. 'I think he put a certain amount of pressure on the poor man to contribute,' she said with uncomfortable memory, raising her eyes to meet Hester's. 'You know, in spite of himself he's awfully proud of you and what we do here.' She bit her lip self-consciously, not because she had said Rathbone was proud of Hester, which was true, but because his emotions were

191

caught up with Margaret, and they both knew that. It had been unmistakable since he had been willing to help gain this building because Margaret had asked him.

Tired as she was, Hester found herself smiling. She understood exactly the mixture of modesty, of hope and fear, that made Margaret phrase it as she had. 'If he's prepared to admit it, then he certainly is,' she agreed. 'And I'm grateful for anything he is able to coerce out of people. I suppose it's the time of year, but we have far more women in here with bronchitis and pneumonia than a month or two ago.'

'I'd have pneumonia if I were walking the streets at night,' Margaret said with feeling. 'I wish I could persuade people to give regularly, but you should see their faces when they think I'm collecting for missionary work, or something like that, and then the change in them when they know it's for street women. I've been sorely tempted to decorate the truth a little, and just take the money.'

'I think it has something to do with acute discomfort that we allowed the misery to happen in the first place,' Hester replied. 'Leprosy isn't our fault, but tuberculosis or syphilis might be. And there's the other side of it, too. We don't mind thinking about leprosy, because we don't believe there's any chance of our catching it. The other things we might, in spite of everything we try to do to prevent it.'

'Syphilis?' Margaret questioned.

'Especially that,' Hester answered. 'Street women are seen as the ones who pass it on. Husbands use them, wives get the disease.' She looked down. 'You can't blame them for anger – and fear.'

'I hadn't thought of it like that,' Margaret admitted. 'No, perhaps I wouldn't be so willing, either, when you think of that. Perhaps my judgement was a little quick.'

Margaret stayed and worked hard all afternoon. She was there to help when an injured woman was brought in, several bones broken in her fingers, but her most serious distress was fever and a hacking cough. She looked worn until her strength and will were exhausted, and when they helped her upstairs and into a bed, she lay silent and white-faced, oblivious of all they could do to help her.

Margaret left shortly after eight in the evening, intending to purchase more of the most important supplies, such as chinchona bark – which was expensive and not easy to find – and such simple things as bandages and good surgical silk and gut.

Hester snatched some sleep for four hours, and woke with a start when it was just after midnight. Claudine Burroughs was standing next to the bed, her long face filled with anxiety and distaste. She also looked annoyed.

'What is it?' Hester sat up slowly, struggling to reach full consciousness. Her head ached and her eyes felt hot and gritty. She would have paid almost any price to slide back into sleep again. The room around her wavered. The cold air chilled her skin. 'What's happened?' she asked.

'The new woman who came in,' Claudine said, framing her words carefully, 'I think she has a . . . a disease of . . . a moral nature.' Her nostrils flared as though she could smell its odour in the room.

Hester had a terse answer on her tongue; then she remembered how much she needed Claudine's help, unskilled as it was. She complained, she disapproved, but through it she kept working, almost as if she found some perverse comfort in it. A thought flickered through Hester's mind as to what her life at home must be like that she came seeking some kind of happiness or purpose for herself here. But she had no time to pursue it.

'What are her symptoms?' she asked, swinging her feet over on to the floor.

'I don't know much about such things,' Claudine defended herself. 'But she has scars like the pox on her shoulders and arms, and other things I'd prefer not to mention.' She stood very stiffly, balanced as if to retreat. Her face was oddly crumpled. 'I think the poor thing is like to die,' she added, a harsh and sudden pity in her voice, and then gone again, as though she were ashamed of it.

For the first time, Hester wondered if Claudine had ever seen death before, and if she were afraid of it. She had not thought to consider that possibility until now. She stood up slowly. She was stiff from lying too heavily asleep in one position.

'I'll come and see what I can do,' she said in answer to the summons. 'There may not be much.'

'I'll help,' Claudine offered. 'You . . . you look tired.'

Hester accepted, asking her to fetch a bowl of water and a cloth.

Claudine was right: the woman looked very ill indeed. She drifted in and out of consciousness, her skin was hot and dry and her breathing rattled, her pulse was weak. Now and again she moved her eyes and tried to speak, but no distinguishable words came.

Hester waited with her, leaving Mercy Louvain to tend to Ruth Clark and try to keep her fever down. Claudine came and went, each time more anxious.

'Can't you do anything for her?' she asked, whispering in deference to the possibility that the sick woman might hear her.

'No. Just be here so she is not alone,' Hester replied. She had a light hold of the woman's hand, just enough to exert a slight pressure in acknowledgement of her presence.

'So many of them . . .' Claudine did not like to say 'die like this', but the thought was in her pale face, the tightness of her lips. She smoothed her apron over her stomach and her hands, red-knuckled, were stiff.

'Yes,' Hester said simply. 'It's a hazard of the job, but it's less certain than starvation.'

'The job!' Claudine all but choked on the word. 'You

make it sound like a decent labour! Have you any idea what heartache they bring to—' She stopped abruptly.

Hester heard the anguish in her voice and the suddenly bitten-back words, as if somehow she had already betrayed herself. She turned and looked up at Claudine. She saw shame in her eyes, and fear, as if Hester might already know more than she could bear.

Hester spoke quietly. 'The best way I have found of dealing with it is to stop imagining the details of other people's lives, particularly the parts that ought to be private, and try to help sort out some of the mess. I've made the odd error myself.'

'Well, we're none of us saints,' Claudine said awkwardly.

Before she could have any further thought the woman on the bed made a dry little sound in her throat, and stopped breathing. Hester leaned closer to her and felt for the pulse in her neck. There was nothing. She folded her hands, and stood up slowly.

Claudine was staring at her, her face ashen. 'Is she . . .'

'Yes.'

'Oh . . .' Suddenly, and to her fury, she started to shiver, and the tears welled up in her eyes. She turned on her heel and marched out of the room, and Hester heard her footsteps along the passageway.

Hester tidied the bed a little, then went out and closed the door. She walked towards Ruth Clark's room, and from several feet away she heard the voices. They were not loud, but tight and hard with anger. The words were muffled, only one or two distinct. There was something about leaving, and a threat so choked with emotion the individual words ran into a blur. Only the rage was clear, a pain so intense and so savage it made the sweat prickle on her skin and her heart pound as if such anger could reach out and damage her where she stood, yards away from it.

She shrank from intruding. She wanted to pretend she

195

had not heard, that the quarrel was some kind of mistake, a momentary nightmare from which she had awoken into reality.

She had not steeled herself to do it when the door opened and Mercy came out, carrying a bowl of cold water and a cloth over her arm. She looked angry and frightened. She stopped abruptly when she saw Hester.

'She thinks she's better,' she said huskily. 'She wants to leave, perhaps tomorrow. She isn't well enough . . . I'm . . . I'm trying to convince her.' Her face was pale, her eyes hollow with exhaustion. She looked close to tears.

'I was told she had family coming for her soon,' Hester replied, trying to be comforting. 'If they do, they will look after her. I imagine that's what she was referring to. Don't worry about it. She isn't well enough to leave without someone to care for her, and she must know that.'

'Family?' Mercy said in amazement. 'Who?'

'I don't know.' She was about to add that it was Clement Louvain who had spoken of them, then she changed her mind. Perhaps Mercy had no idea of her brother's private life, or that of his friend, supposing he existed. 'But don't worry about her,' she said instead. 'We can't keep her here if she wants to leave, but I'll try to persuade her how foolish it would be.' She looked at Mercy's drawn face. 'She's a difficult woman. She's always quarrelling with Flo, even accused her of being a thief, and really upset her. Flo's all kinds of things, and it doesn't matter. But she's not a thief and she really cares about that. If someone comes for Ruth, it will be a good thing.'

Mercy stood still. 'I'm sorry,' she said very quietly.

'Go and have a cup of tea,' Hester said, 'and something to eat. When did you last sit down?' She put her hand on Mercy's arm. 'We can't help everyone – some people just won't be helped. We have to do what we can, and then go on to think of the next person.'

Mercy moved as if to say something, then the words died on her lips.

'I know it's difficult,' Hester smiled very slightly, with warmth rather than humour, 'but it's the only way to survive.'

If Mercy found any comfort in that, it did not reflect in her face. She nodded, but more as a matter of form than agreement, and went on down the stairs.

The rest of the night passed with little incident. Hester managed to get several hours' sleep. In the morning she sent Squeaky to the undertaker to have him come and remove the body of the dead woman, then set about making breakfast for everyone able to eat.

Claudine looked tired and withdrawn, but she carried out her duties with slightly increased skill. She even took a dish of gruel up to Ruth Clark and helped her to eat most of it.

'I'm bothered whether I know if that woman's better or not,' she said when she returned to the kitchen with the dish. 'One minute I think she is, then she has that fever back and looks as if she'll not make it to nightfall.' She put the uneaten gruel down the drain and the dish in the sink. 'I'll go down the street and fetch water,' she added through pursed lips. 'It's as cold as the grave out there.'

Hester thanked her sincerely, and decided to go up and see Ruth herself. She found her propped up very slightly on the pillows, her face flushed, her eyes bright and angry.

'How are you?' she asked briskly. 'Claudine says you were able to eat a little.'

A slightly sour smile touched her lips. 'Better to swallow it than choke. She has hands like a horse, your pinched-up Mrs Burroughs. She despises the rest of your help, but I dare say you can see that.' A curious, knowing look crossed her face. 'Even if you haven't the wit to see why,' she added.

197

Hester felt a moment's chill, an acute ugliness in the room, but she refused to entertain it. 'I am not concerned why, Miss Clark,' she replied sharply. 'Any more than I care why your lover put you out for some friend to bring to a charity clinic to care for you. You are sick and we can help; that is all that concerns me. I am glad you were able to eat a little.'

'Charity clinic!' Ruth said in a choking voice, as if, had she the strength, she would laugh, but there was hatred in her eyes.

Hester looked at her, and saw fear also. 'We'll do our best,' she said more gently. 'See if you can rest for a little. I'll come back soon.'

Ruth did not answer her.

The undertaker came and Squeaky saw to the necessary details, including paying him. It was another strain on their dwindling resources, which he complained about vociferously.

Just before midday the rat-catcher arrived. Hester had completely forgotten she had sent for him, and for a moment she was so startled she did not recognise him. He was thin, a little square-shouldered, only an inch or two taller than she. Then he moved into the light and she saw his wry, humorous face, and the small brown and white terrier at his feet.

'Mr Sutton! You gave me a fright. I'd forgotten what day it is. I'm sorry.'

He smiled at her, lop-sidedly because his face was pleasantly asymmetrical, one eyebrow higher than the other. 'I guess that these rats in't too bad, then, or yer'd be a day ahead o' yerself, rather than a day be'ind. But yer look fair wore out, an' that's the truth.'

'We've got a lot of sick people in just now,' she replied. 'Time of the year, I suppose.'

'It's blowin' fit ter snow out there,' he agreed. 'I reckon as it'll freeze by dark. Even the rats'll 'ave more sense than ter be out then. Got a lot, 'ave yer?' He glanced around the kitchen, noting the food bins, the clean floor, the pails of water. 'Don't take no bad feelin' if you 'ave. Rats don't mind it warm and tidy, no more'n we do. Bit o' spilled flour or crumbs an' they're 'appy.'

'They're not bad, actually,' she answered. 'I just want the few we've got discouraged.'

He grinned broadly. 'Wot'd yer like me ter do, miss? I can sing to 'em? That'd discourage anyone. Rats 'a' got very good 'earin'. 'Alf an hour o' me singin' me 'eart out, an' they'd be beggin' fer peace. Like as not, most of 'em'd be in the next street. An' yer staff wiv 'em.'

Hester smiled at him. 'If that were sufficient, Mr Sutton, I could do that myself. My mother always said I could make money singing – they'd pay me to move on.'

'I thought all young ladies could sing.' He looked at her curiously.

'Most of us can,' she answered, taking a loaf of bread out of the bin and picking up the serrated knife. 'Of those of us who can't, some have the sense not to try, some haven't. I have, so I still need your help with the rats. Would you like some lunch?'

'Yeah, that'd be nice o' yer,' he accepted the invitation, sitting down at the scrubbed wooden table, and motioning the dog to sit also.

She toasted some of the bread, holding it up to the open stove piece by piece on the three-pronged fork, then when it was brown passing it over to him to set in the rack. Then she fetched the butter and cheese, and a fresh pot of tea.

They sat down together in the warm, candlelit kitchen and for over half an hour no one interrupted them. She liked Sutton. He had a vast string of tales about his adventures, and a dry wit describing people and their reactions to rats. It was the first time Hester had laughed in several days, and she felt the knots easing out at the

199

sheer relief of thinking about trivial things that had no relation whatsoever to life and death in Portpool Lane.

'I'll come back this evenin',' Sutton promised, picking up the last piece of toast and finishing his third cup of tea. 'I'll 'ave traps an' me dog an' the lot. We'll get it tidied up for yer – on the 'ouse, like.'

'On the house?' she questioned.

He looked very slightly self-conscious. 'Yeah, why not? Yer in't got money ter spend. Gimme the odd cup o' tea when I'm in this part o' town, an' it'll do.'

'Thank you, Mr Sutton,' she accepted. 'That is very generous of you.'

'I'm glad yer don' stand on no pride.' He looked relieved. 'Daft, it is, when yer can do some real good. An' I reckon yer does.' He stood up and straightened his coat. It was actually rather smart. 'I'll see yer about dark. Good day, Miss 'Ester.' He motioned to the dog. 'C'mon, Snoot.'

'Good day, Mr Sutton,' Hester replied.

She and the others took round bread, gruel, beef tea, whatever they had that their various patients could eat. Mercy had peeled and stewed the apples from Toddy, and that was a very welcome addition.

At three o'clock all seemed quiet. Hester decided to pay another visit to Ruth Clark to try to persuade her to remain in the clinic for at least two days longer, and get her strength back. She was far from well yet, and the bitter air outside could give her a relapse that might even be fatal.

She opened the door and went into the room, closing it behind her because she expected an argument and did not wish it to be overheard, especially by Mercy. It might reveal more things about Ruth's situation and her relationship to Clement Louvain than Mercy would be happy to know, nor did she wish any unkind remarks Ruth might make to be overheard.

Ruth was lying down, her head lower on the pillows than Hester would have left her. Someone had no doubt been trying to ease her, and not known that it was better for those with congestion of the lungs to be raised. She walked over quietly and looked down at the sleeping woman. It was a shame to disturb her; she was resting in profound peace. But she might waken with her lungs choked.

'Ruth,' Hester said quietly.

There was no response. Her breathing was so much impaired there was no sound to it at all, no labouring.

'Ruth,' she said again, this time putting her hand out to touch her through the bedclothes. 'You need to sit up a bit, or you'll feel worse.'

There was still no response.

Hester felt for the pulse in her neck. There was nothing, and her skin was quite cool. She felt again, pushing harder for the pulse. Ruth had seemed to be recovering – she had certainly been quite well enough to quarrel with Mercy, and with Flo again after that.

But there was definitely no pulse, even in the jugular vein, and no breath from her nose or lips when Hester moved the candle closer, then held the back of her polished watch almost touching her. Ruth Clark was dead.

She straightened up and stood still, surprised at how deeply it affected her. It was not that she had liked the woman; she had been graceless, arrogant and devoid of gratitude to those who helped her. It was that she had been so intensely alive, one could not forget or ignore her, one could not be unaware of her passions, the sheer force of her existence. Now, all of a sudden, she had ceased to be.

Why had she died so suddenly, without any warning of deterioration? Was Hester at fault? Had there been something she should have seen, and perhaps treated? If she had liked her more, would she have taken better care of her, seen the symptoms instead of the abrasive character?

She looked down at the calm, dead face, and wondered what Ruth had been like before she became ill, when she was happy and believed she was loved, or at least wanted. Had she been kinder then, and warm, a gentler woman than she had been here? How many people could keep the best of themselves if they were rejected as she had been?

She reached forward to fold the hands in some kind of repose. It was a small act of decency, as if someone cared. It was only when she touched the fingers that she felt the torn nails, and picked up the candle again to look more closely. They were new tears, because the ragged pieces were still there; then she set the candle on the table and examined the other hand. The other nails were perfect, those of a woman who cares for her hands.

Unease rippled through her, not quite fear yet. She looked at Ruth's face again. There was a slight trickle of blood on her lower lip, only the faintest smear, and a trace of mucus on her nose. With the fever and chest congestion she had had, that was hardly surprising. Could she have choked somehow?

She parted the lips slightly, and saw bitten flesh inside, as if it had been pressed close and hard on her teeth. Now the fear was real. It needed disproving. She seized the pillow and jerked it out from under Ruth's head. Clean. She turned it over. There on the underside was blood and mucus.

Slowly she forced herself to open the eyelids one at a time, and look. The tiny pinpoints of blood were there, too, little haemorrhages that turned her stomach sick with misery – and fear. Ruth Clark had been suffocated. The pillow swift and tight over her face, with someone's weight pressing down on it.

Who? And, for heaven's sake, why? There had been quarrels, but they were trivial, stupid. Why murder?

She backed away slowly to lean against the door as if she needed it to hold her up. What should she do? Call the police?

If she did that they would almost certainly suspect Flo because Ruth had accused her of being a thief. But Mercy Louvain had quarrelled with Ruth, too, and so had Claudine Burroughs. That was no proof of anything except that Ruth was a very difficult and ungrateful woman.

Would the police close the clinic? What would happen to the sick women then? It was exactly the sort of thing the authorities would use as an excuse to finish all the good work here. But even if somehow she could persuade them not to, who would come here after this? A place where sick, helpless women were murdered in their beds? Word would spread, vicious and frightening, destroying, causing panic.

If only Monk were not busy now with a case he had to solve, he could have come in, so discreetly that no one but Margaret need have known. But Margaret was not here right now. There was no use asking Bessie – she would have no idea what to do, and only be frightened to no purpose.

She could not trust Squeaky. He was helpful as long as it suited him, and he had no real alternative. But he might see this as the perfect opportunity to win his brothel back, and catch her as neatly as she had caught him. Could he have killed Ruth for that? No – it was absurd. She was losing all sense.

Sutton was coming back. He would understand the problem. He might even have some way to help. First, it would be a good thing if she were to find out all she could. There might be something here to tell her who was last in the room. People made beds in different ways, folded sheets or tidied things, even arranged a sick person's clothes.

And she should prepare Ruth for burial. Should she inform Clement Louvain? Mercy could surely get a message to him. How would Mercy feel? Hester must be careful what she told the other women, and how she worded it.

She straightened up and walked back to the bed again. Was there anything at all that observation could tell her? The bedding was rumpled, but then Ruth had done that herself most of the time when she was feverish. It meant nothing. Hester looked around the floor, and at the way the corners of the sheets were tucked in at the foot. It looked tight, folded left over right. Bessie's work, probably. She examined everything else she could think of. The cup of water was on a small square of cardboard, the way Claudine left it, so as not to make a ring mark on the wood of the table. Flo would not have thought of that. It all told her nothing.

She should wash the body and prepare it for the undertaker. Perhaps she should tell Clement Louvain. Ruth's family might wish to bury her, and he would know who they were. She went downstairs and fetched a bowl of water; it did not matter that it was barely warm. Ruth would not mind. It was just a case of cleaning and making her decent, a gesture of humanity.

She did it alone. There was no need to involve anyone else, and she had not yet decided what to say. Carefully she folded back the bedcovers and took off Ruth's nightgown. It was an awkward job. Perhaps she should have asked someone to help after all. It would not have distressed Bessie; she had washed other dead women with pity and decency, but no fear.

Ruth had had a handsome body, a little shrunken in illness now, but it was easy enough to see how she had been. She was still firm and shapely, except for an odd, dark shadow under her right armpit, a little like a bruise. Funny that she had not complained of an injury. Perhaps it embarrassed her because of where it was.

There was another one, less pronounced, on the other side.

Hester's heart lurched inside her and the room seemed to waver. She could hardly breathe. With her pulse knocking so loudly she was dizzy, she moved Ruth over a little, and saw what she dreaded with fear so overwhelming it made her almost sick. It was there, another dark swelling – what any medical book would have called a 'bubo'. Ruth Clark had not had pneumonia – she had had bubonic plague, the disease that had killed so many people in the middle of the fourteenth century, and was known as the 'Black Death'.

Hester plunged her hands into the water in the bowl, and then as quickly snatched them out again. Her whole body was shaking. Even her teeth were chattering. She must get control of herself! She had to make decisions, do whatever must be done. There was no one else to take over, no one to tell her what was right.

When had the swellings appeared? Who was the last person to wash her or change her gown? It had always been Mercy. Perhaps Ruth had refused to let her see, or Mercy had not known the swellings for what they were.

And what about all the other women with congestion of the chest? Had they got bronchitis, pneumonia – or were they in the earlier, pneumonic stage of plague?

She had no answer. So no one must leave. The disease would spread like fire in tinder. How many people had brought it into the country in 1348? One, a dozen? In weeks it could spread through half of London, and into the countryside beyond. With modern travel, trains the length and breadth of the country, it could be in Scotland and Wales the day after.

Margaret must not come back. And, heaven knew, she would miss Margaret's help, her courage, her companionship. But no one must come in, or go out.

How would she stop that? She would have to have help. Lots of it. But who? What if, when she told the others who were here now, they panicked and left? She had no power to hold them. What on earth was she to do? Was there even any point in trying to see that no one else became infected?

No. That was absurd. Everyone had already been in the room any number of times. It was hideously possible that they had caught it, and it was too late to help and save anything. At least she would prevent anyone else from seeing these bubos, and understanding what they meant. That would stop panic. There was one room with a door that locked. She must wrap the body tightly in a sheet and get Bessie to help her carry it there and lock it in.

She covered Ruth's body again, binding the sheet to leave nothing showing, then went out into the passageway and closed the door. She saw Flo's back as she was about to go downstairs and called to her.

'Find Bessie and send her up here, will you? Immediately, please.'

Flo heard the edge in her voice. 'Summink wrong wi' that miserable cow again?'

'Just do it.' Hester's tone was high and sharp, but she could not help it. 'Now!'

Flo gave a shrug and went off, clearly annoyed at being spoken to that way, but she must have obeyed, because Bessie came within three or four minutes.

'Ruth Clark is dead,' Hester said as soon as Bessie was beside her. 'I want you to help me put her body in the end room that has a lock on it, so Mercy and Claudine don't panic at another death so soon. I . . . I don't want them running off, so say nothing. It matters very much.'

Bessie frowned. 'Yer all right, Miss 'Ester? Yer look terrible pale.'

'Yes, thank you. Just help me to get Ruth into that room before anyone else knows.'

It was difficult. Ruth was heavy, and still limp. It was all they could do not to let her slip through their hands on to the floor. However, Bessie was strong, and Hester at least had some experience with moving the dead. After nearly fifteen minutes of desperate effort they succeeded, and Bessie promised not to say anything to the others yet. At least for the time being it gave Hester a reprieve, and she scrubbed out the room with hot water and vinegar, all the time knowing it was probably useless.

At five o'clock Mercy came to tell her that Sutton was back with his dog and traps.

'Oh – good.' Hester was overwhelmed with relief.

'Are they that bad?' Mercy said with surprise. 'I don't think I've ever seen any. There was one little creature in the laundry, but I thought it was a mouse.'

'Baby rat,' Hester said quickly, no idea whether it had been or not. 'Get a nest sometimes. I'll go and see Sutton now. Thank you.' And she hurried away, leaving Mercy on the landing looking startled.

She found Sutton in the kitchen. Snoot was sitting obediently at his heels, his bright little face full of attention, waiting to begin his job.

'Thank you for coming so promptly,' Hester said straight away. 'May I show you the laundry, where I think they are?'

He sensed something wrong. His face puckered in concern. 'Yer all right, miss? Yer look rotten poorly yerself. Yer comin' down wi' summink? 'Ere, sit down, I can find the rats meself. It's me job. Me an' Snoot 'ere,' he gestured to the little dog, 'we 'ave all we need.'

'I . . . I know you have.' Hester pushed her hand over her brow. Her head was pounding. 'I need to speak to you. I . . .' She gulped and swallowed hard, feeling her stomach knot.

Sutton took a step toward her. 'Wot's the matter?' he said gently. 'Wot's 'appened?'

She felt the tears come to her eyes. She wanted to laugh, and to cry, it was so much worse than anything he was imagining. She wished passionately that she could tell him some quarrel, some domestic tragedy or fear, anything but what was the truth. 'Downstairs,' she said. 'In the laundry, please?'

'If yer want,' he conceded, puzzled now, and worried. 'C'mon, Snoot.'

Hester led the way to the laundry, Sutton and the dog behind her. She asked him to close the door, and he obeyed. She left the one candle burning, and sat down on the single hard-backed chair because she felt her legs weak. Sutton leaned against the wooden tub, his face masklike in the flickering light.

'Yer got me scared for yer,' he said with a frown. 'Wot is it? Wot can be that bad, eh?'

Telling him was a relief so intense it was almost as if it were a solution. 'Ruth Clark is dead,' she said, meeting his eyes. 'Someone suffocated her.'

His face tightened, but there was no horror in it; in fact almost an easing of the fear. He had expected something worse. 'It 'appens,' he pursed his lips. 'Yer wanna tell the rozzers, or get rid of the body quiet? I think gettin' rid of it quiet'd be better. It in't a good thing ter do, but 'avin' the place buzzin' wi' bluebottles'd be worse. I could 'elp yer.'

'She would have died anyway.' Hester heard her voice wobbling. 'You see that isn't the real problem . . . I mean someone suffocating her.'

'Gawd! Then wot is? If she were goin' ter die anyway?' He was confused.

Hester took a deep breath. 'I thought she had pneumonia. When I came to wash her and prepare her for the undertaker, I . . . I discovered what was really wrong with her.'

He frowned. 'Wot could be that bad? So she got

208

syphilis, or summink like that? Jus' keep quiet about it. Lots o' folk do, an' some as yer wouldn't think. We're all 'uman.'

'No, I wouldn't care if it were that.' Suddenly she wondered if she should tell him. What would he do? Would he panic, let everyone know, and run out spreading it everywhere? Would half of England die – again?

He saw the terror in her. 'Yer better tell me, Miss 'Ester.' He dropped into sudden, gentle familiarity.

She knew of nothing else to do. She could not reach Monk, and certainly not Rathbone. Even Callandra was gone. 'Plague,' she whispered.

For a second there was incomprehension in his face, then paralysing horror. 'Jeez! Yer don't mean . . .' He gestured to his chest, just by the armpit.

She nodded. 'Buboes. The Black Death. Sutton, what am I going to do?' She closed her eyes, praying please God he would not run away and leave her.

He leaned against the wooden tub, his legs suddenly weak as well. His face had lost all its colour except a sickly yellow in the candlelight, and slowly he slid down until he was sitting on the floor.

'Gawd 'elp us,' he breathed. 'Well, fer a start, we in't telling nobody, nobody at all. Then we in't letting nobody out of 'ere. It spreads like . . .' he smiled bitterly, his voice catching in his throat, 'like the plague!'

The tears ran down Hester's face and she took several seconds to control them, and to stop her breath coming in gasps and choking her. He was going to help. He had said 'we' not 'you'. She nodded. 'I want to give her a decent burial, but I can't afford to let anyone see her body. Nothing else causes dark swellings like that. Anyone would know.'

He rubbed the heel of his hand across his cheek. 'We gotter stop that at any price at all,' he said hoarsely. 'If folks know, there'd be some as'd mob the place, others as'd put a torch ter it, burn yer down, 'ouse, an' everyone in it. It'd be terrible.'

'It would be better than having the plague spread throughout London,' she pointed out.

'Miss 'Ester—'

'I know. I've no intention of being burned alive. But how can we keep everyone here? How do I stop Claudine going home if she wants to, or Ruby leaving, or anyone who gets better . . . if they do?' Her voice was wavering again. 'How do I get food in, or water, or coal . . . or anything?'

He said nothing for several seconds.

Hester waited. The laundry was strangely silent. It smelled of fat and potash and the steam that filled it during the day. The one candle with its yellow circle of light made the darkness seem endless.

'We gotta make certain no one leaves,' Sutton said finally. 'I got friends as'll 'elp, but it won't be nice.' He looked at her intently. 'We gotta do it fer real, Miss 'Ester. No one gotta leave, no matter wot. In't no room fer "sorry" in this. If yer right, an' that's wot she 'ad, better some dead 'ere fer tryin' ter leave than 'alf o' Europe dead 'cos we let 'em.'

'What can we do?' she asked.

'I got friends wi' dogs, not nice little ratters like Snoot 'ere, but pit bulls as'd tear yer throat out. I'll ask 'em ter patrol round the place, front an' back. They'll make sure fer certain as no one leaves. An' I'll get fellers as'll bring food an' water, an' coal, o' course. An' we'll spread the word as the clinic is full, so yer can't take nobody else in, no matter wot's 'appened to 'em.'

'We can't pay them,' she pointed out. 'And we can't tell them why.'

'They'll do it 'cos I ask 'em,' he answered. 'Yer doin' enough for folks round 'ere. An' I'll tell 'em it's cholera. That'll do.'

She nodded. 'Would . . . would we really set the dogs on anyone? I mean . . . I don't think I . . .'

'Yer won't 'ave ter,' he answered. 'I'll do it.'

'Would you?' she whispered, her throat tight.

'We gotter,' he answered. 'One death, quick. In't that better than lettin' it get out?'

She tried to say yes, but her mouth was so dry the word was a croak.

There was a sound outside the door and a moment later it opened. Mercy Louvain stood in the entrance, a candlestick in her hand.

'I'm sorry to interrupt,' she said a little awkwardly. 'But do you need Claudine to stay tonight?'

Hester glanced at Sutton, then back at Mercy. 'Yes,' she said hoarsely. She swallowed. 'Sorry, I'm so tired my voice is going. Yes, please. Don't let her go home.'

'She won't mind, I don't think,' Mercy answered. 'Are you all right? Do we have a lot of rats?'

'Not bad,' Sutton replied, climbing to his feet. 'But we'll get rid of 'em, don't worry. I just need ter go an' get a few more things done, see a couple o' friends, like, then I'll be back. Yer jus' get yerselves a cup o' tea, or summink. Don't do nothin' till I come back.' That was said firmly, like an order.

'No, of course not,' Hester agreed. 'We'll just . . . get everybody supper. Thank you.'

Sutton left and Hester did as she had said she would, measuring out the food carefully; now it was even more precious than before. She was conscious of Claudine and Mercy both watching her with surprise and a shadow of anxiety. She could not afford to say anything to them. She was deceiving them by silence, but she had no choice. She felt guilty, angry, and above all suffocatingly afraid.

It seemed like hours until Sutton came back. Hester was in the front room. She had given up even pretending that she was not waiting for him. Everyone else had gone to look after the seriously ill or, in Bessie's case, to take a few hours' sleep before relieving Claudine very early in the morning.

'I got 'em,' Sutton said simply. 'They're outside, dogs an' all. I got a sack o' potatoes an' some bones. I'll get cabbages and onions an' the like from Toddy same as usual.'

'Thank you.' Suddenly Hester realised what her own imprisonment was going to mean. Perhaps she would never leave this place. Worse than anything else, she would never see Monk again. There would be no chance for goodbyes, or to tell him how he had given passion, laughter and joy to her life. In his companionship she had become who she was designed to be. All the best in her, the happiest, was made real.

'Can you take a letter to my husband . . . so he knows why I don't come home? And why he can't come here . . .?'

'I'll tell 'im,' Sutton answered.

'And you'd better tell Margaret – Miss Ballinger – too. She can't come back. Anyway, we will need her help raising money even more than before. Make her see that, won't you?'

He nodded. His face was sad and bleak. 'Yer gonna tell 'em 'ere?'

She hesitated.

'Yer gotta,' he said simply.

'I'll tell them.' She stood up slowly and walked over to the door as if she were pushing herself against a tide. She reached it and called out into the passage beyond, 'Claudine! Mercy! Flo! Someone please waken Bessie as well, and Squeaky. I need you all in here. I'm sorry, but you have to come.'

It was ten minutes before they were all there, Bessie still dazed with sleep.

It was Mercy who first realised something terrible had

happened. She sat down hard on one of the chairs, her face white. She looked as if she had not eaten or slept properly in days. 'What is it?' she said quietly.

There was no point in stretching out the fear, which already sat thick and heavy in the room.

'Ruth Clark is dead,' Hester said, looking at the incomprehension in their faces. They saw nothing beyond a small loss in the midst of others. Most of them had not liked her. Hester drew in a shivering breath. 'She did not die of pneumonia – she died of plague.' She watched their faces. One of them knew that was a lie. Had that person any idea at all of the deeper, infinitely more terrible truth than murder? She saw nothing except the slow struggle to understand, to grasp the enormity and the true horror of it.

'Plague?' Claudine said in bewilderment. 'What sort of plague? What do you mean?'

'What the 'ell are you talking about?' Squeaky demanded.

'The bubonic plague,' Hester replied. 'In some cases it starts as pneumonic congestion in the chest. Some people recover, not many. Some die of it in that stage. In others it goes on to the bubonic – the swellings in the armpit and the groin that go black. We call it the Black Death.'

Flo stood motionless. Her mouth open.

Squeaky turned white as a sheet.

Claudine fainted.

Mercy caught her and pushed her head between her knees, holding her until she struggled back to consciousness, gasping and choking.

Bessie sat blinking, her breath rasping in her throat.

'No one can leave, in case we carry it out of here to the rest of London,' Hester went on. 'No one at all, at any time or for any reason. Mr Sutton has already arranged for friends of his, with pit bulls, to patrol outside. If anyone leaves, they will set the dogs on them. Please

213

believe that they will really do that. Whatever happens, we cannot allow the disease to spread. In the fourteenth century it killed nearly half of Britain, man, woman and child. It changed the world. Our few lives are nothing, to stop that happening again.'

'How are we gonna live?' Squeaky asked furiously, as if this were some kind of reason to deny what Hester had said.

'Other people will bring us food, water and coal,' Hester replied. 'They will leave them outside, and we will go and fetch them. We will never meet. We have told them it's cholera, and they must never ever think differently.'

Mercy rubbed her hands up over her face, sweeping her hair back. 'If anyone outside gets to know—'

'They'll burn the place down!' Flo finished for her. 'Mrs Monk's right. We gotta keep it a secret from everyone. It's the only chance we got – God 'elp us.'

'Oh Gawd,' Bessie said, rocking back and forwards in her chair. 'Oh Gawd.'

'I never thought of praying,' Claudine said with wry bitterness, 'but I suppose that's all we have.'

Hester looked across at Sutton. He was the only other person, apart from herself, and one more, who knew that they also had a murderer in the house.

Chapter Nine

✦

Monk was sitting at home, building up the fire to try to create in the house the warmth that was gone from it because Hester was devoting so much time to the clinic. Her absence robbed him of a great deal of the pleasure he would have felt had he been able to share his triumph with her. It had been extraordinarily successful. He had pulled off a master stroke, retrieving the ivory and getting it to Louvain, right under the noses of the thieves, and of Culpepper for whom it was taken, and even of the River Police. Louvain had paid him handsomely, and his reputation was now high. Other jobs would come from it. But there was no one to tell.

He was not finished. He still needed to find out who had killed Hodge, but it had to be either Gould's partner, which was likely only if he had gone on board after Gould, found Hodge stirring, not dead after all, and killed him. That would have been a result of panic, and completely unnecessary – unless the man were someone paid by Louvain, and thus had betrayed him? Louvain would exact a bitter vengeance for that, and it would explain why Hodge had been killed, not merely knocked senseless.

And then there was the other possibility – that he had

been killed by a member of the crew in some personal quarrel that was nothing to do with the theft.

If Monk found out who Gould's partner had been, it might be possible to prove whether he had ever come on board the *Maude Idris*. Gould should be able to remember his own actions, which would at least help. Tusks were difficult things to handle. He would surely know where his partner had been. One could not pass anyone on the gangway to the hold without knowing. The difficulty would be in making sure he was honest. Then, on the other hand, he must have walked close to Hodge's body every time he carried ivory up, or went back down for more.

Louvain would not like it; he might even try to block him, but Monk had taken care of that. He had no intention of allowing Hodge's murderer to escape. He had never known Hodge, and might well have disliked him if he had, but that was irrelevant. The less anyone else cared, the more it mattered that he was given some kind of justice.

He was sitting by the fire, getting too hot but barely noticing it, when he realised there was someone knocking on the door. It could not be Hester; she had a key. Was it a new client? He could not accept one, unless they were prepared to wait. He stood up and went to answer.

The man on the step was lean, and quite smartly dressed, but his shoes were worn. His wry, intelligent face was lined with weariness, and there was a small brown and white terrier at his feet. Monk would be sorry to have to refuse him.

'Mr William Monk?' the man enquired.

'Yes.'

'I have a message for yer, sir. May I come in?'

Monk was puzzled and already concerned. Who would send him a message in this fashion? 'What is it?' he said a little sharply. 'A message from whom?'

'From Mrs Monk. Can I come in?' There was an odd dignity to the man, a confidence despite his obvious lack of education.

Monk opened the door and stepped back to allow him to walk past into the warmth, followed by the dog. Then he closed the door and swung around to face him.

'What is it?' Now his voice was sharp, the edge of fear audible. Why would Hester send a message through a man like this? Why not a note, if she were delayed and wanted to tell him? 'Who are you?' he demanded.

'Sutton,' the man replied. 'I'm a rat-catcher. I've know'd Mrs Monk a while now—'

'What did she say?' Monk cut across him. 'Is she all right?'

'Yeah, she's all right,' Sutton said gravely. 'She's workin' too 'ard, like most times, but she's all right.'

Monk looked at him. There was nothing in his face or his demeanour to ease his growing alarm.

'Wot I got ter tell yer in't a few moments' worth,' Sutton went on. 'So yer'd best sit down an' listen. There in't nothing yer can do 'ceptin' keep yer 'ead, and then 'old yer tongue.'

Monk suddenly found his legs were weak and he felt a rush of panic well up inside him. He was glad to sit down.

Sutton sat in the other chair. 'Thank yer,' he said as if Monk had invited him. He did not tease out the suspense. 'One o' the women wot was brought inter the clinic died today. When Miss 'Ester come ter wash 'er fer the undertaker, she see'd what she really died of, which weren't pneumonia like she thought.' He stopped, his eyes shadowed, his face intensely serious.

Monk leaped to the conclusion that was most familiar to him. 'Murdered?' He leaned forward to stand up. He should go there immediately. Helping Gould would have to wait. He could afford a few days.

'Sit down, Mr Monk,' Sutton said in a low, very clear

voice. 'The trouble in't nothin' ter do wi' murder. It's far more 'orrible than that. An' yer gotta act right, or yer could bring down a disaster like the world in't seen in five 'undred years.'

'What the hell are you talking about?' Monk demanded. Was the man mad? He looked perfectly sane, the gravity in him was saner than in a score of men who governed the fates of businesses and societies. 'What is it?'

'Plague,' Sutton answered, his eyes fixed on Monk. 'Not yer cholera or yer pox, or any o' them diseases – the real thing – the Black Death.'

Monk could not grasp what he had said. It had no reality; it was just huge words, too big to mean anything.

'That's why nobody's goin' in there, an' nobody's comin' out,' Sutton went on quietly. 'They gotta keep the place closed, no matter wot.'

'You did,' Monk said instantly.

'I kept away from Miss 'Ester an' the woman wot nursed 'er as died, an' I in't comin' out again arter this.'

'I'm still going in,' Monk insisted. Hester was there without him. She was facing something worse than any human nightmare. How could he possibly stay out here, safe, doing nothing? 'She'll need help. Anyway, how can you stop people leaving? I mean the sheer practicality? You have to tell the authorities. Get doctors—'

'There in't nothin' a doctor can do fer the Black Death.' Sutton sat almost motionless. His face was impassive, beyond emotion. It was as if the horror of it had drained everything out of him. 'If it takes yer, it takes yer, an' if it leaves yer, it leaves yer. In't no use tellin' the authorities. In't nothin' they can do. An' wot d'yer think'd 'appen then, eh?'

The hideousness of the situation was very slowly becoming real. In his mind Monk could see exactly what this strange, composed man was saying. 'How will you stop people leaving?' he asked.

'Dogs,' Sutton said with a slight movement of his shoulders. 'I got friends with pit bulls. They're guardin' all the outsides. I 'ope nobody runs fer it, but so 'elp me, they'll set the dogs on 'em if they do. Better one torn ter bits than lettin' 'er spread it all over the land, all over the world, mebbe.'

'What if they tell people?'

'We told 'em it's cholera an' they don't know different.'

Monk tried not to think of what his own words meant. 'I must still go and help. I can't leave her alone there. I won't.'

'Yer gotter—' Sutton began.

'I won't come out again.'

Sutton's face softened. 'I know yer won't. Not as I'd let yer, any road. But yer can be more 'elp out 'ere. There's things as needs doin'.'

'Getting food, coal, medicine. I know that. Anyone can do those things.'

''Course they can,' Sutton agreed. 'And I'll see as they do. But in't yer thought where the plague come from? Where'd that poor woman get it, then?'

Monk felt the sweat break out on his skin.

'We gotter find out,' Sutton said wearily. 'An' there in't nobody else as can do that, without settin' the 'ole o' London on fire wi' terror. She come from somewhere, poor creature. Where'd she get it, eh? 'Oo else 'as it? Yer a man as knows 'ow ter ask questions, an' get answers as other people can't. Miss 'Ester says as yer the cleverest man, an' the cussedest, as she ever met. She right?'

Monk buried his head in his hands, his mind whirling, ideas beating against him, bruising in their violence. Hester alone in the clinic with the most terrible disease ever known to man. He would never see her again. He could do nothing to help her. He could not even remember now what were the last words they had said to each other. Did she know how much he loved her, as his wife,

219

his friend, the one person without whom he had no purpose and no joy, the one whose belief in him made everything matter, whose approval was a reward in itself, whose happiness created his?

And the whole of Europe could be riddled with disease. Corpses everywhere, the land itself rotting. History books told how the whole world had changed, the old way of life had perished and a new order been made – it had had to be.

'Is she right?' Sutton asked again.

Monk lifted his head. Did Sutton know that in those words he had made it impossible for Monk to refuse? Yes, almost certainly he did.

'Yes,' he answered. 'What do you know about the woman who died?'

''Er name were Ruth Clark, an' she were brung in by a shipowner called Louvain. 'E said as she were the mistress of a friend of 'is, which is mebbe true an' mebbe not.'

'Louvain?' Monk's body froze.

'Yeah.' Sutton stood up. 'I 'ave ter go. I can't see yer again. Yer just gotta do yer best.' He seemed about to add something, but could not think of words to convey it.

'I know,' Monk said quickly. 'Tell Hester . . .'

'Don't matter now,' Sutton replied simply. 'If she don't know it, words in't gonna 'elp. Find where it come from. An' do it soft, like – very, very soft.'

'I understand.' Monk rose to his feet also, surprised that the room did not sway around him. He followed Sutton and his dog to the door. 'Goodbye.'

Sutton went out into the street, rain drifting in the lamplight, and glistening on the pavement. 'Good night,' he replied, then turned and walked with a peculiar ease, almost a grace of step, into the darkness, the dog still at his heels.

Monk closed the door and went back into the room. It seemed airless and unnaturally silent. He sat down very slowly. His body was shaking. He must control his thoughts. Thought was the only way of keeping command of himself.

Ruth Clark had died of plague. Clement Louvain had brought her there. Where from? Who was she? He had said she was the cast-off mistress of a friend. Was that true? Was she his own mistress? He knew she was ill, but had he any idea what with?

Where had she contracted a disease like that? Not in London. The *Maude Idris* had just come back from Africa. Had she come on it? Was that how it had got here? Did Louvain know that, or guess? And he had taken her to Hester!

For a moment red fury swept over Monk so it almost blinded him. His body trembled and his nails dug into the flesh of his hands till they drew blood.

He must control himself. He had no idea whether Louvain had known what was wrong with her. Why should he? The woman was sick. That was all Hester had known, and Hester was a nurse who had cared for her day and night.

He started to walk back and forth. Should he go to Louvain and tell him? Should he at least tell him that Ruth was dead? If Louvain had known she had plague, he would be expecting it. Would he panic now? Might he cause the very terror they were afraid of? But then if he had not known, and she had been his mistress, would he be distressed? Hardly, or he would have got a nurse in to care for her, not sent her to a clinic for street women to be looked after by strangers. Far better to keep silent. Let him find out in time.

Then another thought struck him. What if Gould had been telling the exact truth, and Hodge had been dead, without a mark on him except the slight bruises of a fall, and his head had been beaten in afterwards, because he had died of plague? Then it was not a murder but the concealment of a death, which could end up killing half the world.

Half the world? Wasn't that a ridiculous exaggeration? Nightmare, hysteria rather than reality? What did the history books say?

Back in 1348 England had been a rural community, ignorant and isolated compared with today. If people travelled at all it was by foot or on horseback. Knowledge of medicine was rudimentary, and filled with superstition.

Monk strode back and forth, trying to picture it. He could not make himself sit down or concentrate his mind in linear reasoning. It had been a barbarous time. Who had been on the throne? One of the Plantagenet kings, long before the Renaissance. It was a hundred and fifty years before they had even learned that the world was round.

There were still forests over England, with wild animals. Nobody would have conceived of such a thing as a train. They burned witches at the stake.

And yet the plague had spread like a stench on the wind. How much further would it spread now, when a man could ride from the south coast of England all the way to Scotland in a day? London was the largest city in the world, crammed cheek by jowl with close to five million people. He had heard someone say recently that there were more Scots in London than in Edinburgh. And more Irish than in Dublin, and more Roman Catholics than in Rome.

It would become a wasteland of the dead and dying, spreading ever outward until it polluted the whole country. It needed only one ship leaving the shores with a sick man, and it would destroy Europe as well.

He had only one choice. He had no power to investigate Hodge's death, or to question anyone. He must find Durban and tell him the whole truth. There was time to pay the price of that afterwards. All that mattered now was to trace the disease, and anyone who might carry it.

Monk slept fitfully, and woke confused and heavy-headed, wondering what was wrong. Then the hideousness of the memory returned, filling him like darkness till he hardly knew how to bear it. He lay frozen, as if time were suspended, until finally intelligence told him the only way to survive was to do something. Action would drive the horror back and leave a fraction of his mind free in which he could live, at least until exhaustion made him too weak to resist.

He dressed quickly in as many clothes as he could, knowing that he would almost certainly spend most of the day on the river. Then he went out and bought hot tea and a sandwich from a street pedlar.

He had turned over a dozen different ways to tell Durban the truth, but there was no good way to say any of this, and it hardly mattered how he expressed it. All personal needs and cares vanished in the enormity of this new, terrible truth that swallowed everything else.

It was a sharp, glittering day, just above freezing but feeling far colder because of the wind that scythed in off the shifting, brilliant surface of the water. Gulls wheeled overhead, flashing white against the sky, and the incoming tide slurped on the wood of piers and the wet stone of steps.

The river was busy this morning. Everywhere Monk looked there were men lifting, wheeling, staggering under the weight of sacks and bales. Their shouts were carried by the wind and blown away. Canvas flapped loose and banged against boards. In the clear air he could see as far as the river bends in both directions, and every mast, spar and line of rigging was sharp as an etching on the sky. Only in the distance above the city was there a thin pall of smoke.

223

Durban was not at the police station. The sergeant informed Monk that he was already out on the water, probably south, but he didn't know.

Monk thanked him and went out immediately. There was nothing to do but find a boat and go to look for him. He could not afford to wait.

A few minutes later he was down by the water again, scanning the river urgently for a boatman willing to take him on a search. At first he barely noticed the voice calling him, and only when his sleeve was plucked did he turn.

'Y' all right, then?' Scuff said in an elaborately casual manner, but his eyes were screwed up and there was an edge of anxiety to his tone.

Monk forced himself to be gentler than he felt. 'Yes. The man with the ivory was very happy.'

'Paid yer?' Scuff asked for the true measure of success.

'Oh, yes.'

'Then why d'yer look like 'e din't?' Now there was real concern in his face.

'It's not money. I'm anxious about someone who might be sick. Do you know Mr Durban of the River Police?' Monk asked.

''Im wi' the grey 'air, walks like a sailor? 'Course I do. Why?'

'I need to speak to him, urgently.'

'I'll find 'im for yer.' Scuff put two fingers in his mouth and let out a piercing whistle, then walked over to the edge and repeated it. Within two minutes there was a boat at the steps. After a hurried conversation Scuff scrambled in and beckoned for Monk to follow.

Monk did not want the child with him. What he had to do was going to be awkward and unpleasant, possibly even dangerous. And he certainly could not afford to have Scuff learn the truth.

'C'mon, then,' Scuff said sharply, his face wrinkled in

224

puzzlement. 'Y' in't gonner find 'im standin' there.'

Monk dropped down into the boat. 'Thank you,' he said politely, but his voice was rough, as if he were trembling. 'I don't need you to come. Go back to your own work.' He was uncertain whether to offer him money or not; he might see it as an insult to friendship.

Scuff pulled a face. 'If yer 'aven't noticed, the tide's up. Like I said, yer shouldn't be out by yerself, yer in't fit.' He sat down in the stern, a self-appointed guardian for someone he obviously felt to be in need of one.

'Word is 'e's gorn down Deptford Creek way,' the boatman said pleasantly. 'Bin a bit o' trouble there yesterday. Yer wanna go or not?'

Monk accepted. If he put Scuff ashore against his will he would lose the boatman's respect, possibly even his co-operation. 'Yes. As quickly as you can, please.'

They pulled out on to the main stream of traffic and went south along Limehouse Reach, weaving in and out of strings of barges, moored ships waiting to unload their cargo, and a few still seeking anchorage.

It took them nearly three-quarters of an hour, but finally Monk recognised Durban's figure on the quayside above a flight of steps near Deptford Creek. Then he saw the police boat on the water just below, with two men at the oars, and Orme standing in the stern.

'Over there,' he told his own boatman. The raw edge to his voice gave it all the urgency he needed. 'How much?'

'A shilling,' the boatman replied instantly.

Monk fished a shilling and threepence out of his pocket and as soon as they pulled in to the steps he passed it over and stood up. Scuff stood up also. 'No!' Monk swung round, all but losing his balance. 'I'll be all right now.'

'Yer might need me,' Scuff argued. 'I can do things.'

There was no time to explain, to be gentle. 'I know. I'll find you when I have something for you to do. For now, 'keep out of the rozzers' way.'

Scuff sank back reluctantly and Monk leaped for the step and went on up without looking back.

Durban turned round just as Monk reached the top. He was about to speak when he saw Monk's face. He looked at the other man, a sullen, weary creature with one shoulder higher than the other. 'Do it again an' I'll have you. Now get gone.'

The man obeyed with alacrity, leaving Monk and Durban alone on the top of the steps in the wind.

'What is it?' Durban asked. 'You look like you've seen hell.'

'Not yet, but that could be truer than you think,' Monk said with bitter humour. How could he laugh at anything now? Except, insane as it seemed, perhaps it was the only sanity left. 'I need to talk to you alone, and it's more important than anything else at all.'

Durban drew in his breath, possibly to tell him not to exaggerate, and then let it out again. 'What is it? If you're going to tell me you were lying about the ivory, and that Gould's innocent of the murder of Hodge, I already know the first, and I might believe the second, with proof. Do you have any?'

Maybe telling the truth was going to be less difficult than Monk had thought, and facing Durban's contempt was going to be more. Already guilt was eating him inside. 'It might be proof, but that isn't what matters,' he replied. 'It's not quick, or easy to tell.'

Durban stood motionless, waiting, his hands in his pockets. He did not ask or prompt. Somehow that made it harder. 'There were fourteen tusks originally,' Monk began. 'I found all of them on Jacob's Island, and hid one as proof.'

'And gave the rest to Louvain, which I presume is what you were hired for.' Durban nodded.

Monk had no time to indulge in excuses. He was

226

conscious of the other police in the boat a few yards away, and that at any moment Orme might come up to see what was the matter.

'I saw Hodge's body when Louvain first told me about the robbery,' he answered. 'It was a condition of doing the job that I found whoever killed him and handed them to you. I only looked at the back of his head, nothing else.'

Durban's eyebrows rose, questioning what any of this mattered. There was no open contempt in his face, but it lay only just beneath the surface. 'Does this matter, Mr Monk? His head was beaten in. What did you see that proves Gould's innocence, or anyone else's?'

Monk was losing control of the story. Orme was out of the boat and on the steps, and any patience Durban might have had was slipping away. For the first time since he had resigned from the police in fury, Monk felt grubby for treating crime as a way of earning a living rather than a matter of the law. That was unfair; he solved the crimes other law officers did not, and he wanted to show Durban that, but there was no time, and no reason except pride.

'My wife nursed in the Crimea,' he said roughly. 'Now she runs a clinic for sick and injured prostitutes, in Portpool Lane.' He saw Durban's contempt deepening. It was difficult not to reach out a hand and physically hold him from turning away. 'A few days ago Clement Louvain brought a woman to her who was very ill. It looked like pneumonia. Yesterday afternoon she died.'

Durban was watching him closely now, but his face was still full of scepticism. He did not interrupt.

'When Hester came to wash her body for the undertaker . . .' Monk found his breath rasping in his throat. Please God Orme stayed out of earshot '. . . she found what she had really died of.' He swallowed hard and nearly choked. Would Durban realise the shattering enormity of what he said? Would he understand?

Durban was waiting, his brows puckered. He lifted a

hand in a gesture to stop Orme, who was halfway up the steps.

It was senseless to prevaricate. If Monk was not doing this the right way, it was too late to do it better now. 'Plague,' he whispered, even though the wind was carrying his words to Durban, not to Orme. 'I mean bubonic plague – the Black Death.'

Durban started to speak, and then changed his mind. He stood perfectly motionless, even through the wind, now cutting them both like ice on the skin. The air was still bright around them. The gulls circled above, the strings of barges moved slowly past on the tide going up to the Pool.

'Plague?' His voice was hoarse.

Monk nodded. 'The rat-catcher, Sutton, employed at the clinic told me last night, late. He came to my house, and he'll tell Margaret Ballinger, who works there, too, but no one else. If he did there'd be panic. People might even try to burn them out.'

Durban ran his hand over his face. Suddenly he was so pale his skin looked almost grey. 'We can't let them out.'

'I know,' Monk said softly. 'Sutton already has friends patrolling all the ways in or out with pit bulls. They'll take anyone down who tries to leave.'

Durban rubbed the heel of his hand over his face again. 'Oh God!' he whispered. 'Who . . .?'

'No one,' Monk replied. 'We've got to deal with it ourselves. Margaret Ballinger will do all she can outside – getting food, water, coal and medicine to them, leaving it somewhere they can pick it up after dark. At least at this time of year the nights are long, and Portpool Lane's well lit. Hester and the women already there will nurse the sick . . . as long as . . .' He could not bring himself to say the rest, even though the words beat in his head: as long as they live.

Durban did not say anything, but his eyes were filled

with a terrible, drowning pity.

Monk swallowed down the terror inside him, fear not of the disease, but of losing everything he loved. 'We have to find where it came from,' he went on, his voice almost steady now. 'We don't have plague in England. The *Maude Idris*, on which the ivory came in, has just returned from Africa. It is Louvain's ship. Louvain took Ruth Clark to the clinic.'

'Yes . . . I see,' Durban answered. 'She probably came off the ship. Maybe Hodge knew that, in which case his death could have more to do with plague than with theft. Either way, we have to know. God in heaven! Once plague gets hold it could sweep the country. The question is, who on the *Maude Idris* knows? And what about Louvain?'

'I don't know that,' Monk admitted. 'I . . . I promised Gould I'd do what I could to see he didn't hang if he was innocent of Hodge's death.'

'Hang?' Durban said with dawning disbelief. 'Great God, man! If what you say is true, the whole world could die in a far worse way than hanging – which is brutal, but it's quick. What's one man, compared with that?'

'We aren't going to let that happen,' Monk replied between his teeth, his voice uneven because his body was beginning to shake. 'Hester will stay locked in the clinic with them. No one will ever come out, except after it's all over, if there's anyone left alive. The world will go on exactly as if nothing had ever happened. And justice will still matter.'

The wash of a string of barges slapped against the stones. 'You and I will be the only ones concerned with Gould's life or death who will know anything about it,' Monk went on. 'Do we hang an innocent man? If we do that because we're frightened sick, then why not two, or ten, or a hundred? How many innocent men are worth trying to save?' He could hear the anger sharp in his words and he knew it was relief because this was something bearable to think about, something they could address. 'We have to know the truth anyway.'

Durban nodded very slowly, his face bleak. Then he walked to the top of the steps and spoke to Orme. Monk could not hear what he said, but he saw Orme acknowledge it, frowning in concern, then go back down towards the other men in the boat. Durban came back.

'Who did Louvain say the dead woman was?' he asked.

'The cast-off mistress of a friend,' Monk replied.

'Is it true?' Durban looked sideways at him.

'I've no idea. Might be, or she could have been his own mistress.'

'Do you think he knew what was wrong with her?'

'If she was the first one he'd seen, no. When Hester took her in, she thought it was pneumonia.'

'Pneumonia kills,' Durban pointed out.

'I know it does. It's still better than plague.'

'Don't keep saying that word,' Durban snapped. 'In fact don't ever say it again!'

Monk ignored the stricture. 'On the other hand, if someone had died of it on his ship, he may well have known,' he went on. 'But if it happened at sea, and the crew buried him over the side, he might, and he might not. Similarly if that's what Hodge died of.'

Durban stared at Monk. 'What are you saying? Hodge had it in the pneumonic stage, and someone killed him to stop him going ashore? Or that he died of it, and they couldn't dispose of the body at sea, because they were here on the river, and they bashed his head so no one would look too closely at the rest of the body?'

'Probably the second,' Monk replied. 'Louvain could be innocent or guilty of knowing what happened.'

'We have to find out whose mistress she was.' Durban's voice was urgent, edged with fear. 'Whoever he is, he could have it too. But worse than that, what about the rest of the crew?'

'Louvain told me that he paid off five, and there are three men left, now Hodge is dead. You'll have to have a boat of men to keep them there. Shoot them if you have to,' Monk answered. 'There's not much point in sending a doctor to them. There's no cure.'

'We can't let them unload, either,' Durban said thoughtfully. The muscles in his face tightened, his mouth pulling into a thin line. 'I hate lying to my men, but I can't tell them the truth.' There was a question in his eyes, no more than a flicker, as if he still hoped there was another answer and Monk would give it to him.

'Sutton told his men it was cholera,' Monk replied. 'Maybe that's what the crew think it is as well.'

Durban nodded slowly. 'Then we'd best be about it. We've no time to waste.' He started for the steps again and led the way down, Monk on his heels.

Orme was waiting. He regarded Monk with patent curiosity, but little liking. He did not know what to make of him, but he was suspicious.

Durban did not prevaricate. 'The *Maude Idris* has cholera,' he stated quietly, his voice without a tremor as if it were the exact truth he was telling them. 'We must stop them unloading, or anyone at all from coming ashore, until they're cleared of quarantine. Doesn't matter what you have to do; shoot them if it comes to that, but it shouldn't. It'll be easy enough to see they don't get a wharf. I'll do that. We're going there now, at once, to warn them. After that keep your distance – got that?'

'Yes, sir.' The crew spoke as one man.

'You'll get a relief – eight hours on, eight hours off. Don't let anything distract you. Keeping the disease in is the most important thing. If you doubt it, just think of your families,' Durban went on. 'Now let's get back upriver and do it.' He took his place in the boat and motioned Monk to follow him, and almost immediately the oarsmen bent their shoulders and dug the blades deep.

Durban did not speak again, but the other men had an obvious camaraderie, and jokes and good-natured insults were swapped all the way. But when the *Maude Idris* was in sight, suddenly their concentration was complete, as if they were already in the presence of illness.

They came alongside and Orme hailed her. Newbolt's shaven head appeared over the rail. 'River Police!' Orme called back, and the rope ladder came over a moment or two later. Durban glanced at Monk, then went up it hand over hand. Monk followed and heard Orme come up behind him.

Newbolt stood on the deck waiting for them. A heavy coat made him look even more massive, but he was bare-headed and had no gloves on.

'Wot d'yer want this time?' he said expressionlessly. He offered no excuse or explanation, and Monk's judgement of his intelligence was immediately revised – possibly of his knowledge as well. It was those who talked too much who gave themselves away.

Durban stood motionless on the deck, balancing to the ship's slight sway with an innate grace. 'How many are on board?' he asked.

'Three,' Newbolt replied. He seemed about to add something, then changed his mind. That was the moment Monk decided he knew the truth. He glanced at Durban to see if he had understood the same thing, but Durban had not moved his eyes from Newbolt.

'Three,' Durban repeated. 'That would have been four with Hodge?'

'Right.'

'What's your full crew?'

'Nine. Five men paid off downriver. Don't need nine ter watch 'er 'ere.' He did not refer to the fact that the ivory had still been stolen, or Hodge met his death, however that had happened, nor did he ask why Durban wanted to know. It was already a battle of wills, undeclared but intensely real.

'Who were the five paid off?' Durban asked.

'Captain, mate, cook an' cabin boy and one able seaman,' Newbolt answered without hesitation.

'Names?' Durban specified.

'Stope, Carter, Edwards, Jenner an' Briggs,' Newbolt said. He did not ask why Durban might want to know.

'Where'd they go ashore?'

'Gravesend.'

It was Durban who hesitated. 'Do you know their first names?'

'No.' Newbolt did not blink, nor did he turn as the lean man with the scar came up through the hatchway from below. 'There's me an' Atkinson an' McKeever 'ere.'

Durban reached a decision. 'We need to contact your captain.'

Newbolt shrugged.

Durban looked beyond him to Atkinson. 'Was Stope your captain?'

'Yeah,' Atkinson replied. ''E went ashore at Gravesend. Could be any place by now.'

'Did he ever say where he lived?'

'No,' Newbolt cut across. 'Captains don' talk ter the likes o' us; captains give orders.'

'And the other men?' Durban persisted.

'Dunno,' Newbolt replied. 'If they said, I don' 'member. Most likely got no special 'ome. At sea, most o' the time. Thought bein' River P'lice an' all, yer'd 'a' know'd that.'

'Captains have homes,' Durban replied. 'Sometimes wives and families. Where's McKeever?'

'Below,' Newbolt answered. ''E in't feelin' good. Mebbe we should 'a' let 'im go, an' kept the cook.' He grinned mirthlessly.

Durban's face lightened. 'I'll need to see him.' He looked at Atkinson. 'Take me below.'

Monk moved forward to stop him and Durban snapped at him to stay where he was. Atkinson glanced at Newbolt, then obeyed. Monk, Orme and Newbolt remained on deck. No one spoke.

Boats passed them, gulls circled overhead. They could hear the shouts of men working on the shore. The tide was receding, moving more and more rapidly past them, carrying flotsam and refuse out. The mudlarks were beginning to scavenge on the banks. Orme looked at Monk with suspicion, then away again.

Finally Durban came back up through the hatchway, Atkinson immediately behind him. He walked over to Monk with his slightly rolling gait, his face pale. 'Not much to see,' he said briefly. 'We could have a long search ahead of us still.' Then he turned to Newbolt. 'You'll be told when there's a berth for you. Stay on board till then.' He did not add any explanation, simply signalled to Orme, and went to the railing.

Monk followed. Nothing more was said between them until the boat put them ashore and Orme and his men returned to keep watch.

'If Louvain paid 'em off at Gravesend, they could be anywhere,' Durban said grimly. 'We've got a long job.'

'He can't have known what it was,' Monk said, keeping step with Durban as they walked towards the street. 'No sane man would let that loose, whatever the profit. If it spreads, there's nothing for anyone – no clippers, no cargoes, no trade, no life. Louvain's a hard man, but he's not mad.'

'He didn't know,' Durban agreed. 'Not at the time of paying 'em off, anyway. I agree, he's clever, brutal at times, but he respects the laws of the sea; he knows no man wins against nature. He wouldn't last long if he didn't, an' Louvain's done more than last; he's profited, built his own empire.' He came to the kerb, hesitated, and crossed, turning south again. 'He'd be perfectly happy to get rid of

234

a mistress if she no longer interested him, more likely than look after another man's cast-off woman. But I'd still wager he didn't know what she had, or he'd have done something different, maybe even kill her, an' bury her with quicklime.'

Monk shuddered at the thought, and believed it. 'We've got to find those men.'

'I know,' Durban agreed.

'Where would they go?'

Durban gave him a dry look. 'That was nearly a fortnight ago. Where would you be if you'd been at sea for a year?'

'Eat well, drink deep and find a woman,' Monk replied. 'Unless I had family, in which case I'd go home.'

Durban's face pinched tight. He nodded, something inside him too knotted with anger and grief to allow him to speak.

'How do we find out?' Monk went on. There was no time for feelings; they could come afterwards – if there was an afterwards.

'We'll get their names,' Durban replied. 'That'll be a start, at least. Then we look for them.' His face was almost expressionless, just a faint, almost bruised sadness about his mouth, as if he understood the darkness ahead.

Neither of them spoke again as they made their way along the narrow pavement past pawnbrokers, shipwrights, chandlers, rope- and sail-makers and ironmongers and smiths, representatives of all the heavy industry of the shore. They were forced to stop and wait while a man backed four magnificent shire horses out of a yard, with the dray turning a tight corner into the street, wheels bumping over the cobbles. He did it with intense concentration and care, all the while talking to his animals.

A cooper was complaining bitterly about a barrel not to his liking. Monk nursed his anger like a small ray of sanity, a glimpse of the world that seemed to be slipping out of his grasp no matter how hard he clung to it. He was on the edge of an abyss where plague destroyed everything; its spread or its containment was all he could think of. The cooper lived in a world where one badly made barrel mattered to him.

He glanced at Durban and saw a reflection of his own thoughts in his eyes. It was a moment of perfect understanding.

Then the cart was clear of the gateway and Durban strode forward, Monk on his heels.

It was tedious finding the information they needed without arousing suspicion or – worse than that – fear that the police were seeking someone in connection with a crime. A breath of that, and not only would the man disappear, but no one on the river would help them. All doors would be closed.

Durban was endlessly patient, sharing a fact here, a fact there, and it was dusk before they emerged from the last office with all the information they were likely to get: the names, physical descriptions and what was known of the background and tastes of the five men they sought.

They began at Gravesend and worked upriver from one public house to another, drinking half a pint of ale or eating a pie, trying to blend in with the other men, talking of ships, voyages they'd known or heard of, always listening for a name, watching for a man who answered any of the descriptions. All signs of Durban's police status had been removed. His hat was stuffed in his pocket, and his coat collar turned up and a little lop-sided. He looked like a ship's officer ashore a few months too long. They heard nothing of value. No one admitted to having seen any of the men from the *Maude Idris*.

The bright, hard light faded shortly after five, and the sun set in a sea of fire over the water, dazzling the eyes till it hurt to look westwards. Glittering shades of silver and gold edged the ruffles over the surface and marked the wakes of barges.

Monk and Durban stopped at another public house for something to eat, and were glad of the warmth. Outside the wind was rising. Neither of them said anything about the necessity to keep looking. Even the thought of home and sleep had to be pushed from the mind. Every hour counted and they had no lead yet.

They ate in silence, glancing at one another every now and then, mostly listening, watching, trying to catch the odd snatch of conversation that might refer to a sailor by name, or to someone home from Africa and looking for another ship. They had been there three-quarters of an hour and were getting ready to leave when Monk heard a man with a hacking cough, and realised that he had also been listening for word of anyone ill, or even a death.

'Where do sick men go?' he asked Durban abruptly, just as they rose to their feet.

Durban swung round to face him, his eyes wide. 'Sailors' homes, the lucky ones. Dosshouses the others – or worse than that, some pick a nethersken on the street.'

Monk did not need to ask what a nethersken was; he knew the cant names for all the different sorts of cheap lodgings – anything to be in out of the rain and share the warmth of other bodies. However dirty they were, or lice-ridden, their shelter might be the difference between survival and freezing to death.

He made no comment, and neither did Durban. For these few hours, or days, they were both policemen with a single task. Their understanding and their unity of purpose was a bond as deep as brotherhood.

They moved into the back streets of the docks, going from one house to another, always asking discreetly, following any word about a man who might be sick, or one who was free with his money. They did not mention names, they could not afford to alarm anyone. Lies came as easily and inventively as the need arose.

By one in the morning they were cold and exhausted, and had pursued half a dozen dead ends. Durban stood in an alley where the wind moaned up the narrow crack between the buildings, his face half illuminated by the one lamp on the outside wall of a dosshouse. His shoulders were hunched and he was shivering. He looked at Monk wordlessly.

'One more?' Monk suggested. 'Could be lucky? Someone must have seen them.'

Durban's eyes widened a little.

'Or we could sleep on it?' Monk smiled.

Durban's face eased, his eyes softer for a moment. 'Right.' He straightened up, stamping his feet to keep some kind of circulation going, and led the way.

The dosshouse-keeper began to refuse them. She was a thin, angular woman with a tired face, and grey hair that was straggling out of an irregular knot. Then she saw the money Monk offered, and changed her mind.

'Gotta share,' she warned. 'But there's clean straw on the floor, an' yer out o' the wind.' She took the few pence and put it away in a pocket well inside her voluminous skirts, then she led them to a small room at the back of the house. It was as primitive as she had said, and already occupied by two other men, but it was tolerably warm.

Monk found himself a place to lie down in the straw, bunching some of it together to form a pillow, and tried to sleep. He was tired enough, and his muscles ached from walking the endless alleys in the damp with the wind off the water cutting the flesh. But thoughts of his own bed and Hester beside him, not only the warmth of her body but the deeper warmth of her thoughts, her dreams, her whole being, made this sour room with its restless and hopeless men a unique kind of hell.

He drifted into sleep, but it did not last long. He was

too cold and the floor was too hard for him to relax. He could not bear to imagine where she was now, how much worse it was for her than for him, how much greater the danger. He lay in the dark listening to the rustle of straw, the heavy breathing of the men, and forced his mind to think.

He pieced together everything he knew and tried to make sense of it. Where would a sailor ashore go? He and Durban had already tried taverns, brothels and doss-houses along this stretch of the river. They had found a score of men more or less like the ones from the *Maude Idris*, but never the right ones. Was it a hopeless task, one only a desperate man, or a fool, would even try?

What were the alternatives? To alert the police forces everywhere, and hunt down the men as if they were murderers on the loose? Would that catch them? Or drive them so far underground they would never be found? And how many people would they infect in the meantime?

His thoughts drifted, and then suddenly he was awake again. He heard the scrape of rats' feet and felt his flesh cringe. Someone in the next room was coughing over and over again, a raw, hacking sound. They were looking for someone ill! That was how plague started, wasn't it, in the chest, with something like pneumonia? He was too cold to move, but he should go and see if that was one of the crew, or, worse than that, someone already infected by them.

He lay shivering, muscles locked, body curled up, until a long spasm of coughing next door made him force himself to roll over and stand up slowly. He picked his way through the forms of the sleeping men to the door, and went out into the narrow passage. It was faintly lit by one candle on a shelf, so anyone needing to relieve himself would not get lost, or fall over and waken everyone else.

He reached the door of the next room and turned the handle very slowly and pushed. It swung wide with a faint creak. It took him a moment to accustom his eyes to the deeper gloom, then he moved very quietly, stepping over and around the sleeping bodies until he came to the one turning restlessly, hunching his shoulders over, his breath laboured.

Monk bent over and touched him. The next instant the man lashed out, sending Monk flying backwards, landing hard and awkwardly on the sleeping man behind him, who let out a yell of fury. It turned into a mêlée of thrashing arms and legs, yells of 'Thief!' and general cries of outrage.

Monk tried to extricate himself, but he was one against half a dozen. He was generally getting the worst of it and failing to explain his motives when a candle appeared in the doorway and he saw Durban's face with an expression of exasperation and amusement. The next moment the candle was set on a chair and Durban ploughed into the battle with gusto. Yelling at everyone to 'Stop it!' he worked his way closer to where Monk was struggling to avoid being knocked senseless without actually doing the same to anyone else.

Finally Monk leaned against the wall, trying to catch his breath while the original man with the cough sat doubled over on the floor breathing with difficulty. Three other men glared at Durban, who was grinning hugely.

'I only wanted to know . . .' Monk gasped '. . . if any of you are off the *Maude Idris*.'

'Wot d'yer come creepin' in 'ere for like a bleedin' thief, then?' one of the men demanded.

'I wasn't going to waken everyone,' Monk said, he thought reasonably.

He was greeted by hoots and jeers.

'Well, have you?' he shouted.

'Never 'eard of it,' another replied.

''Course yer 'ave, yer fool,' the man next to him

retorted. 'One o' Clem Louvain's ships. Come back from Africa. In't put ashore yet.'

'Paid five men off at Gravesend,' Durban told him.

'In't seen none of 'em,' the man shook his head.

'Stope, Carter and Briggs, Edwards and Jenner,' Monk supplied.

'Stope? Know Cap'n Stope, but I in't seed 'im in more'n a year. Now can I go back ter sleep again, an' yer get the 'ell out of 'ere?'

Monk glanced at the rest of the men, but there was nothing in the faces of any of them to indicate guilt, recognition, or anything beyond weariness and wretchedness.

'Yes,' he said. 'Of course.' He followed Durban out, picking up the candle as he went. By some miracle it was still burning.

He put it back on the shelf in the passage as he passed it. He was beginning to be aware of several bruises, and the fact that he was no longer cold. Durban was laughing to himself. He glanced at Monk as they reached the door of the room they had come from and in the wavering light from the flame his eyes were bright. His expression was as eloquent as a score of words.

In the morning Monk woke stiff and his body ached in every muscle. No doubt if he looked he would have blackening bruises all over. He glanced across at Durban and saw him still smiling. He shrugged, and winced. The whole episode was absurd, and they had learned nothing, but he still felt a warmth inside him that he had not before.

Breakfast was porridge and bread. Only hunger could have driven him to eat it. But with daylight they saw their companions in the room more clearly. One was a heavy-set young man with a sullen face; the other was elderly, his skin pock-marked, one hand missing two fingers. He was a great talker and eager to tell anyone about his adventures. He had been round Cape Horn and dined out more than a few times on his memories of the storms off that notorious coast, the wild weather, waves like moving mountains, winds that tore the breath from a man's lungs, coasts like nightmares drawn from the landscapes of the moon. He had rounded Tierra del Fuego in the teeth of the gale, and that was where a loose halyard had shattered his arm. The ship's surgeon had cauterised the stump, sawing the bone with no more anaesthetic than half a bottle of rum and a leather gag to bite on.

Monk watched the man's face, and then Durban's as he listened. He saw many emotions: respect for courage; awe at the splendour and violence of the sea, and at the audacity of men who built boats of wood and set out to sail. It seemed an impossible hubris; although Durban would probably not be familiar with the word, he certainly understood the concept of mortals daring and defying the gods to snatch glory from the hands of heaven. He saw also a tenderness and willing patience, and he guessed some deep meaning lay behind them.

When they left and were back in the street again in a greyer and slightly milder morning, he asked the question that had taken shape in his mind.

'Was your father at sea?'

Durban looked at him with surprise, then something like pleasure. 'That clear, is it?'

Monk smiled back. 'Just a guess.'

Durban kept his eyes ahead now, avoiding Monk's gaze, which had proved too keen. 'Lost in the Irish Sea in 'thirty-five. I can still remember the day they brought us the news.' His voice was quiet, but there was a gentleness and a pain in it he could not disguise. 'I suppose families of seamen always half expect it, but when you grow used to the fear without the reality, it takes you longer to believe that this time it isn't going to be just a scare. It's here to stay, day in, day out.' He jammed his hands further into his pockets and walked in silence. He

242

expected Monk to understand without words and details.

They went to more dosshouses, more street-corner pedlars, more brothels, taverns and pawnbrokers. No one could help. One even knew the family of the cabin boy, and for an hour and a half hope boiled up that they had achieved one breakthrough at last.

But he was not there, nor had his father heard of him since his ship left for Africa nearly eight months ago. They were confused and then worried when Durban said that the *Maude Idris* had docked and paid off.

'Don' worry yerself, Ma,' his elder brother said gently. ''E's a growed lad. 'E'll be 'avin' 'isself a good time. 'E'll come 'ome when 'e's ready. 'E'll 'ave suffink special for yer from Africa, I'll be bound.'

They left sombrely, with a growing weight of urgency and sadness on them, and moved on southwards along the river.

'Trafalgar,' Durban said with a ham sandwich and a pint of ale in his hands. 'My grandfather fought there. Not on the *Victory*, but he remembers Nelson.' He smiled a little self-consciously. 'I wanted to go to sea when I was a boy.'

Monk waited. It would be indelicate to ask why he had not. The reason might hold any kind of pain. He would speak of it if he wanted to.

They were back at the water's edge again. The sharp light of yesterday was veiled in grey, the distances smudged as drifts of rain hid one part of the skyline, and then another. It was not as cold, but the damp ate into the flesh.

'Then my brothers died of scarlet fever,' Durban said simply. 'So I stayed at home.' He straightened up and walked back towards the street and the next place to ask.

Monk followed. He said nothing. Durban did not want sympathy, or even comment, he was simply revealing something of himself. It was an act of trust.

They worked the rest of the day, occasionally separately, mostly together, because this was not an area where a man should have no one guarding his back. Once they did get involved in one other brief fight, and Monk was startled how hard he struck, how instinctively he looked for the crippling blow.

Afterwards he and Durban leaned against the alley wall, breathing hard and, for no reason whatever, laughing. Possibly it was at their handling of the other absurd fight in the dosshouse. Monk was further bruised, and his cheek was cut, but, extraordinarily, the exertion, even the physical pain, had invigorated him. He looked across at Durban and saw exactly the same thing mirrored in his eyes.

Durban straightened up and pulled his coat neat. He pushed his fingers through his dishevelled hair. 'Next one?' he asked.

'I haven't got a better idea,' Monk replied. 'Do you think it means we're getting closer?'

'No,' Durban said honestly. 'They seem to have vanished.' He did not elaborate his fears that they had taken other ships out straight away, or that they were already dead.

The same thoughts raced through Monk's mind. 'We haven't checked the deaths,' he said aloud.

'I did,' Durban answered. 'When you were talking to the brothel-keeper up in Thames Street. The police have identified everyone who might have been ours.'

'How can you know?' Monk challenged.

'Because they know the ones they have,' Durban said simply. 'Doesn't mean they aren't dead, though, just not found an' not buried.' He looked at Monk and his face was rueful. 'C'mon, let's try the next one.'

244

Chapter Ten

❧

On the day when Monk was visited by Sutton, Margaret was in her bedroom preparing to return to the clinic. She meant to give Hester at least one night's uninterrupted sleep. She was sitting at her dressing table when her mother knocked very briefly and, without waiting, came in.

'Margaret, my dear,' she said, closing the door behind her, 'you must not give up hope, you know. You have a difficult nature, and you certainly have an unfortunate tongue, but you are not unpleasing to look at, and at the moment your reputation is unmarked.' Her tone altered very slightly. 'You are from an acceptable family whose reputation is unblemished. Just a little care, a great deal more discretion about your opinion, a degree of becoming meekness, and you could be very happy. Your intelligence does not need to be your undoing, although I admit I am worried. You seem to have unusually little sense as to when you should display it, and concerning what.'

Margaret would like to have pretended that she had no idea what her mother was talking about, but, since it seemed Lady Hordern had carried out her threat, she could not hope to be believed. She could not think of any answer that her mother would like, so she said nothing, just continued to pin up her hair, a trifle crookedly and too tightly at the back. She could feel the pins digging into her head. She would end up having to take them out again, which was a waste of time.

Her mother's voice became sharper. 'I assume from the fact that you are wearing that shabby blue dress again that you are thinking of going to that miserable institution in the slums. Good works are very worthy, Margaret, but they are no substitute for a social life. I would a great deal rather that you did something connected with the Church. They have lots of suitable endeavours where you could work with people – well-bred people whose background and interests are like your own.'

We are not discussing it, Margaret thought. You are telling me your views, as usual. But she did not say so. 'We may have background in common, Mama, but no interests. And I am more concerned with where I am going than where I have come from.'

'So am I,' Mrs Ballinger said tartly, meeting her eyes in the mirror. 'And where are you going, young lady, is on to the shelf, if you do not look to your behaviour, and bring Sir Oliver to the question very soon. He is eminently suitable – you will not do better – and obviously very taken with you, but it is fast becoming time he declared his intentions and spoke to your father. All it requires is for you to spend less time at that wretched clinic, and pay more attention to him. Now, take off that unbecoming dress, put on something of a nice colour and a proper cut for this season – your father provides you with sufficient means – and go to some social event where you may be seen.' She drew in her breath. 'Nothing concentrates a man's mind so much as the realisation that he is not the only one to appreciate your qualities.'

Margaret turned round, stung to an anger almost beyond her ability to bite her words back. 'Mama—'

'Oh! And there is a most reprehensible-looking person

246

to see you,' Mrs Ballinger went on. 'I have had him wait in Mrs Timpson's sitting room.' She was referring to the housekeeper. 'Please ask him not to call again. I would not have permitted him to remain this time, but he insisted he had some kind of message for you from Mrs Monk. I think you should restrict your association with that woman. She is not entirely respectable. Your father agrees with me. Mr . . . whatever his name is . . . is waiting for you. Don't detain him. I am sure he has drains to clean, or something.'

Margaret was too aware of acute unease to take the time to respond to that last remark. Why would Hester send anyone with a message, unless there were something seriously wrong?

'Thank you,' she said curtly, and went out almost at a run, leaving her mother standing in the middle of the bedroom.

Margaret went through the upstairs door to the servants' quarters and down the staircase to the housekeeper's sitting room. She expected to see Squeaky Robinson there, and was startled when the man standing on the mat in front of the fire was not he. And yet it was someone she had seen before, she simply could not remember when. He was lean, with squarish shoulders and a very weary face, which at this moment looked marked by a deep and irrevocable sadness.

'Evenin', miss,' he said as she closed the door behind her. 'I got a message as I gotter tell yer, an' it's fer you an' nobd'y else, no matter wot. I admit as I'd 'a told yer just wot I 'as ter, but Miss 'Ester said as I gotter tell yer the 'ole truth, an' swear yer in Gawd's name as yer'll tell no one else.'

Margaret felt a flicker of fear tighten in her throat. 'What is it?' Now she remembered who he was: Sutton, the rat-catcher. 'What's happened? Is Hester all right?'

'In a manner o' speakin', yes, she is,' he answered. 'But

in another manner, nobody in't all right. I gotter tell yer, miss, an' yer gotter tell no one else, or yer could kill 'em all.' His eyes were intent on hers, and there was a fear in him which now gripped her also, so hard she could scarcely draw in her breath.

'What is it? I swear – I swear anything you like, just tell me!'

'Ruth Clark died, miss, but it weren't pneumonia like yer all thought, it were the plague.'

'The plague?' Margaret said incredulously. 'You mean like London in sixteen sixty-five, before the Great Fire?'

'No, miss, I mean like in thirteen forty-eight, the Black Death wot killed near 'alf o' the world.'

She thought for a hysterical instant that he was making some stupid joke, then she saw the truth in his eyes, and knew that he meant it. The room swam around her. Before she realised it the chair caught her awkwardly as she fell into it and gripped the arms to keep herself from fainting completely.

'I'm sorry, miss,' Sutton apologised. 'I only told yer 'cos I 'ave ter. Yer can't go back there, an' Miss 'Ester can't come out.'

Margaret lifted up her head and the room steadied. 'Don't be absurd, I've got to go back in. I can't leave Hester to cope with that on her own.'

'There in't no copin', miss,' he said very quietly. 'In't much we can do 'ceptin' see as they 'as food an' water, coal, potash, an' a spot o' brandy. An' then nobody else goes in nor guesses why. That's about the biggest thing, 'cos if they does, sure as night and day someone'll stir 'em up ter go an' mob the place, and set light ter it. Fire's about the only thing ter make sure o' the plague, an' they knows that. Was the Great Fire o' London as killed the pneumonic in sixteen sixty-six, but yer can't set fire ter the 'ole o' England.'

She stared at him, wanting to disbelieve, trying to – and failing.

'Yer more use to 'er outside,' he said with sudden gentleness. 'She's gonna need all the 'elp out 'ere as she can find. And there in't nob'dy but you. Mr Monk's got all 'is work cut out ter find where the plague come from in the first place.'

'Louvain,' she said quickly. 'Clement Louvain brought her in.'

'Yeah, 'e knows. But 'e's gotter do all 'e can ter find it an' stop the others wot got it. I'm goin' back in ter 'elp wi' things inside.'

'You aren't a nurse!' she protested.

His face tightened. 'In't much I can do fer that, but there'll be bodies ter get out an' find burial fer, wi'out nobody seein' wot they died of. An' we gotter keep 'em wot's there from leavin' . . .'

'How can you do that, if they insist? You can't keep them at gunpoint.'

'No, miss, men wi' dogs is much better. Sleep wi' one eye open, them dogs, 'ear a footstep softer'n a snowflake landin'. Give 'em the word an' they'll tear yer ter bits. Rip yer throat out, them pit bulls will, if they 'ave ter.'

'Who? What men?'

'Friends o' mine,' he said more gently. 'They won't 'urt nobody if they don't 'ave ter. But we can't let 'em out.'

'I know . . . I know. But if they say even—'

'They dunno it's plague. They think it's cholera.'

She leaned forward and put her head in her hands. This disaster was too big, too hideous. She had read about the great plague in school, but it had been something unreal, just a date to memorise, like 1066 and the Battle of Hastings, or 1815 and Waterloo. It shaped who we are, but it had no reality today.

Now, suddenly, it had. She must have courage. She must be as brave as Hester was, and she must do it without leaning on anyone else, not even Rathbone. She lifted her head and looked at Sutton. 'Of course. I shall start raising more money immediately – tonight. Tell Hester I shall do everything I can. Will you be back?'

'No,' he said simply. 'When yer get money, buy wot yer reckon we'll need, an' bring it ter the back. Tell the men 'oo yer are, an' they'll take it ter the back door an' leave it. If there's any message left for yer, they'll bring it back, so wait for 'em.'

'I understand. Thank you, Mr Sutton.' She stood up, surprised to find her head clear.

There was admiration in his eyes. 'Yer welcome, miss.'

'Would you like a cup of tea before you leave? And something to eat?' she offered.

'Yeah, but it in't fittin', an' I in't got time. But it was a right gracious thing ter ask. Good night, miss.' And he went to the door and out of it with weary, silent tread, and a moment later he was gone.

Margaret went back upstairs slowly, holding on to the banister to keep her balance, and stopping on the landing as if she were out of breath. She was barely aware of her hands and feet, and the familiar space with its Chinese screen and jardinière with flowers seemed blurred and far away. Plague! One word with so vast a meaning the whole world was changed. Was it really the right thing to stay outside, as Sutton had told her, or should she be there to do the real work, above all to support Hester so she did not face that horror alone?

No. There was no time for personal need or indulgence. They were troops facing an enemy without feeling or discrimination, one that could kill every human being in Europe – or anywhere, for that matter. The wants or hungers, the pain of one individual, could not matter. She must stay outside and raise money, take them supplies, keep them from being cut off from all help. And she should start now. It would be even harder than before because she must watch her tongue all the time. She could not even tell Rathbone the truth, and that silence would cost her dear, but she knew why Sutton had asked it.

She straightened her shoulders and went back to her own room. Her sister had invited her to go to a betrothal party this evening. The motive behind it was the same one as always: everybody's minds would be on marriage, an odd, twisting irony that if Rathbone did not love her enough to propose to her, accepting her dedication to the clinic as well, then she would remain single and make her own way in the best manner she could. She would not give up other friendships or freedom of conscience in order to have social status or financial security.

And she would swallow humble pie this evening, and ask to change her mind about the invitation. She went downstairs at a run to request her mother to send the footman, posthaste, with a message to beg Marielle to wait for her. She would be there as soon as she could dress appropriately and have the carriage convey her.

Her mother was too delighted with victory to question it, and obliged with alacrity.

Margaret had dressed with more flair and high fashion than she normally wished to; it was not really to her taste. This gown in warm pinks with a touch of plum was her mother's choice, and it was more dramatic than she cared to be, but it would draw attention to her, and tonight that was what she needed. She acknowledged Marielle's rather fulsome compliments as graciously as she could, and entered the party with her head high and her teeth gritted.

She was immediately welcomed by her hostess, a large lady full of bustling good will. She had a charming smile and a gown up to the minute in fashion.

'How delightful to see you, Miss Ballinger,' she said, after having welcomed Marielle and her husband. 'It has been far too long.' Her wide eyes and the lift of curiosity

251

in her voice made it a question. Some explanation of Margaret's absence was required.

'Yes, it has,' Margaret agreed, forcing herself to smile. 'I'm afraid I have been involved with work for a charity which has consumed my interest so much I have lost track of time.'

'Oh, good works are most admirable, I'm sure,' her hostess said quickly. 'But you must not rob us of your company altogether. And, of course, your own welfare must also be considered.'

Margaret knew exactly what she meant. It was a young woman's duty to find a husband for herself, and not remain dependent upon her parents. 'I am sure you are right,' she replied, trying to look sweet and agreeable, and finding it required more of an effort than she had anticipated. 'And this is such a happy occasion, we shall all feel uplifted by it.'

'Oh, yes!' And her hostess proceeded to sing the praises of her future son-in-law without wishing for any response except perhaps a little envy.

As soon as she had exhibited all the wished-for signs, Margaret excused herself and, with Marielle, moved to the next compatible group of people. Marielle introduced her, with the greatest of ease allowing them to understand that she was unmarried.

Margaret cringed inside but, knowing she needed Marielle's help, she bore it with grace, but great difficulty. Once or twice the ordeal of the party threatened to become unendurable as her mind was filled with the picture of Hester with her sleeves rolled up, her hair falling out of its pins. She could see her face exhausted with days and nights of snatched sleep, unable either to save the sick or to run away from the horror and the death, even had she wanted to. She was trapped, perhaps until she too succumbed to the most terrible of diseases. She might never leave that place, never see Monk again, or anyone whom she loved. What on earth was a little embarrassment to put up with?

'I am sure we have not met before, Miss Ballinger,' the young man was saying to her. He had been introduced as the Honourable Barker Soames. He had floppy brown hair and a mildly superior air of good humour. His tone invited explanation as to why not. His friend Sir Robert Stark was paying only half attention; the rest was on a young lady with auburn hair who was pretending not to look at him while adjusting her fan.

Margaret forced herself to take notice. She wanted to dismiss him with a cool remark, but her purpose overrode everything else, and she bit her tongue. 'We have not,' she replied with a charming smile. 'I should have recalled it. I am always aware of those I have spoken to on serious matters, and I cannot imagine you are interested in trivia.'

He was startled. It was certainly not the answer he had expected, and it took him several seconds to adjust his thoughts. 'Why no, of course not. I . . . I am concerned in all manner of . . . of subjects of gravity.' Gravity was the greatest of virtues, and he was as aware of it as she. The very mention of it conjured up a picture of the late and still deeply mourned Prince Albert.

'To be of worth, it is absolutely necessary, don't you agree?' she pursued. Then before he could answer and divert the course of the conversation to something easier, she hurried on, 'I have been much involved in raising money to fund medicine for the poor and otherwise disadvantaged. We are so incredibly fortunate! We have homes, food, warmth, and we have the means to keep ourselves from falling into the spiral of despair.'

He frowned, unprepared for the degree of gravity she was touching. He had intended theory; she was speaking of reality. It made him uncomfortable.

She saw his discomfort in his shift of position, the way his weight moved backwards a little. She could not afford to be sensitive either for him or for herself. She gazed very briefly around the room with its bright, chattering company, plump arms of the women, pink cheeks, freshly barbered faces of the men. Then for an instant she saw it in her mind as it would be if they failed: the wasted flesh, the fever, the despair, the sick no one dared go near to nurse, the dead no one buried. In weeks these people could be so many corpses, their laughter silent.

She forced the image away.

'I admire generosity enormously,' she went on. 'Don't you? I see it as a great part of Christian duty.' Now was no time to be squeamish about coercion. She added the final twist. 'Of course, within the bounds of what we can afford. The last thing I should wish is for anyone to feel they have to give what is beyond their means. That would be quite cruel. Debt must be such a misery.'

The Honourable Barker Soames looked urgently at his friend, hoping for rescue. However, Sir Robert was now giving Margaret his full attention, and tasting a certain enjoyment in the situation.

'For the sick, you say, Miss Ballinger? What particular charity would that be? One of the African ones, I dare say?' he asked.

'No, it is one here at home,' Margaret answered, now far more careful. She was perfectly happy to bend the truth a little – the need was desperate – but she did not wish to be caught out. 'For young women and children in the Farringdon Road area. It is a clinic that treats injuries, and at the moment is trying to give food and shelter to many struck down with pneumonia. It is most kind of you to care sufficiently to take an interest.' She put a warmth into her voice as if he had already offered a gift.

He hesitated.

Sir Robert smiled. 'Where may we donate, Miss Ballinger? Would you be able to see that it reached the right people if we gave something to you?'

'Thank you, Sir Robert,' she said with a relief and a gratitude so deep it lit her face. For a moment she was truly beautiful. 'I shall buy the food and coal myself, but of course I am more than happy to send you receipts, so you know what we have done.'

'Then please accept five pounds,' he replied. 'And I'm sure Soames can at least match that, can't you?' He turned to Soames, who was looking distinctly cornered.

Margaret did not care in the slightest. 'That is very kind of you,' she said quickly. 'It will do a great deal of good.'

With intense reluctance Soames obeyed. In a wave of triumph Margaret moved on. The next encounter did not go as fortunately, but by the end of the evening she had elicited promises of a reasonably large sum.

The following morning she took the money she had gained, went to the coal merchant, and bought an entire wagonload. She went with the delivery man to Portpool Lane, instructing him as he tipped it all down the chute from the street into the cellar.

She stood in the sharp wind, flat, grey clouds scudding across the sky, and stared at the walls of the house. It was damp and bitterly cold, and the air smelled of soot and the sour odour of drains, but it was not infected. She breathed it in with a sense of guilt. Hester was only a few yards away behind the blank bricks, but it could have been another world. She looked up at the windows, trying to catch a glimpse of anyone, but there was only blurred movement, no more than light and shadow.

The wind stung her cheeks. She wanted to shout, just to let someone know how much she cared, but it would be worse than pointless; it could be dangerous. Slowly she turned away and walked back towards the coalmen. 'Thank you,' she said simply. 'I'll let you know when they need more.'

Next she purchased oatmeal, salt, two jars of honey, a

sack of potatoes and several strings of onions, and carried them back to give them to one of the men standing discreetly under the eaves in the yard at Portpool Lane. She also went to the butcher and bought as many large bones as he had, and carried them back. Again she gave them to one of the men with the dogs, broad-chested, wide-jawed creatures with sturdy legs and unblinking eyes.

In the evening she accepted, at ungraciously short notice, an invitation to a recital. She accompanied a young woman who was more of an acquaintance than a friend, along with her parents and brother. It was an awkward party, but she was only too aware that last night's success might not be repeated for many days, and while ten pounds was a great deal of money, it had already been used.

The music was not the kind she particularly cared for, and her mind was solely on gaining more support, possibly even recruiting someone else to help in the effort. She found herself in a series of brief and unsatisfactory conversations and was losing heart for the evening when during the second interval she saw Oliver Rathbone. He was standing at the edge of a group of people in earnest discussion, and apparently in the company of a gentleman of portly dimensions with fluffy grey hair, but he was looking at Margaret.

She felt a surge of pleasure just seeing his face and knowing that he was as aware of her as she was of him. Suddenly the lights seemed brighter, the room warmer, and she looked away, smiling to herself, and quite deliberately set about working her way closer to where he was.

It was another ten minutes before he managed to introduce her to his guest, a Mr Huntley, who was both a client and a social acquaintance. It was several moments further before Mr Huntley could be directed to converse with someone else, and Margaret found herself alone with Rathbone.

He regarded her gown, which was again in a more eye-catching colour than was her natural choice, and cut with ostentatious flattery. She saw in his face that he was uncertain whether he cared for it. It was uncharacteristic of her, and the change disconcerted him.

'You look very well,' he observed, watching her eyes for the meaning behind whatever words she used to respond.

She longed to be able to tell him the thoughts and the fears that drove her, but she had promised Sutton not to. Rathbone, of all people, would care about Hester. It was a sort of lying not to tell him, but she was bound.

'I am well,' she replied, meeting his gaze, but without inner honesty. She had to go on. It was not possible to tell how long they would have in which to talk. The music would begin again soon, Huntley might return, or any of a dozen other people interrupt them. 'But I am very exercised trying to raise sufficient money for the clinic.'

He frowned very slightly. 'Does it really need so . . . so much of your time?' He said the word 'time', but she knew he was thinking of the change in her, the single-mindedness that absorbed her now so that she wore clothes to please society and to be noticed. She was here at a function she did not care for, and he knew she did not. The familiar in her was slipping away from him, and he was unhappy. She ached to be able to tell him why it mattered more than anything else, or anyone's personal happiness.

'Just at the moment, it does,' she answered.

'Why? What is different from a few days ago?' he asked.

How could she answer? She had expected the question, but she was still unprepared. Whatever she said, it could only be a lie. Even if she explained to him afterwards, would he understand, or would he feel that she ought to have trusted him? He had been part of

257

everything to do with the clinic, even turning the tables on Squeaky Robinson in order to get the building. Rathbone was proud of the clinic and what it did. He had earned the right to be trusted. But she had promised the rat-catcher, so in effect she had promised Hester.

He was waiting, the unease in him growing.

'We are just short of money,' she answered. 'There are big bills and we have to pay.' It was an evasion. She saw instantly that he knew it. She was not good at lying and she had never done it before to him. Her total candour was one of the qualities he loved in her most, and she knew it more sharply just as she felt him slip from her. He was hurt. Would she lose him over this?

She turned away, her throat tight and tears prickling her eyes. This was ridiculous. There was no time for such personal self-pity.

Rathbone started to say something, and then changed his mind also.

She looked back at him, waiting.

There was a sudden hush in the room.

Huntley came back. 'I say, Sir Oliver, they're about to start again. Do you think we might excuse ourselves before it— Oh. I'm so sorry, Miss – er – I don't mean to . . .' He trailed off, not knowing how to extricate himself.

Margaret could at least help him. 'Not at all,' she said. She wanted to smile at him, but her throat was too tight. 'It's a bit tedious, isn't it? I really think the flute by itself has limited appeal.'

His face flooded with relief. He was completely unaware of any other tension. 'Thank you so much. You are most understanding.' He turned to Rathbone.

Rathbone hesitated.

'Please,' Margaret gestured towards the exit so obviously in Huntley's thoughts. 'I must return to my hostess, or she will begin to realise my lack of enthusiasm.'

Rathbone had no choice but to go with Huntley, leaving Margaret hurting as if she had been physically burned.

Rathbone spent a miserable evening and went home as soon as he could excuse himself. Something had changed in Margaret and it disturbed him profoundly. He woke up several times during the night, puzzled and increasingly unhappy. Had he been mistaken in her all the time? Was she not the startlingly honest person he had thought her? Certainly the clinic would have bills, but suddenly so many, and so large?

Even if that were true, it was not at the core of her behaviour. She was lying. He did not know why, or exactly about what, but the honesty between them was compromised. Her manner of dress was different, bolder, more like everyone else's, as if she cared what Society thought of her and, without any explanation, she needed to conform.

For that matter, why had she gone to the recital at all? She disliked that type of function as much as he did. He was there only because Huntley had invited him and it was politic that he accept.

The morning was little better, and brought no ease to his mind. He went to his chambers as usual, and put aside personal matters with the discipline of concentration he had developed over the years. But all the strength of will at his disposal, intense as it was, could not rid him of his sense of confusion, and even of loss.

It was quite late in the afternoon, with the light already fading as rain set in, when his clerk came to inform him that Mr William Monk had called to see him. It was on a matter he regarded as so urgent that he refused to be put off by the fact that Sir Oliver had other commitments for the rest of the day. He simply would not leave; in fact, he would not even be seated.

Rathbone glanced at his watch. 'You had better ask Mr Styles to wait a moment or two. Apologise to him and say that an emergency has arisen, and send Monk in. Warn him that I have only ten minutes, at the most.'

'Yes, Sir Oliver,' the clerk said obediently, his lips pursed. He did not approve of alteration to arrangements, particularly those made with clients who paid, which he knew that Monk did not. But he also loved order, and obedience was the first rule of his life, so he did as he was told.

The moment Monk came in Rathbone knew that whatever had brought him was extremely serious. He was barely recognisable. His usual elegance had vanished; he looked more like a man of substance fallen on hard times, perhaps sunk to the edges of the criminal world. His trousers were shapeless, his boots built for endurance rather than grace, his jacket such as a labourer might wear, and was definitely soiled, and with a tear in the sleeve.

But all that Rathbone noticed at a glance. It was Monk's face that shocked him and held his attention. His skin had no colour at all beneath the dark stubble of his beard, and his eyes were hollow, shadows around them almost like bruises.

Monk closed the door behind himself, having already sent the clerk away. 'Thank you,' he said simply.

Rathbone felt a flicker of alarm. Surely if something had happened to Hester, Margaret would have told him? He had seen her only yesterday evening, and she had said nothing.

'What is it?' he asked a little abruptly.

Monk took a deep breath. As if he would find the slightest bodily comfort impossible, he did not sit down. 'I have taken a job on the river,' he began, speaking swiftly, as if the whole outline of what he was going to say had been rehearsed. 'On the twenty-first of October, to be precise. It was to find some ivory that had been stolen from the *Maude Idris* while she was moored on the river waiting for a wharf at which to unload.'

Rathbone was puzzled; it was not Monk's usual type of work. It must be either a favour he owed or, more likely, financial pressure that had driven him to accept it.

'Why weren't the River Police involved?' he asked. 'They're good, and as long as you stay clear of the revenue men, for the most part they're honest. You get the odd bad one, but they're few and far between.'

A shadow crossed Monk's eyes. 'The issue that matters is that when the theft was discovered, so was the body of the night watchman from the crew, with his head beaten in.'

'Just a minute,' Rathbone interrupted. He could feel the tension in Monk so powerful it was like a live thing in the air, but looking for stolen goods, rather than reporting and pursuing murder, was so unlike Monk he needed to be certain he had grasped the facts truly. 'Are you saying the man was killed by the thieves, or not? Was the shipowner trying to conceal it? Who is he, anyway?'

'I'm telling you the facts,' Monk snapped back. 'Just listen.' His voice all but choked on the emotion within him. A flicker of self-consciousness appeared and vanished. He did not apologise, but it was implicit. 'Clement Louvain. He showed me the body of the man, named Hodge. His skull was stove in at the back. I saw the ledge inside the hold where he was found, and there was very little blood. I wasn't certain if that was because he had actually been killed on deck, and then carried down there, but I couldn't find any blood on deck, either. I was told he had a woollen hat on, and that might have absorbed a lot of it.' Monk took a deep breath. 'Hodge was buried, even though he may have been murdered, but the morgue attendant and the shipowner made written records of his injuries. Louvain needed to get his money first, before I could look into Hodge's death, or he could lose everything.'

Rathbone found that impossible to believe. 'Why—' he started.

Monk interrupted his question. 'If his rival buys the clipper coming up for sale, he will be first home in every voyage. First home gets the prize, second gets the leavings, if any.'

'I see.' Rathbone was beginning to understand more. 'Now he has no interest in Hodge's death, and you want me to pursue it in law?'

The ghost of a smile crossed Monk's face, but so grim it was worse than nothing at all. 'No. Gould, a boatman, is in custody. He took me to the ivory, and he admits he was the only one to go on board and below deck. The other man stayed above and couldn't have killed Hodge, didn't even know he was there. But Gould swears he found Hodge already dead, but without obvious injury. He thought at first he was just dead drunk. I believe him. And I promised I would get him the best defence I could.'

Rathbone was now deeply troubled. Monk was the least gullible of men, and this story was absurd, on the face of it. There had to be something else of crucial importance that Monk was not telling him. Why not? Rathbone leaned back against his desk. It was uncomfortable, but while Monk was standing he did not feel able to sit. 'Why do you believe him?' he asked.

Monk hesitated.

'I can't help you if I don't know the truth!' Rathbone said with an edge that surprised himself. Something of the darkness inside Monk was disturbing him, although he had heard nothing yet except the story of a very ordinary robbery, and a murder concealed. That was it – why would Monk, of all men, hide a murder in this way? 'The rest of it!' he demanded, leaning forward over the desk. 'For heaven's sake, Monk, haven't you learned to trust me yet?'

Monk flinched. 'You don't know what you're asking.' Now his voice was low. His eyes were hollow, only horror left.

Rathbone was truly afraid. 'I'm asking for the truth.' He felt his throat so tight the words were forced out. 'Why do you think this man is innocent? Nothing you've said so far makes sense of it. If he didn't kill Hodge, who did and why? Are you saying it was one of the crew, or the shipowner himself?' He jerked his hands, slicing the air. 'Why would he? Why would a shipowner give a damn about one of his crewmen? What is it? Blackmail, mutiny, something personal? What would a shipowner have personal with a seaman? I'm no use to you half blind, Monk.'

Monk stood perfectly still, a momentous struggle raging inside him so clearly that Rathbone could only stand and watch, helpless and with a cold hand tightening inside him.

The clerk knocked on the door.

'Not yet,' Rathbone said tensely.

Monk focused his eyes; his face was even whiter than before. 'You must listen . . .' he said hoarsely, his voice a whisper.

Rathbone felt cold. He brushed past Monk to the door, opened it and called for the clerk. The man appeared almost instantly.

'Cancel all my appointments for the rest of the day,' Rathbone told him. 'An emergency has arisen. Apologise and tell them I will see them at their earliest convenience.' He saw the man's face crease in bewilderment and dismay. 'Do it, Coleridge,' he ordered. 'Tell them I am very sorry, but the circumstances are beyond my control. And do not interrupt me or come to the door for any reason until I send for you.'

'Are you all right, Sir Oliver?' Coleridge asked with deep concern.

'Yes, I am. Just deliver my message, thank you.' And without waiting he went back into his office and closed the door. 'Now,' he said to Monk, 'tell me the truth.'

Monk seemed to have ceased struggling with his decision. He was even sitting down, as if exhaustion had finally taken him over. He looked so ashen Rathbone was afraid he was ill. 'Brandy?' Rathbone offered.

'Not yet,' Monk declined.

This time it was Rathbone who could not sit down.

Monk began, looking not at Rathbone but somewhere in the distance. 'Shortly after engaging me, Louvain took a woman to the clinic in Portpool Lane. I don't know whether he learned of Hester because of her connection to me, or if he knew of the clinic before and possibly that was why he hired me rather than someone else. Don't interrupt me! He said the woman was the cast-off mistress of a friend, which may or may not be true.' He ran his hand over his face. 'Two days ago, in the evening, a rat-catcher called Sutton came to me at home with a message from Hester.' At last he looked up at Rathbone and the pain in his eyes was frightening. 'The woman, Ruth Clark, had died, and in dressing her for the undertaker, Hester discovered buboes in her armpits and groin.'

Rathbone had no idea what he was talking about. 'Buboes?' he said.

'Black swellings,' Monk answered, his voice cracking. 'They're called buboes – that's where we get the word "bubonic".' He stopped abruptly.

The silence was as dense as fog while very slowly the meaning of what he had said sank into Rathbone and filled him with indescribable horror.

Monk was staring at him.

'Bubonic?' Rathbone whispered. 'You don't . . . mean . . .' He could not say it.

Monk nodded almost imperceptibly.

'But . . . but that's . . . medieval . . . it's . . .' Rathbone stopped again, refusing to believe it. He could not get his breath; his heart was hammering and the room was swaying around him, the edges of his vision blurred. He reached out his hands to grasp the desk as he over-balanced sideways and sat down hard and awkwardly, oblivious of bruising himself. 'You can't have that . . . now. This is eighteen sixty-three. What do we do? How do they treat it? Who do we tell?'

'No one!' Monk said violently. He was between Rathbone and the door, and he looked as if he would physically prevent him from leaving, with force if necessary. 'For God's sake, Rathbone, Hester's in there. If anyone got even an idea of the disease they'd mob the place and set fire to it. They'd all be burned alive.'

'But we have to tell someone,' Rathbone protested. 'The authorities. Doctors. We can't treat it if no one knows.'

Monk leaned forward, his voice shaking. 'There is no treatment. Either they survive it, or they don't. All we can do is raise money to buy food, coal, medicines for them. We have to contain it, at any cost at all. If we don't, if even one person gets out carrying it, it will spread throughout London, throughout England, then the world. In the Middle Ages, before the British Empire or the opening up of America, it killed twenty-five million people in Europe alone. Imagine what it would do now! Do you see why we must tell no one?'

It was impossible, too hideous for the mind to grasp.

'No one,' Monk repeated. 'They have men with pit bulls patrolling day and night, and anyone attempting to leave will be torn to pieces. Now do you see why I have to find out if the disease came in on the *Maude Idris*, and if Hodge died of the plague, and his head was beaten in so no one would think to look for any other cause of death? He was buried straight away. I don't know whether Louvain knew about him, or the Clark woman, or not. I have to find the source. I can't let Gould be hanged for something he didn't do, but not ever, even to save his life, can I tell what I know. Do you see?'

Rathbone found it almost impossible to move or speak. The room seemed to be far away from him, as if he were dreaming rather than seeing it. Monk's face was the only steady thing in his sight, at once familiar and dreadful. Seconds ticked by in which he expected at any instant to wake up in a sweat and a tangle of bedclothes.

It did not happen. He heard hoofs in the street outside, and the hiss of carriage wheels in the rain. Someone shouted. It was all real. There was no rescue, no escape.

'Do you see?' Monk repeated.

'Yes,' Rathbone replied at last. He was beginning to. There was no one to help, no one could. He frowned. 'Nothing they can do? Doctors? Even now?'

'No.'

'What do you want from me?' He refused to visualise it; the reality was more than he could endure. He needed to be busy. It would excuse him from knowing anything else; he would be doing what he could. 'Did you say the man's name was Gould – the thief, I mean?'

'Yes. He's held at Wapping. The man in charge is called Durban. He knows the truth.'

Rathbone was jolted. 'The truth? You mean he knows whether Gould killed Hodge, or not?'

'No. He knows how Ruth Clark died,' Monk said sharply. 'He knows we have to find the rest of the crew of the *Maude Idris*. He and I have been looking, and we haven't found any trace of them yet.'

'God Almighty! Aren't they on the ship?' Rathbone exclaimed.

'No. Five of them were paid off at Gravesend. The

266

crew now is only skeleton, just four men, including Hodge. They were supposedly enough to guard the ship until she can come in for unloading,' Monk replied.

Rathbone gulped, his heart pounding in his chest. 'Then they could be anywhere. Carrying . . .' He could not even say it.

'That's why I haven't time to search for the truth to clear Gould,' Monk answered, still looking at Rathbone steadily.

Rathbone started to ask what one man mattered when the whole continent was threatened with extinction, and in a manner more hideous than the worst nightmare imaginable. Then he knew that, in its own way, it was the shred of sanity they had to cling on to. It was one thing that perhaps was within their power, and in that they could hold on to reason, and hope. When he spoke his voice was rough-edged, as if his throat pained him. 'I'll do what I can. I'll go and see him. If I can't find out who did kill Hodge, at least I may be able to raise reasonable doubt. But isn't there something else I can do? Anything . . .?'

Monk blinked. There was not even the ghost of his usual humour in his face. 'If you believe in any kind of God, I mean really believe, not as a Sunday conformity, you could try praying. Other than that, probably nothing. If you ask your friends for money for Portpool Lane, if you haven't before, they'll become suspicious, and we can't afford that.'

Rathbone froze. Margaret might go to the clinic. He felt the blood draining from his body. 'Margaret . . .' he whispered.

'She knows,' Monk said very quietly. 'She won't go in.'

Rathbone began to see the full horror of it. Hester was in Portpool Lane, imprisoned beyond all human help. Monk knew it, even as he tried to reassure Rathbone about Margaret, while he himself could do nothing but try to find the rest of the crew. Rathbone could only try to save one thief from hanging for a murder he probably had not committed. And Margaret could do no more than struggle to raise from a blind society, which could never be told the truth, enough money to provide food and heat, as long as there were survivors, and do it without telling anyone the truth – not even him.

'I understand,' he said quietly, overwhelmed with gratitude – and shame. 'I'll give her money myself, but I'll ask no one else. Speak to me when you can, and if there is anything else I can do, tell me.' He stopped abruptly, not knowing how to offer Monk money without offending him. And yet it was absurd to let a fear of asking stand between them now.

'What is it?' Monk asked.

Rathbone put his hand in his pocket and pulled out six gold sovereigns and small change in silver. He passed over the sovereigns. 'In case you need it for transport, or anything else. I don't imagine Louvain is still paying you.'

Monk did not argue. 'Thank you,' he said, picking up the coins and putting them in the inside pocket of his coat. 'I'll tell you what I find, if I do. If you want me for anything, leave a message at the River Police station at Wapping. I'll call in there, or Durban will.' He stood up slowly, as if he were stiff and to move hurt him. He smiled very slightly, to rob his words of offence. 'Nobody's going to pay you for defending Hodge.'

Rathbone shrugged and did not bother to reply.

As soon as Monk had left he poured himself a full glass of brandy, then looked at it for a moment, seeing the light burn through its golden depths, like a topaz in its crystal balloon. Then he thought of Monk going out alone to the dark river and the backstreets where he must look for a ship's crew carrying death, leaving Hester in a place that must surely be as close to hell on earth as was possible, and he poured the brandy back into the decanter, his shaking hand spilling a little of it.

He barely spoke to Coleridge on the way out, only sufficient to be civil to the anxious enquiry for his well-being. Outside on the footpath he hailed the first hansom that passed, running out into the street to clamber into it, and giving Margaret Ballinger's address.

He sat down as the cab started forward. At last he understood her extraordinary behaviour yesterday. She had honour! She must have been desperate to raise money for Hester, and of course she could not possibly tell anyone why. How farcical, like some insane, satanic joke – she was trying to save them all, and she could not tell them.

But why had she not told him? If she had sent him some message he would have come immediately, and she could have told him somewhere in private . . . His brain was racing, skidding off the rails like a high-speed train with a drunken driver, no control. When had Margaret heard? The same day as Monk, or not? Perhaps she had had no time to tell Rathbone? Perhaps she had not trusted him? Or was she protecting him from having to know about it?

Why would she do that? Did she know the horror of disease, which rose like a tide inside him, drowning reason, courage, even sense? He had never been a moral coward in his life, nor a physical one. He had faced danger, not willingly but certainly without ever quailing or even imagining running away.

But disease was different. The terror, the nausea, the delirium, the inescapable certainty of death, helpless and without dignity.

Why was the hansom taking so long? Rain was causing traffic congestion as drays, hansoms, private carriages all fought for space in the narrow, wet streets, trying not to bump into each other and tangle, mash wheels and break them in the dark.

What a relief it would be to see Margaret, tell her that he knew. She would not be able to go to the clinic. Monk had said no one was allowed in or out. Thank heaven for that. His body broke out in a sweat of relief. He was ashamed of it, but it was impossible to deny.

But Hester was in Portpool Lane alone. She had only the street women and Bessie to help her, and Squeaky Robinson, for whatever that was worth – probably nothing. He would be the first to run away. And she would have to set the dogs on him. Rathbone refused to imagine that. But she could. She would do it. She would know what it would mean if he escaped and carried the plague to the rest of London. She would have the courage, the strength of mind.

He had never realised what that meant until now. He remembered some of their early conversations with a stab of self-disgust. He had condescended to her, as if she were a woman finding a second-best kind of career, to fill in the space where her emotional fulfilment ought to have been. And she was stronger and better than any other human being he knew.

If she died in Portpool Lane she would leave an emptiness in his life that nothing else would ever fill.

The hansom stopped and he realised with a jolt that he was at Margaret's home. He got out, standing in the rain to pay the driver, then ran across the footpath and up the steps to pull the bell at the door.

The footman answered, but regretted to tell him that Miss Ballinger was out, and he could not say when she would return.

Rathbone was bereft. What if she had ignored instruction and gone to the clinic after all? Then she would be in as much danger as Hester. She would suffer horribly. He would never see her again, never marry her. Whatever happened to the rest of London, or England, his own personal future was suddenly cold and dark. How could anyone else compare with her? That was a stupid thought. There were no comparisons. However virtuous, gentle, funny or clever anyone else might be, it was Margaret he loved.

The footman was waiting patiently.

Rathbone thanked him and left, back out into the teeming rain, and the darkness. The hansom had already gone. It hardly mattered. He would walk home. If it took an hour and he was soaked to the skin, he would not notice it.

Rathbone could not sleep, and in the morning he had his manservant draw him a hot bath, but he could not enjoy it. By half-past eight he was breakfasted, and had sent a note to his chambers to say he would be late. Then he looked for a hansom to take him back to Margaret's house. He could not even contemplate what he was going to do if she was still not there. He could not think of going to the clinic to find her, nor could he think of not going. He could give her money, and then he had to go and find this wretched thief of Monk's, and see what could be done to serve justice. At least if anyone had the skill for that, it was he.

The traffic was heavy again. It was the time of day when people were going into the city, tradesmen were beginning their rounds, everybody seemed to be jamming the roads.

At the first traffic congestion everything came to a standstill. Two coachmen were arguing over whose fault it was that a horse had tried to bolt, and broken the harness. Rathbone waited a short while, then finally paid his own driver and got out to walk. It was no more than three-quarters of a mile further, and the effort it would take was better than waiting cooped up.

This time he was more fortunate. The footman informed him that Miss Ballinger was taking breakfast,

271

and he would enquire if she would receive him. Rathbone paced back and forth in the morning room until the man returned and invited him through.

Rathbone tried to compose himself, so as not to embarrass Margaret in front of her parents, should they be there. He followed the footman across the hall and into the long, very formal dining room, where he was drenched with relief to find her alone. She was dressed smartly in a dark suit a little like a riding habit. It was fashionable and extremely becoming, but she looked alarmingly pale.

'Good morning, Sir Oliver,' she said with some reserve. Obviously she had not forgotten his coolness of the other evening. 'Would you care for a cup of tea? Or perhaps more? Toast?' she invited him.

'No, thank you.' He sat down, praying she would give the footman leave to go. 'I have a legal matter I wish to discuss with you, of a most confidential nature.' He could not wait upon good luck.

'Really?' She raised her eyebrows slightly. She thanked the footman and asked him to leave. She looked guarded, withdrawn, as if she were afraid he were going to hurt her. He found himself ashamed at the thought.

'I know,' he said simply. 'Monk came to see me yesterday afternoon. He told me of the situation at Portpool Lane.'

Her eyes widened, dark and incredulous. 'He . . . told you?' She reached out instinctively and grasped his wrist. 'You must say nothing. I was sworn to secrecy, absolute. No exceptions at all. It—'

'I understand,' he cut across her. 'Monk told me because he needs me to defend a thief. He believes him to be innocent of murdering a watchman and the case may have some connection with what has happened at the clinic. It is not much – one small act of justice, and to a confessed thief at that – but it's all I can do.' He felt ashamed saying it. 'That, and help with funds. But he warned me not even to ask friends in case my urgency should cause speculation.'

Her face was filled with a relief that set his heart surging, the blood pounding in his veins. There was a wild, almost hysterical gratitude in him that Margaret was not in the clinic, and could not go. Anyway, she was needed to raise funds, to purchase what those inside needed and take it to them.

'I know,' she said gently. 'I am having to be so much more discreet than I want to be.' She met his eyes, her own brimming with tears. 'I think of Hester in there, alone, and how she must feel, and I want to go to help her. I want to tell these people the truth and force them to give all they can, every last penny, but I know it would only drive them into hysterics – at least some of them.' She was shivering, her voice husky. 'Fear does terrible things to people. Anyway, I promised Sutton, which really means Hester, that I would tell no one. I couldn't even tell you.'

'I understand,' he said quickly, closing his hand over hers where it lay on his wrist. 'Be careful. And . . . and when you take food to them, leave it. Don't be . . . don't be tempted to . . .'

He saw an instant of pity in her eyes, not for Hester, or for the sick, but for him, because she recognised his horror of disease. It chilled him like ice at the heart. Suddenly he saw that he could lose her, not to death but to contempt, that awakening of disgust which is the end of love between a woman and a man.

He looked away.

'I will do what I have to,' Margaret said quietly. 'I do not intend to go inside the clinic; I am more use to them out here. But if Hester sends for me, perhaps because she is dying, then I will go. I might lose my life, too, but if I didn't I could lose everything that would make life precious. I am sure you know that.' There was no certainty in her voice or her face. She was full of question. She needed his answer.

'I'm sorry,' he apologised. 'I know you must. It was a moment's complete selfishness because I love you.'

She smiled, and lowered her eyes as the tears slid down her cheeks. 'You must go and defend this thief, if that is what Monk requires. Now I am going to raise some more money. We need vegetables, and tea, and beef if possible.'

He took ten pounds out of his pocket and put it on the table. He was giving money away like water.

'Thank you,' she whispered. 'Now please go, while I can still keep some measure of composure. We both have things to do.'

He obeyed, his emotions storming inside him, his own composure in shreds. He was glad to say goodbye and go as rapidly as he could outside into the anonymous street, and the sharp wind to sting his face and the rain to hide his tears.

Chapter Eleven

Day and night blurred into one exhausting round for Hester. There were over a dozen women in the clinic altogether, counting herself, Bessie, Claudine, Mercy and Flo. Three had been injured by accident or violence, five were suffering fevers and congestion, which might be pneumonia, or early stages of plague – it was too soon to be certain. There had already been two deaths, one apparently from heart failure, the other from internal bleeding.

Of course, to his outrage Squeaky Robinson could not leave, either. Sutton had chosen to return and work with the little terrier, Snoot, to catch the rats. Food, water and coal were left in the yard, and the men with the dogs placed them outside the back door. When Hester went to retrieve them, she caught sight of one of them standing near the wall, half concealed in the shadows, his dog at his feet. It gave her a feeling of safety, and reminded her at the same time that she was as much a prisoner as any of the others.

Mercy helped her carry in the pails of water, which were extremely heavy. They left two in the kitchen, and the other eight along the wall of the laundry.

'We're going to have to use the water several times,' Hester said unhappily. 'It's not the best, but we daren't run out. With fever like this, it's more important to drink than to be clean, and I don't think we can have both.'

Mercy leaned against the washtub into which the mangle drained. She looked pale and very tired, but she was smiling. 'Makes you realise what a blessing it is to have water at home, doesn't it? Ask someone for it, and there it is.'

Hester looked at her with affection. In the few days she had been here she had grown to like her. She still knew very little about her, other than that she was Clement Louvain's sister. She had a gentleness with the sick, an endless patience, and in spite of the utterly different world she must be accustomed to, she never seemed to patronise people – unlike Claudine, whose temper was never far below the surface. Although Hester found she could not dislike Claudine, either.

Now they worked together piling the soiled sheets in the corner, and then Mercy tipped more coal from the scuttle into the boiler to heat it up. It was an awkward job, and she was covered in smuts by the time she had finished. She leaned back, putting the scuttle down, and looked at herself in dismay.

'Why on earth do we wear white aprons?' she said disgustedly. 'Whoever thought of that obviously didn't have to do the laundry.'

Hester smiled. 'Don't worry about it, it's good clean dirt.'

Mercy looked confused for a moment, then realised what she meant, and relaxed, smiling back. It was half-past nine in the evening, and most of the jobs were done for the day, in so far as day and night were any different from each other.

'Were you really in the Crimea?' Mercy asked a little shyly.

Hester was surprised. 'Yes. Most of the time it seems like another world, but right now it's not so hard to remember.' She bit her lip a little ruefully. There had been far more deaths there; they were surrounded by death every day, and it had been brutal and terrible, largely senseless, inflicted by men upon their fellows. But there was a vast difference between war and murder, even if there had seemed times when it would be difficult to explain it. Whole hours went by when Hester completely forgot that Ruth Clark had been murdered, let alone that she should be trying to find out who was responsible.

Did it matter any more – really? She realised with a jolt that she was not even certain that she wanted to know. It had to be someone here, and she cared for each of them. Was the bond of fear and survival greater than whatever had driven one of them to kill? She did not want to know the answer.

'You've not asked to have any message sent to your family,' she said to Mercy. She did not want to intrude. Mercy had never spoken of her home. She had not even said if she knew it was her brother who had brought Ruth Clark here, although Hester had assumed that she must have known. She seemed to be in her early twenties, pleasing to look at, and certainly she had an agreeable nature. Why was she not enjoying the social life her position offered her? Was there a love affair that had gone so badly for her that she was still too hurt to think of someone new? Was that why she was here, to escape a greater pain? Hester realised that that was what she had assumed, but there was no evidence for it.

Mercy shook her head. 'My brother knows I am here,' she replied. 'I left him a letter before I was obliged to stay, saying I would be spending much time here. I cannot tell him why I am remaining now, but he won't worry.'

'I'm sorry,' Hester apologised. 'You must be missing many things you would have attended could you leave.'

'No point in thinking about them,' Mercy shrugged. 'And I don't suppose any of them matter anyway. One puts on one's best clothes and one's best manners, and ends up being so polite that all one ever talks of is the weather, or what book one has just read – as long as it is not controversial, of course. Heaven protect us from having to think! Everybody is hoping to meet someone of such interest you can hardly wait to see them again, but unless you are terribly easily pleased, does it really happen? I am in greater danger of making myself believe it has, when my better self knows it hasn't.' She smiled, rubbing absent-mindedly at the smear of coal dust on her apron. 'I say to myself "next time . . . next time", and then it's exactly the same. At least this is real.'

'Doesn't your mother insist on your meeting as many young gentlemen as possible? Mine did,' Hester remembered with embarrassment, and sadness. Her mother had died of grief, and perhaps shame, after her father's suicide when he had been ruined in a financial scandal. Their deaths had been her reason for returning early from the Crimea.

Mercy must have caught the momentary grief in her face. 'My parents are dead,' she said quietly. 'From the way you speak, your mother is also?'

'Yes, and my father,' Hester acknowledged, straightening up to go over to the table. 'I'm sorry. I shouldn't have asked. I just wanted to send a message if you wished. Sutton would see that it was delivered.'

'There isn't anyone,' Mercy replied, getting the bread out of the bin and passing it to her. 'My elder sister, Charity, married a doctor. That was seven years ago. They stayed in England for a year, then he decided to go abroad, and of course Charity went with him.'

'That must have been hard for you.'

Mercy shrugged very slightly. 'It was at first,' she said, turning her face away so Hester could see only the angle of her cheek and the way the muscles pulled in her neck.

278

'But she is ten years older than I, so we were not as close as we might have been.'

'And your brother is older, too,' Hester observed, remembering Clement Louvain when he had brought Ruth Clark in.

'I was an afterthought,' Mercy said, lifting her chin a little, her wide mouth curved in a smile. 'My mother was nearly forty when I was born. But I think she was especially fond of me, for that.' She turned back to face Hester. 'I'll make us a cup of tea. I expect Claudine would like one, too, and perhaps Mr Robinson.' She did not mention the others because they were taking an hour or two's rest before the night duty.

In the kitchen Claudine was preparing vegetables for soup. Many of the sick women found eating difficult. Fever robbed them of all appetite, but some nourishment was essential, and above all they should drink. She stood at the bench, a large knife in her hand, her lips compressed as she tried to cut a raw carrot into small cubes. She was muttering to herself under her breath.

Hester considered offering to help her, but she had already had a taste of Claudine's temper when she was angry with herself for her ineptitude.

Mercy gave Hester a wry glance, more than a little because she was domestically inexperienced also, and knew that culinary skill did not come easily. She filled the kettle and set it on the hob.

Claudine went on chopping.

Squeaky Robinson came in, looking with disapproval and impatience at Claudine, then hopefully at Mercy.

Claudine glared at him. 'Wonderful how you always know to come when the kettle's on,' she said tartly.

'Saves you having to send for me,' he replied, sitting down at the table ready for Mercy to bring him tea when it was brewed.

'And why would we be sending for you?' Claudine

demanded, her jaw clenched to swallow the words as a piece of carrot jumped off the board under the crooked angle of the knife. She stooped awkwardly to pick it up. She had little grace, and she was hurtingly conscious of it.

Squeaky rolled his eyes.

Mercy glanced at Hester, and swallowed a giggle.

'Probably 'cos you've run out of water again,' Squeaky said wearily. 'Beast of burden, I am.'

'You're only getting it from the back door,' Claudine said crossly. 'Some other poor devil is carrying it the length of the street, and he can only do that in the dark, for fear people'll see him and wonder why we aren't fetching our own. So don't waste it. You were scrubbing the floor yesterday as if you'd half the ocean to play with.'

'Perhaps you'd better scrub the floor, missus,' Squeaky retorted. 'An' leave me to chop them carrots. I couldn't make no worse a job of it than you are. No two bits the same, you haven't.'

'Maybe you haven't noticed it, but the Dear Lord doesn't make any two carrots the same,' Claudine said instantly, her eyes blazing, the knife clutched in her hand as if she were about to use it as a weapon.

'He don't do it with potatoes, neither,' Squeaky said with pleasure. 'Only with peas, and we haven't got none of them. You know what peas are, missus?'

'About a penny a hundred,' Claudine responded. 'Roughly what you're worth.'

Squeaky shot to his feet, his face flushed. 'Now look, you vinegar-faced old cow, I've had as much of your tongue as I'm gonna take. You're bleedin' useless. You can't turn the mangle without tearing the sheets, like we got 'em to spare.' He jabbed his finger towards her. 'You can't make soap, you can't make porridge without more lumps than the coal's got in it. You can't light the bleedin' furnace if it goes out, and you can't cut a carrot without hurling bits all over the floor. That poor cow what died was right – no wonder your poor bleedin' husband don't miss you being here. He's probably got a bit of peace for the first time in his poor bleedin' life.'

Claudine went white. She drew in her breath, but found she had no words to defend herself. Suddenly she looked old and plain, and very vulnerable.

Hester was grasped by a pity so fierce she had no idea how to express it or what to say or do. She stood frozen in the grip of it. The fear and the sense of imprisonment was wearing on everyone's emotions. No one gave it words, but they were all intensely aware that the disease was here with them like a brooding entity, able to strike any of them, or all. Every ache, every weariness, every moment of heat or chill, every twinge of headache could be the beginning. She was not the only one to wonder about every tenderness in the breast or the arm, to look at herself with fear and imagine she could see shadows or the faintest swelling sign.

It was Mercy who interrupted her thoughts. 'Mr Robinson, we appreciate that you are afraid – we all are – but deliberately seeking to hurt each other is only going to make it worse.'

Squeaky blushed, but under his embarrassment he was angry as well. He did not like being criticised, particularly in front of Claudine. He knew he was in the wrong, and it hurt him that Mercy, whom he admired, was the one to point it out. 'She's the one with the tongue pickled in acid,' he said accusingly.

'And you think so well of it you have to do the same?' Mercy raised her eyebrows.

Hester smiled, because the only alternative was to cry, and if she started she might not know how to stop. As it was, she was tired, confused, and would have given any-thing, except what it would actually cost, to have been able to go home.

281

The back door opened, startling them all and making them swing round, setting hearts pounding in sharp, urgent fear.

But it was the little terrier, Snoot, with his face half brown, half white, who came scampering in, wagging his tail, Sutton close behind him. Hester breathed out in relief, realising she should have known it would be he. The men with the dogs would not have permitted anyone else to pass.

Sutton glanced around the room, but if he sensed the tension he did not show it. He was carrying beef bones, two bottles of brandy and a pound of tea. 'Miss Margaret must a' brung 'em,' he said, setting them down on the table. He ran his hand gently over the little dog. 'That's you fer the night,' he said gently. 'Now go ter bed.'

The anger in the room subsided, and everyone returned to their duties.

It was in the middle of the night that the incident occurred. Hester had had a few hours' sleep and was going round the more seriously ill of the women when she heard a noise on the landing a short distance away. She knew Bessie was doing the rounds as well, so at first she took no notice. Then she heard a long wail, rising into a note of sheer terror, and she put down the cup of water in her hand. She excused herself to the languid, feverish woman she was with, and went out into the passage.

Bessie was struggling with a woman called Martha, who had come in with severe bronchitis, which had seemed to be getting a little better. Bessie was broad and strong, but Martha was young and handsomely built as well, and she seemed to have a remarkable strength. Bessie's arms were clasped round her in a bear hug, Martha was leaning away from her, her arms free, fists beating against Bessie's chest. As Hester took a step towards her, Martha's right fist caught Bessie in the face and Bessie let go of her with a yell of pain, blood spurting from her nose.

Martha half fell against the wall, banging herself and twisting awkwardly.

Hester started towards her, but Martha scrambled upright again and charged off along the passage towards the stairs.

'Don't bother wi' me!' Bessie shouted, grasping her apron to her bleeding nose. 'Stop 'er! She's makin' a run fer it! She's got them black swellin's.'

Hester barely hesitated. Bessie would have to wait, Martha must be stopped, at any cost. She was already at the top of the stairs and lurching down them, still screaming.

Flo came out of one of the other bedrooms and saw Bessie, her face and bosom scarlet. She screamed as well and ran floundering forward towards her.

'I'm all right!' Bessie yelled at her. 'Stop that stupid cow from runnin' off! Get 'er! Go 'elp Miss 'Ester, fer Gawd's sake.'

Flo stopped with a jolt as Hester started down the stairs. Martha was already halfway down and Squeaky Robinson was on the way up, holding on to the railings at both sides.

'Stop her!' Hester shouted, 'Martha, stop. You can't leave!'

But Martha was beyond listening to anyone or anything. She charged Squeaky and carried him right off his feet, knocking him backwards down the stairs, his legs in the air. She tried to avoid him and tripped, pitching headlong after him, landing heavily, almost smothering him. He screeched furiously, then started howling with pain.

Hester clung on to the banister and went down as fast as she could without risking breaking her legs.

Martha was still clambering to her feet when Hester

reached the bottom. Squeaky was clutching his right leg and cursing vigorously.

'You can't leave, Martha,' Hester said loudly and very clearly. 'You know that. You'll spread the plague all over London. Come back upstairs and let us look after you. Come on.'

Squeaky was still swearing.

'Shut up,' Hester said to him furiously. 'Get up and hold on to Martha.'

Squeaky tried to do as he was told, grabbing a handful of Martha's nightgown skirts to haul himself up. She lashed out at him and sent him sprawling backwards to land with a thud against the wall. Whether she thought he was molesting her, or she simply was not going to let anyone prevent her escape, was irrelevant.

Squeaky lay where he fell.

Martha blundered away, gathering speed, and Hester ran after her. Martha knew her way and was heading for the kitchen and the back door. Hester called out, desperation making her voice high and shrill. She was not even sure if she was trying to stop Martha, or warn Sutton and call for help. Would she have the nerve to order the dogs set on her? Even with the plague, could she cause the death of someone in such a terrible way?

Claudine was sitting half asleep in a chair in the kitchen. She woke with a start as Martha almost banged into her. She lunged forward, realising instantly what Martha was trying to do. Her weight carried Martha forward and they fell together against the kitchen table. Claudine went down first, Martha on top of her.

There was a high-pitched, ear-splitting series of barks. Snoot shot out of the door from the laundry as it opened and Sutton appeared.

'Wot the 'ell is . . .?' he started.

Martha was the first to her feet. 'Let me go!' she shrieked. 'I gotta get out of 'ere! Let me . . .' And again she plunged towards the back door.

Hester tried to shout, but she could not draw her breath.

'Don't!' Sutton yelled. 'Don't do it!'

But Martha was beyond reach; in her own mind she must escape or die. The plague was here in this house, and beyond in the night was freedom and life. She ran out barefoot into the yard.

Hester propped herself up on to her hands and knees.

Sutton gritted his teeth and closed his eyes for a second, then he opened them again. 'Get 'er!' he shouted.

Martha was floundering across the cobbles of the yard. Out of the shadows, from two different directions, shot two pit bulls. They leaped just as she shrieked, and their weight carried her down hard and heavily. As instinct and training taught them, they went for her throat.

Hester screamed. 'No! No! Oh, God no!' and lurched to her feet.

Claudine was standing as well, one hand across her mouth, the other clenched over her stomach where she had fallen against the table corner.

Sutton stumbled to the door and ran out into the darkness. The men were calling their dogs off. Martha lay motionless, her white nightgown stained with widening blotches of crimson.

Sutton reached her and bent down. He touched her gently, feeling for a pulse. The two dog owners stood by, hands on their animals, reassuring them they had not done wrong, but their voices trembled and Hester knew they were talking as much to themselves as to their animals.

Sutton looked up at them from where he kneeled.

'Thanks, Joe, Arnie. That can't be easy ter do, but yer did right. Please 'eaven, yer won't 'ave ter do it no more, but if yer do, then yer must.' He turned to Hester who was now outside in the light rain almost beside him. 'She in't dead, but she's bleedin' summink 'orrible. Still, I s'pose yer seen that before, yer bein' in the army an' all. We'd best get 'er inside an' see if yer can stitch 'er up, poor little cow. I dunno wot for. This'd be an easier way to go, Gawd 'elp us.'

Claudine was outside now as well. She was gasping for breath, trying to control the hysteria rising in her.

'You murderer!' she choked out the words, staring transfixed with horror at Sutton.

'No, he isn't!' Hester protested, her own voice thick with held-in anguish.

'He set the dogs on her,' Claudine said coldly. 'You saw it. God! Look at her. They've torn her throat out.'

'No they haven't.' Hester bent down to her knees to look at the mangled, scarlet mess, praying that what she said was true. Or maybe that it wasn't.

Claudine began to gasp for breath, the air scraping and wheezing in her chest.

Sutton put his arm round her and with the other hand struck her hard on the back.

She turned on him in fury. 'Going to kill me now, are you?' she shrieked, raising both her fists as if to strike him in the face.

'I might do, missus,' he said grimly. 'I really might do – but not yet. I'll 'ave enough ter bury without you, an' yer getting' ter be more use every day, spite o' yerself. Now get on an' 'elp Miss 'Ester wi' this poor little cow. 'Old the water or the needle or summink. Don't stand there wi' yer bleedin' mouth open. In't no flies ter catch this time o' night.'

Claudine realised she was breathing clearly again. She was beside herself with rage. 'You—' she started.

But Sutton was not listening to her. 'Shut yer face an' be useful, yer great lump,' he told her abruptly. 'Afore she bleeds ter death 'ere in the yard an yer 'ave ter spend yer mornin' wi' a broom and vinegar tryin' ter clean it up.'

Partly out of sheer surprise, Claudine obeyed. Together all three of them managed to carry Martha back inside and lay her on the kitchen table. In the light she looked even worse.

'Can yer stitch 'er?' Sutton whispered.

Hester looked at the blood-soiled clothes and the mangled flesh. Martha was still bleeding freely, but it was not with the brilliant scarlet of arterial blood, and it was still pumping, which meant that she was alive.

'I can try,' she answered. 'But I need to be very quick. Claudine, you'll have to help. Bessie's got what looks like a broken nose, and Mercy'll have to deal with that. Anyway, we've no time. Get my needle and silk out of the top drawer of the cupboard over by the sink.' As she spoke she was tearing out the other sleeve of Martha's nightgown and rolling it up into a pad, holding it to the worst of the wounds. 'Sutton, fetch the bottle of brandy and pour some of it into a dish, then get more towels. Be quick.'

They were ashen-faced, hands trembling, but they did exactly as she told them. Mercy came while they were busy, and said in a low voice that Bessie's nose was broken, but she had managed to stop the bleeding. Bessie would be all right, and so would Squeaky. He was bruised but nothing was broken. Flo was doing what she could for the rest of the sick women, and what would Hester like her to do now?

'Put a pot of tea outside for the men in the yard,' Hester answered. 'And thank them. Tell them we are grateful.' She did not look away from her work. 'Put your finger there,' she instructed Claudine, indicating a raw vein from which blood was running. 'Hold it. I'll stitch it as fast as I can. I've got to do this one first.'

Without hesitation Claudine stretched out her finger and pressed.

Hester was oblivious of time. It could have been a

quarter of an hour, or three-quarters, when she finally realised she had done all she could. With Claudine's help she bound the last bandage on Martha's neck and shoulder and the top of her arm. She looked only once at the purplish patch near the armpit. She did not know if it was a bruise or the beginning of a bubo. She did not want to know. They washed her as best they could, put a clean gown on her, then called for Squeaky to help them carry her to one of the downstairs rooms. He appeared, limping a little but not badly injured. They laid her on the bed and covered her over.

Claudine looked at Hester questioningly, but she did not ask if Martha would live or not. 'I'll go and clean up the kitchen,' she said ruefully. 'It looks like a butcher's shop.'

'Thank you,' Hester answered with profound sincerity. She did not add any praise. Claudine knew she had earned approval, and that was all that mattered to her. She went out, even smiling very slightly at Squeaky as she passed him on her way to the door.

Hester took the blood-stained clothes to the laundry, where she found Sutton looking exhausted. His lean face was shadowed as if with bruising, his eyes hollow, the stubble on his chin patched with white.

'Was the Crimea like that?' he said with a twisted smile. 'Gawd 'elp the army if it were.'

She thought of it with an effort. It seemed like another world now. She had been younger, had so much less that was precious to her to live for. One did not allow oneself to think about the violence and the pain in a rational way, or it became too much to bear.

'Pretty much,' she replied, dropping the clothes on the floor. The real answer was too long, and she was too tired, and perhaps Sutton did not really want to hear it anyway.

'Iggerant an' mad, in't we?' he said with startling

288

gentleness. 'Makes you wonder why we bother wi' ourselves, don't it? 'Ceptin' we in't got nobody else, an' yer gotter care about summink.' He shook his head and turned to walk away. 'Snoot,' he called when he was outside in the passage. 'Where are yer, yer useless little article?'

There was an enthusiastic scampering of feet. Hester smiled as the little dog shot out of the shadows and caught up with his master.

After putting the clothes into cold water she went back upstairs. There was not much she could do for Martha except sit with her, make sure the bandages did not work loose, give her water if she woke, bathe her brow with a cool cloth and try to keep the fever down.

When she'd been sitting there for five minutes, Claudine came to the door with a cup of hot tea and passed it to her. 'It's ready to drink,' she said simply.

It was. It was just cool enough not to scald. It was also powerfully laced with brandy that Hester felt she should be careful not to breathe near the candle flame.

'Oh!' she said as the inner fire of it hit her stomach. 'Thank you.'

'Thought you needed it,' Claudine replied, turning to go. Then she stopped. 'Want me to watch her for a bit? I'll call you if anything happens, I swear.'

Hester's head was pounding and she was so tired her eyes felt gritty. If she closed them for longer than a second she might drift off to sleep. The thought of letting go and allowing herself to be carried away into unconsciousness, without fighting, was the best thing she could imagine, better than laughter, good food, warmth, even love – just to stop struggling for a while. 'I can't.' She heard the words and wondered how she could make herself say them.

'I'll get another chair to sit here,' Claudine replied. 'Then if she needs you I can wake you just by speaking. I wouldn't have to leave her.'

Hester accepted. She was asleep even before Claudine sat down.

She sat up with a gasp an hour later when Claudine woke her to say that Martha was very restless and seemed to be in a lot of pain. One of the wounds was bleeding again.

They did what they could to help her, working with surprising ease together, but it was little enough. Hester was grateful not to be alone, and she told Claudine so as they sat down again to watch and wait.

Claudine was embarrassed. She was not used to being thanked; twice in one night was overwhelming and she did not know how to answer. She looked away, her face pink.

Hester wondered what her marriage was like that she apparently lived in such bitter loneliness, uncomplimented, without laughter or sharing. Was it filled with quarrels, or silence, two people within one house, one name, one legal entity, who never touched each other at heart? How could she reach out to Claudine without making it worse, or ask anything without prying and perhaps exposing a wound that could be endured only because no one else saw it? She remembered Ruth Clark's cruel words and the mockery and contempt in them, as if she really had known something about Claudine, not just guessed at it. Perhaps she had, and perhaps it was bitter and wounding enough that Claudine had seen the chance to kill her, and protect herself. But Hester refused even to allow that thought into her mind. One day she might have to, but not now.

'Would you like Sutton to have another message sent to your home?' she asked. 'You could let them know you are all right, but that with so many ill we can't do without you. That would be more or less the truth, or at any rate it's not a lie.'

'It doesn't matter,' Claudine replied, her eyes fixed

steadily on Martha. 'I said that in the first message.' She was silent for a moment or two. 'My husband will be annoyed, because it is a break in his routine, and he was not consulted,' she went on. 'There may be social events he would like me to have attended, but otherwise it will not matter.' Her voice caught for a moment. 'I don't wish to appear to be explaining myself. For the first time in my life I am doing something that matters, and I don't intend to stop.'

She had said little, and yet beneath the surface it was an explanation for everything. Hester heard the emptiness behind the words, a whole bruised and aching lifetime of it. But there was no answer to give, nothing to make it different, or better. The only decent response was silence.

She drifted back into sleep again, and Claudine woke her a little before four. Martha was slipping into deeper unconsciousness. Claudine stared at Hester, the question in her eyes, the answer already known. Martha was dying.

'Is it the plague, or the dogs?' Claudine asked in a whisper.

'I don't know,' Hester said honestly. 'But if it is the dogs, perhaps that isn't a bad thing. I—'

'I know,' Claudine interrupted. 'Best thing not to linger.'

Martha was struggling for breath. Every few moments she stopped altogether, then gasped again. Hester and Claudine looked at each other, then at Martha. Finally it was the last time, and she lay still.

Claudine shivered. 'Poor soul,' she said softly. 'I hope there's some kind of peace for her now. Do . . . I mean, should we . . .' she blinked rapidly 'say something?'

'Yes, we should,' Hester answered without any doubt at all. 'Will you say it with me?'

Claudine was startled. 'I don't know what.'

'How about the Lord's Prayer?'

Claudine nodded. Together they pronounced the familiar words slowly, a little huskily. Then Claudine folded the dead woman's hands, and Hester went to fetch Sutton and ask his help.

He was in the laundry, rewarding Snoot for having found a rats' nest. He looked up as Hester came in. His face was grave, expectant. He saw her expression. 'She go?' he asked. 'Poor soul. 'Oo knows?'

'Just Claudine and I,' she replied.

'Good. We better get 'er out before light.' He straightened up. 'Go ter bed, Snoot. Good boy. You stay there like yer told.' He turned back to Hester. 'I'll get the fellers ter take 'er. Sorry, but we'll 'ave ter wind 'er in a sheet. I know yer can't afford ter lose no more, but there in't no better way. 'Ceptin' a blanket, mebbe, if yer got a dark one? Less easy seen.'

'I'll find you a dark grey blanket,' she promised. 'But what will they do with her? She can't just be . . . I mean, she has to be buried, too.' She thought of the silent, miserable business of taking Ruth Clark's body out and leaving it on the cobbles in the rain for the men to take to an unknown grave, wrapped in blankets for decency, and so they would not have to touch it. She had not asked where then; it was more than she wanted to know.

No doctor had seen Ruth, nor could anyone see Martha, not even an undertaker: he would see her throat and think she had been murdered. There was an irony in that she had not, not morally, anyway. Ruth had, but Hester had barely turned her mind to the question of who had done it, or why. Now it was poor, stupid, terrified Martha who mattered. That hysteria lay close under the surface in all of them.

Hester licked her lips. They were so dry they hurt. 'In hallowed ground?' she asked tentatively. 'Is that impossible? I just can't bear to think of her being pushed away somewhere in a drain, or something.'

'Don' worry,' Sutton said gently. 'I got friends as can do all sorts o' things. There's graves in corners o' proper places as got more bodies in than they 'ave names on the stones. The dead don' care if they share a bit. She won't be left unblessed, or unprayed for. Nor Ruth Clark, neither.'

She felt the tears prickle in her eyes and the sheer weight of exhaustion, loneliness, pity and fear over-whelmed her. His kindness sharpened it almost beyond bearing. She wanted to thank him, but her throat was choked.

He nodded, his face hollow in the candlelight. 'Go find the blanket,' he told her.

Claudine helped her roll the body and very quickly stitch the makeshift shroud around it, catching it in places so it would not fall undone if she were carried hastily, and perhaps with little skill. They did not speak, but every few moments their eyes met, and a kind of understanding made them move in unison, each reaching to help the other.

Squeaky came to help again. The three of them took Martha with stumbling steps, awkwardly, their backs aching, along the passage and to the back door, then outside into the yard. Hester raised her arm in signal to the men. In the faint streetlamps twenty yards away they looked huge and untidy, coats flapping in the rising wind, bare-headed, hair plastered down. The rain made their skins shiny, almost masklike in the unnatural shadows. They acknowledged Hester and Claudine, but waited until they had gone back inside before they approached.

Sutton went out alone and spoke to the men.

The larger of the two nodded and beckoned his com-panion. Carefully they picked up the corpse, and without speaking again they turned and walked slowly away in the rain. They stayed very upright with the weight balanced between them as if they were used to such a thing.

Hester and Claudine stood side by side at the doorway, so close their bodies touched, watching as the men passed under the streetlamp. For a moment the rain was lit above them in bright streams. Then it glimmered pale on their backs as they retreated into the darkness. The van at the end of the street was little more than a greater denseness in the shadows.

No one spoke. It was quite unnecessary, and there was nothing to say. In a few hours another day would begin.

Chapter Twelve

❦

Rathbone went to visit Gould in prison because he had promised Monk that he would. He had expected to find a man he was morally obliged to defend, not for the man's sake, or because he was moved by any conviction that he was innocent, but because it was a clear duty. He realised as he left that he was inclined towards accepting Gould's story that he really had found Hodge dead, but without apparent injury. He admitted freely that he had stolen the ivory, but his indignation at the charge of murder had a ring of honesty that Rathbone had not expected.

However, on speaking to the undertaker who had buried Hodge, there could be no doubt whatever that he had suffered an appalling blow to the head. It had crushed the back of his skull, and was presumably the cause of his death. The undertaker had done as he was asked in burying Hodge, being assured both by Louvain and by Monk that all evidence had been recorded under oath, and would be passed to the appropriate authorities. The perpetrator of the crime was being sought, and when found would be brought to justice.

Rathbone returned to his office and began to consider what possible courses were open to him. He was thus occupied when Coleridge informed him that Monk was at the door. It was a little after half-past eight in the morning.

'Now?' he said incredulously.

Coleridge's face was studiously without expression. 'Yes, sir. I dare say he is also concerned about the case.' He had no idea what the 'case' was, and he was offended by the omission. He also desired Rathbone to realise that Monk was not the only person working long and remarkable hours.

'Yes, of course,' Rathbone acknowledged. He had no intention of telling Coleridge what the case was; he could not afford to until it was absolutely necessary. Even then, he would impart only what he was going to say in court, and not include the reason for any of his extraordinary silences. But Coleridge did deserve to be treated with consideration. 'He will be,' he said, referring to Monk. 'It is a grave matter. Will you show him in, please.'

'Would you like a cup of tea, Sir Oliver? Mr Monk looks unusually . . .' he searched for an adequate phrase '. . . in need of one,' he finished.

Rathbone smiled. 'Yes, please. That is most thoughtful of you.'

Coleridge retreated, mollified.

Monk came in a moment later, and Rathbone saw immediately what Coleridge had meant. Monk was wearing the same clothes he had had on last time and his face looked even hollower, as though he had neither eaten nor slept well since then. He came into the office and closed the door behind him.

'Coleridge is coming back with tea in a few minutes,' Rathbone warned. 'Have you found any of the crew yet? You'll have to tell them, even if you keep them by force. You can't put them into the clinic, can you?'

'We haven't found them,' Monk replied, his voice low and rasping with exhaustion. 'Not any of them. They could be anywhere in the country, or back at sea on other ships, going God knows where.'

He remained standing. Rathbone noticed that Monk's body was rigid. His right hand flexed and unflexed and the muscles of his jaw twitched in nervous reaction. He must be in agony over Hester alone in Portpool Lane. He would have no idea whether there were more people dead, plague raging through the place with all its horror and its obscenity. Or if they were cooped up waiting, dreading every cough, every chill or flush of heat, every moment of faintness, whether mere exhaustion or the beginning of the measured agony of fever, swelling, pain and then death.

Rathbone was overcome with relief that Margaret was not in there. It welled up inside him like an almost physical escape from pain, like the fire of brandy in the stomach and the blood when one has been numb with cold.

He stood facing Monk, who was grey with the dread of losing all that mattered most to him and gave his life purpose and joy. If Hester died, he would be alone in a way that would be a constant ache inside him, increasing every burden, dulling any possible happiness. And Rathbone was awash with relief at his own safety. It filled him with shame.

'I saw Gould,' he said aloud, trying, for his own sake almost as much as Monk's, to occupy their minds with the practical. Pity would be no help. 'I believed him.' He saw the slight lift of surprise in Monk's face. 'I didn't expect to,' he agreed. 'He'll make a good witness, if I have to put him on the stand. The trouble is, I don't know what the truth is, so I'm afraid of what I'll uncover.'

Monk was pensive. 'Well, so far as we know there was no one on board the ship apart from the skeleton crew and Gould, so the only defence can be that if Gould didn't kill Hodge, then one of the crew did, or else it was an accident.'

'If it was an accident then he fell and cracked his head open, possibly breaking his neck,' Rathbone reasoned. 'And if that were the case, it should have been apparent to whoever found him. Was his neck broken? You didn't say so.'

'No, it wasn't.'

'And you said there was so little blood you thought he was actually killed somewhere else,' Rathbone went on. 'You said—'

'I know what I said,' Monk snapped. 'That was before I knew about the plague.'

'Don't say that word!' Rathbone said sharply, his voice rising. 'Coleridge will be back any minute.'

Monk winced, as though in sudden pain.

Rathbone drew in his breath to apologise, although he knew it was the truth that hurt Monk, not his words. Just at that moment there was a brisk tap on the door, and Coleridge opened it, carrying in a tea tray and setting it on the table.

Rathbone thanked him and he withdrew again.

'Are you saying he died of . . . illness?' Rathbone asked, passing the tea as he spoke.

'It fits the facts if Gould is telling the truth,' Monk replied, sitting down at last. He looked so weary it was going to be an effort for him to stand up again. 'Hodge had to be accounted for. They couldn't just get rid of the body, so someone took a shovel to the back of his head to make that seem the cause of death.'

Rathbone believed it. 'But that's no use as a defence for Gould,' he pointed out. 'All I can think of so far is reasonable doubt, and I don't know how to raise that without going too close to the truth.' He shivered and put his hands into his pockets. It was an uncharacteristic gesture because it pushed his trousers out of shape, and above all he was elegant. 'Who can I call?' he went on. 'The prosecution will call the crew, who will say they know nothing. I daren't call any medical evidence, because if I question them we would raise the issue of whether he was dead already, and, if so, what caused it. His neck wasn't broken, there was nothing to suggest heart attack or apoplexy, and the last thing on earth we can afford is to have them dig him up again.'

Monk shook his head slowly, like a man in a fog of thought, too harried on every side to find his way. 'You'll have to play for time,' he said unhappily. 'I need to find something to raise a doubt.'

Rathbone hated forcing the issue. Monk was exhausted and he could barely guess at the fear that must be eating him alive. Margaret was safe. Rathbone had everything to look forward to. If he lost her it would be his own doing: his cowardice, moral or emotional. The solution to their relationship lay in his own hands. But Monk was powerless. There was nothing he could do to help. He did not even know from hour to hour if Hester was alive, still well, or already infected, suffering terribly. She was imprisoned with virtual strangers. Would they even care for her in her moments of extremity? Would they stay to nurse her, as she had nursed so many others? Or would they run away in terror or inadequacy? Or would they be too close to death themselves to be able to raise a hand to fetch water, or whatever one did to ease the terror or pain of the dying? The thought made him sick with misery.

'What is it?' Monk demanded, cutting across his thoughts.

Rathbone recalled himself. 'To raise reasonable doubt I have to suggest a believable alternative,' he answered. 'If Gould didn't kill him, either someone else did, or it was an accident. Can you get evidence to go back on your original decision? Louvain wrote that paper swearing that Hodge was murdered, and the circumstances in which he was found. That'll come out, because the undertaker will swear to the injuries and what was agreed about allowing burial to protect himself. I can't afford to question the medical evidence at all. They would dig the body up, and that's a nightmare I don't even want to imagine.'

Monk said nothing. He seemed to be lost in thought. As if noticing the tea for the first time, he poured himself a cup and drank it, wincing at the heat, and yet obviously grateful for it.

Rathbone poured some for himself as well. 'Does Louvain know the truth?' he asked.

Monk looked up at him. 'I really don't know.'

'Then you've got to find out. At least, one of us has to. If you—'

'I'll do it,' Monk said with such biting decision that Rathbone knew he would not raise the question again.

'If he doesn't know,' Rathbone said quietly, 'then you will have to tell him. The only way he can protect himself is to testify that he was mistaken, and Hodge could have fallen and hit his head.'

'Or that Gould killed him, exactly as we first believed,' Monk replied bitterly.

'Do you believe it now?'

'No.' Again there was no hesitation.

'Then we'll have to find a way of getting Louvain to testify for him, or he'll hang,' Rathbone warned him. 'We can't let the plague loose in London to save one man, however innocent.'

Monk took a deep breath and rubbed the heel of his hand over his face. 'I know. How many days till the trial?'

'Day after tomorrow.'

'I'll see Louvain,' Monk promised. He straightened up, but there was a weariness inside him that bowed his shoulders and his face was ashen. 'Durban is still hoping to find the crew.' His face crumpled. 'How many people are there, Rathbone, who disappear and no one misses? How many can fall, and we all just press onward without even seeing the space they've left? Does anyone care? Or are there people suffering, crippled with grief, and we don't notice that, either?'

Rathbone wished he had a lie good enough to be even the remotest comfort, but he hadn't. Whether anyone missed the crewmen he had no idea. They might be dead of plague in any town in the south of England, or more probably already at sea on another ship. There was no terror spreading, no cry of quarantine, evacuation, fire to burn it out, exorcise it like a thing from hell. But Monk was speaking of the void in his own life that Hester's loss would create, and Rathbone knew that.

And he was contemplating allowing himself to love Margaret just as deeply – wasn't he? With all the strength of emotion he possessed. It defied every instinct of self-preservation he had followed all his life. It was a denial of sanity, the ultimate madness.

Had he any choice? Can one decide whether to love or not? Yes, probably. One could walk away from life, and choose half-life, paralysis of the soul.

He had walked away from Hester, and she had been wise enough to refuse him anyway, perhaps for precisely that reason. Monk had had the courage of spirit to care, and she knew that and valued it. Now Monk would be racked by his caring for ever if she died.

Margaret was safe, as much as anything warm and living and vulnerable was ever safe. If he, Rathbone, wanted to be part of life, not merely a watcher, then he would let himself love as well. Perhaps it was the nature of caring that you could not help it. There was no choice to make; your own nature had already made it. If you could pull back then you were not wholly involved. He had never admired Monk more than he did at this moment, for the courage it had taken him to risk everything.

There was nothing to say or do as Monk turned and walked to the door. The friendship between them was deeper than Rathbone had acknowledged to himself before, and it was on the brink of being destroyed, because part of Monk himself would be lost.

If friendship could hurt so profoundly, what in heaven's name would love do?

Rathbone spent the rest of the day catching up on other work he had put aside in order to prepare for the Gould case, and much of the following morning also.

However, his mind was made up regarding Margaret. Time was precious, far more so than he had appreciated until now. He had dithered on the brink of asking her to marry him. It was both cowardly and foolish. He had written to her and dispatched the letter by messenger, inviting her to a dinner party that evening, and rather than wait till this crisis was past, whatever the relief, or the irretrievable loss, he would tell her his feelings and ask her to marry him.

As he dressed, regarding himself unusually critically in the glass, he was aware with surprise that he had taken it for granted that she would accept. It had not occurred to him until this moment that it was possible she would not.

Then he realised why the nerves in his stomach were jumping, and there was a tightness in his throat. It was not that she might decline. Everything in society and in her personal circumstances dictated that she accept, and he was perfectly certain that there was no other suitor she was considering. She was far too honest to have allowed him to court her had there been. She would accept him. The question that turned and twisted inside him was: would she love him? She would be loyal, because loyalty was in her nature. She would be gentle, even-tempered, generous of spirit, but she would have done that for anyone. It was not enough. To have all that, not because she loved him but because it was a matter of her honour that she should give it, would be a refinement of torture he could not bear to face. Yet if he did not ask her, he had already chosen failure.

He took a hansom to call on her, and this time he found Mrs Ballinger's attentions even more difficult to receive gracefully. His emotions were far too raw to expose them to her acute perception. He had no layer of wit with which to defend himself, and he found parrying her enquiries extremely hard work. He was relieved when Margaret was unfashionably punctual; in fact, he was deeply grateful for it.

He offered her his arm, bade Mrs Ballinger a good evening, and went out to the waiting hansom just a fraction more hastily than was graceful.

'Have you heard anything more from Monk?' Margaret asked as soon as he had given the cabbie instructions. 'What is happening? Has he heard from Hester?'

'Yes, I have seen Monk again,' he replied. 'He came to my chambers yesterday morning, but he had heard nothing from Portpool Lane. I know no more than you do.'

She made a tiny sound of desperation. 'How was he?'

How could he protect her from pain? To love and cherish her was the privilege he was seeking to obtain for the rest of their lives. Surely he should begin now?

'He is trying very hard to find evidence to help Gould in the trial,' he replied. 'It starts tomorrow.'

'Sir Oliver,' she said simply, 'please do not patronise me. I asked you because I wish to know the truth. If it is a confidence you cannot tell me, then say so, but do not tell me something untrue simply because you believe it is what I wish to hear. How is Monk?'

He felt powerfully rebuked. 'He looks dreadful,' he said honestly. 'I have never seen anyone suffer as he is doing now. And I know of no way to help him. I feel as if I am watching a man drown, and standing by with my arms folded.'

She turned to face him, the carriage lamps of the

passing traffic throwing a flickering light on her face. 'Thank you,' she said softly. 'That at least I believe. And please don't blame yourself like that; no one can help. There are not many occasions that friendship cannot improve, but I think this might be one of them. We can only do our best, and be there if the time should come when there is something to do.'

There was no answer that was large enough for the occasion, so Rathbone made none. A kind of peace settled between them. He thought how fortunate he was to be sitting beside her, and the resolve within him to ask her to marry him became even more certain.

They arrived at the home of their hosts and alighted. They were welcomed in their turn, there being above a score of guests. It was a very formal affair, women in magnificent gowns, richly embroidered, jewelled combs and tiaras glittering in their hair, diamonds on earlobes and around pale throats.

Margaret wore very little adornment, only a simple pearl necklace, and he was surprised that anything so modest could please him so much. It had a purity that was like a quiet statement of her own worth.

Within a few moments they were absorbed into the buzz of conversation. He had been accustomed to such parties for years, but he had never found it quite so intensely difficult to chatter politely without saying anything of meaning. He recognised several people here, and did not wish to become involved in exchanges with them because he knew he could not concentrate. His usual ease of manner was impossible. Emotions threatened to break through his composure and it required a constant vigilance to conceal them. He wanted to protect Margaret from the intrusive speculation that was customary. He had escorted her several times now and it was inevitable that many would be waiting for him to make some declaration. They would be watching her for pride, disappointment, desperation. It was all intrusive, unintentionally cruel, and a part of society they both took for granted.

Far more deeply than that, he wanted to protect her from the fear she felt for Hester, and the sense of helplessness because there was nothing she could do beyond continuing to raise money.

'How charming to see you again, Miss Ballinger,' Mrs Northwood said meaningfully, looking first at Margaret, then at Rathbone.

Rathbone drew in his breath to answer her, then saw Margaret's face and realised she did not care. She had caught the implication and it barely touched her. He felt a rush of admiration for her. How beautiful she was in her passion and integrity, beside these bright and trivial women. What did a little social prurience matter, compared with the horror that was going on less than two miles away in Portpool Lane?

He moved a little closer to her.

Mrs Northwood noticed it, and her eyes widened.

There was at least half an hour before dinner would be announced, but they were hemmed in by people on all sides. He could hardly ask her to find a place where they could speak alone. He did not even know exactly what he was going to say. Such things should be graceful, romantic, not blurted out in the fear they would be interrupted or overheard. He should have invited her to a completely different kind of function. What on earth had made him choose this?

But he knew the answer. She would accept this, because it gave her the opportunity to seek funds again. A more charming situation, more romantic, and where they could be alone, she would have refused, and then it would have become embarrassing and, worst of all, contrived. And he enjoyed being with her in company. He looked around at the other people present, and was proud that it was she on his arm and not one of them. He found himself smiling. He would create a situation where he could speak to her, even if it was on the way home.

Lady Pamela Brimcott was coming towards them. She was in her mid-thirties, handsome and formidable. He had defended her brother Gerald on a charge of embezzlement – unsuccessfully. At least she had considered it so, because Gerald had been found guilty, even though the sentence had been relatively lenient, due to Rathbone's plea of mitigating circumstances. Actually, Gerald was greedy and selfish, and Rathbone had believed him guilty as charged. But it was his duty to be advocate, not judge.

'Good evening, Oliver,' Pamela said coolly. Her gaze moved to Margaret. 'I presume this is Miss Ballinger, whom I hear about so often? I dare say Oliver has told you as much about me?'

Rathbone felt the heat flood up his face. At one time he had courted Pamela, and even considered she would be a suitable wife. That had been before he met Hester, and realised that 'suitable' was a description without passion or laughter, or necessarily even friendship. Thank heaven that his instinct had prevailed. He could see the enmity in Pamela's eyes, and knew she had not forgiven him for either of the things in which she believed he had let her down. She very probably would not have married him then – he had had no title – but she would have liked to be asked.

'I'm afraid he has not mentioned you,' Margaret replied, her tone polite and implying regret.

Pamela smiled. 'How discreet of him.' She let the layers of hidden meaning unfold.

Rathbone felt the heat increase in his face. He would love to have had a crushing response, but he cared too much to think of one. He knew Hester would have, and wished she were here to defend them both.

Margaret grasped the implication immediately. Her body stiffened; Rathbone could feel it almost as if she were actually touching him. But she smiled with startling sweetness, and looked unblinkingly at Pamela. 'He never discusses past cases with me,' she responded.

Rathbone gasped.

There was utter silence for a second, two seconds. Then Pamela's face went white as she understood what she had heard. For the first time in years she struggled to find a response. The remark had been truer than Margaret could have known and she could not fling it back.

Margaret waited, refusing to help her.

'He certainly wouldn't discuss this one,' Pamela said at last. 'He doesn't care to speak of failures, and this was a disaster. He defended a member of my family who was charged with an act of which he was completely innocent, but suffered in spite of it.'

Now Margaret's face was tense and pale also. She raised her eyebrows very slightly. 'Really?' she said with disbelief. 'That must have been most distressing for you. I admire your courage in speaking of it so frankly to a stranger.' Her tone implied it was also indiscreet.

'We are not really strangers, when we share so much,' Pamela replied between her teeth.

Margaret lifted her chin even higher. 'Do we? I had not realised, but I am delighted to know it. Then you will be as keen as I on giving to charitable causes. I am presently concerned with a clinic which treats sick and injured women in the Farringdon area. Even a few pounds is sufficient to provide heating and medicines so the most desperate cases can have time to recover a little. I shall give you an account of how it is spent, naturally.'

Pamela looked startled, and cornered. 'I admit you have surprised me, Miss Ballinger. I did not expect you to ask me for money.'

Margaret contrived to look even more surprised. 'Have

you something else I might wish?'

Rathbone could feel his stomach clenched and his face burning, and yet he wanted to laugh. The whole evening was escaping him. He had failed Pamela's brother, not in that Gerald was found guilty, but in arguing the case at all. He should have persuaded him to admit his guilt and repay the money. He could have done; he had had the means. He had bent to pressure from the family, and because he was fond of Pamela he had not wanted to tell her that her brother was a thief. He did not want Margaret to know that.

'Nothing that I could pass to you, my dear,' Pamela said icily, her meaning perfectly plain.

Margaret smiled radiantly. 'I'm so glad,' she whispered, and turned to walk away, leaving Pamela utterly confused, feeling she had been bested without knowing exactly how.

Rathbone was amazed, and a little startled how pleased he was that Margaret had defended herself so very effectively. He caught up with her in a glow of satisfaction, almost pride. He took her arm, but as soon as they were a few yards away she stopped and faced him with all trace of humour gone.

'Oliver, I would like to be able to speak to you for a few moments without interruption. I believe there is a conservatory; would you mind if we went to it? There would surely be a discreet corner.' She smiled a trifle self-consciously. 'Without people leaping to romantic conclusions.'

He felt oddly crushed. He did not wish her to take the lead; it was vaguely unbecoming. And yet she had made it plain that her intention was not romantic, and he was disappointed. 'Of course,' he replied, hearing the coolness in his voice and wishing it were not there. She must surely have heard it also. 'It is this way.'

It was a marvellous room, full of wrought-iron arches

and filled to the roof with exotic plants. The sound of falling water was delightful, and the smell of damp earth and flowers filled the air.

Margaret stopped as soon as they were several yards from the nearest person who might overhear them. Her face was extremely grave, and in the dappled light looked almost colourless.

Rathbone felt alarmed. This was not even remotely how he had intended it to be. 'What is it?' His voice sounded nervous, scratchy.

'Have you heard from Hester?' she asked, but there was no lift of expectation in her.

'No. Have you?'

'I don't even know if she is well or ill,' she admitted. 'But I do know that it is not over, or she would have returned home.' She looked at him very steadily. 'She is still in there, with only the help of unskilled women, and Squeaky and the rat-catcher. There is no one to look after her, if she should need it, or even to be with her so she does not face this alone. I am going tomorrow morning, early, before light. Please don't try to argue with me. It is the right thing to do and there is no alternative.'

It was terrible. Unbearable. 'You can't!' He reached out and took her hands, clasping them hard. She did not resist, but neither did she respond. 'Margaret, no one is allowed in – or out,' he said urgently. 'I understand your wishing to help, but . . .' His mind was filled with horror, as if a pit had suddenly yawned open at his feet, and he and all he loved were teetering on the rim.

She pulled her hands away sharply. 'Yes I can. I shall write a message for the men with the dogs to take to the rat-catcher. Hester may not let me in, but Sutton will, for her sake.' She looked so white now that he was afraid she might faint. She was as terrified as he was, just as aware of the horror of the disease and the chances of her contracting it and dying a swift and vile death. And yet she intended to go.

He had to stop her. The irony of it was devastating. 'I was going to ask you to come to the conservatory so that we might speak alone, for an utterly different reason.'

'What?' She was startled, as if she thought she might have misheard him.

'I was going to ask you to marry me. I love you, Margaret, more than I have ever loved anyone else, more than I realised I could. I am very afraid of caring so intensely, but I find I do not have a choice in the matter.' How stilted he sounded, as if he were addressing a judge before a more impassioned plea to a jury.

Her eyes filled with tears, which amazed him.

'Please?' he said gently. 'I love you far too much to give up asking. For me there is no second best, nothing else to fall back on.'

'I love you too, Oliver,' she said in little more than a whisper. 'But this is not the time to be thinking of ourselves. And we do not know if there will be a future after this.' There was reproach in her voice; it was infinitely gentle, but it was also impossible to mistake.

His heart plunged. She had seen his terror of disease, and while she might understand it, she could conquer her own fear and she expected as much from him. Had he lost her already, not to plague but to contempt, or even to its kinder and devastating likeness, pity? And yet he had no power to govern the churning of his stomach, the feeling as if everything strong and in control inside him had suddenly turned to water.

He closed his eyes. 'It is precisely because there may be no future after this that I had to tell you how I feel.' He heard his voice hollow, shaky rather than passionate. 'Tomorrow, or next week, may be too late. I could merely have said I love you, but I imagine you already know that – the important part is that I wish to marry you. I have never asked a woman that before.'

310

She turned away from him, smiling in spite of her tears. 'Of course not, Oliver. If you had, they would have accepted you. But I can't, not with things as they are. I hope you will forgive me, and take my place in the raising of funds. We will still need them desperately. But others apart from me can do that. No one else can be there, nor should they.' She turned back. 'I am not asking because you love me, or because I love you, but because it is right.'

'Of course.' He did not have to give it an instant's thought. He wanted to argue with her, say anything, do anything, to prevent her going, but he knew if he did, it was rooted in selfishness, and it would destroy both of them. He offered her his arm, and they went back to join the party, and proceed in to dinner.

When he took her home it was not late because they both could think of nothing but the fact that she must be up early in the morning, to reach the clinic before dawn.

He alighted from the hansom and offered his arm to hand her out. He hesitated for a moment, hoping to kiss her. She must have sensed it, because she pulled away.

'No,' she said quietly. 'Goodbye is difficult enough. Please don't say anything, just let me walk away. Apart from anything else, I do not wish to have to explain myself to my mother. Good night.' And she walked across the footpath as the front door of the house opened. She went in, leaving him as utterly alone as if he were the only man alive in a deserted city.

He slept badly and at half-past four gave up the attempt altogether. He rose, shaved in tepid water, and dressed. Without bothering with breakfast, he took a hansom cab and gave the driver the address of his father's house in Primrose Hill.

It was nearly six when he arrived, and still as dark as midnight. It took him almost five minutes on the front doorstep before Henry Rathbone's manservant let him in.

'Good gracious, Mr Oliver! Whatever's wrong?' he said with horror. 'Come in, sir. Let me get you a brandy. I'll go an' fetch the master.'

'Thank you,' Rathbone accepted. 'That's very good of you. Please tell him that I am quite unhurt, and so far as I know in perfectly good health.'

Henry Rathbone arrived some ten minutes later, accepting the offer of a cup of tea from his manservant. Then he sat down in the armchair opposite Oliver, who was nursing a brandy. He did not cross his legs as usual but leaned forward, giving Rathbone his whole attention. The room was cold, no one having risen yet to clean out the grate, set and light a new fire.

'What is it?' he said simply. He was a taller man than his son, lean with a gentle, aquiline face and steady, very clear blue eyes. He had been a mathematician and some-time inventor in his earlier years, and the lucidity of his mind and its gentle reasonableness had often assisted in Oliver's more desperate cases.

Oliver remembered Henry's profound affection for Hester, and it made what he had to say almost impossibly difficult. He hesitated, now that the moment was here, lost for words.

'I cannot help if I do not know what it is,' Henry reminded him reasonably. 'You have come this far, before dawn, and you are obviously beside yourself with anxiety over something. You had better say what it is.'

Rathbone looked up. His father's mere presence made it both better and worse. It brought all his own emotions so much closer to the surface. 'It is something that can be told to no one else at all. I should not tell you, but I am at my wits' end,' he said.

'Yes, I see that,' Henry agreed. 'Wait till we have the tea, and can be uninterrupted.'

Oliver obeyed, marshalling his thoughts into some kind of rational order.

When the tea had been brought and they were alone, he began. He told the story very simply and as devoid of emotion as he could manage. Rather than robbing it of feeling, this added to it.

Henry said nothing whatever until Oliver stopped speaking and waited for a comment.

'How like Hester,' Henry said at last. 'I am sure Margaret Ballinger is a fine woman, that much is quite clear, and perhaps Hester would not have made you happy, nor you her. But I have never known anyone else whom I liked quite so much.'

'What can I do?' Oliver asked.

'Defend the thief to the best of your ability,' Henry told him, 'as long as you do not ever allow anyone to guess, as wildly as they may, that you are concealing a disease of any nature, let alone this one. You would create a panic which might end in mass destruction. Neither Hester nor Margaret would survive it, and it would not even necessarily contain the plague. Whatever you do, Oliver, you must let no one suspect. It will be very dreadful if the thief is hanged for a crime of which he is innocent, but for once injustice is not the greatest evil.'

'I know,' Oliver agreed quietly. 'I do know.'

'And poor Monk is doing what he can to trace the members of the crew who were paid off?'

'Yes. The last time I spoke to him, he had had no success at all.'

'They may already be dead,' Henry pointed out. 'It is even possible they died at sea, and Monk can find no trace of them because there is none to find.'

'I hadn't thought of that,' Oliver admitted.

'Is there any reason to believe this man Louvain?'

'None at all.'

'Then you had better appeal to his interest rather than his honour.'

'Now that Margaret is no longer able to raise money

313

for food, coal, medicines, it is up to me. People don't want to give to street women in London. They all prefer to give more exotic causes, lepers or missions in Africa.'

Henry sighed. 'People's gullibility never ceases to annoy me.'

'Gullibility?' Oliver was startled. 'It's not that, it's a fear of immorality and disease in our midst. We don't like to be reminded of such things so close to home. We feel guilty that it happens and we are perfectly well and comfortable ourselves. Africa is too far away to be our fault.'

'Personally,' Henry agreed drily. 'It is too far away for us to feel accountable for it and it is equally too far away for them to be accountable to us.'

Oliver was too tired to grasp his meaning. He was cold and exhausted deep to his bones. 'What do you mean?'

'That we give money, and feel our duty is discharged,' Henry replied. 'There is no probability of seeing that it goes to the cause we have been told, so we feel virtuous, and ignore the rest.'

'Well, of course, it—' Oliver stopped.

Henry reached for the teapot and topped up his cup. 'I shall help. It will not be difficult for me to raise money for you. You attend to rescuing the thief from the gallows. I shall bring money for you tomorrow. For today I have about seven pounds in the house. Take that and begin. I shall get more, however I do it.'

'However?' Oliver said sharply. He glanced around the room at various pieces of pewter, silver, a couple of wooden carvings.

'Can you think of anything better I could do with whatever I have?' Henry asked.

'No. No, of course not.' Oliver rose to his feet stiffly. 'I must get back to town. Thank you.'

As darkness shrouded the river on the evening when

Rathbone took Margaret to dinner, Monk was standing on the shore at Wapping Stairs waiting for Durban. He heard the boat scraping against the stones and moved forward out of the shadows.

Durban came up the steps slowly, coughing in the raw night air. For a brief moment he was silhouetted against the water where the riding lights of a moored boat shimmered behind him, then he was in the dark. But Monk had seen him for that moment, and knew from the hunch of his shoulders that he had found nothing.

'Neither did I,' he said quietly. He voiced the thought that had been in his mind for some time. 'Do you think they could have died at sea and simply been put overboard, and that's why there is no trace?'

'Of plague?' Durban asked, standing close beside Monk so he did not have to raise his voice. 'And the rest of the crew got the ships here?'

'Why not? Couldn't four men do it, if they had to?'

'Probably, and they wouldn't all go at once. But that isn't the issue. If the men died of an ordinary illness they'd report it. Why not? And Louvain would know.'

'Yes,' Monk agreed. 'But if they died of plague, they wouldn't. The ship would be barred from landing and Louvain would lose his cargo, and we already know he can't afford that.'

'You saw Newbolt and the others,' Durban responded. 'Do you think they'd stay on a plague ship out of loyalty to Louvain?'

'No.' There was no argument, the idea was ludicrous. 'So where are the other five?'

'Paid off, as Louvain said, and either lucky enough not to have got the plague, or dead of it by now,' Durban answered, his voice soft in the darkness and the gentle slurping of the tide against the stones.

'Gould goes to trial tomorrow,' Monk said. 'I believe Hodge died of plague, and someone beat his head in to hide the fact. They didn't dare put him over the side once they were in port, which means Gould had nothing to do with it. We can't prove that, and wouldn't even if we could. We daren't even suggest it was one of the crew, or the whole thing could come out. We daren't give them any cause to dig up the body, so we can't call medical evidence.'

Durban did not ask if Monk knew anything from the clinic; they had spent enough time together that he would have heard it in Monk's voice – in what he didn't say as well as what he did. Durban never once offered pity, just a quiet understanding of pain.

'It wasn't any of the crew who killed Hodge,' he agreed. 'If they knew it was plague they'd have been off that ship if they'd had to swim. It must have been Louvain himself. But we'll not get him to testify to that.'

'What would be "reasonable doubt"?' Monk was thinking aloud. 'Dead drunk and fell?'

'It would mean Louvain would have to go back on his word in the first place,' Durban warned. 'He'd not like that.'

'He'd not like the alternative, either,' Monk said with growing conviction. 'I need to make it sufficiently unpleasant he'll be glad to say he was mistaken. Hodge was drunk and he fell and hit his head so hard it killed him. There was more blood around him than he first realised.'

'Hodge was a drunkard?' Durban asked dubiously. 'They left a known drunkard on watch at night on the river, with the cargo still on board? That's incompetent.'

'They're short-handed.'

'Then put your drunkard on during daylight.'

'Then you're right, they're incompetent,' Monk agreed bitterly. 'That's still better than plague-ridden, and that's Louvain's choice.'

'You going to tell him?'

'Can you think of anything better?'

'You want me to come?'

Monk heard the exhaustion in Durban's voice. 'No. Anyway, I'd like to see that bastard alone. I want to be the one to force him to save Gould. It's not much, but I'd like to.'

'I understand. But be careful,' Durban warned, and suddenly the edge was back in his tone, the tiredness gone. 'Make sure he knows you are not working alone. The River Police know everything. Make absolutely certain he understands that.'

'You think he'd kill me?' Monk was only mildly surprised, and he acknowledged a strange, flat emptiness inside that meant he did not really care. He was exhausted with plunging between hope and despair for Hester. Hope was agonising – sometimes almost unbearable to cherish. Better to accept that this was the end. Sooner or later she would catch the disease. She had given her life to save London, maybe Europe. He was passionately proud of her, so angry he could have killed Louvain with his bare hands and felt the life choke out of him with the nearest he could know to pleasure. He was so full of pain he was buckling under the weight of it. He did not want to eat, and could not sleep, only succumb to unconsciousness now and then.

'Actually, I think you might kill him,' Durban said reasonably. 'So I'll come with you anyway. You can be the one to talk, I'll just be there.'

'And if he has men there, and kills both of us?' Monk asked.

'Chance I'll take,' Durban replied drily. 'We'll take him with us, that'll be something.'

'Won't help Gould much.'

'No, it won't, will it?' Durban agreed. 'Come on. Let's go and see him.'

This time it was less easy to gain entrance to Louvain's

office, even though the clerk readily admitted that Mr Louvain was still in, and there was no one with him.

'It's to do with the *Maude Idris* and the theft of the ivory,' Monk said curtly.

'Yes, sir. We have the ivory back, thank you.'

'I know, damn it! I'm the one who got it back for you. The thief goes on trial tomorrow. A matter has arisen which I need to speak to Mr Louvain about before then.'

'I'll ask, sir. And the gentlemen with you?'

'Inspector Durban, of the River Police.'

Ten minutes later they were in Louvain's office, the fire still burning, the room warm, the gaslight gleaming on the polished surface of his desk. He was standing with his back to the window, as he had been when Monk was here last time, the lights of the Thames flickering in the dark window behind him. He looked tense and tired.

'What is it?' he said as soon as the door was closed. 'I know the thief goes on trial tomorrow. What of it?' He did not bother to hide his irritation, as he and Monk faced each other across the room, anger brittle in the air between them. 'What the hell have you got the River Police here for?'

'Gould didn't kill Hodge,' Monk stated. 'I didn't look at the body closely. As I was meant to, I saw only the back of his head.'

Louvain's eyes were hard and steady. Not once did they look at Durban. 'And what more did you wish to see?' he asked.

'The cause of death,' Monk replied instantly. 'Or the cause of Ruth Clark's death – whoever she was.'

Louvain's face paled under the windburn on his skin. 'She has nothing to do with them,' he said gruffly. For the first time there was an emotion in him quite different from anger.

Monk wondered if she had been Louvain's mistress, after all. Had it even hurt him to take her to the clinic and leave her there? He had thought it possible Louvain had not known it was plague, believed it to be simply pneumonia, but Durban's logic was relentless. If Gould had not killed Hodge, then it had to be Louvain who had disguised the cause of his death. If the crew had known the truth, nothing on earth would have kept them on the ship. Which also meant that the other five had been paid off rather than died at sea.

'She had everything to do with it,' Monk said with a choking hatred inside him. 'You took her to the Portpool Lane clinic, knowing she had the plague.' He ignored Louvain's wince of pain. However much he might have cared for her, it would not excuse him taking her to where she could pass on the disease to other people, women other men loved. In fact, the depth of his own loss made it worse. 'That is what Hodge died of – isn't it?' he accused. 'It was you who took the shovel to the back of his head to make it look like murder, so he would be buried quickly, and no one would ever know the truth. You didn't care a toss that an innocent man might hang for it.'

'He's a thief,' Louvain said bitterly, anger in his voice at being held to account.

'Is that why you're hanging him?' Monk was incredulous, and yet the more he thought of it, the more he believed it. 'Because he stole from you?'

Louvain's mouth twisted. 'You think you're a worldly man, Monk, and that no one dares to defy you, but you're naïve. You're hobbled by your own morals. You're too weak to survive on the river.'

A few days ago that insult would have bothered Monk. Today it was too trivial even to answer. What was vanity in the face of the loss that gaped in front of him?

'Gould is not going to hang,' he answered instead, 'because we are going to see he is acquitted, on the grounds of reasonable doubt.'

Louvain bared his teeth in something like a smile. 'Reasonable doubt as to what? You're not going to tell anyone Hodge died of plague.' Even as he said the word his voice caught, and Monk realised for the first time the horror that turned him sick at even speaking the word. It was anger, greed and pride that drove him, but it was fear that beaded the sweat on his skin and drained the blood from it. 'You'll have panic like forest fire,' he went on. 'Your own wife will be one of the first to be killed. The mob would torch the clinic, and you know that.' A glitter of triumph lit his eyes, thin as melting ice.

Monk was drenched with the sense of the power in Louvain, the intelligence and the violence held in check only by judgement of his own need. Now he knew exactly why the shipowner had been so willing to sign the paper testifying to Hodge's injury. He had intended even then to hold Hester and the clinic to ransom. That was why he had chosen Monk. It made the most perfect sense.

'Of course I won't tell anyone what Hodge died from,' Monk agreed, his voice shaking, and almost oblivious now of Durban behind him. 'And neither will you, because if you do you'll be mobbed as well. I'll see to it. The river wouldn't thank you for bringing plague into London. You'll not only lose your ship, and the cargo still in it, but you'll be lucky if they don't burn your ware-house, your offices and your home. They'd string you up for the pleasure of it.' He smiled back. 'I'll make damn sure of it – if I have to.'

He saw the sweat of fear on Louvain's lip and brow, and the hatred in his eyes.

'So you are going to testify that you were mistaken,' Monk said in a hard, level voice, holding Louvain's eyes. 'You did not want everyone to know that you had a watchman on duty who was a drunkard – bad for your reputation. But you realise now that you have to be more precise with the truth. Hodge drank too much, he smelled of it, and he must have overbalanced and fallen, hitting his head, because that's how you found him. Gould will change his story about Hodge being dead but without apparent injury when he saw him. It will be reasonable enough to think that's what happened.'

'And if I refuse?' Louvain said very carefully. He stood stiffly, his body balanced as if for a physical fight, shoulders high, weight on the balls of his feet. 'You're not going to let the plague story out, any more than I am. We are hoist with the same petard, Monk. I say Gould hangs. The next thief will think twice before stealing from a Louvain ship.'

'How clever do you think Gould is?' Monk asked, as if it were merely a matter of curiosity. 'How moral?'

'Not much – in either case,' Louvain answered, shifting his weight a little. 'Why?'

'He didn't kill Hodge. What are you prepared to gamble on his willingness to hang in order to protect your interests?'

Louvain's eyes were bright, but the last vestige of colour had drained from his face, making the stubble on it look grey rather than brown. 'You wouldn't tell him,' he stated.

'I wouldn't have to,' Monk replied. 'He might be able to work it out. Not plague, perhaps, but yellow fever, typhus, cholera. Are you willing to have them dig up Hodge's body to see if he's right? Once it gets that far, none of us will be able to prevent it.'

There was silence in the room. Suddenly the ticking of the chronometer on the table became audible, counting away the moments of eternity.

'What do you want me to say?' Louvain spoke at last. His skin was white and sheened in sweat, but there was black rage in his eyes.

Monk told him, slowly and carefully, then he and Durban went out into the rain-washed, blustery darkness,

Monk with a small triumph like a pin-dot of warmth inside him, too tiny to ease the vast fear of loss.

In the morning Rathbone was preparing to go into court when Monk came to him in the corridor. He looked ashen-faced and his clothes were ragged. He was thinner than a couple of weeks ago and there were hollows around his eyes.

'Sorry,' he apologised. 'I lost track of the time. I should have been here earlier. Louvain will testify that Hodge was a drinker, and when he found him he was on the ledge at the bottom of the steps, dead drunk, his head bashed in from the fall.'

Rathbone stared at him. 'You're sure?'

'Yes. He dare not do anything else.' Monk blinked. 'You look terrible.' His voice caught in his throat, fear naked in his eyes, his face, the wild, angular rigidity of his body.

Rathbone felt an overwhelming sense of brotherhood with him, a bond shared so profoundly it changed something inside him in that moment. All he could think of was getting rid of the terror in Monk's eyes. He understood it because it was his own. 'Margaret has gone to the clinic to help Hester,' he answered. 'I don't know any more, good or bad, but I'm taking money and supplies.'

The momentary relief left Monk speechless. His eyes filled with tears and he turned away.

Rathbone let him go. There was no need for words between them.

The trial lasted for three days. On the first the prosecution began with the undertaker who had buried Hodge, and his evidence seemed damning. There was little Rathbone could have done to shake him, and he knew he would only make himself unpopular with the jury, were he to try. The undertaker was an honest man and it was quite clear he believed utterly what he said. He behaved with both dignity and compassion.

In the early afternoon Hodge's widow gave evidence as to the identity of the body – not that anyone had doubted it. It was her quiet grief that the prosecution wished the jury to see.

Rathbone rose to his feet. 'I have nothing to ask this witness, my lord. I would merely like to offer my condolences upon her loss.' And he sat down again to a murmur of approval from the crowd.

Next to be called was Clement Louvain. Rathbone found his heart beating faster, his hands clenched and slick with sweat. There was more than a man's life depending upon him. If he probed too far, asked too much, he might let out a secret that could destroy Europe. And no one in the room knew it but Louvain and himself.

Louvain took the oath. He looked tired, as if he had been up all night, and his face was deep-lined with the ravages of emotion. Rathbone wondered briefly what part of it might be grief at the loss of the woman Ruth Clark.

The prosecution led Louvain through the finding of Hodge's body and the description of the terrible wound in his head.

'And why did you not call in the police, Mr Louvain?' he enquired mildly.

Rathbone waited.

Louvain stood silent.

The judge stared at him, his eyebrows raised.

Louvain cleared his throat. 'Part of my cargo had been stolen. I wanted it recovered before my competitors were aware of it. It ruins business. I employed a man to do that. It was he who caught Gould.'

'That would be Mr William Monk?'

'Yes.'

The prosecution's tone was audibly sarcastic. 'And now

that you have your cargo back, you are ready to co-operate with the law, and the people of London, not to mention Her Majesty, and help us to obtain justice. Do I understand you correctly, Mr Louvain?'

Louvain's face was twisted with fury, but there was nothing he could do. Watching him, Rathbone had a sense of the power in him, the strength of his will, and was glad he had not incurred such hatred.

Louvain leaned forward over the railing of the witness box. 'No you don't,' he snarled. 'You have no idea of life at sea. You dress in smart suits and eat food brought you by a servant, and you've never fought anything except with words. One day on the river and you'd heave up your guts with fear. I got the thief and I got back my cargo, and I did it without anyone getting hurt, or spending the public money on police time. What else do you want?'

'For you to follow the law like anyone else, Mr Louvain,' the prosecution replied. 'But perhaps you will tell me exactly what you found when you went to your ship, the *Maude Idris*, and discovered the body of Mr Hodge?'

Louvain did as he was bidden, and the prosecution thanked him and invited Rathbone to question the witness if he wished.

'Thank you,' Rathbone said courteously. He turned to Louvain. 'You have described the scene very vividly, sir, the dim light of the hold, the necessity of carrying a lantern, the height of the steps. We feel as if we have been there with you.'

The judge raised his eyebrows. 'Sir Oliver, if you have a question, please ask it. The hour is growing late.'

'Yes, my lord.' Rathbone refused to be rushed, his tone was easy, almost casual. 'Mr Louvain, is it as awkward to climb the steps into the hold as you seem to suggest?'

'Not if you're used to it,' Louvain answered.

'And sober, I presume?' Rathbone added.

Louvain's shoulders clenched under his jacket, and his hands on the railing looked as if he might break the wood. 'A drunken man could miss his footing,' he conceded.

'And fall a considerable distance. I believe you said eight or ten feet?'

'Yes.'

'And sustain serious injuries?'

'Yes.'

'And was Hodge sober?'

Louvain's eyes narrowed. 'Not from the smell of him, no.'

'Then what makes you believe he was murdered, rather than simply having missed his footing, slipped and fallen?' Rathbone walked a step further forward into the middle of the floor. 'Let me assist you, Mr Louvain. Could it be that, since some of your cargo had been stolen, you automatically assumed that the watchman was a victim of the same crime? You looked at the scene, and concluded that the thief had come aboard your ship, attacked your watchman and stolen your goods, rather than that your watchman had died an accidental death. His absence from his post had allowed a thief to come aboard your ship, and steal your goods? Is that possible, Mr Louvain?'

'Yes,' Louvain said bitterly. 'That is possible.' His voice was barely audible. 'In fact, I believe that is what happened.'

'Thank you, sir.' Rathbone returned to his seat.

The rest of the trial was a formality. The other witnesses gave their evidence, including Monk the following day, substantiating all that Louvain had said. The jury returned a verdict on the third day, Gould was guilty of theft, as he had pleaded, but there

325

was more than reasonable doubt that any murder had been committed at all. Of that charge he was not guilty.

Rathbone walked out into the mid-morning rain with a sense of one very small victory, one man's life saved, at least for the time being.

Chapter Thirteen

❦

In Portpool Lane time was measured not in nights and days but in loads of laundry, whether it was light enough to blow out the candles, or dark enough to ask the men in the yard to fetch water from the well at the end of the street. Everything still had to be done by signs from the back door. No one must come close enough to risk catching the contagion.

Four women had died now, including Ruth Clark and Martha, leaving nine alive. Hester went to each survivor as often as she could. For those with pneumonia or bronchitis it was a matter of keeping the fever down and making sure they drank as much as possible: water, tea, soup, anything to make up for the fluid loss.

For the three whose illness was recognisably plague there was less to be done, and a more desperate desire to try anything at all to lessen the pain, which was acute. It was not only the knowledge of almost certain death, but the poison that raged through their bodies before it erupted in the blackened, putrefying flesh of the buboes, that made the person so ill that they longed for oblivion. The moments of awareness between one delirium and another were so agonising they cried out, and there was nothing Hester or any of the others could do but administer cool cloths, a sip of water, and not leave them alone.

'I wouldn't wish that on anyone,' Flo said softly, pulling uncomfortably on the sleeve of her blouse, like all of them conscious every moment of her armpits and groin. She set down another bowl of water on the table outside one of the rooms so Hester could wring out cloths in it from the woman inside. 'Not even that Ruth Clark, the lyin' bampot.' Her face was pale with tiredness, the freckles on it standing out like dirty marks, her eyes dark-ringed. 'I may be a tart, Miss 'Ester, an' a few other things I dare say, but I in't never bin a thief. I got a name like anybody else, an' she got no right to take it from me by telling lies. Why'd she do that? I in't never done nothin' to 'er.'

'She was an angry woman,' Hester replied, putting the cloths over her arm, then picking up the bowl. 'A man she trusted, maybe even loved, threw her aside like so much rubbish when she most needed him. She just lashed out at everyone.'

Flo shrugged. 'If she trusted a man wot paid for 'er, the more fool 'er.' She looked at Hester defiantly and Hester stared straight back at her. Flo sighed and lowered her gaze. 'Well . . . I s'pose we're all stupid sometimes, poor cow,' she said reluctantly. Then she smiled. 'I'm alive, an' she ain't, so I reckon I don't 'old no grudges. I won, eh?'

Hester felt the cold grasp her as if the outside door had been opened on to the night. 'Is that what you call winning, Flo?'

'Well . . .' Flo started, then she froze. 'Jeez! I din' do nothin' to 'er, Miss 'Ester.'

The cold deepened inside Hester, gripping like ice. 'Why would I think you would, Flo?' she asked very quietly.

''Cos she called me a thief, an' I in't!' Flo said indignantly. 'That's a nice thing ter say. If yer'd believed 'er yer coulda put me out on the street, fer Gawd's sake. I could die out there!' A wry, miserable smile flickered across her face. 'Come ter think on it, I could die in 'ere, too. But in 'ere I'm wi' friends, and that counts.'

'I never thought you were a thief, Flo,' Hester said, surprised how completely she meant it.

Flo's face lit with amazement, and joy. 'Din't yer? Really?'

Hester felt tears prickle in her eyes. It must be tiredness. She could not remember when she had last slept more than an hour at a time. 'No, I didn't.'

Flo shook her head, still smiling. 'Then I'm glad I never fetched the poor sod in the chops – an' b'lieve me, I thought of it. D'yer want some more towels, then?'

'Yes, yes, please,' Hester accepted. 'Bring them next time you come.'

Another woman died and Hester and Mercy tied her in one of the dark-blankets as a winding sheet. When they were finished Hester looked across and saw how white-faced Mercy was, and when she turned her head, hearing footsteps on the stairs, the candlelight accentuated the hollowness around her eyes.

'We'll get Squeaky to help us carry her down,' she said. 'Don't you do it.'

Mercy started to argue, then gave up. 'Perhaps you're right,' she conceded. 'It would be terrible to drop her – poor soul.' Her face was filled with pity and there was also a note of anger. Hester wondered why, but she was too tired to pursue it.

Claudine stood in the doorway. She looked at Hester for a moment, then at the bundle on the bed. The body was that of a woman she had despised, but even a glance at her face showed that death had cleansed judgement from her and left only a common humanity.

'I'll tell the men,' she said. She turned from Hester to Mercy. 'You don't look as if you could lift your own feet, let alone anyone else's. I'd better fetch that useless man away from his books.' And without asking Hester's agreement she withdrew. They heard her feet going down the passageway, still sharp-heeled on the wood, but slower than before. She too was on the edge of exhaustion. It would soon be time for Bessie and Flo to take over for the rest of the night.

'We can manage,' Hester said to Mercy. 'Go to bed now. I'll wake you when it's time.'

For once Mercy made no demur.

Claudine returned with Squeaky a step behind her, grizzling all the way.

'Isn't my job to be a bleedin' undertaker,' he complained. 'What if I get the plague, eh? What then? Carrying bodies! Mr Bleedin' Rathbone didn't say as I had to be carrying bodies – that weren't part of the agreement. What if I get it, eh? You didn't answer me that, did you?'

'You didn't hold your tongue long enough to give me the chance,' Claudine responded tartly. 'But if you can't work out the answer for yourself, then I'll tell you. You'll die of it, that's what. Exactly the same as the rest of us.'

'You'd like that, wouldn't you?' he accused her, glaring at her where she stood just inside the door, her head high, hair untidy, hands on her wide hips.

'Of course I wouldn't like that,' she snapped. 'If you were dead I would have to carry all the water myself, instead of just most of it, as I do now. Apart from that, who'd carry you out?'

'You're a cold and heartless woman,' he said miserably. 'And you don't carry most of the water; you carries half, just like I does.'

'Well, carry half that poor woman's body,' she ordered. 'Not the bottom half, the top.'

'Why?'

'Because it's heavier, of course. Use the wits you were born with, man.'

'Poor woman, is it?' he sneered. 'That's not what you called her a couple of days ago. Nothing weren't bad enough for her then, 'cos she made her living on her back, like most of 'em here. You just despises her 'cos you wouldn't 'a made an 'a'penny yourself, not even in the dark.'

Hester tensed, ready to stem the onslaught she expected in reply to this insult.

But Claudine remained perfectly calm. 'Don't put words in my mouth, you stupid little man,' she said wearily. 'Just pick her up and help me carry her down the stairs. And do it discreetly. She's not so much dirty laundry to be slung about.'

Squeaky obeyed. 'You've changed your tune, haven't you? So tarts off the street are all right again, as long as they're dead, eh?' He bent and picked up the wrapped bundle approximately where her shoulders were, and staggered a little under the weight.

'Well, there isn't much point in criticising the dead, is there?' Claudine challenged him. 'Poor soul's God's problem now.'

Squeaky let out a high-pitched expletive. 'She's my bleedin' problem if I rips me guts out carrying her. D'you put a couple of lead bricks in with her?'

'For heaven's sake, man!' Claudine exploded. 'Bend your knees. Straighten your back. What's the matter with you? Haven't you ever picked up anything before?' She gave an exasperated sigh. 'Here.' She bent down carefully and, with surprising grace, keeping her back perfectly straight, picked up the dead woman's feet. 'Come on,' she ordered.

Squeaky copied Claudine exactly, his face twisted in concentration, then lifted the other end of the corpse. He did it with comparative care, hesitated, transparently doubting within himself whether to thank her or not, and very graciously decided to do so. 'Yeah,' he said. 'It isn't so hard.'

'Oh, get on with it,' Claudine told him impatiently. 'What are you waiting for, a round of applause?'

He glared at her, and set off backwards down the candlelit corridor towards the stairs.

Hester followed, calling out and warning just as Squeaky reached the top of the stairs and looked like falling backwards down them.

'You fool!' Claudine said in utter exasperation, probably because she had not thought to warn him herself.

'I dunno why we bother with Sutton and his bleedin' dogs,' Squeaky said indignantly. 'Got a mouth like a rat trap, you have. Catch all the bleedin' rats in the place, yer would. Mebbe that's what's wrong with you. Swallowing too many bleedin' rats.'

'Stop complaining and carry this poor woman to her grave,' Claudine responded, apparently unmoved.

Squeaky steadied himself and started backwards down the stairs. Claudine went gently, with considerable regard for his balance and speed, waiting whenever it was necessary, and without further criticism. When they reached the bottom she told Squeaky when to go left, when right, and when he seemed lost she waited.

Finally they reached the back door and Sutton, who was standing beside it, opened it on to the rain-soaked night. The lamplight gleamed on the stones, and the gutters were awash. Under the eaves two men were waiting, dogs sitting patiently at their heels. Two more detached themselves from the shadows, ready to come forward for the body when the door was closed. The rat cart would be waiting at the kerb, but it was out of sight.

Squeaky let go of the body with relief and then Claudine let go of her end in turn. To everyone's amazement she stood quite still, in the rain, her head bowed.

'May the Good Lord have mercy on her soul, and remember only what was good in her,' she said quietly.

'Amen.' She jerked her head up. 'What are you staring at?'

Squeaky glowered at her, his body hunched and tight, shivering in the cold.

'Amen,' he replied, then splashed back over the cobbles to the kitchen door, scattering water everywhere, Claudine immediately behind him.

Hester smiled, thanking them both, just as Bessie appeared, announcing her arrival to take over for a while. Hester excused herself and went upstairs again to find a quiet place and snatch a few hours of sleep, sinking into oblivion with immeasurable gratitude.

She woke what seemed only a few minutes later, but must actually have been several hours because the thin winter daylight came in through the window. Flo was standing beside her, her long, freckled face filled with misery.

Hester dragged herself into consciousness and forced herself to sit up. The air was cold and her head ached. 'What is it, Flo?' she asked.

'I went ter waken Miss Mercy,' Flo replied. 'She looks 'orrible pale, an' I can't get 'er ter waken proper.'

'She's probably exhausted,' Hester answered, pulling the bedclothes around herself. 'She's been working almost without a stop for days. We can leave her for a little longer. I'll get up. Has anything happened during the night? How is everyone?' As she straightened up she touched her fingers under her armpits, dreading to feel the tenderness, and only half believing it was not there.

'That Minnie looks worse,' Flo replied, pretending she had not noticed the gesture. She understood it perfectly. 'Coughin' fit to bring her guts up, she is,' she went on. 'But still got plenty ter say fer 'erself, so I reckon's she's good fer another day or two, poor little cow. Kettle's on when yer ready.'

'Thank you.'

Flo went out, closing the door behind her, and stiffly,

shivering as the air hit her skin, Hester got up. She dressed again, and splashed her face from the small dish of cold water she had spared herself. Then she started to go downstairs for the tea Flo had offered, and a slice or two of toast. Thanks to Margaret's constant efforts, they had sufficient food and fuel. She pushed the thought of Margaret out of her mind because she missed her company, her encouragement, just the knowledge that she could glance at her and know that they understood each other in unique ways. The loneliness might cripple her if she allowed it.

If she thought of Monk she would find herself in tears. She could not bear to think of being with him again – his voice, his touch, the feel of his lips on her face – because the sweetness of it was everything she longed for. Nor could she think of the possibility that she would not, because that robbed her of hope. He was the only reward that mattered and was enough to drive her through exhaustion and pity and grief.

She was halfway down the stairs when she thought she had better go to see if Mercy was all right. She was probably just exhausted. She was a young woman of good birth and a fairly sheltered upbringing. This kind of physical labour, let alone the constant fear, would have crippled most girls like her.

Hester knocked lightly on the door, and there was no answer. She pushed it open and went in. Mercy looked to be sound asleep, but not motionless. She moved very slightly, took an unsteady breath, then turned her head.

'Mercy?' Hester said quietly.

There was no answer.

Hester walked over to her. Even in the dim daylight through the curtains she could see that Mercy was not awake. She was tossing and turning in fever, her cheeks flushed, a beading of sweat on her lip.

Hester felt a slow settling of pain inside her and fear

took hold of her stomach, knotting it tight. With a trembling hand she reached over and pulled the bed-clothes back. Her fingers rested lightly over the place where the sleeve of the nightgown met the bodice: she felt the hard lumps. Perhaps it was going to happen to all of them. It was only sooner or later, that was all. Now for Mercy it was a terrible certainty.

Hester's throat was thick with tears. She found it suddenly hard to breathe. Looking down at the flushed face and the fair, tangled hair, she realised how much she liked Mercy. She was angry that this should happen to her, and not someone who had less to lose, or who would not be missed so much. It was a stupid emotion, and she should have known better than to allow herself to feel it, but all the reason in the world made no difference.

Slowly she turned and walked away, closing the door of the room behind her and going down the stairs as if in a dream. She must get something to eat, stay strong. She would nurse Mercy herself, make sure she never woke alone. No one could help, no one could remove the physical pain, the horror or the inevitability of death. Lies would be no comfort, would only dig a gulf between them. She could do nothing but simply be there.

She walked down the stairs and into the kitchen. They all turned to look at her, but it was Sutton who spoke. He came over to her, his face pinched with concern.

'Tea,' he ordered Flo. 'Then get yerself off.' To Claudine he just waved a hand, and, white-faced, she went to resume the endless laundry. There was little water left, but she did not mention it, and certainly did not complain. She would reuse what was there if it proved necessary. Squeaky was nowhere to be seen. Fear was in the air, like the cold.

Flo poured the tea and excused herself. Hester sat down, still without having spoken. She placed her hands round the steaming mug and let the warmth run through them.

'D'yer know 'oo did it?' Sutton said quietly.

'Killed Ruth?' She was surprised. It seemed to matter so little now. 'No, I don't. I'm not sure how much I care. The poor woman was dying anyway, she just took longer than some of these. Partly it was because of the way the disease went, and partly because she was strong, not living on the streets half starved. I think if I had plague, I wouldn't mind a lot if someone just snuffed me out a little faster. And don't bother to tell me you shouldn't do that. I know. I'm just admitting that I haven't even thought about it lately. Have you?'

'Not much,' he replied. 'She quarrelled a lot with Claudine and Flo. Mercy was the only one 'oo 'ad the measure of 'er, but then seems it were Mercy 'oo looked after 'er, as it were 'er brother wot brung 'er 'ere, so mebbe she knowed plenty about 'er. Could a' bin 'er as done it.' He pulled his face into a gruesome expression of disbelief. 'Or it could a' bin anybody else. Ruth were a nasty piece o' work, Gawd rest 'er.'

'I don't think it's going to matter if Mercy did it,' Hester said quietly, her voice flat.

Sutton caught the tone and he looked at her with intense sorrow. 'She got it, too?'

Hester took a shuddering breath. 'Yes . . .' It ended in a sob.

Automatically, he put out his hand to touch hers, very lightly, as if he did not want to intrude. She felt the warmth of it and ached to be able to hold on to him. But it would have embarrassed him. She was here to be a leader, not to turn to others for comfort as if she were just as terrified as they were. They might guess it, but they must never know.

She sat there silently for a moment longer, forcing her breathing to become even again, and the tears to choke back out of her throat. Then she brought her head up and began to drink her tea.

Ten minutes later she went back upstairs to sit with Mercy. She spoke to her every so often, not certain if she were awake enough to hear, or understand. She talked about all sorts of things: past experiences, things she had seen, like the first Christmas in the Crimea, the beauty of the landscape, snowbound under a full moon. And she described other things, closer to home, wandering in her memories at random, simply for the sake of talking.

Once or twice Mercy opened her eyes and smiled. Hester tried to get her to drink a little beef tea, and she managed a mouthful or two, but she was very weak. How she had kept going for so long was hard to imagine. She must have been in great pain.

Hester thanked her for all she had done, above all for her gentleness, for her friendship. And she praised her, hoping she would understand at least some of it. Late in the afternoon she seemed to find almost an hour of sleep.

In the evening Hester went downstairs again to see how everything else was doing, if there was enough water, food, soap, and to fetch another candle. Her head was aching, her eyes prickled with weariness and her mouth was dry. She had just started back upstairs when she was aware of the room blurring a little, sliding away from her vision. The next thing she lost her balance and slipped into total darkness, only vaguely aware of something hitting her head on the left side.

She opened her eyes to see the smoke-stained patch on the ceiling, then Claudine's face, ashen with fear, tears on her cheeks.

With a wave of terror so intense the room spun around again, she remembered the moment she had touched Mercy's armpit and felt the hard swelling. Had she looked as Claudine did now? It was the end; she had got it after all. She would never see Monk again.

Sutton was beside her, his arm round her, holding her head up a little. Snoot was pushing against him, wagging his tail.

'Yer've no right to give up yet,' Sutton said scathingly. 'Yer've nothing ter give up for. Yer not ill, yer just daft.' He gulped. 'Beggin' yer pardon fer the familiarity, but there in't nuffin' under yer arms. Yer just too skinny ter stand the pace.'

'What?' she mumbled.

'Yer not got the plague,' he hissed at her. 'Yer just got a fit o' the vapours, like any other lady wot's bin brung up right. Claudine'll get yer ter yer bed, an' yer ter stay there until yer told yer can come out. Sent ter yer room, like. In't that wot yer ma did to yer when yer was full o' lip?'

'Sent to my room . . .' Hester wanted to giggle, but she hadn't the strength. 'But Mercy—'

'The world in't gonna stop just 'cos yer in't pushin' it round,' Sutton said disgustedly, but his hand on her was as gentle and his eyes as soft as when he fondled the little dog. 'Just do as yer told, for once,' he snapped, his voice suddenly choking. 'We in't got time ter be pickin' yer up off the floor every five minutes.' He turned away quickly, blushing hard.

Claudine bent down and helped Hester up, holding her so tightly she couldn't have buckled at the knees if she had wanted to. Together, awkwardly, trying to keep in step and not trip each other, they made their way back up the stairs, passing a horrified Squeaky Robinson on the landing.

'Don't look like that, you daft ha'porth.' Claudine shot a furious glare at him. 'She's just tired. If you want to be useful, go and fetch some water from the yard. And if there isn't any there, tell those blasted men to go and get some.' And without waiting to see if he was going to obey her, she swept Hester along to the bedroom and half heaved her on to the bed. 'Now go to sleep,' she ordered furiously. 'Just do it. I'll look after everything.'

Hester stopped struggling and let go. She thought she said 'thank you', but was not certain if the words were simply in her mind.

She woke with a start. The only light in the room was from the candle burning on the small table beside her. In its flame she could see Margaret sitting on the chair, looking back at her, a little anxious, but smiling.

Hester shook her head, trying to clear her thoughts. She sat up slowly, blinking, but Margaret was still there. Horror welled up inside her. 'You can't have . . .'

'I haven't.' Margaret understood immediately. She leaned forward and took Hester's arm. 'Neither have you. You were just exhausted. You'll be all right.'

'They shouldn't have told you,' Hester protested, struggling to sit up. Now fear for Margaret was drowning out all other thoughts.

Margaret shook her head. 'They didn't. I came because I couldn't leave you here alone.' She said it quite simply, without protestations of morality or friendship. It was simply a fact.

Hester smiled widely, and lay back, filled with warmth, just for now refusing to think beyond the moment.

Later they met together over toast and jam and a cup of tea, while Hester told Margaret all that had happened since she had left.

'I'm sorry about Mercy,' Margaret said quietly. 'I liked her. It seems a terrible sacrifice. She's so young, and had everything before her. At least . . .' She frowned. 'I don't really know anything except that she is Clement Louvain's sister. One tends to think that if people have a good family, and are more than pleasing to look at, they will be happy, and that's silly, really. She may have all kinds of private griefs we know nothing of.' Her face became reflective, deep in her own thoughts, and there was more than a shadow of pain in them.

Hester knew what it was; there was only one thing that would trouble Margaret in such a way. There was all the difference in the world between the ache in the heart caused by love, its disillusion and loneliness, and the fear of any other kind of calamity. She had realised it even more intensely these last days, that the passion, the tenderness, above all the companionship of heart and mind, were the gifts that gave light and meaning to all others, or took it from them.

'Oliver?' she said gently.

Margaret's eyes opened wide, then she blushed. 'Am I so transparent?'

Hester smiled. 'To another woman, yes, of course you are.'

'He asked me to marry him,' Margaret said quietly. She bit her lip. 'I had been waiting for him to do that, dreaming of it, and it was all exactly as it should have been.' She gave a rueful, bewildered little laugh. 'Except that nothing was really right. How could I possibly accept marriage now, and go away leaving you here alone to cope with this? What would I be worth if I could, and how could he not know that? What does he believe of me that he would even ask?'

Hester watched Margaret's face. 'What did you say?'

Margaret took a sharp breath. 'That I could not, of course. I told him that I was coming here. He didn't want me to, at least, part of him didn't. Illness . . . frightens him.' She said it with hesitation, as if betraying a confidence and yet unable to bear it alone.

'I know,' Hester smiled. 'He's not perfect. It cost him all the courage he has even to think of it, let alone come close to it.'

Margaret said nothing.

'Perhaps he can face things we find harder, or even turn away from,' Hester went on. 'If he were afraid of nothing, if he had never run away, never failed or been ashamed, never needed time and another chance, what would he have in common with the rest of us, and how would he learn to be gentle with us?'

Margaret looked at her steadily, searching her eyes.

'You're disappointed?' Hester asked.

'No,' Margaret answered instantly, then looked away. 'I . . . I'm afraid he'll think I am, because I was for a moment or two. And maybe he won't ask me again. Maybe nobody will, but that doesn't matter, because I really don't want anyone else. Apart from you, there's nobody else I . . . like so much.' She looked up again. 'Do you understand?'

'Absolutely. I believe he will ask you, but if he is cautious, you will have to deal with that.'

'You mean be patient, wait?'

'No, I don't,' Hester responded instantly. 'I mean do something about it. Put him in a situation where he is obliged to speak – not that I am the least use at doing that sort of thing myself, but I know it can be done.'

Sutton came in through the back door, Snoot at his heels. Hester poured tea for him, offered him toast and invited him to sit down.

'It's good to see you, miss,' he said to Margaret, accepting the invitation. The words were bare enough, but the expression in his face was profound approval, and Margaret found herself colouring at the unspoken praise.

Hester took the crusts from her toast and gave them to Snoot. 'I know I shouldn't,' she acknowledged to Sutton. 'But he's done such a good job.'

'He's a beggar,' Sutton said tartly. ''Ow many times 'ave I told yer not to beg, yer little 'ound?' His voice was full of pride. ''E 'as done a good job, Miss 'Ester. I in't see'd a rat fer two days now.'

Hester realised how much she relied upon him, even

with Margaret back – his resourcefulness, his wry, brave wit, his companionship.

'Show me where they were,' she said, sensing he had more to say.

She finished her tea, and when he had also she followed him to the laundry. It smelled of carbolic, wet stone and cotton.

'We in't had no more new cases o' the plague since Miss Mercy. Mebbe we're gonna get the better of it,' he said softly. 'But I in't goin' even when I can till yer find out 'oo killed that Clark woman. Not as she din't deserve it, like, but nobody can't take the law into their own 'ands.' He looked at her in the dim light. 'I bin thinkin', it's gotta be between Flo, Miss Claudine, an' Miss Mercy, though why Miss Mercy should wanta kill 'er I in't got no idea. Summink ter do wi' 'er brother, mebbe. Bessie could've, o' course, but she in't like that. The rest of 'em were too poorly, accordin' ter Bessie, an' din't never see 'er.'

'Or Squeaky,' Hester added. 'But so far as I know, he didn't see her, either. And why on earth would he want to kill her?'

'That's exactly it,' Sutton said unhappily. 'An' as yer said, it were Mr Louvain as brung 'er in?'

'Yes. He said she was the mistress of a friend of his.'

He raised an eyebrow in a lop-sided expression of doubt. 'Or mebbe not? 'Ave yer thought as mebbe she were 'is own mistress, like?'

'Yes, of course, I have.' A coldness touched her. 'You mean that Mercy knew that, perhaps even knew her?'

'In't wot I wanna think,' he said sadly. 'Nor I wouldn't wanta think as mebbe that's why she come 'ere ter 'elp.'

'Just to murder Ruth Clark?' Hester refused to believe it. 'She was here for days before Ruth was killed. If that's what she came for, why would she wait?'

'I dunno. Mebbe she wanted ter argue the Clark woman inter leavin' the family alone?' he suggested, his face pinched with weariness. 'But p'raps the Clark woman 'ad ideas o' becomin' Mrs Louvain? Or mebbe just o' bleedin' 'im o' money. Miss Mercy could a' bin protectin' 'im.'

'No.' This time she was quite certain. 'He doesn't need anyone to do that. If Ruth Clark were trying to blackmail him, or get money in any way, he'd simply have dumped her in the river himself.'

He looked at her, shaking his head a little. 'Somebody put a piller over 'er 'ead. D'yer reckon as it were Flo, or Miss Claudine? Miss Claudine got a tongue on 'er as'd slice bacon, but she wouldn't stoop 'erself to 'it anybody. I seen 'er wi' Squeaky. She'd fair bust 'er stays, but she wouldn't 'it 'im. Flo's a different kettle o' fish. She'd a' throttled 'er, if she'd really lost 'er rag, like. But d'yer reckon as she'd a' carried it off after, all cool an' surprised, like? An' nobody'd guessed it were 'er?'

'No . . .'

'Then I reckon yer've gotter think as it were Miss Mercy.' His face was marked with weariness and sorrow. 'I wish I 'adn't 'ad ter say that.'

'I was just putting off thinking it,' Hester admitted. 'I sensed emotion between them, but I really didn't think it was hatred, and I would have sworn that Ruth wasn't afraid of her. If there'd been that kind of threat between them, if Ruth were blackmailing Clement Louvain, or imagining she would marry him, then surely she'd know Mercy would try to stop it? Wouldn't she have been afraid?'

Sutton was disconcerted. ''Ow daft were she?'

'Not at all. She was quick, well-educated, in fact they seemed to belong to the same social class, except that Ruth was possibly Louvain's mistress, whereas Mercy is his sister.'

There was a sound at the doorway, and Claudine came in, aware that she was probably interrupting, and ignoring

343

the fact. Her eyes were bleak and she held her voice in control with difficulty. 'Mrs Monk, I think Mercy is sinking. Flo is with her, but I thought you'd like to be there yourself, if she rallies long enough to know.'

Hester was not ready. Her thoughts were in turmoil and she needed to know the truth, however deeply it hurt, if only to free Flo and Claudine from suspicion. Nor was she ready emotionally. She liked Mercy, liked her patience, her curiosity, the way she was willing to learn skills totally outside her class or style of life, her generosity of spirit, her readiness to praise others, even her occasional flashes of temper. She was not prepared to accept her death with so much turbulence of heart, so many painful questions unanswered.

But time would not wait; the hand of plague waited for nothing.

'I'm coming,' she said, glancing once at Sutton. Then she followed Claudine out through the kitchen and up the stairs to Mercy's room.

Flo was sitting beside the bed, leaning forward a little to hold Mercy's hand. Mercy lay quite still, her eyes closed. She was breathing heavily and the sweat stood out on her skin.

Flo rose and allowed Hester to take her place, moving silently to the door.

Hester touched Mercy's head, then wrung out the cloth in the dish of water and placed it on her brow. A few minutes later Mercy opened her eyes. She saw Hester and smiled, just the corner of her lips moving a fraction.

'I'm here,' Hester whispered. 'I won't leave you.'

Mercy seemed to be struggling to say something. Hester wet her lips with the cloth.

'Are there any more?' Mercy breathed, the words barely audible.

'Any more?' Hester did not understand what she meant, but she could see that it was of intense importance to her.

344

'Any more . . . sick?' Mercy whispered.

'No, no more,' Hester answered.

There were several more minutes of silence. Mercy was blue about the lips and she was obviously in severe pain. The poison that blackened the buboes in her arms and groin was racking her whole body now. Hester had seen death often enough to know that it would not be long. She would have to get word out to Clement Louvain when it was over and they could communicate with the outside world. She would have to tell him about Ruth Clark as well, whatever the truth of his regard for her had been. Odd, such lovely words, Mercy and Clement. And the sister was Charity. And Ruth Clark too. The word was usually used in the negative – ruthless, so Ruth must be a kind of mercy and forbearance, a gentleness of spirit. Presumably Clement Louvain would tell Charity. What a lot of grief for one man to bear.

Had he known that Ruth had plague? Was that why he had brought her here, instead of having her nursed in his own home? If she had been his mistress, then he could well have it too by now.

Mercy's eyes were open.

Hester looked at her. 'Did you know that Ruth Clark had the plague?'

Mercy blinked. 'Ruth?' It was almost as if she did not know who Hester meant.

'Ruth Clark, the first one to die,' Hester reminded her. 'She was suffocated. Someone put a pillow over her face and stifled her, but she would have died of plague anyway – almost certainly. Hardly anyone ever recovers.'

'Leaving . . .' Mercy said hoarsely. 'Not listen to me. Spread it . . .'

'No she didn't,' Hester assured her gently, her eyes brimming with tears. 'She never went outside the clinic, except to be buried.' She put her hand on Mercy's and felt the fingers respond very slightly. 'That's why you killed her, isn't it?' Her throat was tight and aching. 'To stop her leaving. You knew she had plague, didn't you?'

'Yes.' It was hardly more than a breath.

'How? Was she your brother's mistress?'

Mercy made a funny little sound in her throat, a gasping as if she had something caught in it, and it was a couple of seconds before Hester realised it was laughter.

'Wasn't she?' she asked. 'Who was Ruth Clark?'

'Charity . . .' Mercy answered. 'My sister. Stanley died at sea, but Charity thought she could escape. I wouldn't let her . . . not with plague. I . . .' But she had no more strength. Her eyelids fluttered and her breath eased out slowly and did not come again.

Hester reached for her pulse, but she knew it would not be there. She sat motionless, overwhelmed with the reality of the loss. She had not known Mercy long, but they had shared sorrow, pity and laughter, shared grubby manual duties, fear and hope, and feelings that mattered. Now she knew that Mercy had come here deliberately, knowing what it might cost her, to stop her sister from carrying plague away into the city, the country. She had paid the price to the last drop.

Slowly Hester moved from the chair and sank to her knees. She had prayed often for the dead – it was a natural thing to do – but before now it had been for the comfort of those remaining. This time it was for Mercy, and it was directed to no listener except that divine power who judges and forgives the souls of men.

'Forgive her,' she said in her mind. 'Please – she didn't know anything better to do – please! Please?'

She did not know how long she kneeled, saying the words over and over until she felt a hand on her shoulder and flinched as if she had been struck.

'If she's gone, Miss 'Ester, we gotter get 'er away from 'ere, an' buried proper.' It was Sutton.

'Yes, I know.' She climbed to her feet. 'She has to be

buried in a graveyard.' She stated it as a fact. She had already decided to tell no one what Mercy had said. As far as they were concerned Ruth Clark was a prostitute who had died of pneumonia and no more.

'She will, Miss 'Ester,' Sutton bit his lip. 'I told the men yesterday. They got a place. But we gotta 'urry. There's a grave new-dug not far from 'ere, mile an' a 'alf, mebbe. It's rainin' like stair rods, which'll keep folk off the streets. Flo's bringin' one o' them dark blankets as we'll wrap 'er up. But we in't got time ter grieve . . . I'm sorry.'

Hester felt her eyes hot and stinging with unshed tears, but she obeyed. When Flo came with the blanket she took it from her and insisted on wrapping Mercy in it herself. Then the three of them, Sutton at the feet and the two women at the head, carried her down to the back door. Squeaky, Claudine and Margaret were waiting, heads bowed, faces pale. No one spoke. Margaret looked at Hester, a question in her eyes.

Hester shook her head. She turned to Sutton. 'I'm going with them.' It was a statement.

'Yer can't do that . . .' he started, then he saw the blind grief in her face. 'Yer can't go out now,' he said gently. 'Yer've kept in all this time—'

'I won't go near anyone,' she cut across him. 'I'll walk behind, by myself.'

He shook his head, but it was in defeat rather than denial, and his eyes were swimming in tears.

Flo sniffed fiercely. 'Don' yer forget yer goin' fer all of us. An' for all of them as we buried as 'as got no one else to grieve for 'em, or care where they are.'

'Say something for us as well,' Claudine agreed.

Hester nodded. 'Of course I will,' and before anyone could say anything more and break what little composure she had left, she opened the door and Sutton helped them carry the body outside into the yard and lay it down.

'Look after 'er,' he said to the men, when they came for it.

Hester waited until they were almost to the street, then she pulled her shawl over her head and followed over the cobbles, in the drenching rain, Sutton's coat around her shoulders. She waited under the arch of the gate as they passed under the streetlamp, and across the footpath and placed the body gently in the rat cart. One man picked up the shafts and started to pull, his dog beside him, the other went behind, his dog at his heels.

Hester went after them, about twenty feet behind. They knew she was there, and possibly they walked a little more slowly to allow her to keep up. They moved through the sodden night unspeaking, but every now and then glancing backwards to make sure she was still there.

She thought of the other women who had been buried this way, unmarked and unmourned. Whoever had loved them would never know where they were, nor at the very least that someone had dealt with them with some reverence.

The rain was turning to sleet, drifting across the arcs of light shed by the streetlamps and disappearing into the darkness again. Hester pulled Sutton's coat more tightly around her.

Without warning they came to a stop and she stood, still twenty feet away, while the two men took the body out of the cart and led the way very slowly, guided by the bull's-eye lanterns, through the graveyard gates. She waited until they were almost out of sight before she went after them along the paths between the stones.

A thin figure loomed up ahead, standing by the earth of a new grave, dug ready for the morning. The mound of fresher earth, excavated deeper, was barely visible in the darkness.

'Quick!' was the only word spoken, but she heard the slither of soil and then a thud as shovel blades hit harder ground. There was a minute's silence. Dimly she saw the figures straighten, and bend again as they lowered Mercy down. Then all three piled the earth back in. It was bitterly cold, and she heard the faint splash of water in the bottom of the grave. At least the downpour would wash the mud from their hands afterwards.

It seemed an age until Mercy was completely covered, but at last it was done.

One of the men walked over and stopped about ten feet from Hester. 'Yer wanner say summink?' he asked quietly.

'Yes.' Hester took a step sideways, closer to the grave, but away from him. 'Rest in peace,' she said clearly, the rain icy in her face, washing away the tears. 'If we loved you as much as we did, and could understand, you have no need to fear God – He has to love you more, and understand even better. Don't be afraid. Goodbye, Mercy.'

'Amen,' the others said in unison, then led the way ahead of her between the gravestones back to the rat cart, and the cold, bitter journey home.

The next day passed with no one else developing symptoms. They waited in dread and hope, listening for every cough, feeling for tenderness, watching for an awkward movement. They worked together to scrub, launder, cook, change bandages for the injured still trapped with them, and tend to those recovering from what now seemed to have been only pneumonia or bronchitis.

No one spoke much. They were all deeply subdued by Mercy's death. Even Snoot seemed to have lost heart for ratting, although he had possibly got them all anyway.

Once or twice Claudine seemed about to say something, deliberately filling her expression with hope, then as if it were too fragile to expose to reality, she changed her mind and kept silent, redoubling her efforts at scrubbing or mixing or whatever else she was doing.

Flo chopped vegetables as if she were slitting the throat

349

of an enemy, biting back tears all the time, and Bessie banged pots, pans and folded linen around and grunted. But whether it was out of satisfaction, the ache in her shoulders and back, or too much hope bottled up inside her, she did not allow anyone to know.

In the evening they sat together round the kitchen table and ate the last of the soup. From now on there would be nothing except gruel, but no one complained. In everyone's mind there was just the one prayer: that the plague was gone.

In the morning one of the men with the dogs knocked on the back door. When Claudine allowed him time, then went to answer it, she found a box of food, three pails of fresh water, and two envelopes tucked where they were kept dry. She carried them inside in triumph.

One note was for Margaret. Hester watched as she opened it and her face filled with joy, her eyes brimming. She read it twice, regardless of her tears, then looked across at Hester, whose note was still unopened.

'It's Oliver,' she said, gulping. 'He brought the food himself.' Involuntarily she glanced at the courtyard. 'He was right outside the door.' She did not offer any further comment. They both knew the effort it must have cost him, and the victory.

Hester tore hers open as well, and read:

My dearest Hester,
The thing you will care most about is that Monk is well, but he looks exhausted, and his fear for your welfare is eating him alive. He is working night and day to find the crew of the *Maude Idris* who were paid off before the ship reached the Pool of London, but we fear they may already be dead, or else have gone back to sea in new ships.

However, we have succeeded in saving the life of the thief, Gould, with a verdict of 'not guilty' because of reasonable doubt, and thus justice is served, without the terror of the truth being known.

When I last saw Monk, after the trial, I did not yet know that I would find the courage to deliver this myself, or I could have brought you a letter from him. But you will already know all that he would have written.

My admiration for you was always greater than I told you, but now it grows beyond my ability to measure. I shall be proud if you still wish to consider me a friend.

Yours as always,
Oliver

She smiled, folding the letter to put into her pocket, then looked up at Margaret. 'I told you he would,' she said with infinite satisfaction.

They spent the day scrubbing everything they could reach. Rathbone had thoughtfully included carbolic among the things he had left. By suppertime they were exhausted, but every room was clean and the sharp, stinging odour of the carbolic was everywhere. At any other time it would have been offensive; now they stood in the kitchen and inhaled it with pleasure.

That night they all slept, except that Bessie now and again walked the corridors just to make certain there was still no one worse, or complaining of new symptoms.

In the morning there was a crisp, hard frost and the light was sharp with the pale sun of winter. It was 11 November, twenty-one days since Clement Louvain had called Monk in to find his ivory, and see the dead body of Hodge.

'Yer beat it,' Sutton said with a huge grin. 'Yer beat the plague, Miss 'Ester. I'll take yer 'ome.'

'We beat it,' she corrected him, grinning back at him. She lifted her hands tentatively, wanting to touch him, shake his hand, something. Then she abandoned conventions, even the fear of embarrassing him, and did what she wished. She threw her arms round him and hugged him.

He stood frozen for a moment, then responded, gently at first, as if she might break, then strongly with sheer joy.

Claudine came into the room, gasped, then whisked round and took hold of Flo behind her, and hugged her, too, almost bumping into Margaret.

There was a knock on the door and Sutton stepped over and threw it open, blinking in amazement when he saw a smartly dressed man with fair hair and a long, intelligent face, at the moment filled with overwhelming emotion.

'Oliver!' Hester said in disbelief.

Rathbone looked questioningly from one to another of them, then solely at Margaret.

'Come in,' Margaret invited him. 'Have breakfast with us. It's perfectly all right.' Then she smiled hugely as well. 'We've beaten it.'

He did not hesitate an instant. He strode in and took her in his arms, hugging her just as all the others had, in a bewilderment of happiness.

Finally he turned to Hester. 'You haven't been home for well over a week. I'll take you now.' It was not a question.

She smiled at him, shaking her head. 'Thank you, Oliver, but—'

'No,' he cut across her. 'Margaret will stay here now. You must go home. Even if you don't think you deserve it, Monk does.'

'I'll go home,' she said meekly. 'I'll just go with Sutton, if you don't mind.'

He hesitated only an instant. 'Of course I don't mind,' he replied. 'Mr Sutton deserves that honour.'

So Hester walked home beside Sutton, who was pulling

the rat cart, smiling all the way. Snoot sat upright in the front, quivering with excitement at all the new sights and smells, and the infinite possibilities of ratting ahead of him.

Sutton put the cart down in Fitzroy Street, and turned to Hester.

'Thank you,' she said with profound sincerity. 'That is far too small a word for what I feel, but I don't know any large enough.' She offered him her hand.

He took it a little awkwardly. 'Yer don't need ter thank me, Miss 'Ester. We done well together.'

'Yes, we did.' She shook his hand, then let it go and turned to walk up to the door. She would have to knock, or look for her key. She thought Rathbone had said Monk was home, but perhaps she only wanted to believe that. How absurd it would be if he were not!

The door opened, as if Monk had been watching for her. He stood just inside the hall looking thin and ashen-faced, his eyes shining with joy so intense he could not speak.

Rathbone had planned this – she knew it now – but there was no time even to think of him. She walked straight into Monk's arms and clung to him so fiercely she must have bruised his body. She felt him shudder, holding on to her with such passion he could scarcely breathe, and his tears were wet on her face.

It was the rat-catcher who softly closed the door, leaving them alone.

Chapter Fourteen

❧

Monk stood in the bedroom in the wan morning light looking at Hester still sleeping. He wanted to stay, simply to be as close to her as he could. He would like to wait until she woke, however long it was, and light the fire downstairs, regardless of expense. He would make the room warm for her, bring her whatever she wanted – tea, toast, go out in the rain and buy what else she would like, and bring it back for her. Then, when she was ready, talk about everything, tell her all that had mattered to him, and learn more than the few bare facts she had told him of her time in Portpool Lane. He wanted to hear the details, how she had felt in all the victories and the pain, so he could be closer to her.

But he had unfinished business with Louvain. Not only were there the five men from the crew still unaccounted for, but he must face Louvain himself.

But before that he had one more idea to pursue. He knew nothing about any of the missing crewmen except Hodge. He was apparently the only one married. It was perhaps intrusive to go to his widow now, but it was just possible that Hodge might have told her something about one of the missing men: a woman, a place, anything at all to help find them.

He went downstairs and cleaned out the grate, clumsily. It was not a job he was accustomed to doing, and at the end he found himself with rather more cleaning up to do than he had expected. Then he laid a new fire and lit it. When it was drawing nicely, he damped it down so it would last. He filled the coal buckets to the top, and wrote a note for Hester, saying simply that he loved her. At any other time he would have thought it ridiculous, but today it was the most natural thing to do. He only became self-conscious after he had propped it up on the table and had gone as far as the door, coat collar turned up. He smiled for a moment, then went out into the wind and sleet.

He had no idea of Hodge's widow's address, but Louvain's office was the obvious place to ask. However, the surgeon or the morgue attendant might also know, and he would far rather ask them. He had too much other business to address with Louvain: the deaths of his sisters, the whereabouts of his missing crew, and Monk's own black rage with him for deliberately sending Ruth Clark to Hester, knowing she had plague, to use it to manipulate Monk. He dared not even think of that: the raw emotion it woke in him robbed him of reason, of any kind of judgement. He wanted to beat him physically with his own hands, until he was a bloody pulp and too helpless even to ask for mercy. And that blind rage frightened him; it woke old memories of another rage that had ended in murder, and only by the grace of God had he not been guilty.

So instead he set out to look for the attendant at the morgue. He was walking along the embankment again when he heard a scampering of feet. The next moment Scuff's voice was demanding to know what was the matter with him.

'In't yer talkin' ter me no more?'

Monk stopped, taken aback at how pleased he was to

355

see him. 'I was thinking,' he excused himself.

'Think that 'ard an' you'll walk straight inter the river,' Scuff said disgustedly. 'Wot yer looking fer now?'

Monk smiled at him. 'How about a hot pie? Then I need to find where the widow of the man from the ship lives, the one who was killed.'

'Wot fell down the 'ole an broke 'is 'ead?' Scuff asked. ''Odge?'

'Yes.'

''Ow yer gonna do that?'

'Ask the man at the morgue. Presumably she came to see the body.'

Scuff gave an exaggerated shudder. ''E won't tell yer. In't none o' yer business. But we could ask Crow. 'E'd find out fer yer.' Now he was eager.

'Do you think so?'

'Yeah. C'mon. We'll get a pie, eh?' Scuff looked acutely hopeful.

Monk did as was expected of him, with pleasure. Three-quarters of an hour later they were walking back along the street towards the river, the wind in their faces. Crow was concocting a vivid and rather unlikely story in order to obtain the necessary information from the morgue attendant. He did not once ask Monk why he wanted it. He seemed to consider it some kind of professional courtesy.

They reached the morgue and Monk and Scuff remained outside while Crow went in. He emerged fifteen minutes later, black hair flying in the wind, and a smile of triumph showing brilliant teeth.

'Got it,' he said, waving a piece of paper in his hand.

Monk thanked him, took the paper and read it, then put it in his pocket.

'Now what?' Crow asked with interest.

'Now I treat you to the best pie I can afford, and a cup of hot tea, then I go about my business, and leave you to

356

'go about yours,' Monk replied with a smile.

'You're almighty pleased with yourself,' Crow said suspiciously.

'Only half,' Monk replied with sudden honesty. 'I've still got the rest to do. Do you want that pie or not?'

He treated them handsomely, but refused to allow either of them to go with him. Scuff objected strongly, insisting that Monk was not safe on his own and unquestionably needed someone to advise him and watch his back. While Monk reluctantly agreed with him, nevertheless he still would not allow the boy to come. With a show of suffering fortitude, Scuff finally resigned himself to going with Crow instead, just this once.

It took Monk little more than an hour to find the right small brick house. It was in the middle of a long row of similar houses built back to back near the docks in Rotherhithe. When he knocked on the door she opened it and he recognised her immediately, as much for her resemblance to Newbolt as from memory of her at the morgue.

'Yeah?' she said suspiciously. He knew she was trying to think where she had seen him before.

'Good morning, Mrs Hodge,' he said respectfully. 'I am hoping that you can help me—'

'Can't 'elp no one,' she replied without hesitation, beginning to close the door.

'I should not be ungrateful for it.' He forced himself to smile at her. She was graceless and abrupt, but she must also be frightened and, whatever her relationship with her husband had been, she must still be raw from his loss, and the implied disgrace that he had died of his own drunken carelessness. 'I regret your loss, Mrs Hodge,' he added quite genuinely. 'It is a terrible thing when a husband or wife dies. I don't think anyone else can comprehend it.'

'You lost someone?' she said with surprise.

'No, but I am fortunate. I very nearly did, and only late yesterday evening did I learn that she was all right.'

'Wot d'you want?' she asked reluctantly. 'I s'pose you'd better come in, but don't get in my way. I in't got all morning. Some of us 'as gotter work.' She pulled the door wider and turned to allow him to follow her into the small kitchen at the back. Seemingly it was the only warm room in the house. The black stove was burning and it gave off considerable heat, and a smell of soot and smoke that caught in his throat and made his eyes water. She seemed oblivious of it.

He looked around without having intended to. There was a stone sink, but no drain. That would be in the yard at the back, with the privy. Water would be collected from the nearest well or standing pump. There were wooden bins for flour or oats, several strings of onions hanging from the ceiling and a sack of potatoes leaning against the wall, with two turnips and a large white cabbage beside it.

Two scuttles were nearly full of coal, and on the wall were hanging three very handsome copper pans.

She saw his glance. 'I in't sellin' 'em,' she said tartly. 'Wot is it yer want?'

'I was simply admiring your pans,' he told her. 'It's information I'm looking for.'

'I don't grass.' It was a flat statement. 'An' before yer ask, they wasn't stole. Me bruvver give 'em me, back in August. 'E bought 'em fair, at a shop up west. Could prove it!'

'I don't doubt you, Mrs Hodge,' Monk answered her. 'Do you have several brothers?'

'Just the one. Why?'

'I suppose one like that is more than most people have,' he said evasively. 'The information I wanted has to do with the other men your husband served with on the *Maude Idris*. I wondered if you knew where any of them lived.'

'Lived?' she said in amazement. "Ow the 'ell should I know? You think wi' three kids I got time ter go around visitin'?"

'Only if they were close, a street or two away.'

'Maybe they are, but I dunno,' she replied. 'Is that all?'

'Yes. Thank you. I'm sorry to have wasted your time.'

She frowned. 'Why d'yer wanna know?'

He created the best lie he could think of. 'Actually, it was the captain I wanted to find, but I'll just have to keep looking. Thank you for your courtesy.'

She shrugged, not knowing how to reply.

He excused himself and went out into the street, his mind racing. He had the beginning of an idea, a wild, terrible possibility that explained everything.

He was bitterly cold by the time he crossed the river to the north bank again at Wapping Stairs and the River Police station. He found Durban looking tired and pale, sitting at his desk with a mug of hot tea in his hands.

He regarded Monk curiously, seeing the relief in him and not knowing what it was.

Monk walked across to the chair opposite him and sat down. 'It's over at the clinic,' he said, unable to keep the emotion out of his voice. 'No new cases in days, and it's three weeks now since Hodge's death. Hester came home last night.'

Durban smiled, a sweet, gentle expression. 'I'm glad.' He stood up and walked over to the window, away from Monk.

'I know we haven't finished with Louvain,' Monk conceded. 'What he did to the people in the clinic was inhuman. Eight of them died, and it could have been all. And if they hadn't been prepared to sacrifice their own lives to stay there and keep it in, it could have been all London, all England, and God only knows what beyond.'

Durban pursed his lips. 'I think he knew who he was dealing with,' he answered. 'Mrs Monk's reputation is not unknown. It was the best gamble he had, other than to kill Ruth Clark and bury her somewhere. I'm not surprised he couldn't bring himself to do that, if she was actually his own mistress.' His voice dropped. 'He wouldn't be sure she had plague then, it was only a danger. She might simply have had pneumonia.'

'She wasn't his mistress,' Monk replied. 'She was his sister; her real name was Charity Bradshaw. She and her husband were coming back from Africa. He died at sea.'

Durban's eyes widened. 'I'm not surprised Louvain wanted her cared for, but he should have told Mrs Monk what the illness could be. Although I dare say he believed she'd refuse her if she knew.'

'You think Clement Louvain, the hard man of the river, couldn't kill his own sister, even if she carried the plague?' Monk asked, his voice grating with the dreadful irony of the idea now in his mind.

Durban blinked; his eyes were pink-rimmed with exhaustion. 'Could you?' he asked. 'Wouldn't you have to try every last thing you could to save her?'

Monk brushed his hands over his face. For all his joy at Hester's return, he, too, was physically drained. 'If she was going to spread the disease, I don't know. But Mercy Louvain went there to help in the clinic, as a volunteer.'

'To nurse her sister?' Durban's face was gentle, his eyes shining. 'What sublime devotion.'

'She went there to nurse her,' Monk replied. 'She certainly killed her rather than let her leave carrying the plague with her.'

Durban stared at him in growing horror. He started to speak, then stopped, still incredulous. 'Oh God,' he said at last. 'I wish you hadn't told me.'

'You can't do anything,' Monk said, looking up at him. 'If you could, I wouldn't have said it. She's dead, too.'

'Plague?' The word was a whisper, said with fierce, hurting pity. It seemed to be torn from somewhere deep inside him as if all his passion were in it.

Monk nodded. 'They buried her properly.'

Durban turned his back to Monk, staring out of the small window, the cold light picking out the grey in his hair.

Now was the time Monk had to speak, no matter how preposterous, even if Durban thought him insane.

'I went to see Mrs Hodge today.'

Durban was puzzled. 'What for? Did you think she would know anything about the crew?' He smiled very slightly, hardly a movement of the lips. 'Did you think I hadn't thought of that?'

Monk was momentarily embarrassed, but the idea in him overrode everything else. 'I'm sorry. Did you see the copper saucepans in the kitchen?'

'I didn't go, Orme did.' Durban was frowning. 'What about them? What does it matter? I can't afford to care about petty theft now.' Again the fraction of a smile touched his mouth and disappeared.

'They weren't stolen, so far as I know,' Monk answered. 'She saw me looking at them and said her brother gave them to her.'

'I'm too tired to play games, Monk,' Durban said wearily. He looked grey-faced, close to collapse.

'I'm sorry,' Monk said quickly, and he meant it. He liked Durban as much as anyone he had known in years. 'She told me she has only one brother and he gave them to her in August. She said she could prove that.'

Durban blinked, frowning harder. 'She can't. He was off the coast of Africa in August. Are you saying the *Maude Idris* was here then? Or that Newbolt wasn't on her?'

'Not exactly either,' Monk said very quietly. 'We checked the names of the crew.'

'Of course.'

'But not their appearances.'

361

Durban steadied himself, leaning back against the sill. 'For God's sake, what are you saying?' But the hideousness of the deduction was already in his eyes. He shook his head. 'But they're still there – on the ship.'

'You told your men to keep them there because it was typhoid,' Monk reminded him. 'Maybe Louvain told them the same, or close enough?'

Durban rubbed his hand over his face like a man trying to dispel a nightmare.

'Then we'd better find out. Can you use a pistol?'

'Of course,' Monk replied, no idea whether he could or not.

Durban straightened up. 'I'll get Orme, and half a dozen men, but I'm the only one going below.' He stared very levelly at Monk, his eyes seeming to look into his brain. 'That is an order.' He did not elaborate but walked past him and through the outside office, calling for Orme as he went.

He gave his orders concisely and with a clarity no man could misunderstand, like a commander going into a last battle.

The rain had cleared away and the water was bright and choppy with a knife-edge wind blowing from the west when they rowed out.

Monk sat in the stern of the boat, cradling his loaded gun as they plied between the ships, and the *Maude Idris* came clearly into view.

Durban sat in the bow, a little apart. He glanced at each of his men, then gave a barely discernible nod as they drew alongside and he stood up, balancing easily even in the pitching boat. He hailed the ship, and Newbolt's head appeared over the railing.

'River Police!' Durban called out. 'Coming aboard.'

Newbolt hesitated, then disappeared. The next moment the rope ladder came pitching over, uncurling to fall almost in Durban's hands. He caught it and climbed up – it seemed to Monk, watching from below, less agilely than before.

Two of the River Police went up after him, Orme and another man, guns tucked in their belts, and lastly Monk, leaving only the oarsmen in the boat. He climbed over the rail on to the deck where the three River Police faced Newbolt and Atkinson. There was no sound except the whine of the wind in the rigging and the slap of water against the hull below them.

'What d'yer want this time?' Newbolt asked, staring sullenly at Durban. 'None of us killed 'Odge, and none of us 'elped anyone take the bleedin' ivory.'

'I know,' Durban replied steadily. 'We don't think anyone killed Hodge; he died by accident. And we know that Gould stole the ivory, because we have it back.'

'So wot d'yer want 'ere then?' Newbolt said irritably. 'If yer wanter do summink useful, get bleedin' Louvain ter unload this ship an' pay us off.'

'I want to see below decks, then we might do that,' Durban replied, watching him curiously, his face intent. 'Where's McKeever?'

'Dead,' Newbolt said tersely. 'We got the typhoid. Still wanna go below?'

'I know you have,' Durban replied. 'That's why you've not berthed. Now open the hatch.'

Newbolt's eyes flickered and his head came up as if at last he were paying real attention. 'Right. Wot d'yer wanter see?'

'I'll find it for myself,' Durban said grimly. 'You stay up here.'

'I'm comin wi' yer,' Newbolt insisted.

Durban took the gun out of his belt and glanced at Orme, who did the same. 'No you aren't.'

Newbolt looked startled, then suspicious. 'Yer no better than the bleedin' revenue men,' he snarled. 'Bloody thieves, the lot o' yer.'

Durban ignored him. 'Keep them here,' he ordered his men. 'Shoot them if you have to.' There was no possibility whatever of doubting his intent. He took a bull's-eye lantern from Orme and walked over to the hatch. Monk followed him. As Durban reached it he yanked it open, and the stench of the enclosed air caught in Monk's throat, turning his stomach. He had not remembered it being so strong. 'I'm going down,' Durban said, his face pinched with revulsion. 'You stay here. I'll tell you if I find anything.'

'I'm coming—' Monk started.

'You're doing as you're told,' Durban snapped at him. 'That's an order. Or I'll have Orme hold you at gunpoint!'

Monk saw in Durban's eyes that there was no point in arguing, and no time. He stood back and watched as Durban swung over the edge, found the ladder, then took the lantern in his other hand and started down. He saw him reach the ledge, and look up, his eyes dark in the small circle of yellow light. He knew as well as Monk did that, had any of the jury seen the hold of the *Maude Idris*, they would have known that a man who slipped off the ladder would not land on the ledge, injure his head fatally and then lie there. His body would have pitched off and gone on down, probably breaking his neck or his back when he hit the bottom.

Then he turned and held the lantern out so he could see as much as possible of the stacked wood and the boxes of spice. As far as Monk could remember, peering down from the top, it all seemed exactly the same as when he had been here three weeks ago with Louvain.

Durban went on down. At the bottom he stood still. He was directly above the ship's bilges.

Monk could not wait. He threw his leg over the hatching and started down. Durban shouted at him, and he ignored it. He could not leave him alone with what he now dreaded they would find.

Below him Durban kneeled down, holding the light only inches from the boards. The marks of a crowbar were clear, indentations, splintered wood, rat droppings.

Durban's face was grey, even in the yellow light. 'Go back up,' he ordered as Monk reached the ledge above him. 'It doesn't need two of us.'

Monk found himself shaking and he had trouble swallowing the nausea down from the sickening smell in the air. He ignored the command.

'Do as you're told,' Durban said between his teeth.

Monk stayed exactly where he was. 'What's under there?'

'The bilges, of course,' Durban said irritably.

'Somebody's taken them up,' Monk observed.

Durban's eyes flashed. 'I can see that. Get out.'

Monk was frozen, unable to move even if he had wanted to. His skin crawled with the horror he imagined.

'Get out,' Durban said, looking up at him, emotion naked on his face. 'There's no point in both of us being here. Pass me the crowbar from over there, then go back to the deck. I'll not tell you again.'

Somewhere in the darkness a rat dropped on to the floor and scuttled away. At last Monk obeyed, climbing his way up hand over hand, until he reached the air and gasped it, freezing and clean, into his lungs.

'What is it?' Orme said hoarsely. 'What's down there?' He put out his hand and half hauled Monk over the hatchway and on to the deck.

'I don't know,' Monk replied, straightening up. 'Nothing yet.'

'Then what are you doing back here? Why 'ave you left 'im down there? Smell o' bilges got to yer, 'as it?' There was infinite contempt in Orme's voice and in the curl of his lip, not for a queasy stomach, but for a man who deserted another in the face of trouble.

'I came back up because he ordered me to,' Monk said

365

wretchedly. 'He wouldn't move until I did.'

Orme stared at him coldly. 'What's 'e doin'?'

'You'll find out when he wants to tell you,' Monk retorted.

They looked at each other, but remained silent. Newbolt and Atkinson were standing near the rail, sullen and anxious. No one moved, because the police pistols were at the ready and there was enough fire power to stop both of them.

The wind was whining more shrilly in the rigging. A large schooner passed going upriver, tacking back and forth. Its wake rocked the ship slightly, making everyone adjust their balance.

Finally Durban's head appeared above the hatching. Monk was the first to move, striding over towards him, clasping his hand and hauling him out. He looked paperwhite, his eyes red-rimmed and shocked, as if he had seen hell.

'Was it . . .?' Monk said.

'Yes.' He was shuddering uncontrollably. 'With their throats cut, all eight of them, even the cabin boy.'

'Not—'

'No. I told you – throats cut.'

Monk wanted to say something, but what words could possibly carry the horror that was in him?

Durban stood on the deck breathing slowly, trying to gain control of his limbs, his racing heart, the trembling of his body. Finally he looked at Orme. 'Arrest those men for murder,' he commanded, pointing at Newbolt and Atkinson. 'Mass murder. If they try to escape, shoot them – not to kill, just to cripple. Shoot them in the stomach.

'The third one is down below, possibly dead. Leave him. Just batten down the hatch. That's an order. No one is to go below. Do you understand me?'

Orme stared at him in disbelief, then slowly understanding came, at least partially. 'They're river pirates.'

366

'Yes.'

Orme was white. 'They killed the whole crew?'

'Except Hodge. I suppose they left him because he was married to Newbolt's sister.'

Orme rubbed his hands over his face, staring at Durban. Then suddenly he came to attention and did as he was commanded.

Durban walked over to the rail and leaned against it. Monk followed him.

'Are you going to arrest Louvain?' he asked.

Durban stared ahead of him at the churning water and the shoreline where the tide was rising against the pier stakes and washing ever higher over the steps. 'For what?' he asked.

'Murder.'

'The men will no doubt say he ordered them, even paid them,' Durban replied. 'But he'll say he didn't, and there's no proof.'

'For God's sake!' Monk exploded. 'He knows these aren't his crew. He has to know they murdered them, except Hodge. It doesn't matter whether he knows it was because they had plague, or because they simply wanted to take the ship!' He gulped. 'Anyway, who the hell would believe that? The ship's here, and the cargo's here.'

Durban said nothing.

'If Louvain paid these men,' Monk went on, turning to face Durban, the knife-edge wind stinging his face, 'he must have been aboard the ship to do it. Someone will have taken him, seen him. There'll be a chain of proof. We can't let him get away with it. I won't.'

'There are a dozen arguments he can come up with,' Durban said wearily. 'These are the men who killed the crew. We won't prove that Louvain even knew about it, much less ordered it. We can't tell anyone his reason, and he knows that.'

'I'm going to find him,' Monk said, rage almost choking the air out of his lungs.

'Monk!'

But Monk would not listen. If Durban would not, or could not, make Louvain answer for what he had done, then Monk would, no matter what it cost. He strode along to the ladder, swung over the rail and scrambled down it to the boat, not caring if he skinned his knuckles, or bruised his elbows. Louvain had been responsible for Mercy's death, and the death of eight other women. It was only by the grace of God that it had not been Hester and Margaret as well. It could have been half of London – half of Europe. He had gambled that Hester would be prepared to give her own life to prevent it.

He landed in the boat. 'Take me ashore,' he ordered. 'Now.'

The oarsman took one look at his face and obeyed, digging the blades into the water with all his strength.

As soon as they reached the shore Monk thanked him and stepped out, his foot sliding on the wet stone. He grasped at the wall and went up as fast as he could. At the top he turned straight for Louvain's office without even glancing behind him to see the boat begin its journey back.

'You can't go in there, sir. Mr Louvain's busy!' the clerk shouted at Monk as he went past, bumping into another clerk with a pile of ledgers and only just avoiding knocking the man over. He apologised without turning around.

He reached Louvain's office door, lifted his hand to knock, then changed his mind and simply opened it.

Louvain was at his desk, a pile of papers in front of him, a pen in his hand. He looked up at the interruption, but without alarm. Then he saw Monk and his face darkened.

'What do you want?' he said sharply. 'I'm busy. Your thief got off. Isn't that enough for you?'

Monk had to make an intense effort to control himself, even to keep his voice from shaking. He realised with amazement that part of him had respected Louvain, even liked him. It was that which made his rage so nearly uncontrollable now. This was the man who had been dazed by the beauty of the great landscapes of the world, who had longed to sail beyond the horizon in the great clippers with their staggering beauty, a man he had almost confided in.

'Did anyone tell you that your sister died?' he asked instead. He was not even certain what made him say it.

Louvain's face tightened. It hurt him, and he could not conceal it. 'She was very ill,' he said softly.

'Not Charity.' Monk saw Louvain's eyes widen. In using her name he had at once told Louvain how much more he knew. He drove home the far deeper pain. 'I meant Mercy. You knew Charity would die when you took her to Portpool Lane, and you didn't care. Eight other women died as well.'

Louvain was staring at him, his eyes wide, his hands on the desk top white-knuckled. 'You're speaking as if it's over?' he said hoarsely.

'In Portpool Lane it is.'

Louvain leaned back and let his breath out slowly. 'Then it is over everywhere.' His body went limp. He almost smiled. 'It's finished.'

Monk forced the words through clenched jaws. 'And what about the crew of the *Maude Idris*? Bradshaw died of it, and so did Hodge. How about the rest of them?' He watched Louvain intently.

'If they haven't got it now, they won't,' he answered, and Monk saw barely a flicker of regret in his face.

'Let's go and see,' Monk suggested, straightening his body, his hands sweating, his breath uneven.

'I'm busy,' Louvain answered. His eyes met Monk's and they stared at each other across the silent room.

Monk thought of Mercy, of Margaret Ballinger, of Bessie and the other women whose names he did not know, but mostly of Hester, and the hell it would have been for him without her.

Louvain became aware of a change in the air between them. He sat back. The moment of understanding was gone. They were enemies again. 'I'm busy,' he repeated, challenging Monk to act.

Monk wanted to smile, but his face was stiff. 'Come with me to see them now,' he said softly. 'Or I shall tell Newbolt and Atkinson what kind of a ship they're on. Do you think they will wait there then? Don't you think they'll hunt you down, anywhere, everywhere, for the rest of your life?'

Louvain's skin blanched of every trace of colour, leaving him grey-white. He drew in his breath to defy Monk, but knew that his face had betrayed him.

This time Monk could laugh; it was a grating sound, choked inside him. 'You know what they are,' he said. 'You know what they'll do to you. Now, are you coming or do I tell them?'

Louvain stood up very slowly. 'What for? You'll get nothing, Monk. You can't prove I knew. I'll say I paid off the others at Gravesend, and these men brought the ship up to the Pool.'

'If you like,' Monk replied. In that instant he knew exactly what he was going to do; the resolve inside him set like steel.

Louvain sensed the change, and he also knew that he could not fight it. He straightened up and came round the desk. He was moving slowly, with the tense, animal grace of a man who knows his own physical power. 'What if I say you attacked me?' he asked almost curiously, as if the answer did not really matter.

'You won't,' Monk replied. 'Because if you do I'll make it true, but you'll be dead. I will have shot you. And

Newbolt and Atkinson will still be there. McKeever's dead, by the way. Plague, I imagine.'

Louvain stood still. 'What do you want, Monk?'

'I want you on the *Maude Idris*. Go ahead of me – now!'

Slowly, both of them moving as if wading against the tide, they went out through the office. Clerks looked up but no one spoke. Louvain opened the outer door and winced as the icy air struck him, but Monk allowed him no time to collect a coat. There might have been a weapon in the pocket.

They walked across the street and on to the quayside, Louvain shuddering with cold. It was a brilliant afternoon, the sun low in the west in the shortening day, light dancing gold on the water.

They had only a few minutes to wait for a boat, and Monk ordered the oarsmen to take them out. Neither of them spoke as they sat, the waves slapping against the wood of the hull. The occasional spray was like ice.

When they reached the *Maude Idris*, Monk told Louvain to go up the ladder, then followed after him. Durban was alone.

Louvain looked startled. He swung around to Monk.

Monk took the gun out of his belt. 'I'm taking Mr Louvain down to see the crew,' he told Durban. 'May I borrow the lantern again?'

'I'll take him,' Durban answered. 'You stay up here.'

Monk stared at him. He looked exhausted, his face flushed, his eyes sunken. 'No. I'm doing this. Besides, the state you're in, he might jump you.'

Durban started to argue, and Monk pushed past him, thrusting the lantern into Louvain's hands. 'You go first,' he ordered. 'All the way down. If you stop I'll shoot you, and believe me, I will.'

Durban leaned against the rail. 'Don't be long,' he said. 'The tide turns in a quarter of an hour. I need you to go ashore then.' There was a finality in his eyes and his voice.

Louvain started down the ladder and Monk followed, one hand on the rungs, the other holding his gun. He had to do this. He had to see Louvain's face when he stood on the floor and looked down into the bilges. Monk needed him to smell the plague, breathe it in, to know the stench of it so that for the rest of his life it would stalk his dreams. As an old man he would wake screaming, soaked in sweat, enclosed again in the creaking, rolling ship with the corpses of the men he had had killed.

The smell was far worse. It was like a thickness in the air as they went down, hand over hand, towards the ledge.

Louvain stopped. Monk could hear his breathing, gasping, laboured. He looked down at his face and saw the sweat standing out on it, his eyes like holes in his head, sockets dark.

'Keep moving,' Monk ordered. 'What's the matter? Can you smell them?' Then as he looked past Louvain at the open bilges where Durban had torn up the wood, his stomach heaved so violently he nearly lost his grip on the ladder. The boat swayed in the wash of something passing, and the water in the bilges slopped forward, carrying the bloated head and shoulders of a dead man. His eyes were eaten out, and his face rotted, but the fearful gash in his throat was still plain, and the stench so overpowering it made Monk's senses swim.

'That's your crew, Louvain,' Monk said, gasping to control his own nausea. 'Can you smell the plague? It's the Black Death.'

There was a scrabbling of clawed-feet and a flurry of squeaks, then a rat dropped into the bilges with a plop.

Louvain screamed and flung himself upwards, the lantern falling from his hands to land with a crash, and the light went out. Louvain was still screaming.

Monk started up again, desperate for the air. He reached the ledge, panic welling up inside him, horror inconceivable at what lay below him in the dark, and the madman at his heels.

He saw the square of sky at the hatch darken for a moment as Durban began to climb down.

'We're coming up,' he shouted. 'It's all right.'

Durban hesitated.

Louvain reached the ledge and Monk realised it half a second too late. He caught the movement out of the corner of his eye and then Louvain's arms were round him, clinging as if to squeeze the air out of him, break his ribs and crush his lungs and his heart.

He could not escape. His only choice was to lunge forward with his head. Louvain did not let go. Monk twisted sideways and bit Louvain's wrist as hard as he could, feeling his teeth break skin and his mouth fill with blood.

Louvain yelled and his grip loosened, but he was blind with terror. He swung at Monk, but Monk moved and was caught only a glancing blow on the shoulder.

'You had their throats cut,' Monk gasped out. 'Even the poor bloody cabin boy.'

'They'd have died anyway, you fool,' Louvain said between his teeth, his hands reaching after Monk's throat. 'But I couldn't tell anyone that. If you'd had the stomach for it, you'd have done the same.'

'I'd have taken the ship out again.' Monk lunged at him, fist clenched, and Louvain sidestepped, bringing them closer so they were locked together, muscles straining.

'And lose my cargo?' Louvain replied, grunting with effort. His face was running with sweat. 'I need that clipper. This was quick – better than dying of the plague. I thought you'd see that.' He punched Monk hard, but caught him on the hip instead of the stomach.

Monk gagged with pain, doubling forward. 'But you took your sister to Portpool Lane, to spread the plague there.'

'So London's got a few whores the less,' Louvain retorted. 'I knew your wife wouldn't let it go beyond that. I couldn't kill Charity – she was my sister.'

Monk swung his legs back and kicked him as hard as he could on the shin. When Louvain's hold weakened for a moment, Monk struck him with all the force of rage he possessed, all the horror and loss that had drenched him night and day for the last week.

Louvain staggered, lifting his own arm to strike back. He teetered on the rim for wild, hideous seconds, then plunged over the edge, limbs flailing, and landed with a crash on the broken boards of the hold floor, his head a foot away from the swirling bilges awash with blood and their cargo of dead men, flesh bloated and eaten, throats gaping in eternal silence.

Monk dropped to his knees and was sick. Then he crept to the edge and started down. Vertigo made him grasp the wood as if it were salvation, although it was no more than twelve or fourteen feet below. There was no sound but the slurp of water, and the scraping of rats. Louvain lay on his back. His eyes were open and Monk knew instantly that he could see, but he could not move. His back was broken.

The ship swayed. Monk clung on even harder, horror at what lay below him crawling over his skin and running off him in cold sweat.

Louvain slid closer to the yawning bilges, the weight of his body carrying him along the slimy, angled floor.

Monk stared at him, knowing what was going to happen with the next lurch of the ship, and seeing in Louvain's eyes that he knew it also. The moment froze like an everlasting hell.

The ship swayed again. Louvain slithered to the edge of the boards, hesitated a ghastly moment, then helpless to save himself, slipped into the nightmare of the bilges, bumping against the swollen body of the cabin boy, and two dead rats. His own weight took him down. Monk saw his white face for a moment, then the putrid water closed over him, and he was no longer distinguishable from the rest of the corpses slewing back and forth.

Monk closed his eyes, and saw in his mind the same scene burned into his brain. Time seemed to have stopped. He saw it frozen for ever.

'Help me get the sails up.' It was Durban's voice at his shoulder.

He avoided his eyes, and grasped the hand held out to help him. He staggered to his feet.

'Help me get the sails up,' Durban repeated. 'The tide's turning and there's a stiff breeze from the west. Two should do it, three at most.'

'Sails?' Monk said stupidly. 'What for?'

'She's a plague ship,' Durban replied. 'We can't let her put ashore, not here, not anywhere.'

Monk was reeling with fearful, inescapable thoughts. 'You mean . . .?'

'Can you think of anything else?' Durban said quickly. His face looked grey in the light from the hatch.

'Your men . . .' Monk began.

'Ashore. I told Orme. Had to, or he'd not have understood why I have to take Newbolt and Atkinson with me, and McKeever's body. Help me get the sails up, then you can go, too. There's the lifeboat you can take.'

Monk was balancing with difficulty. It was not with the faint rolling of the ship, but sick horror in his mind. 'You can't sail her alone. Where to? There's nowhere you can take her.'

'Out beyond Gravesend, and open the seacocks,' Durban answered, his voice little above a whisper. 'The sea'll clean her. Way down the bottom it'll be a good burial. Now let's get out of here and up into the air. The smell is making me sick.' As he spoke he turned and started climbing up again. Monk followed, hand over hand, until he stood on the deck, gasping the ice-cold evening air, sweet as the light that poured across from the west, etching the waves with fire.

He could not remember much about raising a sail, but Durban told him what to do. Some familiarity from childhood on the north-eastern seaboard gave skill to his fingers. One great canvas slowly unfurled, and with the combined weight and strength of the two men, began to crawl up the mainmast. They lashed it close, straight into the wind, then moved to the second.

Together they went to the winch and lifted the anchor. Monk completed the last few turns as Durban went back to the wheel and slowly turned her to catch the wind in one sail, then the next. It was hard work, and, with only two of them, dangerous. As the canvas billowed out and they picked up speed, Monk turned to look at Durban. It was a kind of insane and terrible triumph. They were sailing a drowned ship on a sea of gold, heading towards the shadows of the east and the dying day.

'It's time you went,' Durban said raising his voice above the wind and the water. 'Before we put on speed. I'll help you launch the longboat.'

Monk was stunned. 'What do you mean? If I take the longboat now, how will you get ashore?'

Durban's face was quite calm, the wind burning his cheeks to scarlet. 'I won't. I'll go down with her. It's a better way than waiting for the other death.'

Monk was too shattered to speak. He opened his mouth to deny it, to refuse to grant the possibility, but it was foolish even as the thought entered his mind. He should have seen it before, and he had not: the sweating, the burning cheeks, the exhaustion, the carefully bitten-back pain, and above all the way recently he had kept a distance between himself and Monk, or his own men.

'Go,' Durban said again.

'No! I can't . . .' They were near the rail; the ship was

376

gathering speed, the water churning alongside them. The words were the last Monk said before he felt a weight jolting hard against him; the rail had caught him in the back. Then the water closed over his head, cripplingly cold, smothering, drowning everything else.

He fought to hold his breath, to beat his way up to the surface, for seconds the will to live driving out everything else. He broke into the air, gasping, and saw the huge bulk of the *Maude Idris* already fifty feet away and moving faster. He shouted after her, no idea what he was saying, just bellowing in fury and grief. For an instant he saw Durban's figure in the stern, his arm lifted in salute, then he moved away and Monk was left to thrash around and think how he was going to make his way to shore, without being drowned, run down by another ship, or simply frozen to death.

He had only swum a few strokes, hampered by his sodden clothes, and was already overwhelmed, when he heard a shout, and then another. With a mighty effort he twisted round in the water and saw a boat with at least four men at the oars bearing down on him rapidly. He recognised Orme leaning over the side of the bow, arms out.

The boat reached him, and even though they shipped the oars, the speed of it made it a desperate, arm-wrenching struggle to grasp Monk. It took three men to haul him on board. Then the moment he landed they threw their weight behind the oars again, hurling them forwards after the *Maude Idris*, which was going ever faster as the wind filled her sails.

But she was a heavy ship, and the lighter boat was closing the gap. Monk sat shuddering with cold in the stern. The wind was making his wet clothes like ice on his skin, but he was only peripherally aware of it; all his thoughts were on Durban. Would it help to rescue him? It was the action of instinct, of the heart, the driving compulsion of a friend, but was it really the best thing to do? Did honour and dignity not require that he be allowed to die his own way? Is that not what Monk, or any of these men around him, would choose for himself?

Did they know? Had Durban told them? No – he couldn't have, or they might have prevented him, guessing what he might do. They would not believe the enormity of plague, the certain death, the hideousness of it. Dare he tell them now?

They were still closing on the *Maude Idris*. The lowering sun made her spread sails gleam like the wings of a great bird as she cut the water. They were clear of the Pool of London and the other ships were behind them. She was heading down Limehouse Reach past the Isle of Dogs, but it was a long way to the sea, with many places where she would have to come about and go on the other tack. Could Durban manage alone, guts apart from his weakened condition; could any man? Perhaps Orme guessed. Was that what these men around him, breaking their backs at the oars, really wanted – to make sure that the *Maude Idris* did not crash into a pier, another ship, or run aground?

He hoped not; he prayed their pursuit was out of concern for Durban.

Durban was struggling with another sail. Slowly, agonising with the strain, it went up the mast, a foot at a time. Monk did not even realise that he was leaning forward on his seat, his muscles aching with the effort as if he were hauling the great sail himself, pitting his own strength against the heavy canvas, the sun in his eyes, the light blinding him off the river. Slowly the *Maude Idris* pulled ahead of them again, widening the distance.

Not a man in the longboat spoke. The oarsmen moved with steady rhythm, faces intent, breath forced from their lungs. Beside Monk Orme never took his eyes off the ship ahead. Her sails were bellying full now, the white wake

creaming behind her as she sped down Limehouse Reach
with the Isle of Dogs to the left. Monk looked at Orme
and saw the horror and grief in his face, seawater mixed
with tears.

Durban was forced to come about clumsily on the
bend. For a moment he lost control, and they closed in on
him again. Monk ached as he watched. They were within
twenty yards of the *Maude Idris*. They could see Durban
working frantically to control the great booms and stop
her from broaching and going over.

Orme was standing up, half crouching forward, his
face a mask of passion and despair. Monk did not even
realise that he, too, was shouting.

But Durban took no notice. He succeeded in coming
about and righting the ship. All the sails filled again, and
the *Maude Idris* pulled away from them past Greenwich.
The sun was low, a pool of fire on the horizon behind
them. Only the gathering purple of the evening lay ahead,
and the darkness over Bugsby's Marsh to the south.

Durban was on deck again, black against the shining
gold of the sails. He raised both arms in a signal, a
gesture of victory and farewell, then he disappeared down
the forward hatch.

Monk clung to the gunwale of the boat, his hands
frozen, his body shaking and numb with cold. He could
hardly breathe for it. Seconds went by, a minute – it
seemed like eternity – then another minute. The *Maude
Idris* was still gaining speed.

Then it happened. At first it was only a dull sound.
Monk did not even realise what it was, until he saw the
sparks, and then a gout of flame. The second crash was
far louder as the ship's magazine exploded and the flames
roared upward, engulfing the decks and leaping up the
sails. Soon she was a pillar of fire in the encroaching
night, an inferno, a holocaust of burning wood and
canvas sweeping towards the deserted mud of the shore,

carrying with it Durban, Louvain, the river pirates and the corpses of the crew.

It was at once a Viking's pyre, and a plague ship's burial. She lurched into the shallows and stuck, the white heat gone, the light dying red, the water rushing in.

Monk stood in the boat beside Orme, freezing and exhausted, his mind burned through to the core with grief and pride. The tears were wet on his face and his hands too numb to feel Orme reach out and grip hold of him in a moment of understanding, a loss too deep to endure alone. He was barely aware of one of the other men at last taking off his coat and putting it round his shoulders.

The warmth would come later, in the time still ahead.

Headline hope you have enjoyed THE SHIFTING TIDE, and invite you to sample the beginning of SHOULDER THE SKY, the next novel in Anne Perry's new compelling series set during World War I.

Chapter One

❧

It was shortly after three in the afternoon. Joseph Reavley was half asleep in the April sun, his back to the pale clay wall of the trench, when he heard the angry voices.

'They be moi boots, Tucky Nunn, an' you know that well as Oi do! Yours be over there, wi' holes in 'em!' It was Plugger Arnold, a seasoned soldier of twenty, big-boned, a son of the village blacksmith. He had been in Flanders since the outbreak of war last August. Although he was angry, he kept his voice low. He knew it carried in the afternoon stillness when the men snatched the three or four hours of sleep they could. The German trenches were only seventy yards away across this stretch of the Ypres Salient. Anyone foolish enough to reach a hand up above the parapet would be likely to get it shot. The snipers seldom needed a second chance. Added to which, getting yourself injured on purpose was a court-martial offence.

Tucky Nunn, nineteen and new this far forward, was standing on the duckboards that floored the trench. They were there to keep the men's feet above the icy water that sloshed around, but this seldom worked. The water level was too high. Every time you thought the ground was drying out at last, it rained again.

'Yeah?' Tucky said, his eyebrows raised. 'Fit me perfect, they do. Didn't see your name on 'em. Must 'ave wore off.' He grinned, making no move to bend and unlace the offending boots and hand them back.

Plugger was sitting half sideways on the fire-step. A few yards away the sentry was standing with his back to them, staring through the periscope over the wire and mud of no man's land. He could not afford to lose concentration even for a moment, regardless of what went on behind him.

'They's moi boots,' Plugger said between his teeth. 'Take 'em off yer soddin' feet an' give 'em back to me, or Oi'll take 'em off yer and give yer to the rats!'

Tucky bounced on the balls of his feet, hunching his shoulders a little. 'You want to try?' he invited.

Doughy Ward crawled out of his dugout, fully dressed as they all were: webbing and rifle with bayonet attached. His fair-skinned face was crumpled with annoyance at being robbed of any part of his few hours of sleep. He glared at Joseph. ' "Thou shalt not steal." Isn't that right, Chaplain?'

It was a demand that even here in the mud and the cold, the boredom and sporadic violence, Joseph should do his job and stand for the values of justice that must remain, or all this would sink into a purposeless hell. Without right and wrong there was no sanity.

'Oi didn't steal them!' Tucky said angrily. 'They were—' He did not finish the sentence because Plugger hit him, a rolling blow that caught the side of his jaw as he ducked and struck back.

There was no point in shouting at them, and the sound would carry. Added to which, Joseph did not want to let the whole trench know that there was a discipline problem. Both men could end up on charges, and that was not the way for a chaplain to resolve anything. He moved forward, careful to avoid being struck himself, and grasped hold of

Tucky, taking him off balance and knocking him against the uprights that held the trench wall.

'The Germans are that way!' he said tartly, jerking his head back towards the parapet and no man's land beyond.

Plugger was up on his feet, slithering in the mud on the duckboards, his socks filthy and sodden wet. 'Good oidea to send him over the top, Captain, where he belongs! But not in moi boots!' He was floundering towards them, arms flailing as if to carry on the fight.

Joseph stepped between them, risking being caught by both, which would make charges unavoidable. 'Stop it!' he ordered briskly. 'Take the boots off, Nunn!'

'Thank you, Chaplain,' Plugger responded with a smile of satisfaction.

Tucky stood unmoving, his face set, ignoring the blood. 'They ain't his boots oither!' he said sullenly, his eyes meeting Joseph's.

A man appeared around the dogleg corner. No stretch of the trench was more than ten or twelve yards long, to prevent shellfire taking out a whole platoon of men – or in case a German raiding party made it through the wire. The trenches were deep-sided, shored up against mud slides, and barely wide enough for two men to pass each other. The man coming was tall and lean, with wide shoulders, and he walked with a certain elegance, even on the slopping duckboards. His face was dark, long-nosed, and there was a wry humour in it.

'Early for tea, aren't you?' he asked, his eyes going from one to another.

Tucky and Plugger reluctantly stood to attention. 'Yes, Major Wetherall,' they said almost in unison.

Sam Wetherall glanced down at Plugger's stocking feet, his eyebrows raised. 'Thinking of creeping up on the cook, are you? Or making a quick recce over the top first?'

'Soon as Oi get moi boots back from that thievin' sod, Oi'll put 'em on again,' Plugger replied, gesturing towards Tucky.

'I'd wash them first if I were you,' Sam advised with a smile.

'Oi will,' Plugger agreed. 'Oi don't want to catch nothin'!'

'I meant your feet,' Sam corrected him.

Tucky Nunn roared with laughter, in spite of the bruise darkening on his jaw where Plugger had caught him.

'Whose boots are they?' Joseph asked, smiling as well.

'Moine!' both men said together.

'Whose boots are they?' Joseph repeated.

There was a moment's silence.

'Oi saw 'em first,' Plugger answered.

'You didn't take them,' Tucky pointed out. 'If you 'ad, you'd 'ave them now, wouldn't you?'

'Come on, Solomon.' Sam looked at Joseph, his mouth pulled into an ironic twist.

'Right,' Joseph said decisively. 'Left boot, Nunn. Right boot, Arnold.'

There was considerable grumbling, but Tucky took off the right boot and passed it over, reaching for one of the worn boots where Plugger had been sitting.

'Shouldn't have had them off now anyway,' Sam said disapprovingly. 'You know better than that. What if Fritz'd made a sudden attack?'

Plugger's eyebrows shot up, his blue eyes wide open. 'At half-past three in the afternoon? It's tea-toime in a minute. They may be soddin' Germans, but they're not uncivilized. They still got to eat an' sleep, same as us.'

'You stick your head up above the parapet, and you'll find he's nowhere near asleep, I promise you,' Sam warned.

Tucky was about to reply when there was a shouting about twenty yards along the line, and a moment later a young soldier lurched around the corner, his face white. He stared at Sam.

'One of your sappers has taken half his hand off!' he said, his voice high-pitched and jerky.

'Where is he, Charlie?' Joseph said quickly. 'We'll get him to the first-aid post.'

Sam was rigid. 'Who is it?' He started forward, pushing ahead of both of them, ignoring the rats scattering in both directions.

Charlie Gee swivelled and went on his heels; Joseph stopped to duck into the connecting trench leading back to the second line, then picked out a first-aid pack in case they needed more than the field dressing the wounded man should be carrying himself.

When he caught up with them Sam was bent over, one arm around a man sitting on the duckboards. The sapper was rocking back and forth, clutching the stump of his hand to his chest, scarlet blood streaming from it.

Joseph had lost count of how many wounded and dead he had seen, but each man's horror was new and real, and it looked as if in this case the man might have lost a good deal of his right hand.

Sam was ashen, his jaw clenched so tight the muscles stood out like cords. 'We have to see it, Corliss!' His voice shook in spite of everything he could do to steady it. 'We have to stop the bleeding!' He looked at Joseph, his eyes desperate.

Joseph tore open the dressing and, speaking gently to the injured man, took his hand and, without examining it, pressed the bandage and the lint over the streaming wound, then bound it as well as he could. He had very little idea how many fingers were left.

'Come on, ol' feller,' Charlie said, trying to help Corliss to his feet. 'Oi'll get you back to the doc's and they'll do it for you proper.'

Sam climbed to his feet and pulled Joseph aside as

Charlie and Corliss stumbled past.

'Joe, can you go with them?' Sam said urgently. He swallowed, gulping. 'Corliss is in a hell of a state. He's been on the edge of funking it for days. I've got to find out what happened, put in a report, but the medics'll ask him what caused it . . . Answer for him, will you?' He stopped, but it was painfully apparent he wanted to say more.

Suddenly Joseph understood. Sam was terrified the man had injured himself deliberately. Some men panicked, worn down by fear, cold and horror, and put their hands up above the parapet precisely so a sniper would get them. A hand maimed was 'a Blighty one', and they got sent home. But if it was self-inflicted, it was considered cowardice in the face of the enemy. It warranted a court martial, and possibly even the death sentence. Corliss's nerves may have snapped. It happened to men sometimes. Anything could trigger it off: the incessant noise of bombardment, the dirt, body lice; for some it was waking in the night with rats crawling over your body – or worse, your face. The horror of talking one moment to a man you had grown up with, the next seeing him blown to bits, perhaps armless and legless but still alive, taking minutes of screaming in agony to die – it was more than some could take. For others it was the guilt of knowing that your bullets or your bayonet were doing the same to a German you had never met, but who was your own age, and essentially just like you – warm, breathing, laughing, eating. Sometimes they crept over no man's land at night and swapped food. Occasionally you could even hear them singing. Different things broke different men. Corliss was a sapper. His nerve could have gone at the claustrophobia of crawling inside the tunnels under the earth, the terror of being buried alive.

'Help him,' Sam begged. 'I can't go . . . and they won't believe me anyway.'

'Of course.' Joseph did not hesitate. He grasped Sam's arm for an instant, then turned and made his way back over the duckboards to the opening of the communication trench. Charlie Gee and Corliss were far enough ahead of him to be out of sight round one of the numerous dogleg bends. He hurried, his feet slithering on the wet boards. In some places chicken wire had been tacked over them to give a grip, but no one had bothered here. He must catch up with them before they reached the supply trench and someone else started asking questions.

Morale was Joseph's job – to keep up courage and belief, to help the injured, too often the dying. He wrote letters home for those who could not, either through injury or inability to put into words emotions that overwhelmed them, and for which there was no common understanding. He tried to offer some meaning to pain almost beyond bearing. They were already in the ninth month of the bitterest and most all-consuming war the world had even seen.

To begin with they had believed it would be over by Christmas, but that had been December 1914. Now it was April 1915, the British Expeditionary Force of almost one hundred thousand men was wiped out, either dead or injured, and it was desperate that new recruits were found. Kitchener had called for a million men, and they would be fresh, healthy, not having endured a winter in the open in the unceasing cold and rain. They would not have lice, swollen and peeling feet, or a dozen other miseries to debilitate them.

Joseph crossed the reserve trench and saw men moving. A soldier was singing to himself 'It's a Long Way to Tipperary' as he poured water out of a petrol can, wrinkling his nose at the smell. He balanced the dixie tin over a precarious arrangement of candles to heat it. He raised a hand to Joseph and smiled without distracting his attention from his task.

The men in this segment were from the Cambridgeshire villages around Joseph's home of Selbourne St Giles. Most of them knew each other by their local nicknames. Joseph was thirty-six, and for the years leading up to the war had been a lecturer in Biblical languages at St John's College in Cambridge. Before that he had been in the ministry. He knew most of these men's families. His own youngest sister, Judith, was twenty-four, older than many of these.

He thought of her with a twisting confusion of emotions. He was intensely proud that she had volunteered to use her one distinctive skill, driving, to come here and work wherever she could help. She had been both a joy and a menace on the roads at home, but here she coped with the mud, the breakdowns, the long hours and the horror of wounded and dying men with a courage he had not known she possessed.

The trench was climbing a bit, and drier. The slit of sky overhead was blue, with a thin drift of clouds, like mares' tails.

Joseph was afraid for Judith in many ways. The obvious danger of injury or even death was only a part of it. There was also the vulnerability of the mind and heart to the destruction around her: the drowning in pain, the loss of so many young men, and the inability of the ambulances to do more than carry them from one place to another, very often too late. He knew the questions that tormented his own mind. No sane person could be whole-hearted about war, not if they had seen it. It was one thing to stand in England in the early spring with the hedgerows beginning to bud, wild birds singing and daffodils in the gardens and along the banks under the trees, and speak of the nobility of war. It was an idea, even at times a noble one. Most people despised the thought of surrender.

Out here it was a reality. You were always cold –

frozen at times – and usually wet. All waking hours were occupied with monotonous routine: carrying, cleaning, digging, shoring up walls, trying to heat food and find drinkable water. You were always tired. And then there were the short interludes of horror: fear crawling in your stomach, shattering noise, and the blood and the pain, men dead – young men you had known and liked. Some would still be crippled long after the war passed into history; the nightmares would never be over for them.

And maybe Germany had invaded 'poor little' Belgium, and a matter of honour rested on it. Invasion was wrong; that was the one thing about which there was no question in anyone's mind. But the few German soldiers Joseph had seen were in every way but uniform indistinguishable from the Englishmen beside him. They were young, tired, dirty, and confused like everyone else.

When a successful raiding party captured someone and brought him back, Joseph had often been chosen to question the prisoner because before the war he had spent time in Germany and spoke the language not only fluently but with pleasure. Looking back on those times now was a wrenching, muddled sort of pain. He had been treated with such courtesy, laughed with them, shared their food. It was the land of Beethoven and Goethe, of science and philosophy and vast myths and dreams. How could they now be doing this to each other?

Joseph turned the last corner, and up a couple of steps he caught up with Charlie Gee and Corliss, but the trench was still too narrow for him to help. Two men could barely walk side by side, let alone three abreast.

The main dressing station was in a tent a few yards away. At least it was dry, and no more of a target than any other structure. It was quite spacious inside. After a bad raid they had to deal with dozens of men, moving them in and out as rapidly as ambulances could take them back to proper hospitals. Just now there was a lull. Only two men were inside, grey-faced, their uniforms blood-stained, waiting to be moved.

Charlie Gee gave a shout, and a young doctor appeared, saw Corliss and immediately went to him.

'Come on, we'll get that fixed up,' he said calmly. His eyes flickered to Joseph and then back again. It was easy enough to see in his haggard, hollow-eyed face the fear that a hand wound was a self-inflicted.

Joseph moved forward quickly. 'We did what we could to help the bleeding, Doctor, but I don't know exactly what happened. He's a sapper; I imagine something collapsed underground. Maybe one of the props gave way.'

The doctor's face eased a little. 'Right.' He turned back to Corliss and took him inside.

Joseph thanked Charlie Gee and watched him amble back up the connecting trench towards the front line again.

An ambulance pulled up, a square-bodied Ford Model T, a bit like a delivery van. It was open at the front, and with a closed part at the back, which could carry up to five men laid out in stretchers, more if they were sitting up. The driver jumped out. He was a broad-shouldered young man with short hair that sat up on the crown of his head. He saluted Joseph, then looked at the more seriously injured of the two men waiting, whose right leg was heavily splinted.

'Don't need ter carry yer,' he said cheerfully. 'Reckon an arm round yer and yer'll be fine. 'Ave yer in 'ospital in an hour, or mebbe less, if Jerry don't make too much of a mess o' them roads. Cut 'em up terrible around Wipers, they 'ave, an' 'Ellfire Corner's a right shootin' gallery. Still, we'll cut up a few o' them, an' all. Looks broke all right.' He regarded the splinted leg cheerfully. 'Reckon that's a Blighty one, at least for a while, eh?'

'Oi'll be back!' the soldier said quietly. 'Oi've seen a lot worse than broken legs.'

'So've I, mate, so've I.' The ambulance driver pursed his lips. 'But this'll do for now. Now let's be 'avin' yer.'

Joseph moved forward. 'Can I help?' he offered.

'Blimey! 'E don' need the last rites yet, Padre. It's only 'is leg! The rest of 'im's right as rain,' the ambulance driver said with a grin. 'Still – I s'pose yer could take the other side of 'im, stop 'im fallin' that way, like?'

A quarter of an hour later Joseph was refreshed by really quite drinkable tea. Unlike in the front trenches, there was plenty of it, almost too hot to drink, and strong enough to disguise the other tastes in the water.

He had almost finished it when a car drove up. It was a long, low-slung Aston Martin, and out of it stepped a slim, upright young man with very fair hair and a fresh complexion. He wore uniform, but with no rank. He ignored Joseph and went straight into the tent, leaving the flap open. He stopped in front of the surgeon, who was now tidying up his instruments, almost at attention.

'Eldon Prentice, war correspondent,' he announced.

Joseph followed him in. 'Bit dangerous up here, Mr Prentice,' he said, carefully not looking towards Corliss, who was lying on one of the palliasses, his bandaged hand already stained with blood again. 'I'd go a bit further back, if I were you,' he added.

Prentice stared at him, his chin lifted a little, his blunt face smooth, perfectly certain of himself. 'And who are you, sir?'

'Captain Reavley, chaplain,' Joseph replied.

'Good. You can probably give me some accurate first-hand information,' Prentice said. 'Or at least second-hand.'

Joseph heard the challenge in his voice. 'It's cold, wet and dirty,' he replied, looking at Prentice's clean trousers and only faintly dusty boots. 'And, of course, you'll have to walk! And carry your rations. You do have rations, don't you?'

Prentice looked at him curiously. 'A chaplain is just the sort of man I'd like to talk to. You'd be able to give me a unique view of how the men feel, what their thoughts and fears are.'

Joseph instinctively disliked the man. There was an arrogance in his manner that offended him. 'Perhaps you haven't heard, Mr Prentice, but priests don't repeat what people tell them, if it's of any importance.'

Prentice smiled. 'Yes, I imagine you have heard a great many stories of pain, fear and horror, Captain. Some of them must be heart-rending, and leave you feeling utterly helpless. After all, what can you do?' It was a rhetorical question, and yet he seemed to be waiting for an answer.

He had described exactly Joseph's dilemma, and the emotions that most troubled him, awakening a feeling of inadequacy, even failure. There was so little he could do to help, and even then it was trivial, but he was damned if he would admit it to this correspondent. The feeling of inadequacy caused too deep a hurt to speak of, even to himself.

'Nothing that is really your concern, Mr Prentice,' he said aloud. 'A man's troubles, whatever they are, are private to him. That is one of the few decencies we can grant.'

Prentice stood still for a moment, and then he turned very slowly and looked at Corliss. 'What happened to him?' he asked curiously. 'Bad ammunition exploded and took off his fingers?'

'He was down the saps,' Joseph said tartly.

Prentice looked blank.

'Tunnels,' Joseph explained. 'The intention is that the Germans won't know where the tunnels are. They get within a yard or two of their trenches, then lay mines. If a mine had exploded there'd be nothing left of any of them.'

'He's a sapper? I hear that men reaching their hands

393

above the parapet level sometimes get hit by snipers.'
Prentice was watching Joseph intently.

Joseph drew in breath to reply, and then changed his mind. Prentice was a war correspondent, like any other. They all pooled their information anyway – he knew that. He had seen them meeting together in the cafés when he had been behind the lines in one of the towns at Brigade Headquarters, or even further back at Divisional Headquarters. Nobody could see everything; the differences in their stories depended upon interpretation, what they selected and how they wrote it up.

There was movement at the entrance, and a sergeant came in. He saluted Joseph, ignored Prentice and spoke to the doctor, then went to Corliss.

'What happened, soldier?'

Corliss stared up at him. 'Not sure, sir. Bit of the wall fell in. Something landed on my hand.'

'What? A pick?'

'Could be, I suppose.'

'Hurts?'

'Yes, sir, but not too much. I expect I'll be all right.'

'Sapper without 'is fingers is not much use. Looks like a Blighty one.' The sergeant pushed out his lip dubiously, but his voice was not unkind.

Joseph took a deep breath and let it out, feeling his muscles ease a little. If Corliss had been as close to the edge as Sam feared, he might have been careless, might even have been partly responsible for the accident, but that was still not a crime. If someone else had been injured he should be put on a charge, but he was the one in pain, the one who would spend the rest of his life with half a hand.

'Nasty injury,' Prentice remarked, taking a couple of steps towards the sergeant. 'Eldon Prentice. I'm press.' He looked down at Corliss where he was lying. 'Looks like you'll see home before the rest of your mates.'

Corliss gulped and the fraction of colour that was in his face vanished. His teeth were chattering and he was beginning to shake. Perhaps Sam had been right and his nerves were shot.

There was a long silence. Suddenly Joseph was aware of the tent being cold. The air smelled of blood, the sweat of pain, disinfectant. There was noise outside, someone shouting, the faint patter of rain on canvas. The light was fading.

Should he say anything, or might he only make it worse? The doctor was unhappy – that was wretchedly clear in his tired face. He was a young man himself. He had seen too many bodies broken, too much hideous injury he could not help. He was trying to dam rivers of blood with little more than his hands. The shadows under his eyes looked even more pronounced.

Joseph knew the sergeant vaguely. His name was Watkins. He was regular army. He had probably seen most of his friends killed or injured already. He believed in discipline; he knew the cost of cowardice, even one man breaking the line. He also knew what it was like to face fire, to go over the top into a hail of bullets. He had heard the screams of men caught on the wire.

Joseph turned to Prentice. 'It's a pity you won't get to go along the saps some time,' he said, his voice drier and more brittle than he had meant it to be. 'You could write a good piece about what it feels like to crawl on your hands and knees through a hole in the ground under no man's land, hear the water dripping and the bits of earth falling. A bit close to the rats down there, but it can't be helped. They're everywhere, as I expect you've noticed. Thousands of the things, big as cats, some of them. They feed on the dead, especially the eyes. You want to cover your face when you're asleep.' He felt an acute satisfaction as he saw Prentice shiver. 'But then you won't be able to go that far forward, will you? War correspondents don't.

They'd get in the way. You only have to watch what other men do, and then go off somewhere safe and talk about it.'

'And what do you do? Pray about it, Chaplain?' Prentice snapped. 'God Almighty! You're a joke!' His voice was shrill with contempt. 'You're no more use here than a maiden aunt in a whorehouse. If your God gives a damn about us, where is He?' He jabbed his hand viciously in the direction of the front line, and no man's land beyond. 'Ask him,' he pointed at Corliss, 'if he believes in God when he's down one of his saps!'

'If you had ever been out there at night, when they're shooting, you would know there's nothing else to believe in except God,' Joseph answered him with bitter certainty. 'If there's any real, physical place to convince you there is a hell, try no man's land in winter. To sit in a nice warm pub with a glass of beer and write stories for the breakfast tables in England sounds like heaven in comparison.'

'Look—' Prentice began.

He was cut off by the sergeant. 'I think you'd better go back to your pub and your beer, Mr Prentice,' he said in a hard, level voice. 'What the captain says is right. And you may be an atheist yourself and believe in nothing at all, but you've got no place coming out here and making mock of other men's faith. When it gets bad, it may be all you've got. But you wouldn't know that, seeing as you aren't a soldier.' He was a big man, heavier than Prentice, though not as tall, and he was seven or eight years older, probably nearer forty.

'Any officer can have you arrested at any time,' he went on. 'King's Regulations. So it might be a good idea to be polite to the captain, don't you think?'

Prentice stood facing him, measuring his resolve.

Joseph waited without moving.

Prentice retreated, his face tight with anger.

The sergeant smiled. 'Ambulance'll be here soon,' he

said to Corliss. 'Take you back to a proper hospital, then Blighty in time.' His voice was strong, comfortable, but Joseph knew from his face that he had no inner certainty that the wound was not self-inflicted. He would not report it as such because Prentice had angered him. He was an outsider who had come in and tried to tell him his job. It was soldiers closing ranks against civilians.

Outside there was a splash and crunch as an ambulance drew up, and a moment later a loose-limbed young man came in. He was sodden wet, and his dark hair dripped down his face. As soon as he spoke it was obvious that he was American.

'Hi, you got anyone for me, Doc?' He saw Joseph. 'Hi, Padre, how's it going?'

'Fine, thank you, Wil,' Joseph replied. 'Yes, there's one for you there.'

Wil walked over to Corliss. 'Looks like it hurts,' he said sympathetically.

Corliss tried to smile. 'Yes, but not too much,' he answered, his voice rasping between dry lips.

Prentice grunted, and smiled sarcastically.

'That's what everyone says!' Joseph told him, not bothering to suppress his anger. 'If they're dying, they still say that!'

'But he's not dying, is he, Chaplain?' Prentice responded. 'And he won't! In a week or two he'll be home in England, warm and safe!'

'So will you!' Joseph told him. 'Only you'll have all your fingers.' And he turned to help Wil Sloan get Corliss to his feet and out to the ambulance in the rain.

Matthew Reavley drove along the open road in the April sunshine. He was heading south from London towards the outskirts of Brighton and he had a sense of exhilaration to be out of the city and, at last, after nine months of frustration and failure, to be on the brink of a real step forward.

The events of the previous summer, even before the outbreak of war, had altered his life irrevocably. At the end of June, on the same day as the assassination of the Archduke Franz Ferdinand in Sarajevo, Matthew's parents had been killed in a car crash, which at first had seemed simply an accident. On the previous evening John Reavley had called his son Matthew on the telephone and said that he had found a document that outlined a plan that, if carried out, would ruin England's honour, and change the history of the world. It was in bringing the document from his home in St Giles to Matthew in London that the accident had happened.

But when Matthew and Joseph had examined their father's possessions, taken from the wreck, there was no document. Nor was it in the shattered car. They had searched the house and found nothing even resembling such a thing.

The car crash had proved to be a careful and deliberate murder, although the police had never known that. John Reavley had also warned Matthew, in their last brief conversation, that the conspiracy touched even as high as the Royal Family, and he could trust no one.

Matthew and Joseph, seven years his junior, had uncovered the painful and ultimately tragic truth of what had happened. They had found the document where John Reavley had hidden it, and what it contained was far worse than he had painted it. Even as Matthew sped between the hedgerows, with their new leaves translucent green, a soft veil of rain misting the copse of woodland in the distance, he remembered the numbing horror with which he and Joseph had read the paper. The proposal was beyond anything they had imagined: a treaty between Kaiser Wilhelm II and King George V, agreeing that England should abandon France and Belgium to the German conquering army, in return for which England and Germany together would form an empire to divide the world between them. Most of Europe would fall to Germany, who would then help Britain to keep its present empire and add to it the old colonies of the Americas, including the entire United States. It was a betrayal almost inconceivable.

And yet it would have avoided the slaughter that was now staining the battlefields of Europe, a carnage that looked set to continue if Kitchener raised a million more men to go voluntarily into that hell of pain and destruction.

The brothers knew who had killed John and Alys Reavley, and why. The young man himself was now dead, as was his brother, but the instigator of it all, almost certainly the man who had believed he could convince King George to sign the treaty, was still unknown, and free to continue in whatever way he could to further the creation of his empire of subjugation and dishonourable peace.

Joseph was serving in Flanders and had no opportunity to pursue 'the Peacemaker', as they had called him. Hannah, Joseph and Matthew's elder sister, had moved back to the family home in St Giles, with her three children. Her husband, Archie, was in the Royal Navy and at sea most of the time. Hannah had been the closest to their mother, and in many ways was trying to take her place in the village, close to the familiar lanes and fields of her childhood, the families she knew, the routines of domestic care and the small duties and kindnesses that were the fabric of life.

Matthew himself had naturally continued in his career in the Secret Intelligence Service, which his father had so deplored. It surprised him how much it still hurt that the one time John Reavley would have turned to him for professional help it had been too late, and he still, nearly a year later, could not complete the task.

Judith, five years younger than Matthew, was using

the only real skill she had and harnessing her aimless impetuosity somewhere in the Ypres area, as a VAD – a part of the Voluntary Aid Detachment – driving ambulances, staff cars, whatever she was asked. Her letters sounded as if finally she had found a sense of consuming purpose, and even a fellowship, which gave her a kind of happiness in spite of the frequent danger and the almost perpetual physical hardship.

That meant it was only Matthew who was able to pursue the little knowledge they had in order to find the Peacemaker, not for personal vengeance or even some abstract of justice, but to stop him in whatever alternative way he was pursuing his goal. And none of them had ever imagined he would abandon it.

He drew up at the crossroads. A team of horses – heavy and patient creatures – was drawing a harrow over the field to his left, and he could smell the turned earth, a rich, clinging fragrance. The rain had passed and the sunlight glittered on the dripping leaves in the hedge.

He accelerated and moved forward. He could trust no one outside the family, not even his own superior in the SIS – in fact, possibly him least of all. He could only rehearse the facts that were indisputable and deduce from them what else had to be true.

John Reavley had finished his university education in mathematics in Germany, and had many German friends. One of them had been Reisenburg, the man whose calligraphic skills had been used to draft both copies of the treaty. He had been appalled by what he saw, and had stolen them, bringing them to England, to the one man he trusted and believed might be able to stop the conspiracy.

Reisenburg had passed the documents to John Reavley, who had within hours telephoned Matthew in London, saying he would bring them the following day. But he had got no further than a few miles when he had been sabotaged on the road by Sebastian Allard, Joseph's favourite student at St John's College, passionate, idealistic and terrified of the destruction, not only to life but to the very spirit of civilization, that war would bring. He had believed the Peacemaker's plan to be the lesser evil. Then, after he had committed double murder in its cause, and seen with horror the reality of violent death, he had found he could not live with it.

That had been followed by the murder of Harry Beecher, Joseph's oldest and dearest friend, and finally by yet another suicide. Reisenburg too had been killed, but Matthew had no idea by whom.

And on 4 August Britain had been plunged into war.

Who was the Peacemaker? A man with allies, who had access to the German royal court, almost certainly to the Kaiser himself, and who also had private and personal access to King George V. No one would conceive of such a plan, let alone put it into action, without knowing both men. He was also quite obviously politically astute, had a soaring and utterly ruthless imagination, and yet, in his own way, a passionate morality.

He and his disciples had desperately wanted the treaty document back because there was neither time nor opportunity to redraft it and get the Kaiser to sign it again before offering it to the King, but also it was imperative it did not fall into the hands of anyone who would make it public.

When they had discovered it was gone, they must have known it was Reisenburg who had taken it, but not in time to follow him. If they had, they would have taken it from him and killed him then. Similarly they could not have seen him pass it to John Reavley, or again they would have acted at the time.

And yet they had instructed Sebastian Allard to kill John Reavley the very next day. Therefore they had to have known that he had it, and that he would be driving down that particular stretch of road that morning.

The Peacemaker could only be someone who knew John Reavley personally, and also knew that his second son worked in London in the Intelligence Services, and would be the obvious person to whom to take the document.

Who had contacted Sebastian Allard with information and instructions in the few hours of the afternoon or evening after Reisenburg had given John Reavley the document, and before he had set out the next day for London?

Sebastian was dead, as was his brother, Elwyn. Their father, Gerald, was drowned deeper than ever in the brandy bottle, and their mother, Mary, was broken by the fury and shame of the scandal. She had changed her name and left Cambridgeshire, with its unbearable past, behind her. She had not adopted any family name, either on her parents' side, or Gerald's, but something totally unconnected. It had taken Matthew this long to find her where she worked as a voluntary aide in a military hospital outside Brighton.

It was early afternoon when he parked in the gravel space outside the entrance and climbed out, grateful to stretch his legs after the two-hour drive. He went up the steps, enquired in the hallway if he could speak with Mrs Allan, and was directed to one of the wards.

On the way there he passed a young man, looking no more than twenty, sitting in a wheelchair. The way the rug fell over his lap made it apparent he had only one leg.

Matthew did not want to look at it. He was twisted with pity, guilty for being able to stride out easily himself, and he was in a hurry. He was acutely aware that Joseph would have felt the same, and would have stopped. It often surprised him how much he missed Joseph now. Since he lived in London and Joseph had lived in Cambridge, he had not expected to.

'Good afternoon,' he said with a smile. 'Am I heading the right way for Ward Three?'

'Yes, sir,' the man assured him with a sudden light in his face. He looked at Matthew's uniform but saw no regimental insignia on it. 'Straight ahead.'

'Thanks,' Matthew acknowledged, and went the rest of the way and through the door. He saw Mary as soon as he was inside. She was wearing a grey skirt and blouse with a white apron over it, rather than the fashionable unrelieved black silk of mourning that he had last seen her in, but she was still gaunt-faced, her body almost fleshless, shoulders high and thin, backbone like a ramrod. She took no notice of him, concentrating on her task of rolling bandages. She was probably used to people coming and going in the ward.

'Good afternoon, Mrs Allan,' he said quietly, using her new name in order not to embarrass her. 'Can you spare me a few minutes of your time?'

She stopped, her hands motionless, the bandage in the air. Very slowly she turned, but he knew that she had already recognized his voice. Her angular features were pinched with fear and her dark eyes shadowed. She stared at him without speaking.

'I'm sorry to disturb you, Mrs Allan,' he repeated her new name to let her know he had no intention of ripping away the mask she had so carefully constructed. There was such tragedy between them, wounds to which healing could not be imagined. Both his parents were dead at her son's hands, both her sons were guilty of murder and suicide, the scandal had destroyed everything she cared about – and it was his brother who had exposed it. She had no dreams left and the emptiness was there as she looked at him.

'I assume you have some reason, Captain Reavley,' she replied without expression in her voice.

'Maybe we could walk outside?' he suggested, glancing

403

towards the door, which opened on to a terrace and then the lawn, where he could see at least half a dozen young men in chairs of one sort or another.

'If it is necessary,' she answered. She did not betray any interest in what he wanted, nor did she ask how any of his family were, although she must have known Joseph and Judith were both in Flanders, because it had been general knowledge in the area before she had left it.

He led the way, their footsteps hard on the wooden floor of the ward. He was aware of at least two men lying silently in beds watching them as they went.

Outside the air was mild and still, sheltered by the high walls covered with roses and honeysuckle, not yet in full leaf. The sky above was milky blue.

'What is it you wish?' she asked, stopping well short of any of the other occupants of the garden.

He had given a great deal of thought to what he would say to her, but nothing had ever been free from the pain of the past. There was no clean or kind way of phrasing it. Perhaps simple was the best.

He had decided to tell her as much of the truth as he dared. She was owed that much; she had lost more than any of them, and he saw no added danger in it.

'Sebastian did not act alone,' he began. 'Someone taught him ideas and beliefs, then told him what to do. He obeyed, thinking it would avert war. That person, apart from individual guilt for death in your family and mine, is also still free to commit treason and sabotage of England, and to help Germany in any way they can. Their motives don't matter, they must still be prevented. I cannot ask official help in this because I don't know whom I can trust.'

The faintest, most bitter humour touched her face for an instant, then vanished, her black eyebrows rising so slightly it could have been only a trick of the light. 'And you imagine you can trust me?'

404

'I've told you little you don't already know,' he replied. 'Added to which, I'm at a dead end. I cannot believe that you have any kinder feelings towards this man than I do.'

The emotion was nowhere in her face except her eyes, which suddenly sprang to smouldering life. 'I would kill him if I could,' she replied. 'I would like to do it with my own hands, and watch him go. I would like to see the knowledge in him, and the pain. I would make sure that he went slowly, and that he knew who I was.'

The implacable hate in her frightened him, but he did not doubt her words. He found his mouth dry. Could he ever hate like that? He had lost his parents, and the grief might never completely leave him, but their deaths had been swift and honourable. Both her sons, the passion and the hope of her life, had been turned into murderers, and died by suicide. And yet neither of them had been evil – he knew that as clearly as he saw the sunlight on the grass. They had been deceived and destroyed by others, and, in the end, crucified by shame.

'Unfortunately I haven't yet found him,' Matthew said to her with a gentleness that amazed him that he could feel for her. She looked like some mythical fury rather than an ordinary twentieth-century woman standing on the lawn of a Brighton hospital. But then surely myth survived because it was a distillation of human truth? 'You can help me,' he added.

'How?' she asked, looking at the wheelchair-bound soldiers, not at him.

'Who contacted Sebastian the afternoon before the crash in which my parents died? In any way – telephone, letter, personally, anything at all.'

'How excruciatingly delicate of you, Captain Reavley.' There was a hint of mockery in her voice. 'You mean the day before Sebastian killed your mother and father!'

'Yes. The morning would have been too early; anything from lunch time onwards.'

She considered for a moment or two before answering. 'He had two or three letters in the early afternoon delivery. One telephone call, I remember. No one visited, but he did go out, and was troubled when he returned. I have no idea whom he could have met then.'

'Did the letters come through the post?'

'Of course they came through the post! What were you imagining? Letters by pigeon? Or a liveried footman dropping something off in a carriage?'

'A message by hand,' he replied. 'It is simple enough to put something through a letter box, but it wouldn't have a franked stamp on it.'

She let out her breath in a sigh. 'Do you really think this is going to help you find him? Or that it will bring any kind of justice if you do? You won't be able to prove anything. You will look ridiculous, and whoever you accuse will walk away. You'll be fortunate if he doesn't ruin you for slander.'

'You underestimate me, Mrs Allan. I didn't have anything so straightforward in mind.'

She stared at him. It was not hope in her eyes, making them so alive, but it was a flicker of something better than the dead anger before. 'There was a telephone call, from Aidan Thyer, and then half an hour after that, Sebastian went out.'

Aidan Thyer. He was Master of St John's College in Cambridge, a position of extraordinary, almost unique, influence. Many young men's dreams and ambitions had been moulded by whoever had been Master of their college in their first formative years as adults, away from home, beginning to taste the wild new freedoms of intellectual adventure. Matthew could remember his own Master, the brilliance of his mind, the dreams he had started, worlds he had opened for his students. Who better to teach Sebastian to be an idealist who would kill for peace?

406

If it were Thyer, it would hit Joseph profoundly. But pain had nothing to do with truth.

'Nothing between?' he asked Mary Allan. 'No one to the door, even at the back? No deliveries, no tradesmen?'

'No,' she answered.

Was she being careful, or trying to avoid an answer that would hurt so deeply? But the contact had to be someone John Reavley had known, and presumably trusted. It had to be someone close enough and with the intellectual and moral power to have influenced Sebastian to kill two people he had known for years, the parents of the man who had tutored and helped him even before he went up to university and even more afterwards.

'Did he say anything about where he was going?'

'No. Do you think it was to see Aidan Thyer?' Her voice was crowded with disbelief. After Sebastian's death she had stayed in Thyer's house! He had witnessed her grief, and appeared to do all he could to help.

'I don't know,' Matthew replied truthfully. 'There are lots of possible explanations. But it is at least somewhere to begin. Someone told Sebastian what to do, and where my father would be.'

'Why could it not have been at any time?' she asked, frowning slightly. 'Why only in the afternoon of the day before? Why did he do it? Your brother was Sebastian's closest friend.'

'I know. It had nothing to do with Joseph. It was political.' That was as close to the truth as he would come.

'That's absurd!' she retorted. 'Your father used to be a member of Parliament, I know, but he didn't stand for any convictions Sebastian was against. He didn't stand for anything out of the ordinary. There were scores of men like him, maybe even hundreds.' It was possibly not intended to be rude, but her tone was dismissive and she made no effort to hide it.

Matthew pictured his father's mild, ascetic face with its incisive intelligence, and the honesty that was so clear it was sometimes almost childlike. Yes, there were many men who believed as he had, but he himself had been unique! No one could fill the emptiness his death had created. Suddenly it was almost impossible for Matthew not to snap back at Mary's callous remark. It required all his self-control to answer civilly.

'And had any of those hundreds been the ones to learn the information he had, and had the courage to act on it,' he said carefully, 'then they would have been the ones killed.' He deliberately avoided using the word 'murdered'.

Her face pulled tight and she turned away. 'What information?'

'Political. I can't tell you more than that.'

'Then go and talk to Aidan Thyer,' she told him. 'There's nothing I can do to help you.' And without waiting for him to say anything more, or to wish him goodbye, she turned and walked back towards the door inside, a stiff-backed figure, every other passion consumed in grief, oddly dignified, and yet completely without grace.

Matthew remained outside, and went back to the car along the grass and around the footpath.